Lilli
Chernofsky

a novel

Nina Vida

Brick Mantel Books
Bloomington, Indiana

Published by Brick Mantel Books, USA

Brick Mantel
BOOKS

www.BrickMantelBooks.com
info@BrickMantelBooks.com

An imprint of Pen & Publish, Inc.
www.PenandPublish.com
Bloomington, Indiana
(314) 827-6567

Print ISBN: 978-1-941799-97-0
e-book ISBN: 978-1-941799-98-7

Library of Congress Control Number: 2017947064

Cover Credit:
Darker Shadows Texture Stock by redwolf518stock

Printed on acid-free paper.

In memory of Jacob Margolis, my grandfather

Acknowledgments

In 1990 a reunion of Old China Hands, Jews who had fled Hitler's Europe for Shanghai during World War II, was held in a hotel in Anaheim, California. Since I live not far from the hotel where the reunion was held, I attended one of the public events. I was moved by the joyously emotional gathering, and, as a writer, I wanted to know more. Through friends in Leisure World, California, and with a few well-placed ads, during the next few months I was able to meet and interview Irving Bikel, Victor Donath, Ursula Melchior, Gussie Koster, Margot Weiss, Henry Rossetty, Dorothy Fleischner, Frank Wachsner, Hildegard Bikel, and Jonny Teicher. I'm grateful to them for sharing with me their memories of Shanghai, a place of rescue, but also a place of disrupted lives, violence, hunger, disease, and, too often, death. My novel *Lilli Chernofsky* is a salute to them.

Thanks to Arthur Frumkin for his reminiscences of "flying the Hump" as a pilot in the Air Transport Command in 1942.

And special thanks to Jennifer Geist, publisher of Brick Mantel Books, for giving *Lilli Chernofsky* a home.

Chapter 1

Kovno, Lithuania
July 1940

The Soviets marched into Kovno, and Mama's hair turned white. It used to be the color of used bricks. Now silken sprigs of hair as shiny white as salt burst from beneath her mouse-gray wig, which in the heat of the kitchen, with cooking pots full and steaming, sat like a dried bird's nest on her head.

"Stir the *kreplach*, Lilli," Mama said.

"Yes, Mama."

Lilli was hypnotized by the turbulence the spoon created. A person could learn a lot by studying the way *kreplach* struggled to keep afloat in boiling water, spinning and twirling like tiny rafts, then tipping sideways, ribbons of yellow fat staining the water as the meat-filled pockets were sucked into the vortex, sank to the bottom, then bobbed up again.

"Are you stirring, Lilli?" Mama said.

"I'm stirring, Mama."

There was more cooking to be done now that there were five extra mouths to feed, *yeshiva* students who'd escaped Poland one step ahead of Hitler and arrived in Kovno with eyes like graven pits and clothes that looked as if they had been chewed on by wild animals. Mama had never been a meticulous housekeeper, but her superficial neatness was now overwhelmed by too many bodies in too few rooms. Two of the students occupied Lilli's room, and two others slept on the floor in her brother Aaron's room. (Lilli slept with Mama in the feather bed that had been Grandma Chernofsky's wedding present to Mama and Papa; Papa slept in a chair in his study.) Moses Zuckerman, at twenty-two *di firer*, the leader of the group, the one who led the students through the Polish forests to escape the Nazis, occupied the sagging couch in the parlor, long arms and legs hanging over the cushions and onto the floor like a toppled tree.

The house was upside down: teetering alps of books to be scaled, battered suitcases to be bumped into, Hebrew prayers chanted from early morning to late evening. The yeshiva students made no concession to the heat. They sat by the open window in threadbare suits and calf-length coats, black felt hats pulled all the way down to the tops of their ears, not even unbuttoning their shirts to let a slice of air tickle their necks. At night they sprawled on their mattresses, fully dressed in their torn suits and coats and cracked shoes, their black hats on the floor beside them so that if the house caught fire and they had to run outside, they wouldn't be without a head covering to remind them that God was right above them. Lilli could hear their voices now in the dining room, strips of sound like the yapping of hatchlings in a nest.

"Moses says we have to leave Kovno," Lilli murmured to Mama.

"He speaks to you?" Mama said.

"Yes."

"You must be careful, Lilli. Papa will send him and his yeshiva buchers out of the house if he finds out."

"He's a Jewish boy, Mama."

"He's not a boy; he's a man, a stranger. What do we know about him? There are questions to be answered, Lilli. He says he got out of Poland with the Nazis shooting people in the streets. Nazis shooting people in the streets? Who can believe him? Would even Nazis do such things? He's someone to be treated cautiously. Who knows who he is. He appears out of nowhere with his *farloyrn menschen* following after him like sheep, and Papa takes him in and blesses him. And never mind the Nazis—maybe he's running away from something bad he's done." Mama lowered her voice. "Maybe he's a *golem*, a handful of dust kneaded into the shape of a man."

Before the Soviets invaded, it was Hitler that Mama had worried about. She had sent Lilli to stay with Papa's sister, Rose Chernofsky, in Stuttgart. Tante Rose, Hitler's favorite actress in the halcyon days of Jewish actors, had been reduced to performing obscure plays with the Stuttgart Repertory Theater in a half-timbered abandoned factory on a cobblestone street in the doll-like, thirteenth-century city of Stuttgart. In the four months Lilli was there with Tante Rose, she turned seventeen, her body slimmed and lengthened, her baby cheeks sleekened, and the skin beneath its drizzle of cinnamon freckles turned as rosy as a summer flush. In those four months the Nazis closed the synagogues and began snatching Jews off the street and pulling them off the trams. Stuttgart, a gold-dipped, solemn city, its flower-blanketed hills bleeding head-spinning perfume into the air, became an iron-hard city spitting its Jews out as smoothly as peanut shells.

When Milton Gorstein, the theater company's manager, disappeared while walking from his apartment to the theater, Tante Rose sent Lilli home.

"Tell your mama it's no safer here than it is in Kovno."

"Who dresses a child like a harlot?" Papa asked when Lilli got off the train wearing a silk shirtwaist and bow-toed pumps, her hair marcelled, eyes mascaraed, cheeks rouged.

Mama washed Lilli's face, and Aaron said, "I knew Tante Rose would ruin her."

The dress and shoes were now in a box in the closet, the makeup in a drawer, and Lilli wore the same puff-sleeved dirndls and laced shoes she'd worn before she went away, her behavior once again as circumscribed as the earth's orbit, the same restrictions and forbiddances blooming like holy writ in every corner of the dusty house.

"You'll fall asleep if you stir the soup any slower, Lilli," Mama said now. "Take some honey cake to Papa."

"And a man must not sit when others are standing nor stand when others are sitting," Papa was saying as Lilli opened the dining room door. The yeshiva students glanced up, then rapidly averted their eyes as Lilli set the plate of sliced honey cake in the center of the table amidst the papers, books, and cold cups of tea sopping onto the pink roses in Mama's embroidered tablecloth. It made Lilli smile the way the yeshiva students tried to avoid looking at her, how they examined their fingernails, bent to tie their shoes, murmured snatches of prayer. If she had been certain it wouldn't make Papa angry, she would have picked out one of the yeshiva students and squeezed his hand to prove her touch wasn't fatal.

Moses wasn't afraid to look at her. The week before he had opened the door to Mama's bedroom when Lilli was dressing. She was naked from the waist up, the chemise she was about to put on still in her hand. She didn't cover herself. It was too late. She let him look.

Moses was extremely tall, taller than the lintel above the synagogue doors. His voice held inside it the rustle of someone who had crawled up out of the grave. Papa said Moses' escape from Poland was proof that the *Mashiach*'s protective hand had crowned him with the force of a thousand suns. Aaron said Moses was like the Moses of the Pentateuch, a wanderer in the wilderness, only tied to the earth by the string of hapless yeshiva buchers he dragged along behind him. Only Mama worried about who he really was.

Mama worried about everything. It seemed to Lilli that Mama must wake up every day with a schedule of things she should worry about. Hitler and Stalin, of course, but also about Papa's headaches and Aaron's lack of appetite and whether there will be enough *kreplach* for the soup. Mainly she worried about Lilli.

"What will happen to you if Papa and I aren't here to protect you?" Mama said this afternoon while Lilli was scrubbing vegetables and Mama was grinding chicken for the *kreplach*. "Aaron is a good boy, but he doesn't pay attention, he's always with his nose in the Mishnah. The house could catch fire; he wouldn't notice. You have to take care of yourself, Lilli. The Soviets are here and no one is shooting at us now, but what about tomorrow, do we know what will happen tomorrow? You have to be careful not to go too far from the house, and when you walk to the bakery make sure your arms are covered, and if someone talks to you don't answer. Even a neighbor can be dangerous in times like these."

What if Lilli had told Mama that Moses had seen her naked? Or that he had kissed her—once in the fallow yard behind the house, once in the kitchen, and once in the dark dining room when everyone was asleep? Surprise kisses that gathered Lilli in and held her fast. She had never been kissed by anyone before Moses, and she fell into the bower of his soft beard and kissed him back, their lips like the press of a moist flower between the pages of a book.

If Lilli were still in Stuttgart she could talk to Tante Rose about Moses. Tante Rose had never been married, but she had told Lilli about all the lovers she had had. The last one, the one who had promised to take Tante Rose to America, wasn't even Jewish.

"What does it feel like to be in love, Tante Rose?" Lilli once asked her.

"Romantic love, Lilli?"

"Like in books and plays."

"Don't waste your time. A woman has to be practical. A man has to have qualities that are useful. This is the real world with real situations. You have to be particular who you choose to give your favors to. An earner is all right, but a businessman is better. Artists are too risky. They make promises they don't keep. And watch out for the *kohanim* in your papa's *shtibl*. You should avoid them like the plague. Your papa will marry you off to one of them and they'll be a stone around your neck. Too much praying, too little money-making. And don't tell your Papa that my latest isn't Jewish."

Aaron was still reading from the Mishnah, the book gripped between thin fingers, his murmured readings as smooth as birdsong.

"And a man must not sleep when others are awake, nor should he remain awake among those who sleep," Aaron said. His face was dense with freckles above a beard suspended from his chin like a tomatoey mop. Lilli resembled him in the high yoke of cheekbone and constellation of freckles, but her hair was the color of soft-washed flax, and her lips were plump and her nose was narrow, while his face had a wandering lumpiness.

"I dreamed that Hitler came to Kovno, Papa," Lilli said. "Mr. Gorstein, the stage manager of the Stuttgart Repertory, was in my dream."

"And what did Mr. Gorstein have to say in your dream, Lilli?"

"He said we should leave Kovno. You always say that dreams are messages, Papa. Well, Mr. Gorstein sent me a message in my dream."

"And where should we go, Lilli?"

"Spain would be a fine place."

Aaron looked up from the text. "You're so dumb you probably don't even know where Spain is."

"Don't talk to her like that," Moses said.

"When she becomes your sister you can talk to her the way you want. Meanwhile I'm her brother, and I'm talking to her. Besides, we have no passports, no transit visas, and the Soviets want two hundred American dollars for every exit visa. If you try to sell your belongings on the black market, they shoot you. Two men from Vilna were found dead in the street yesterday after trying to sell an overcoat for a sack of potatoes. Impossible."

When Lilli was younger, Aaron brought her squares of buttery *mandel-brot* from the study hall and read Torah stories to her in the evenings, but, as though he were afraid that Tante Rose's bohemian ways had tainted her, he now spoke to her with a look in his bay-colored eyes that reminded Lilli of the drawing of a Spanish inquisitor in one of Papa's books.

Before Lilli went to Stuttgart, she had been an invisible person, rarely speaking above a whisper, sure that what she had to say about anything had no worth. In Stuttgart she lost her smothering timidity and for the first time felt the first bud of self apart from family and tradition and ritual. Maybe that was the awakening of the mysterious soul that Papa was always talking about. She wouldn't tell anyone in the world—not even Tante Rose—that if there were no Stalin or Hitler in the world, she would have stayed in Stuttgart and would never have come back to Kovno except to visit. She might have become an actress like Tante Rose. ("She has my quickness and lack of fear," Lilli heard Tante Rose tell Mr. Gorstein before he disappeared.) She might have sold books in a shop in the city center on subjects that no one in Kovno had ever heard of. Or maybe she would have opened a *kinderheim* and filled it with cast-off, unwanted children like cousin Masha, who died of diphtheria before Lilli was born. Although Lilli was too young to remember her, sometimes she imagined she saw her sitting in a chair in the kitchen, her hair lying in gold-streaked curls across her forehead.

"Your head is uncovered," Papa said, staring at Lilli's headscarf, at the exposed crown where wisps of hair as fine as duck down had escaped the heavy twist of hair.

"The scarf is too small."

"Here." Aaron handed her his handkerchief, which was almost as big as the dishtowels stacked in a drawer in the kitchen.

"You blew your nose in it."

"I only wiped it."

"Enough!" Papa said.

Papa looked like the picture of Abraham hanging on the dining room wall, fierce-faced, his eyes two burnt holes in their creased beds. Unlike Abraham's flowing white beard and uncovered head, Papa's beard was a gray-flecked brown, and he always wore a hat, even in the house. When studying at the dining room table, he wore a small black satin yarmulke and a long silk morning coat. When visitors came, he put on his high-domed sable hat and a full-length black coat. In the synagogue he donned his rabbinical robes and embroidered silk *tallit*. Papa didn't seem concerned that the Russians had smashed open the gates and, like a burglar, snatched the city up.

Papa now pointed to the cake in the middle of the table.

"What's this?" he said.

"Cake, Papa," Lilli replied.

"I see that it's cake. Take it away. We're not through."

Lilli took the cake back into the kitchen and set it on the counter.

"What?" Mama said. "Is there something wrong with the cake?"

"They're not through," Lilli replied.

She took off her apron and opened the door to the side yard, a nubbly space full of sinkholes and rocks. When Lilli left for Stuttgart, the single tree in the corner of the yard had been alive, its winter drapes shed and green buds rippling along its branches. Now it was a seared-brown scarecrow. Aaron said that nothing grew in the yard because of the constant dampness where the water pipes had leaked onto the ground. Too much water robs plants of oxygen, he said. It was a mystery how Aaron knew so much about so many things, since he spent all his waking hours at Papa's side, his body bent over the holy texts.

Lilli had lived in this house most of her life, but since her return from Stuttgart it felt smaller than she remembered, its walls grown trembly, and there was a definite sensation of its foundation having slipped away, so that when she closed her eyes, she imagined the tile-roofed house gliding unfettered across the sky, open doors like sails catching the wind. But it was the same house. The same gray wallpaper peeled off the walls like a serpent shedding its skin. The same pots bubbled on the iron stove.

The meandering unpaved dirt streets of the city's Jewish section hadn't changed; when the wind blew the air was still choked with silt that grayed the buildings and sifted through ill-fitting door frames and window sills. The wood-frame synagogue was still across the street, the kosher meat and poultry market a block away, the bakery and fruit market still standing between the *mikveh* and tailor shop.

Before the Soviets annexed Lithuania, Papa and Aaron had argued about whether it was more dangerous to leave Kovno or to stay.

"Moses says we should leave," Aaron said.

Papa said, "A man doesn't leave his home and go out into the wilderness for no reason."

"But the Jews, Papa . . ."

"We have to have trust in God, Aaron, and not be afraid. We are citizens. This is our country. Who will harm us if we stay and are quiet and make no trouble?

"Moses saw terrible things done to the Jews in Warsaw."

"Kovno isn't Warsaw. No place is exactly like another place. Kovno is our home. Jews have always lived here. The Soviets aren't like Hitler. Nothing as terrible as what happened in Warsaw will happen here."

Shortly after that the Soviets arrived in Kovno. First they closed the Jewish schools, then foreign consulates were shuttered, communal meetings forbidden. The few people on the streets hurried to their destinations with quick, fearful looks.

"Zev Mandelbaum was taken away in the middle of the night, Papa," Aaron said. "Who knows where he was taken or what was done to him."

"He must have done something wrong."

"What wrong could Zev Mandelbaum have done? He spent his days reading Torah."

"We don't know the truth of everything, Aaron. Only God knows."

Refugees from Nazi-occupied Poland continued to pour into the city, bringing with them stories of attacks on Jews too wild, too preposterous, too horrific, to believe.

The telegraph office was jammed with people waiting to send cables to American relatives, however distant, begging for dollars with which to buy exit visas. American dollars—not zlotys or rubles or litai—was the only currency the Soviets would accept, and yet Jews caught selling their belongings for dollars or found with dollars in their possession were executed.

Aaron and Papa no longer argued about leaving, and Moses stayed on in the Chernofsky house with his retinue of followers, his arms stretched out to catch Lilli in shadowed corners and clutch her to him in dangerous ways, but at every unusual sound he would go to the front door and look out as though he were waiting for a summer storm to descend on Kovno and hollow out the skies.

One afternoon he left the house and came back with news.

"If you give the Dutch consul a piece of paper, he'll stamp the words *No visa is required to Curaçao* on it."

"A piece of paper?" Aaron said. "What are you talking about?"

"I'm talking about not needing a visa to go to Curaçao."

"So what? How do we get there? You make no sense."

"The Japanese consul is willing to grant twenty-one-day transit visas through Japan to the holders of Dutch visas.

"Through Japan? Through? Then what? Will we then be abandoned?"

"The Japanese control Shanghai," Moses said. "We might be able to get to Shanghai."

"Might," Aaron moaned. "Might."

Chapter 2

Moses and Lilli left the house at dawn, Moses carrying the precious Torah scroll in his arms, Lilli, a bright blue scarf over her sheaf of oaten hair, walking beside him. It was a dawn like any other summer dawn, warm beneath a faltering sky of winged clouds, the sun-ruddled linden trees kiting the breeze through their lacy leaves, dun-colored horses pulling milk wagons, the noisome clatter of their hooves shaking the morning sloth. A good day to be outside in the summer air walking, as though walking were the purpose.

By the time they reached the neighborhood where Gentiles lived in frame houses on cobblestoned streets, the sun was fully up. Lilli had walked this far from home only twice before, once to the train station to take the train to Stuttgart and once when she returned home.

The iron fence of the Japanese consulate lay ahead, a press of people like a raised scar winding around the small house and spilling off the sidewalk into the street.

Moses handed the scroll to Lilli.

"Are you nervous?" he said.

"No."

"I'll wait for you here."

Lilli took her place in line behind a woman carrying a baby.

"My husband is sick in bed and now the baby is coughing," the woman said. "You should stand as far away from me as you can."

"Someone will step in front of me if I leave a space," Lilli said. "I'm not afraid of getting sick. I never get sick. Your baby is very pretty."

Lilli looked behind her. She couldn't see the end of the line now. In the few moments she had been standing here, it had grown past the fence and down the block and had begun to turn the corner.

"We could have gone to New York," the woman said. "The Soviets came before we could leave."

"I'm sorry."

"Everyone is sorry for something. You should put your bundle down on the ground. You'll hurt your back."

"It isn't heavy."

"I've cried and cried. I have no more tears. But what good is regret for what I should have done? Can a person see into the future? Life is *beshert*. We can plan what we're going to do and how we're going to do it, but God has other ideas. Anyway, what happens to us in life is over in the blink of an eye. So is what you're carrying valuable?"

"No. Hardly worth anything."

"Still, every little bit of money you can get for it is a good thing. I have a pair of diamond earrings pinned to Freyda's diaper. Maybe they will bring enough to take my family away from here."

The baby began coughing. The woman opened her blouse and put the baby to her breast. "She's not hungry, but it quiets her," she said.

It was hot. There was exhaustion in everyone's face. Those closest to the iron fence leaned on it, draped their arms over it. Some merely sat on the curb and stared at the white house with the brown door and narrow windows. There were no trees here, no shade, merely an unruly line of shoving, stumbling, benumbed people, some pushing baby carriages, some holding children in their arms, some lugging paper-wrapped parcels, boxes or suitcases, everyone with a sheet of paper or a passport stamped with the words *No Visa Is Required to Curaçao.*

The scroll was heavy. Lilli had never held it before. It had sat in its ark in Papa's study, only taken out on holy days and then only Aaron was allowed to carry it from the house to the synagogue.

The line didn't seem to move. A battalion of people stretched out behind her. Maybe Aaron was right. Maybe he should have been the one to do this. She clasped the scroll more tightly, worried now that someone would steal it out of her arms or she would collapse in the hot sun and the scroll would roll away while she lay unconscious on the pavement.

She tried to concentrate on what was being said around her. Wild stories. Rumors. *The Soviets are filming everyone in front of the consulate; they will arrest you, take you away for interrogation, send you to Siberia. The Japanese have arrested Consul Sugihara and closed the consulate and there will be no more visas. Consul Sugihara will defy the authorities and issue visas. Consul Sugihara is lying dead in his office, shot by a German assassin. Consul Sugihara is still in his office, but he has been wounded (luckily in the left arm—he's still free to stamp transit visas with his right hand).*

At mid-morning Consul Sugihara himself came out of the house. Lilli had thought he would be wearing a uniform and that his head would be shaved like the pictures of the Japanese in the newspapers, but he had bristly hair tamed by a layer of pomade and was wearing an ordinary gray suit and large striped tie.

"I will give a transit visa to everyone here," he said in halting Lithuanian. "I will write and stamp visas as long as I can. You have my promise." He took a handkerchief out of his pocket, wiped his brow, and then went back inside.

A drenching summer storm came suddenly. Shirts, cotton dresses, bundles of paper, carried children and wobble-wheeled prams seemed to sink beneath cascading waves of water. Mama had wrapped the Torah in a raincoat and newspapers. Ink now streamed down Lilli's legs and into her shoes. In a few moments the rain was gone, and the sun was brighter and hotter than before. Coils of steam spiraled up like cigarette smoke from scattered pools of rainwater, some no bigger than a baby's fist, others as large as small ponds to be stepped in and sloshed through.

The line was moving slowly, but Lilli was now close enough to the house to smell the flowers blooming beneath the windows. There was a line at the side of the house, too, where a Lithuanian woman in a print housedress, a hairnet on her gray hair, was letting people into the basement of the house, one at a time, to use the toilet.

Mama had prepared a bowl of boiled oats and milk for Lilli before she left the house. "You'll need your strength," Mama said. But Lilli hadn't been able to eat. Now she felt the flag of an empty stomach.

By late afternoon Lilli had passed the iron gate and was walking up the steps to the house. A young Japanese woman in a gray skirt and white blouse, her black hair as straight as a wire brush, opened the door and let Lilli in. The woman motioned for Lilli to wipe her shoes on the towel on the floor of the entryway, and then led her through a sparsely furnished living room, then past the kitchen where another Japanese woman (Consul Sugihara's wife?) held a baby in her lap while a toddler crawled on the floor and a child sat at a table tearing an orange into segments. The woman holding the baby smiled at Lilli.

Then to the end of a short hall and into Consul Sugihara's office.

The office was plain: an umbrella stand with an umbrella in it, file cabinets, a typewriter on a small table next to Consul Sugihara's desk. Sun shone through the single bare window onto walls as white as boiled potatoes, their plainness interrupted only by a picture of a lone tree on a hill.

Consul Sugihara was seated behind a desk strewn with an assortment of papers, inkpots, and stamp pads.

"What is your name?" he said.

"Lilli Chernofsky."

He stared at her for a moment. "How old are you?"

"Seventeen."

"Where are your parents?"

"Here in Kovno. Also my brother Aaron. Also five others. We have no passports. We're all from Poland. Papa is a rabbi. He left Warsaw for Kovno when I was a baby. We have pieces of paper with a Dutch stamp for Curaçao."

"Why isn't your father here with you?"

"He never leaves the house except to go to the synagogue. My brother is older and very smart, but he sometimes forgets to say what he intended to say and then says the wrong thing."

Consul Sugihara nodded his head, was quiet for a while, then picked up his pen and filled out nine transit visas, stamped them and handed them to her.

She put the visas in the pocket of her jacket, but didn't move toward the door.

"I have something to sell."

He sighed. "Everyone with something to sell. I'm sorry, but it's not possible."

Moses had asked Lilli if she was nervous. How could she explain that nervousness was what she felt when she stood on the stage in Stuttgart and said a few lines in one of Tante Rose's plays. What she felt now was excitement.

He turned away, was writing something on the pad in front of him.

"You'll change your mind when you see what I've brought you," she said. "I know how easy it is to say no before you even have a chance to look at something. I would do the same if I were in your place because I know everyone waiting in line outside has something to sell and you're tired of looking at old relics and broken treasures. But this is something that museums want, a rare object."

"Please, please, there are others waiting."

"You can buy it from me, and then you can sell it. You can become rich because you have never seen anything like what I'm going to show you. It's been in our family since 1862. It's Papa's most precious possession. Mama said that when Uncle Samuel bought the scroll he didn't know that he would be performing a *mitzvah* by dying and leaving it to Papa and that if you didn't want to buy it then you were a fool. Mama never says things like that. She's very quiet, speaks about everyone with respect, but she's worried about what will happen to us if we stay in Kovno. Papa doesn't want to emigrate. He doesn't know I've taken the scroll. I don't think you're a fool. I think you're going to buy the scroll and we're going to leave Kovno."

He shook his head. "I have no time for this. I'm sorry."

Lilli could feel his impatience. He was waiting for her to leave, wanted her to leave, but she had already decided it didn't matter how many people before her had brought things to sell, she wouldn't leave until he had bought the scroll.

She laid the scroll on the floor in front of Consul Sugihara's desk and began to tear away the feathery layers of rain-melted newsprint.

"No, no, there are people waiting."

"Mama didn't know it would rain, but she always prepares for the worst, so she wrapped the scroll in a raincoat I wore when I was ten years old. Mama never throws anything away."

"No, Miss Chernofsky."

"Mama always says no to the pots-and-pans man, but he just stands in the doorway and doesn't leave until Mama buys something. Have you ever heard of anyone so stubborn? And what's a pot or a pan to something as beautiful as what I'm going to show you? When Aaron carries it into the synagogue everyone loses their breath at the sight."

Consul Sugihara got up from his chair and was now watching as Lilli began to unwind the raincoat.

"Look at the way the sun shines the silver," she said as the last fold of raincoat fell away. "It's bright enough to hurt your eyes."

"I'm sorry, the authorities watch everything I do."

"Great Uncle Samuel Chernofsky read in a book that there was a synagogue in Kaifeng, China, so he boarded a ship and went to China to look for Chinese Jews. The synagogue had been turned into a public urinal, but there were Chinese who claimed to be descended from Jewish traders who came from Baghdad in the twelfth century. They didn't look like Jews—how could they when they only had Chinese to marry?"

"I'd like to buy it, but I can't."

This was always the moment when the pots-and-pans man said his wife sent Mama her regards and said to be sure and tell Mama she could make a tastier *cholent* if she bought a new pot.

"Imagine—a Torah scroll in Hebrew and Chinese. No one could imagine such a thing. Papa always says he can feel the holy spirit enter a room when he opens the scroll."

"I'm being sent to Berlin. I'm not free to do what I want."

"Do you have American dollars?"

"I can't buy it. I'm sorry."

"It has to be American dollars. Zlotys are no good. I need American dollars for nine exit visas."

"Surely someone will buy it."

"There's no time. The Soviets will kill me first. Two thousand American dollars and the scroll is yours."

"Everyone in Kovno wants American dollars," he said. "There aren't enough American dollars in Kovno for everyone."

"Look at the parchment; there is no parchment in Europe to equal this. Look at the engraving in the breastplate, the bells, and flowers. Only a great artist could have made a Torah case like this one. You see how it opens, the Sephardic way, on a hinge, two pieces and then the scroll."

"You have to understand that I have sympathy, but . . ."

"The Hebrew script was written by stylus, and the Chinese was written with a Chinese brush pen. It dates from the year 1642 when the Yellow River dikes broke. The synagogue and nearly the whole city of Kaifeng were drowned in water. You can see the water stains on the paper. Minor stains. Nothing to ruin the beauty."

"I can't buy everything that's offered to me."

"In 1930 the English Historical Society offered Papa fifteen thousand pounds."

"My currency transactions are watched."

"You can make money on it; sell it wherever you want."

"Can you leave it here?"

"Leave it here?"

The sun was overbright; its rays dazed her.

"I take the morning train for Berlin tomorrow. Come to the station, and I'll have your money for you."

*   *   *

"Everything is lost, hopeless," Aaron said. "How could you have left the scroll with someone you don't even know, who isn't even Jewish? Are you so stupid you think a promise of money is the same as real money?"

"It was the only way."

"She did the best she could," Moses said.

Lilli wasn't sure that it was the best she could do. Mama had given Papa some headache medicine and they were both now in Papa's study with the door closed.

"I should have been the one to take the scroll," Aaron said. "The man fooled you. What did you think, that he was your friend? He probably has contempt for Jews. What does he care what happens to us after he's gone to Berlin?"

"He promised he would get the money for me. We'll be able to buy exit visas," Lilli said.

"'He promised.' What do you know about anything? You're just a child. You're too young and stupid to even know what you've done."

Lilli could hear the ragged voices of yeshiva buchers *davening* at the eastern wall of the living room as though what was happening had nothing to do with them.

"Consul Sugihara said he will bring the money to the train station," she said.

"A lie. Do you think you are smarter than he is? You've given away the only thing of worth in the family and now Papa is sick because of it. It will be on your head, Lilli, if something bad happens to him because of this. You know how important the scroll is to him. Do you think scrolls like that are in every home, that everyone has a museum piece like that and can trust a non-Jew to promise to pay money for it and tell you to leave it with him, and you listen to him and go away and leave the scroll with him and that's the end of it? Do you?"

"Don't shout at her," Moses said.

"It's all right," Lilli said.

"Yes, Moses. Listen to Lilli. This is my family. This is my sister. And I'll shout if I want to shout."

"I don't mind your shouting, Aaron," Lilli said, "but you're making yourself hoarse."

Aaron put his hand to his throat. "I think maybe I *am* getting a cold. Feel my head, Lilli. Do I have a fever?"

Lilli held her hand to Aaron's forehead. "No fever, but I'll make you some tea and lemon."

Aaron cleared his throat, then coughed a few times.

"You think we can control everything that happens, Aaron, but we can't," Lilli said.

*   *   *

Consul Sugihara and the woman Lilli had seen in the consulate kitchen were at the train window signing and stamping passports, birth certificates, notepapers, letters, old lists, receipts, ledger sheets, tattered strips of newspaper, pages torn from books, covers of magazines, even matchboxes. Particles of paper floated through the air like rain, like snow, like rainbows. Specks, shreds, bits of paper fluttered onto the tracks. Hands clawed at the train's metal body, held papers up to the open window. There was barely room to move on the station platform. No one would give up an inch of hard-earned space.

Moses took Lilli's hand and pushed through the crowd until they were within reach of the train window.

The train had begun to move.

"Now," Lilli said.

Moses lifted Lilli up above the heads of the crowd and Consul Sugihara leaned as far as he could out the window. Lilli felt Consul Sugihara's fingers first, and then the envelope as it dropped into her hands.

Chapter 3

Aaron said he felt sick before they left the house, and had been complaining of stomach pains since they crossed the bridge. He leaned over now, icicles twining like white cotton thread through his red beard, and retched onto the berm of gravelly snow bordering the river.

"I don't know," Aaron said and wiped his mouth on his sleeve.

"What don't you know?" Moses asked him.

"What it feels like to die, if there is some sign in the moment before. Holy men talk about a blinding light."

"We don't have to do this today," Moses said. "We can try again tomorrow or next week."

"No, we'll do it today. Just make sure every piece of my body is recovered for burial. I don't want even a fingernail left behind in this *gehenna*."

They had started out on Mapu Street, because Aaron said it was a good street, but Moses had seen Soviet patrols on Mapu and decided the river route would be safer. Aaron had argued that Moses was a stranger to Kovno, what did he know about what street to take, and Moses retorted that Aaron might have lived in Kovno all his life, but he didn't know a good street from a bad street. Moses didn't dislike him, but he had no patience for his erratic behavior and unpredictable, maddening opinions. Torah and synagogue were all he knew. He studied the holy books for so many hours a day he forgot to eat. What did he know about anything outside of the holy texts? He barely saw the sky. He didn't even notice the beauty of the linden trees standing like ermine-trimmed stanchions along the city streets, had no interest in the ancient churches and castles that loomed over the city in the same way they had in the twelfth century. He studied the holy books and accepted the inerrancy of God's word, but without scripture to guide him he intuited the world, imagined motives, created evidence, pronounced verdicts. He belittled Lilli, forced her to bite off her words, to trim them syllable by syllable. It was all Moses could do to hide his contempt for him.

Aaron stopped to rest again, holding his stomach with both hands. Every day he had changed his mind about when it would be safe to leave Kovno.

We don't have to rush to get exit visas. We should wait until the Soviets relax their restrictions. We should wait until the weather warms. We should wait to hear from those who have gone ahead.

Then came news that eight hundred Jews had been murdered by a Lithuanian militia and he decided it was time to leave.

It was quiet by the river. Tranquil. The great confluence of the Nieman and Neris reeled out into the distance, its purple-tinged water turgid and swollen, steamboats moored on the tributaries waiting for spring. There was no sign here that the city was crushed and dying.

"Are you all right?" Moses asked.

"I'm breathing," Aaron replied.

He didn't look well, but then he never looked particularly healthy. His arms were untoned slags of skin, his legs skinny appendages. Still, he was dangerous to Moses. There was always the possibility in his obsession with Talmudic knots that a random bit of knowledge annealed in some forgotten store in his brain would awaken, or some of his rambling thoughts would cohere and he would question Moses more closely, would want to know more than Moses had limpingly told him about the escape from Warsaw, the trek through farm land and forest, the finding of the four yeshiva students sitting in the open on the side of the road. All of that had no complicated parts, but what would he do if he knew who and what Moses really was?

They headed away from the river now down a street of slope-roofed, unpainted wooden houses, front gardens bare, fences little more than sticks to keep in the chickens, the houses so close together it was as if there were no walls to separate them. From open windows came the smell of sausages and soggy wool and rancid cooking oil.

The stone Commissariat building was ahead.

A Russian soldier guarded the door. Moses had heard that people had been shot in front of that door, pockets emptied, shoes and mufflers and hats and coats taken by scavengers, bodies unclaimed. Blood still stained the steps. There. And there. And there. But on the other side of the door was the place where Aaron and Moses will rip open the lining of their coats and spill American dollars onto some official's desk for nine exit visas.

Moses handed the soldier forty litai.

The soldier spat in Moses' face. "Parasites! Blood suckers!"

"Give him more money," Aaron said, bent over, mouth open, as though he were starving for air.

Moses turned his back on the Russian and opened the oak-plank door.

"Let him shoot us," he said. "I gave him enough."

* * *

The names of those approved to receive exit visas were posted on the wall of the Commissariat building once a week. On Tuesday the Chernofsky name was on the list. Nine visas.

No one slept. Cold meals were eaten at odd hours. Marathon discussions lasted into the night.

Papa didn't take part in the discussions. He no longer suppled and smoothed the meanings of ancient texts. He had aged, his shoulders were fallen and curved, his head a lion's mane of gray waves and snarls, his gaze, once lashed with light, now fettered and dull.

"Papa is not coming with us," Mama said, her eyes as red as torn skin.

Chapter 4

December 1940

Forty people—young, old, babies, small children—waited at the train station, bundled up in heavy coats, extra socks tucked into waterproof boots, thick scarves wound around necks, the yeshiva students shivery in the same destroyed clothes they were wearing when they arrived in Kovno. Moses had given the youngest his coat and now stood in his thin black suit with his back hunched against the gale gusting in from the east.

At seven-thirty the locomotive roared toward them, a screen of lavender smoke scumbling its shape and turning the black blot a frost gray. The men, Intourist travel vouchers safe in their pockets, carried suitcases, packets of food, paper bags filled with breakable items. The women held the children. Warm breaths gauzed the frigid air.

Papa had been at his desk when they left, the window curtain behind him leaking light, the air smelling of seeping frost and the velvety soap that sat in the dish in the bathroom. The eggs Mama prepared for him sat untouched on a plate.

"Please come with us, Papa," Lilli said.

"When the world is perfect I will come to you."

She felt the heat of his hand through her headscarf as he gave her his blessing.

"And I will carry you on eagles' wings and I will deliver you to Me," he murmured in her ear.

Lilli looked back at Kovno. She could see children skating on a frozen pond. Snow drifted across rooftops, scuffed up against the trunks of trees and lay in slate piles at street corners. She wished she had a camera. She wished she could run home and tell Papa she loved him, but Moses had his arm around her waist and was pulling her toward the train.

The tracks hummed, the train's wheels squealed, metal sparks flew into the cold air, and suddenly everyone was in one small spot. Arms and legs flailed, small packages fell, a child screamed, an old man's cane stabbed the air like an errant saber.

"Be a good girl, Lilli, and take care of your brother," Mama said, her lips like a smooth cube of ice on Lilli's cheek. "And always remember that it is a *mitzvah* to be kind to the less fortunate."

"But you're coming with us."

"Not now."

"When?"

"Soon."

"Hurry," Aaron hollered from the train steps.

For a moment Lilli thought of letting the train go. Trains came and went. There would be another train.

"Go, Lilli," Mama said and gave Lilli a small shove.

"No."

"We'll come, I promise you."

Moses lifted Lilli in his arms and carried her up the steps into the train.

"Do you know how foolish you are, how stupid?" Aaron said, his lips cracked with cold, his eyes glistening. "You knew she wouldn't leave him. What were you thinking, that you can stay behind and let me go without you, that I would leave you here?"

It began to snow again, soft white sheets covering the broken bits left behind on the station platform. The train was moving, the pavement slipping by, crack joining crack joining crack until it was just a dizzyingly smooth gray surface gliding by. Mama looked tall standing on the platform by herself, the wind blowing the spent curls of her wig, her hand waving and waving and waving.

*   *   *

By the time the train pulled into the Kazansky terminal in Moscow there was a definite ebbing of apprehension. The men laughed and joked, the women held their children less tightly.

A small, stout man in an ill-fitting overcoat with cat-fur hat and earmuffs, greeted them in Yiddish.

"Welcome to Moscow, my fellow Jews. My name is Mandel Bornstein. I am your Intourist representative here in beautiful Moscow. As you can see, in honor of your arrival the snow has stopped and the sun is out. This augurs well for the continued success of your journey. You will remain in Moscow two days. There are rooms reserved for you at the Nova-Moscova Hotel. A beautiful hotel, the best. There is a kosher dining room on the fourth floor that Intourist has generously provided for your use. Your rooms are comfortable. No one has an uncomfortable room. I myself have seen the rooms. They are good rooms, beautiful, the best. We want you to have a happy, carefree time here in Moscow. It will be a good place for you to rest before you continue on to Vladivostok."

"Will we be interrogated while we're here?" Moses asked.

"Those stories are fascist propaganda. I, as a Russian Jew, and my wife Ida and our daughter Shaya are happy citizens of Soviet Russia."

"His smile winks on and off like a broken lamp," Aaron said.

"His smile is his smile," Lilli said.

"If you would for once agree with something I say."

"Let her be," Moses said.

"Mind your own business."

"You make a slave of her."

"If you say he winks, then he winks," Lilli said.

* * *

The Nova-Moscova Hotel was old but elegant, with marble floors that rasped, clicked, and squeaked as the various shoe soles rubbed against its surface. Some of the refugees were from *shtetlekh* in the Polish countryside and had never been in a hotel before, had never even seen an elevator. There was a picnic atmosphere in the lobby as they watched the iron cage move up and down between floors. When they tired of that, they walked around the lobby, fingering the leaves of the giant palms or watching the blinking lights of the telephone switchboard.

The rooms were well furnished. French-style bureaus, soft beds, German engravings of Russian cathedrals on the walls. Lilli shared a room with a Mrs. Lipsky and her middle-aged daughter Fanny. The mother, white-haired and fat, had no teeth (she ate nothing but mashed groats, her daughter said) and spoke only Yiddish. The daughter, narrow-faced, her straight hair wrapped around her ears like two empty snail shells, was short and thin with a complexion the color of weak tea.

For two days the refugees were taken on bus tours of the city with Mandel Bornstein providing lengthy commentaries on Russian history.

"I have never heard such tales as he spins," Aaron said as they waited in Red Square to view Lenin's tomb. "That he should make things up when there are books to be consulted is the work of a charlatan or a madman."

"There are radio transmitters in the rooms and the Soviets monitor every-thing we say," Moses whispered to Lilli. "Speak kindly of Stalin."

On their last night in Moscow they attended a performance of the Yid-dish State Theatre. Some in the audience had brought food and were spooning it out of paper bags. The odor of chicken and *grivines* was mixed with the boggy wetland smell of steeped leather and sodden wool.

Lilli and Moses were seated next to Mandel Bornstein and his wife Ida, who held their daughter Shaya on her lap. Ida was a tiny woman in a rab-bit-trimmed greatcoat, lank brown hair fastened into a pompadour which curved away from the sides of her head like the wings of a bird. Shaya, a red wool hat on her buff-colored hair, her small body packaged in a padded jacket and leggings, teetered uncertainly on Ida's knee. The yeshiva students, afraid they might accidentally touch elbows with a strange woman, had stayed behind in the hotel, but Aaron, who had never been to the theater before, decided to attend (as an *experiment*, he said), and was sitting with Fanny and Mrs. Lipsky.

The curtain rose suddenly, and the emcee, a wooly-haired man in a lime-green business suit, introduced an actor in silk pantaloons and a belted smock who recited Hamlet's soliloquy in Yiddish. It was greeted with solemn quiet and polite applause.

A tenor was next. He began the first few strains of a Jewish folk song and there were sighs from the audience. A few people picked up the melody, some knew the words, and soon everyone was singing. They didn't stop when the tenor left the stage.

The emcee returned, but no one could hear him over the singing.

The emcee departed and the stage was bare until a comic in purple spats and cowboy hat appeared.

Voices shouted, "Go home! We want the singer!"

The comic gave up trying to make himself heard and began doing hand-stands and somersaults while balloons twirled above his head and flew into the audience like red and yellow dirigibles. Lilli caught one of the balloons and handed it to Ida.

"For your little girl."

The emcee tried to pull the comic off the stage, but he wouldn't go. Some of the refugees joined the comic on the stage and were dancing the *kazatskeh*, while everyone else clapped and sang and stamped their feet.

Aaron got out of his seat and stood in the aisle, a wild look on his face.

"Is this how we fall into the pit?" he shouted. "While Jews vanish into the icy wastes of the Arctic, into the disease-riddled heat of the steppes of Kazakhstan and Samarkand, we, a trickle in the ocean, sit like stepchildren in a Moscow theater, banging our feet and bellowing?"

Lilli got up and led Aaron back to his seat.

"What is happening to us, Lilli?" he said.

"Nothing is happening. When people feel afraid, they make noise."

* * *

Bornstein stood on a box in the train terminal shouting to be heard. He wasn't wearing his overcoat, although the temperature was well below freezing. His hat and earmuffs were gone, his hair uncombed, the bald spot laid bare, small brown freckles, like islands on a map, visible on his scalp. He looked as if he had had a shock or was about to be sick; instead he gave a speech.

"I am here to see you on your way, to make sure everyone is present that should be present, that no one has been accidentally left behind. I apologize for the opening and checking of the contents of suitcases and for the wait while items in the hotel rooms were inventoried to make sure nothing was stolen. Not that we believe anything was stolen, but it's a formality, something that's done for no reason other than to give the people who check those things something to do."

He had no winking smiles today. He said everything in a loud rush, as though expecting someone to come before he had finished and pull him away. He had brought his wife and daughter with him. His daughter stood near a lamppost looking bewildered. His wife paid no attention to her but walked up and back through the station throngs, as though she had a destination in mind but couldn't remember what it was. Lilli couldn't stop looking at the little girl, worried that she might wander away.

"If you would be so generous as to take the form and fill it out on the train and mail it back to Intourist," Bornstein said. "Future clients will benefit, and I'm sure you will take note of my service, you will rate it as at least satisfactory, my job depends on it, as you must know, because service must be beautiful, the best, or everything is lost. I'm sure you understand my position and will say the service has been beautiful, the best. Still, there is no such thing as perfection, anyone can tell you that who has ever tried to achieve it. Perfection? I for one will tell you it's impossible. Don't forget: fill it out and mail it back."

"Mail it back?" Aaron said to Moses. "Perfection? He's lost his mind."

"It's his job," Lilli said.

"Do you even know what you're saying?"

"Then throw it away," Moses told him.

"Your name is good enough," Bornstein was saying. "Don't concern your-self about an address. There will be time for that later."

"When later?" Aaron said to Moses. "Where?"

"It's just an expression. Let the man talk."

"I don't believe in expressions. A person should be precise and say what he means."

"He's just doing what he's been told," Lilli said.

"You make judgments out of the air," Aaron told her. "No one told him to say what he's saying. Madmen talk the way he does."

"He can hear you."

"I don't care if he can hear me or not. And a Jewish Communist? He should be ashamed."

"The Soviet government wants nothing more than to serve you," Bornstein continued. "Satisfaction. They want satisfaction. For myself, I have enjoyed our encounter, but it has been too short, you should have come in June when the weather was warm, we could have sat in the park and played chess, but I am sure you have enjoyed your stay in Moscow and there is no doubt you will enjoy your stay in Vladivostok and will be treated in the most beautiful way, the best."

"He doesn't know how we will be treated," Aaron said. "And does he think we are roaming the earth looking for a chess game?"

"He doesn't want us to worry," Lilli replied.

"Don't defend him. 'Beautiful'? 'The best'? Twenty times he said it. I counted."

"Enough," Moses said. "Enough."

"Enough? Who are you to say what is enough? Did you hear him, Lilli, telling me 'enough' as if he were the *Mashiach*?"

The train arrived on schedule. A third-class train, bench seats with thin mattresses for sleeping, a few bare hanging light bulbs, some water kettles, an iron stove in the middle of the car.

The train was barely stopped when it began hissing to be gone again.

"One last heartfelt good-bye to my dear Jewish comrades," Bornstein said and bounded onto the train, carrying the little girl and holding his wife's hand, while the refugees clambered aboard behind him. Fanny found a bench near a flyspecked, dirt-covered window. Moses helped Mrs. Lipsky up the steps (actually carried her heavy weight in his arms) and then joined the four yeshiva students, who had settled themselves in the rear of the car and were already arguing among themselves as to whether or not sitting as close as they were to women was a breach of Talmudic law. Lilli checked to see that Aaron didn't leave his suitcase in the train station and then pushed two benches together before he could complain about the lack of room for his books.

The train whistle was now blowing for a second time and Bornstein and his wife and daughter still hadn't gotten off the train.

"Well, I wish good health to all of you, and a beautiful trip, the best," he said, and then he embraced his wife. "Take care of Shaya. Be careful. There are dangers, Ida, you have to pay attention and look in all directions and make sure you always have Shaya with you, that she doesn't get lost. Anything can happen. Make sure she eats well. That's the important thing, that she isn't hungry. A child needs food to grow. Watch her carefully. I have only one child, one wife. Don't forget to write to me, let me know where you are, I won't rest until I hear from you."

"I see that the Jews of Russia are no happier than they've ever been," Aaron said.

* * *

They had been on the train for six days. Up until yesterday there had been an occasional village, primitive buildings sunk on chunks of icy plain. Today the view was monotonously white and flat, power lines and leafless trees the only relief from the geometric sameness.

"We must not ride on the Sabbath unless our lives are in danger," Aaron said, the Mishnah open on a desk he had made out of pieces of kindling the conductor said was to be used for the stove.

"Our lives *are* in danger," Moses said.

"Not *imminent* danger. It says here, Moses, right here in the Mishnah that riding in a conveyance on the Sabbath is not permitted *unless* your life is in danger. Is this not the Sabbath and are we not in a conveyance, and are we not in as perfect health as the circumstances allow?"

"If you get off the train, you'll die. Is that danger enough for you?"

"But *on* the train, Moses, *on* the train. That is the question. Are we in danger *on* the train?"

"I can only speak about the danger if you leave the train, not if you stay on it."

"The Mishnah is quite clear, Moses, that the danger must be present for you to remain on the conveyance on the Sabbath."

"It's no good for his eyes, reading while the train is jumping up and down," Fanny Lipsky said from where she sat next to her mother, who had lost her appetite for groats and appeared to have shrunk some during the journey.

"Your interpretation is too narrow," Moses said. "The question is broader than that."

"If I accept your interpretation, tell me what guarantee there is I will die if I get off the train."

"That isn't the question, Aaron."

"I know what the question is. Don't you think I know what the question is?"

"If you want me to make comments, you'll have to let me make them."

"Make them. What do I care?"

Everyone occupied their time in their own way. The yeshiva students slept during the day and were awake at night so they could walk through the car without accidentally touching one of the women. Ida kept Shaya close to her and didn't talk to anyone. Lilli tended the iron stove (adding kindling when the car grew too cold), filled the water kettles when the train stopped to let another one go past, helped Fanny when Mrs. Lipsky had to use the toilet (Fanny holding one arm and Lilli the other while they lowered Mrs. Lipsky onto the filthy seat), and took care of Aaron (making sure he wasn't so absorbed in Talmudic reasoning that he forgot to eat and sleep). As for the rest, when they weren't eating, sleeping, smoking, and praying, they sniped at each other. *You sit too close. You smell bad. Why do you keep saying the same things over and over? You ate more of the bread than I did. So sleep if you want to sleep. Am I the one who told you to leave Kovno? So go back. How do I know what's going to happen? Is it my fault you refused to go to America when we had the chance?*

Lilli looked out at the passing landscape. The voices around her crested then receded, a nattering whine of panic and dread. At the next stop she would refill the water kettles and maybe there would be someone selling something to eat.

* * *

"How much for the bread?" Lilli asked the peasant woman.

"Five kopecks," she said and held up a lumpy wheel of black bread.

Lilli looked longingly at the shiny loaf. Meat had to be kosher or Aaron wouldn't eat it, but peasant bread, black as dirt, was neutral, unless, of course, it was made with lard, and then, according to the laws of *kashrut*, it was *treyf*. Aaron would starve before he would eat *treyf*. She couldn't tell if it had lard in it or not. All she could smell was the goodness of flour and water and coarsely ground grains.

She counted out the money. Her leather change purse jangled more loudly now that there were fewer coins in it.

"Did you get some dried fish?" Aaron asked when she climbed aboard again.

"I bought black bread."

"I wanted fish."

"I have some salami," Fanny offered.

"Is it kosher?"

"I don't know."

"Don't eat it, Lilli. It's *treyf.*"

"I have groats if you want groats," Fanny said.

Aaron had already turned back to his book.

"Aaron won't eat anything that isn't kosher," Lilli whispered, "but I will."

Fanny opened the cloth bag containing the remnants of the cured meat and cheese she had bought in Moscow and gave a piece of salami to Lilli.

"I didn't ask if it's kosher," Fanny said apologetically. "I just bought it. I knew we had to eat."

* * *

Lilli couldn't sleep. Moses was awake, too, both of them standing in the small vestibule at the rear of the car, the cold sleeking their cheeks—a dry, smoked cold, not the damp cold produced by sleeping bodies and warm breaths that froze beards and long hair to the train's timber walls.

"Are you sure we're going east?" Lilli said.

"I'm sure," Moses replied. "According to my pocket map we're now in Siberia. Every time the train stops I watch for Russian soldiers. I imagine I can see them coming down from the steppes on horses and yanking us from the train."

Moses stepped back toward the bleared-white window and pulled her with him. He leaned into the mitered corner, his spine like a toothed comb against the cold iron. She didn't yield. He should have expected that. A rabbi's daughter. A child of the *shetl.* An innocent young girl in stiffening retreat. After three or four kisses did he think she would raise her skirts to him and guide his hand?

Her body relented, then bent toward him. He kissed her again and she pressed against him and opened her mouth to his. She didn't stop his hand this time, but let his palm wander her smooth inner thigh toward the flap of cotton, the warmth of moist flesh rising now against his cupped hand. She surprised him. She flouted danger here in the dark. Her spread legs mocked her sheltered image. How far could he go before she resisted? She enticed him, but she was an inexperienced girl who expected romance. He had no time for romance. He held her away from him now, his caution an alarm set to ring. He should not have stopped in Kovno. He would not have were it not for the four yeshiva buchers wilting like parched plants, and he would not have stayed if not for Lilli, who broke his urge for flight with a single gated glance.

She took his hand and held it to her breast. Her breast was like she was, soft and compliant, her heartbeat a promise of ease and peace.

"I was mistaken," he said and pulled his hand away.

"You aren't mistaken. I'm old enough. I'm seventeen, and the world is ending."

Aaron had stepped into the vestibule.

"You take advantage, Moses. I go to sleep and you take advantage."

"He didn't take advantage," Lilli said.

"What are you saying? Do you even know what you're saying? He stands here in the dark with you. That's enough of an advantage. How do we know who he is, what he intends? You never think, Lilli. Do I have to watch you every minute? You have to be more suspicious of men, especially men who have lived in the world."

"You needn't worry," Moses said. "Go back to your prayer books."

"So you can do what you want with her?"

"Stop it," Lilli said.

"Stop it? You ask me to stop it? I'm your brother. I promised Papa I would take care of you, and you tell me to stop it?"

Moses laughed.

"Is something funny?" Aaron said. "Am I a comedian?"

"No, you're just foolish."

"I'm foolish? Because I don't want you to defile my sister? I won't move until you apologize. And I don't like the way you keep laughing at me. This isn't something to be laughed at. If you had a sister, you would know what I'm talking about."

Moses nodded. "You're right."

"Then you apologize?"

"Let's not argue."

"I accept your apology." Aaron stretched and yawned. "I'm hungry, Lilli. Do you have an egg?"

"I don't have an egg, but I have bread."

She walked back through the train, past the sleeping bodies. The swaying of the train made the wet between her legs feel strange. It ached right in the place where Moses had touched her with his fingers. She wondered if the skin was red there, if his touching her had damaged something. But the ache wasn't a painful ache, it was a sucking ache that was both pleasurably warm and mildly worrisome. It was as though Moses had wrenched a trembly bit of flesh out of its proper place, and she needed him to put it back. Aaron was so funny in his anger, all red-faced and wild-eyed, and then nothing, as if he really didn't care what she and Moses had been doing, as if he didn't want to know, but needed to act as if he did. She didn't suppose he had ever touched a girl where Moses had touched her. God forbid! As far as she knew, Aaron had never even held a girl's hand. He ran the other way if a girl so much as glanced at him. If Aaron weren't so hard to talk to she would have asked him what the Talmud said about touching and pleasure, whether there was a special *gehenna* for girls who opened their bodies to a man before they were married. Tante Rose said that if something gave you pleasure there could be no harm in it and that being with a man was as natural as breathing or eating or sleeping. *But there are precautions you must take. When you are ready, I will explain what they are.* But Tante Rose was in Stuttgart and the precautions remained a mystery, along with why Moses' browsing fingers had made her ache, and why he looked at her the way he did while he was touching her, and why when he kissed her she had felt so weak she would have fallen down if he hadn't been pressing her up against the wall of the train.

Moses was right. Aaron *was* foolish. He didn't know who she was or what she wanted. Sometimes she felt as though he had a chain around her neck. Papa may have told Aaron to take care of his sister, but Mama knew the truth of everything, and she told Lilli to take care of her brother. It was a mystery how different men and women were, how they didn't even know the simplest things about each other. What if he had come into the vestibule a few moments earlier and seen what she and Moses were doing?

The bread was hard. Probably baked four days ago. Probably made with pencil shavings. Aaron wanted an egg. Maybe on the next stop there would be eggs. She still had coins left, enough for one small egg for Aaron.

People made the oddest noises when they slept. Grunts and groans and snores, even a few whistles that joined with the loose clacking of the train on its tracks. Shaya was asleep, her breath leaving a wispy trail. How old was she? Two? Three? Ida was awake. She had wrapped Shaya in her coat and sat now with nothing but a sweater on.

"Where are we?"

"Siberia," Lilli said. She handed her a piece of bread, then reached for her suitcase, retrieved the jacket Mama knitted with wool from an old afghan and put it around Ida's shoulders, then walked back to the rear of the car.

"I still say that putting wood even into a stove on a train violates the Sabbath," Aaron was saying. "The Mishnah says that on the Sabbath we must not empty carts of their planks nor load planks into empty carts."

"The Mishnah says nothing about stoves on trains," Moses said and smiled a dark, secret smile at Lilli.

"God would want us to be warm," Lilli said and handed Aaron and Moses each a piece of bread.

"Look how she interprets the Mishnah for us, Moses." Aaron bit into the bread and grimaced. "It's stale. It hurts my teeth."

"Keep it in your mouth a few seconds and it will get soft," she said and walked back through the train again and lay down on her bench.

It was snowing again, moonlight splintering the windows. The landscape shifted. Hills became mountains. A sleek plateau became a glacial stage, frosted larch trees pirouetting across it. She closed her eyes and let the sleep of exhaustion swallow her up.

She was startled to hear Mama call her name. She sat up and looked out the window. Mama and Papa were galloping toward the train on golden horses, Papa in his fur-trimmed caftan, white beard its own whirling gale against the snowy steppes, Mama in her Sabbath black silk, her natural hair speckled with snow. Lilli held out her arms.

"I told you we would come to you soon," Mama said.

* * *

The train arrived in Vladivostok on the twelfth day. Its occupants staggered off, blinking in the sea-drenched light, then stood in line while Russian officials confiscated their money, their watches and rings, their fountain pens and stamps and books—even the books Aaron had lovingly guarded all the way from Kovno.

"My books, Lilli. My books."

"There will be more books, Aaron, I promise you."

Ida let go of Shaya's hand and stood at the brink of the dock, waving at the empty ship.

"More books, more books, more books," she sang in a childish lilt.

"Is she crazy, Lilli?" Aaron said. "Has Bornstein burdened us with a *meshuge* wife?"

"She's just homesick."

Dock workers fed the refugees fried fish and boiled potatoes, and in two hours the benumbed refugees were in a rusted, leaky ship that had been a trawler and reeked of rotted fish. The refugees were led down steps into a dark compartment that held packing boxes and foul-smelling nets, one person leading another through the enveloping murk to find an open space on the oil-stained deck on which to place a blanket, a suitcase, a child.

Ancient engines thundered and strained as the ship steamed across the Sea of Japan. Waves as tall as mountains tossed the ship from crest to crest. No one could stand upright. Soon the cramped compartment was littered with prostrate, vomiting bodies. Lilli heard Aaron calling to her, felt Moses holding a wet rag to her forehead. Shaya was whimpering somewhere. Ida was shrieking. Someone was sobbing. All thought was gone. Time was lost. Purpose spun away into emptiness.

"We're coming into the bay, Lilli," Moses said. "The water is calmer here."

Chapter 5

The ship had been docked in Tsuruga Bay for three days, the refugees in their shredded clothes hanging like peeling paint over the rail, too spent, too apprehensive to appreciate the shimmery green-blue water, the pine trees and rocky inlets dipping in and out of the gently undulating shoreline, the filigree beaches beneath a pearl-gray gossamer sky as shiny as copper beads in the winter sun. No one knew what was happening. Rumors seeded, then bloomed and spread like noxious weeds.

On the afternoon of the third day a rotund man in a lumpy gray suit appeared on the wharf.

"This is the crisis I anticipated, the one I have been preparing for in my mind, the one I knew would come." Aaron said to Moses as they watched the ship's captain, a lumbering man in a faded blue uniform, his right leg favoring a rachitic left knee, limp down the gangway toward the man. "It's the end. We're to be turned back. We're finished. I knew it would happen, leaping out of Europe the way we did, without preparation, without thought."

"We didn't leap, and it's meaningless to say we did," Moses snapped.

"In Kovno we at least knew where we were and what was going to happen."

"Have you forgotten about Hitler? Do you think you would still be praying in your father's house while Hitler and Stalin fight over who will kill us first?"

"Did I say I forgot about Hitler? All I'm saying is that we are like worms crawling from hole to hole."

"Shush, everyone can hear you, and they believe what you say," Fanny said.

"Let them hear. Let them believe."

"There might be an egg when we get off the ship," Lilli said.

"Listen to the remark she makes. An egg. She talks about an egg while we can see our deaths in front of us."

The conversation on the wharf was over. The captain's rolling gait was more pronounced as he pulled himself back up the gangway.

"Who is he?" Aaron asked him. "What does he want? He's not Japanese. He doesn't look Jewish. Everything is *farfaln*, hopeless."

"His name is Adolph Budin," the captain said. "He says he's from the Kobe Jewish Committee."

"He says? Either he is or he isn't."

"Calm down, Aaron," Moses said.

"He wants to talk to someone in charge and he can't wait long," the captain said. "He took the train from Kobe and is due back before dark."

"That's it?" Aaron said. "He has appointments? He has no time for us? I don't think he's a Jew at all. He has no beard, no *tzitzis*. What kind of Jew is he? A few gray hairs, a fat middle, a ring on his finger. I can predict to you right now that he is against us already. It's clear that we're lost."

"You don't want to hear what he has to say?" Moses said. "You're willing to sit on this ship until it turns around and goes back to Russia? Is that what you want?"

"If he's a Jew, why doesn't he come up on the ship? We're kept waiting for three days, like lepers. What have we done except try to save our lives? I'll speak to the man. What harm can it do to talk to him, even if he isn't a Jew. A human being, after all, can have compassion, no matter what he is. And I see what you're doing with Lilli, the way you encourage her to talk in the middle of conversations and influence her to behave in alien ways. If we live through this, she will be ruined as a Jewish woman."

"You hop from subject to subject, Aaron," Fanny said. "It can make a person dizzy. Moses should speak to him."

"Moses will antagonize him. I can approach him softly. A Jew who is not a Jew cannot be talked to roughly."

"It's decided. I'll go," Moses said.

"You've decided? Just like that?"

"You can come. But I'll be the one to speak to him."

"I might have something to say. He might find you too short-tempered. Don't you think so, Lilli, that Moses has a short temper?"

"I think the three of us will go together, and Moses will talk to him, and if you have anything to add, you'll add it."

"How will that work? It will be confusion. Anarchy. Someone always has to speak for the common good. It's the way politicians do it." He cradled his thick beard in his hands and fretted his shoulders as though his neck ached.

"All right. I'll let you speak, Moses, but I'll be right beside you, and if I think you have left something out or have mischaracterized something, I will interrupt immediately to make it right. I'll be judicious, of course, but I have a right to speak."

Moses started down the gangway. Aaron followed, Lilli a few steps behind.

At a distance Adolph Budin's stance was that of a soldier warding off the enemy. Closer up he seemed less a soldier than a guardian of the spot he occupied. An ordinary man with an open, clean-shaven face. His dark-brown tie lay like a rope around his neck lifting the points of his collar and fluting the skin beneath his jaw.

"I said I would talk to one person," Budin said.

"I'm one person. Moses Zuckerman."

"And the other two?"

"Aaron Chernofsky and his sister Lilli. They'll listen, but you can talk to me."

"Good, very good. And how was the crossing?"

"Bad. Everyone was sick."

"Terrible."

"So if you want to talk, then talk, but I'll tell you first that everything is black for us, there is no way back."

"You put all of history on my shoulders."

"I will put our deaths on your shoulders. Do you hear that wailing? Who knows? Maybe they'll jump off the ship now. Maybe they won't wait until they're sent back to die. I can't predict. It's never easy to know what desperate people might do."

"Who said easy? I would be the last person to say easy."

"The problem is you're not letting them off the ship."

"You grant me too much power."

"Then let them off."

"It's a problem. This is not easy, believe me, what I have to say to you."

"Say it."

"You can't stay in Japan."

"We don't intend to stay in Japan. But we're here."

"I know you're here. Don't you think I know you're here?"

"And we're not going back to Russia."

"I would say the same thing in your place. You have no idea of the pity I feel, the compassion, the understanding, the sympathy."

"Good."

"Yes, good. Of course good."

"Then we are in agreement that we're here and we have no choice but to stay."

"It's not so simple."

"How hard can it be?"

"The Germans."

"Ah, the Germans."

"They pressure the Japanese not to let any more Jews in, and the Japanese pressure the Jews, and that puts us all in danger. And believe me when I tell you that I understand your situation. What could be worse than what's going on in Europe? But our situation is getting worse, too. We few Jewish families cultivated our position in Kobe before this crisis. We're traders, we run businesses, we speak Japanese, we're accepted. Now there are Jews everywhere you look. Everything we do is watched, examined. The Japanese gave extensions to refugees in the beginning, but now there are too many. And believe me when I tell you we turned no one away at first. It was a *mitzvah* to house and feed the less fortunate. But now . . . now . . . so many Jews coming here. We can't keep up. Suddenly we're noticed, paid attention to. We have problems with money, with everything."

"Go to Europe," Moses said, "and you'll see that the pressure you're under is nothing."

"He says he has problems, Moses," Aaron said. "If he says he has problems, we should believe him."

"Too many people in a lifeboat, and the lifeboat sinks," Budin said. "There are Germans on the streets of Kobe. The Kobe newspaper is beginning to speak against the Jewish invasion. It's possible there will be a favorable change in the Japanese position in a few months if conditions in Europe get better."

"Maybe it's better in Europe already, Moses," Aaron said. "How much worse can it be? We have put too much trust in Mammon. We should trust in God. The Midrash states that during our future redemption the night will be as light as the day. Maybe if we had gone west instead of east it would have been better. We left too quickly, without planning, without thought. I wanted more time. You wanted to rush, leave, hurry."

"Now that we've come this far and are actually standing with our feet on a piece of Japan, you quote rabbinical commentary as a rationale for giving up?"

"I merely said that black is not always black, white is not always white. The Talmud says . . ."

"You have to be reasonable," Budin said. "I've been in Japan for ten years. Maybe the Germans will make the Japanese get rid of me, too."

"Our purpose in life is not to endanger others, Moses," Aaron said.

"Let Moses speak," Lilli said, her headscarf barely covering her hair, coat buttoned to her neck, a sprinkle of arctic sun glazing her curls.

"What?"

"Let Moses speak. You're too excited."

"Do we need you here with your childish advice?"

"We've crawled out of Europe," Moses said to Budin. "Will you throw us out? Do you have the nerve and the strength to send fellow Jews back into the inferno? We have come from hell to get here."

"Maybe Palestine . . ."

"Impossible."

"Perhaps a milder tone, Moses," Aaron said.

"Be quiet."

"What about affidavits for the United States?" Budin said.

"Do you think we would be here, that we would have traveled six thousand miles to get here, if there were an alternative, if we had certificates and passports and affidavits? We were promised twenty-one days in Japan."

"It's been changed. The Japanese will now only allow me to give you two days. God knows what they'll do if you try to stay longer."

Moses had seen Jewish men in Warsaw who were like Budin. Merchants, doctors, furriers, lawyers who had never set foot in a *shetl*. They donated to Jewish causes, were always ready to make a *minyan* at the synagogue, and yet here one of them stood safe in Japan giving the almost-dead nothing more than his sympathy.

"I'm standing in front of you. Those that are with me are real, made of flesh and blood, and you don't know the injury I'm capable of inflicting on anyone who tries to send us back."

Budin looked up at the ship, at the drawn faces and faded scraps of cloth.

"Two days, then," Budin said.

"And destination papers."

"You push too hard."

"I can push you into the ground."

"Please. I have a difficult job. My heart is weak."

"And I have no heart. I threw it away in Poland. I want two days and destination papers."

"All right, all right. Fifty German Jews are arriving in Kobe tomorrow. Heinrich Strauss and his family are traveling with the group. He owned the *Tageblatt Hamburg* newspaper. A very important man, with great friends. I knew him well when I traveled for business in Germany."

"Who cares who he is?" Aaron said. "German Jews aren't Jews. They don't speak Yiddish. They eat *treyf*, they treat Polish Jews like worms, they . . . ."

"He has destination papers. I don't know for where. Maybe certificates for Palestine, maybe affidavits for the United States. I can't promise that he can help you."

"If not, what else can you offer?" Moses said.

"How can I offer anything? It's out of my hands. You'll come with me by train to Kobe, and in a few hours we'll see if you're lucky or not."

* * *

Moses explained the uncertainty of the situation to the refugees, that the trip to Kobe may not solve anything, that they may still be turned back. No one wanted his opinion.

Possibilities are opening up, some said.

God sees our distress and is saving us, others said.

They walked happily from the battered ship to the train station, then applauded and whooped at the sight of the train, not caring what the destination was, just exulting that the death sentence was being reviewed, the final execution stayed.

The train to Kobe was a modern one with padded seats. The conductor, a Japanese man in a dark blue uniform with gold braid on both shoulders, collected the tickets from Budin while children ran up and down the aisle, women marveled at the clean windows, men silently studied the passing scenery, and the yeshiva students (ever vigilant against seduction-by-proximity keeping their distance from the women by opening a suitcase and planting its contents over the last six rows of seats) prayed, their voices as deep and sonorous as the pluckings of a cello. Budin was a few rows up with Aaron, listening, as though interested, to Aaron's analysis of the mysteries at the heart of Maimonides' philosophy.

Moses sat in the middle of the car next to Lilli, close enough that small tendrils of her hair escaped their prison scarf and tickled his ear. He had regained his senses. The blaze of desire was extinguished. How could he have forgotten the strictures of Jewish life? Had he become such a renegade, so used to grabbing whatever appealed to him that he mistook Lilli for a piece of ripe fruit? He who was always so careful in plotting out every step in advance, yet playing at lovemaking with the daughter of a rabbi, a shtetl girl who held secret yearnings in her, who would no doubt misconstrue what almost happened between them as the beginning of some romantic tale. And what did it matter that in selling the scroll she discovered a talent for cunning?

She sat so straight beside him, her small back no wider than the span of two hands. She had a familiar face: the short nose, the dusting of freckles on ivory skin, the cleaving sun slanting gently across the deep-hued blue of her eyes. How different she looked in the daylight, no longer the innocent temptress, merely a girl no different than any other girl, prettier than some, but poison just the same.

History marched beside them twined with murder and mayhem and he sat like a school boy studying the way she licked her lip with the tip of her velvet tongue, the way she folded her handkerchief into the shape of a dagger and slipped it into the sleeve of her jacket.

She was too young. The time and place were all wrong. What to do with the yeshiva students when he ran again weighed on him. Maybe he would take her with him, steal her like some flaming jewel of the orient wrapped in the knitted afghan Mrs. Lipsky wrapped around her fat knees.

"Why do you let Aaron talk to you the way he does?"

"He doesn't mean it."

"He'll destroy you."

"Aaron can't destroy a mouse, Moses. Anyway, people don't destroy that easily. Aaron is just frightened because I've grown up and he doesn't know who I am anymore. He worries that something will happen to me, that I'll get lost or sick. He worries about what will happen to us when we get to Kobe."

"There is nothing to worry about. We will either stay or be sent back."

"No one believes we'll be sent back. They're already giving thanks to God for their deliverance."

"They should wait a little while before they give thanks. Nothing has been promised. Maybe the rich German Jew has gone in another direction and won't appear in Kobe at all. Maybe he will be there, but will have nothing to offer us."

Ida Bornstein walked down the aisle toward them.

"More books, more books, more books," she said, then took off her right shoe, scraped at a blob on its sole with her fingernails, then reached over and kissed Lilli's cheek.

"You are my best friend," she said.

*　*　*

The weather in Kobe was mild, the Buddhist temples tucked into the mountains above the city glowing in the winter sun. Japanese women peered out of doorways at the bedraggled band of refugees marching single-file down the hilly, twisting street, the yeshiva students in their long black coats and scraggly beards, the women in their heavy layers of clothing, children balanced in their arms, the men carrying suitcases that had been soaked in seawater, stomped on, rent from seam to seam, then tied back together with string.

Ida's suitcase was gone. Fanny said she saw her throw it off the ship in Tsuruga, the contents flying over the water as delicately as flounced birds. Fanny now had her by the hand, jerking her toward her every once in a while like a dog on a leash while Moses helped Mrs. Lipsky maneuver the uneven stone pavement and Lilli carried Shaya.

"Who knew Budin would change his mind?" Aaron said to Moses. "But your words could have been kinder. When you talk to a person like you did, you make him an enemy instead of a friend. Do you see the way he walks way ahead of us, as if being too close to you is dangerous?"

"He may not be a friend, but he's not an enemy. He's just a man who has lost a fight."

"The Talmud says that to achieve one's ends by threatening a person's life is forbidden."

"I didn't threaten his life."

"You did."

"If I did, it's not important."

"Not important? Would you turn into a savage like the savages tormenting you?"

"Moses said what needed to be said, and now we are here," Lilli said.

"Do you take his side now?"

"What side is that, Aaron?"

"When you can reason intelligently, I'll allow you to interrupt. I might even listen."

"It isn't savage to want to live, Aaron."

"By any means? Is that what you're saying? Is that what we've come to?"

"Moses didn't hurt anyone. They were just words."

"Be grateful we're here," Moses said.

"But for how long?" Aaron asked him.

"What difference does it make for how long? Do we know anything in life? We will be here the allotted time, and then we will either stay or we will go somewhere else."

"Well, however long we're here, I will eat only kosher food. Do you think the food will be kosher, Lilli?"

"I don't know, but I'm sure there will be bread."

"The Japanese eat rice," Fanny said.

"My mother will be so happy to see me," Ida said. "Her house isn't too far. Hurry up or we'll be late."

"She thinks we're in Kiev," Fanny said.

"There is plenty of kosher food in Kiev," Ida said. "The store is right around the corner."

They were now on a lane of shops and fragile-looking wooden houses; iron lanterns stood at slatted doors, roofs leaned toward each other like trees in a forest.

The hotel was at the foot of the hill, a bamboo grove to one side, a small canal with a footbridge on the other. An outside wall hid a small garden. Stepping-stones led to a wooden gate, and beyond that to a matchbox-shaped building rising up out of a hummock of tufted grass.

"Take your shoes off," Budin said, and soon there was a pile of ragged, dusty, smelly shoes beside the slab-wood door.

"Be quiet inside."

They walked through the door into a small anteroom in their torn socks and ripped stockings, then passed through a curtain into a small lobby. The interior was spare, a pot of bamboo against the red clay wall, a woven-reed basket in the shape of a boat on a pedestal, a few low settees.

"Four people to a room, and adjoining toilet," Budin said. "Men and boys will bathe at three in the afternoon, women and girls at five. Kosher food will be brought in later this evening. The water is safe to drink. No loud talking or motioning or pointing. Keep your opinions of the way the Japanese look and dress to yourself. You are the foreigners here, not the Japanese. And keep your children from touching anything. The Japanese don't like strangers with peculiar habits."

The communal bath was in a corner of the hotel. A barefoot Japanese woman in a long dress that had been wrapped and tucked and wound and folded and then fastened together with a broad band around her waist was instructing the refugee women in sign language to use the bars of soap and thick sponges to wash themselves and their children and then to dip the wooden ladles into the buckets of fresh water to rinse off. When this was finally accomplished they walked down a short set of steps, through a sliding paper door, and into a room with glazy tiled walls and a pool as big as the Chernofskys' kitchen. Everything was milk white—walls, paper doors, the steam clouding the surface of the water.

They stepped one by one into the pool. Ida Bornstein first, Shaya in her arms, then the other mothers and their children, followed by the Lipskys and Lilli.

"The water feels like silk," Fanny said.

"Such a pleasure," Mrs. Lipsky said.

"Sit here on the ledge next to me, Mrs. Lipsky," Lilli said. "There's enough room for you to put your feet up."

"Our bathtub at home is in a closet," Fanny said. "Mama covers it with a board when we're not using it. In the summer she piles the board high with winter clothes. In the winter she piles it with summer clothes. If we got rid of the bathtub, we would have a closet, but then we wouldn't be able to take a bath."

"Look at how Shaya is laughing at that," Lilli said.

"She's too young to understand."

"It's better if she doesn't know what's going on," Mrs. Lipsky said.

"Our bathtub in Moscow is iron," Ida remarked with no sign of craziness at all. "The hot water is only on for two hours a day."

"A bath like this saves water," Fanny said.

"I wonder if Shaya will remember this journey," Ida said. She kissed Shaya's cheek, then dipped her under the water and held her there.

For a moment Lilli stared at the bubbles on the surface of the water and at Shaya's curls floating upward like a gently unfurling ball of yarn.

By the time Fanny shrieked, Lilli had reached into the water and lifted the sputtering child out.

"My God," Fanny said.

"Is she all right?" Mrs. Lipsky asked.

"She's all right," Lilli said. "She's fine."

"Too many people make the water dirty," Ida said, and she stepped out of the pool as if nothing had happened and disappeared through the paper door into the dressing room.

"Maybe the woman was crazy before and her husband just wanted to get rid of her," Fanny said.

"Should we splash a little bit, Shaya?" Lilli said. "Look how the water jumps up and down when you pat it."

"A woman in Vilna once drowned her twin boys," Mrs. Lipsky said. "A Jewish woman, too. It was winter. She took them down to the river, dug a hole in the ice and threw them in."

*   *   *

There were straw mats on the floor, a pile of bedding beside each one. Fanny and Mrs. Lipsky each took a mat (after a few moments of discussion as to what to do with them and some uncertain moments while Fanny and Lilli lowered Mrs. Lipsky to the floor). Ida Bornstein took the other two, just lay down across them both, arms and legs spread out, body as still as a corpse, and wouldn't get up. Lilli whispered in her ear, then pulled at her arms to try to move her over, then tried to slide one of the mats from under her, then checked to see if she was breathing.

"Go away," Ida said.

Lilli took what was left of the bedding and settled Shaya in a corner of the room, then wrapped herself in her coat and lay down on the bare floor beside her. She dozed in intervals throughout the night, waking periodically, sitting up, peering through the dark at Ida, then at Shaya, noting the shift of moonlight across the room, listening to the mild sound of snoring from the men's rooms down the hall, then lying down again, as if this were the natural way to sleep, the way it should be, the way it always would be, the only way it could possibly be, putting herself between this madwoman and her child.

Chapter 6

The German Jews had arrived.

"Look at how they sniff at the rest of us, Lilli, keeping to themselves in one corner of the lobby," Aaron said. "They think if they get too close to us our *shmuts* will rub off on them. They think we're *shlepers*, not good for anything. In my opinion, they're not really Jews."

"Why do you say that?"

"Because they look like Gentiles, the men in their modern suits and the women with their hair uncovered. They probably have never been inside a synagogue in their lives. They don't even speak Yiddish. It's a joke to call them Jews." He glanced at Shaya. "Where is her mother?"

"Still sleeping."

"We have enough without taking on the responsibility of a crazy woman's child."

"There's no responsibility, Aaron. I'm just taking care of her while Ida is asleep."

"Well, Moses and I are going to talk to Budin. You wait for us here, and don't mix with the Germans while we're gone."

"What are you going to talk to Budin about?"

"Do I have to tell you everything? Just be a good girl and do what I said."

The few settees in the lobby were already taken. Lilli found a place on the floor against the wall, and pulled Shaya onto her lap. It was comfortable here out of the way. Shaya turned her head, looked up at Lilli, then turned away again. She hadn't asked for her mother at breakfast. Lilli wasn't sure she could speak. She had never heard her say a word. Not in Moscow, not on the train, not ever.

"What is your favorite color, Shaya?"

No answer.

"It's all right not to have a favorite color. We'll just sit here and watch what everyone is doing."

Lilli didn't believe Aaron about the Germans not being Jewish. If there had been Jews in China, surely there were Jews in Germany. But they did look different, the women in fur-trimmed coats, the men in tweeds, the children in arm-stiffening padded suits. And they were so clean. It was as if they had been packed away in one of their large suitcases and had now emerged, slightly wrinkled, ready to examine their surroundings, make a few comments, and if need be, pose for photographs. And their children were so well-behaved, while the Polish children ran through the lobby swatting at the hanging lanterns and skipping through the loose stones of the adjoining garden.

She found herself focusing on a family standing together not far from where she sat with Shaya. The mother, pink-faced and golden-haired; the son, tall and fair; the daughter, dark-eyed like the father, her hands in a fur muff, sniping at her brother about a small suitcase left behind when they fled Germany.

The daughter, who had caught Lilli's gaze, walked toward her.

"You've been staring at us," she said to Lilli in German. "Do you like what you see?"

"I was admiring how good-looking you all are," she replied in German.

"Where did you learn to speak German?"

"The Kovno German Language High School, but I speak mainly Yiddish."

"German is the best language there is. Vati says Yiddish is German's bastard child. The little girl . . . is she yours?"

"No."

"What's her name?"

"Shaya Bornstein."

"Are you her mother's maid?"

"No."

"Her hair is very pretty. I like blonde hair. Is she an orphan?"

"Her mother is here, but she's sick."

"My father is Heinrich Strauss. I'm sure you've heard of him. Everyone knows him. He's very famous in Germany. My brother Sigmund is very fond of horses. Do you ride?"

"No."

"Why do you cover your hair with a handkerchief?"

"It's a rule."

"Do you speak English?"

"School English. I like English books."

"All educated people speak English. I have English friends. They all say how well I speak. I never say 'trink' for 'drink' like some people do. Vati arranged for us to come here. Vati knows everyone there is to know and can arrange anything a person wants or needs. He used to publish the biggest newspaper in Hamburg. Vati's picture was always in the newspaper before Hitler came. Mutti didn't want to leave Hamburg. We had a very big house there and I had everything I wanted. I'm Hannah Strauss. What's your name?"

"Lilli Chernofsky. I've never known anyone who had their picture in a newspaper, except for an uncle who went to China and came back with a Sephardic Torah. He died before I was born. Mama kept the newspaper in a closet, and it mildewed."

"I have no idea what you're talking about, but you seem very nice for a Polish Jew. Vati says Polish Jews are backward and superstitious and that they smell bad and stick together."

"I don't think I'm backward or superstitious. Do I smell bad?"

"Not really." She pulled a cigarette from her muff and lit it. "Stand in front of me so they can't see me. I don't smoke in front of them. Do you want one?"

"I've never tried."

"Really? That's a peculiar thing. What's wrong with Shaya's mother?"

"She left her husband in Moscow, and I think it affected her mind. She tried to drown Shaya in the bath yesterday. She didn't know what she was doing, but I can't take a chance that she'll do something else to hurt her."

"I suppose so. Have you ever been engaged?"

"Engaged? To be married?"

"Of course to be married."

"No. Never."

"I was engaged to be married last year. He was very handsome, but Mutti said he only wanted to marry me for Vati's money, so I broke it off. Was that your brother I saw you with at breakfast, the one with the red hair?"

"Yes."

"What's his name?"

"Aaron."

"He's very thin."

"He only ate a banana for breakfast. He wouldn't eat the cereal. He worries that the *milkhik* and *fleyshik* dishes have been mixed together."

"What does that mean?"

"Meat and dairy have to be kept separate."

"Really?"

"I don't care if meat and dairy are mixed, but my brother can lose his mind over things like that. He's very religious."

"He looks like you. Of course, you're pretty and he's peculiar looking. All that hair on his face. And the others, too. Why don't they shave?"

"They're not supposed to put metal to their hair. It's in the Talmud."

"What's that?"

"You don't know what the Talmud is?"

"If it has to do with Jews, I don't want to know. My family doesn't believe in religion. Vati says if there were no Jews, we would all be as happy as could be. When girls at school would ask me if I was related to the Jew Strauss, the one who owns the *Tageblatt Hamburg*, I would say, 'No, I'm related to the Strausses of Munich. Richard Strauss, Hitler's favorite composer, is my uncle.' Of course, everyone would find out eventually. Vati is too famous. I just wish I could have stayed behind in Hamburg. My mother didn't want to leave either. Her name used to be Margot Rosenthal. The Rosenthals owned a textile mill in Dresden, and they were even richer than Vati, but they were taken away in December." Hannah took a puff of her cigarette. "Mutti doesn't speak to Vati. She blames him for everything that's happened to us. She used to call him darling. Now she hates him. I would go back to Hamburg right now if I could. I'm not afraid of Hitler."

"She might change her mind."

"Who?"

"Your mother. People say things they don't mean when they're unhappy. When she isn't unhappy anymore, she might stop hating him. I used to hate my brother because he was a boy and I was a girl. Papa let me go to school, but most Orthodox girls can't do very much except work in the house. Boys are like princes. I don't hate him at all now, because it's not his fault."

"Is the tall man your lover, the one who looks at you like you're a juicy chop? Your face has turned red. Do you mind the way I talk?"

"I don't think so. No, it's fine, although I'm always careful about the words I use. I don't like to upset Aaron. He says I'll be ruined if I lose my modesty."

"Really? How would you lose it?"

"By talking too much, by uncovering my hair and wearing colorful clothes and speaking to men outside the family. There are lots of rules. I could write them all down for you if you're interested."

"No, thank you. It sounds awful."

"It isn't really. You get used to it."

"You shouldn't cover up your hair. What I can see of it is pretty in an ordinary sort of way."

"When Aaron isn't around I do what I please."

"Vati says there are lots of Jews like your brother in Vienna, all of them with flowing beards and silky hats and flapping coats, and that they're always praying. Sigmund can imitate it. He makes me laugh when he does it. He looks like a bird pecking for worms in the grass. Sigmund is very clever. Is your brother clever?"

"Papa says he could be a rabbi he's so smart. Aaron can read a book and tell you everything that's in it, every detail, perfectly. I think sometimes he's the smartest person I know, except that he would forget to tie his shoes if I didn't remind him."

"Do rabbis have money?"

"Not usually. If they have a rich congregation, they might have money. Papa's congregation was large and poor, but since so many Jews have left Kovno it's now small and poor."

"Hmm. Have you ever had a lover?"

"To do what?"

"You know. Like married people."

"No."

"Have you ever kissed a boy?"

"A few times."

"Did you get a tickly feeling?"

"Where?"

"Down there."

"I don't think so."

"You're lying. I can tell. It's all right, though, I don't care if you lie. I lie sometimes, too. Not about lovers, though. About other things that really don't matter. Lovers are easy to get. All my friends have had them. I had my first one at sixteen. There's nothing to talk about with your friends if you don't do it. Sigmund noticed you at breakfast. He told me that he thinks you're pretty, but without style. He says you remind him of a chambermaid in his apartment hotel when he was at the preparatory school in Frankfurt. He never brought her home, and, of course, she wasn't Jewish. Can you see anyone looking at me?"

"Who would be looking at you?"

"Vati or Sigmund—either one—are they looking at me?"

"Your brother looked this way once, but he turned away again."

"What is he doing now?"

"Looking this way again."

She dropped the cigarette into the potted plant.

"Well, good-bye," she said and walked away.

* * *

"Look how Budin treats the Germans, like royalty," Aaron said to Moses, "like they're tourists who've come to Kobe to see the sights and when they're finished they'll go back to their castles in Bavaria. He doesn't talk to them the way he talks to us. It's disgusting. We wasted our breath talking to him. Did you hear what he said? No guarantees that we wouldn't be sent back to Moscow. After he made promises to us."

"He didn't make promises. Maybe you should get something to eat before the food is gone."

"I knew it from the first moment I set eyes on Budin that he couldn't be trusted. Do you think he's going to talk to Strauss about us?"

"I don't know, Aaron."

"We should keep our few belongings close, we won't be here long. It's obvious. Look at the way he walks around the room, laughing and joking like a *knaker*. He tricked us into coming here, into raising our hopes."

"I hadn't noticed that your hopes were raised, Aaron."

"They were elevated slightly. But I knew better than to trust an unorthodox Jew. Just like Bornstein, pretending to love the Soviets so much and dropping his wife and daughter on us. Budin is the same. I can see that now. It's very plain. He talks about Heinrich Strauss like he knows him, like he's his best friend, but he only says it to inflate himself. What does he know about him except that he owned a newspaper in Hamburg? I've heard of that newspaper. It was a rag, an excuse for common sense. What makes Strauss so special that he knows how to get out of here and we don't? Is he a rabbi? A learned man? May we be saved from it. That's Strauss over there. Look at him, no better than we are. Where is his gold watch? And shouldn't his wife have a fur coat? And the daughter, look how she pouts and preens. I'll have to watch out for Lilli, keep her away from such a girl. Ruination comes unbidden, like the plague."

"You'll feel better if you eat something."

"And the son doesn't look like a Jew, I don't think the mother is Jewish, the two of them are too blonde, and it's clear that he has no Jewish learning, he looks like an empty glass, a whipped dog. And see how Strauss stands in one place and struts. I never saw a man who could stand and strut at the same time. It's a gift. A definite gift. A talent for looking important when he has holes in his socks just like the rest of us. And did you notice when breakfast was served the way the Germans ate, without chewing, pretending they're so polite and then eating everything before anyone else can get a finger in?"

"You don't have to stand here with me," Moses said.

"And where should I stand?"

"Go find Lilli."

"I don't want to find Lilli. Lilli is turning as crazy as that Bornstein woman, carrying that child around with her, the mother trailing behind her like a *golem*. Lilli says the woman doesn't speak anymore. Who needs to hear a crazy woman talk, anyway? I don't even know if the food is really kosher. Lilli is too busy to find out. She said to ask Budin, but what does Budin know about kosher food? We should have stayed in Kovno. I shouldn't have listened to you. The whole thing is a disaster."

"He's talking to him."

"He is?"

"Yes."

"So what if he's talking to him? A person can talk to anyone they want. What does it mean? Nothing, that's what it means. Is Strauss the *macher* of the world, the only one who knows how to get out of here, who knows where to go? And see how he puts his hand in his pocket and then looks surprised because there is no big fat wallet there. Maybe he thinks Budin stole it."

"You should go eat before the food runs out," Moses said.

"I'm not hungry."

"Then stop making comments. It doesn't help."

Budin came toward them.

"I congratulate you. Your luck is good. There are permits for Shanghai still available. American Jewish aid will take care of it, the permits, the boat, everything. Someone will be here this afternoon to make the arrangements and take you by bus to catch the boat."

"But what will we do in Shanghai?" Aaron said.

* * *

Lilli was ready. She combed Ida's hair and sat her down on the floor in a corner of the lobby next to Fanny and piled two suitcases up for Mrs. Lipsky to sit on. She fed Shaya a bean-filled *anpan* (Ida took a bite, then spit it out) and convinced Aaron to eat two hard-boiled eggs, and there was nothing to do but wait for the bus to take them to the ship.

The aid worker, her jumble of hair the color of lemons, had arrived a little while ago, then lined everyone up, checked their documents and handed out

Shanghai permits. Moses was talking to her now, his timbery frame in contrast to her spare, lightly fleshed figure. An American Jew, someone said. Lilli liked the way she talked, as though she were the only one in the room and didn't care whether anyone was listening or not. She didn't dress like an American, at least not like the Americans in the movies Tante Rose took Lilli to see in Stuttgart. She had a flyaway look, as though the print skirt and flowered blouse fell out of the sky and landed on her without her noticing. She didn't seem healthy; the spots of color in her cheeks were a little too red, her arms a little too thin. She'd just gotten through telling everyone in Yiddish to keep track of their children, that she won't go hunting for lost children, it wasn't her job, and right after that she picked up a little boy who was crying and held him until his mother appeared. What must it be like to be an American girl who could tell men as well as women what to do and answer questions with a sharp edge in her voice and an impatient glance and still look like someone Lilli would want to know? And why was she here when she could be safe in America?

The bus came and everyone got on without saying anything, as though by their silence they could preserve some fine thread of hope that they really were going to go to Shanghai.

The ship had staterooms and deck chairs and a lounge where the aid worker—her name was Rachel Shapiro—had arranged for kosher meals to be served. The Germans had already reserved the best staterooms. The Poles scurried through the corridors looking for vacant rooms. By afternoon everyone had settled in, and some had gone up on deck as the ship moved out of the harbor and the islands of Japan receded, beaches and mountains and forests vanishing behind a curtain of green mist.

"This reminds me of the ship we took on our cruise through the Greek Isles," Heinrich Strauss remarked to his wife, who sat in a deck chair reading a book. She didn't look up.

"Look how she ignores him," Aaron said to Lilli. "A real *prietzteh*."

Aaron was now staring at Hannah, who was standing at the rail with her brother Sigmund. "And stay away from the daughter, Lilli. Such a girl can put bad ideas in your head. She has no modesty, and the way she bares her hair, she doesn't look like a Jewish girl at all."

"But she is."

"Aren't you listening to me? I'm telling you, Jewish girls don't look like her. No good Jewish man will marry a girl like that."

Moses said, "You won't have to worry, Aaron. She won't marry someone like you either."

"Siggie, take my picture," Hannah said.

"Where did you get the camera?" Fanny asked him.

"In Berlin."

"How did you manage to keep it hidden?" Moses said.

"I didn't."

"Shaya is my niece," Ida Bornstein said to Mrs. Lipsky. "Lilli is my sister. I had a husband, but he's dead."

*   *   *

They left the open sea and were now sailing through the silty waters of the Whangpoo River. It had been raining for two days, a cold drizzle that had turned to sleet, but everyone was on deck as the soaring spires and rounded domes of Shanghai appeared out of the blurry gale like a European postage stamp pasted on a Chinese fan. As the ship slid closer to shore, what at a distance had resembled a color-stained carpet along the foreshore became a flooded boulevard jammed with bicycles and rickshaws and pedicabs. The air turned caustic and bitter, then sweetly decaying, then nauseatingly ripe. Like rotten fruit. Like coal fires and spices and human waste. Like corpses left out in the sun to rot.

The landing in Shanghai was chaos. As they waded through eddies of garbage-laden water to where two trucks waited, beggars and lepers surrounded them; filthy children jabbering in pidgin poked foul-smelling fingers into their faces.

There was no clear distinction now between the Germans and the Poles, everyone scrambling up onto the nearest truck, grabbing at the wooden rails, scuffling for a toehold, jostling for room on a step, dragging soggy suitcases up behind them, everyone shrieking at everyone else to move, help me up, take my hand.

"You're in the wrong truck," Aaron shouted at Sigmund as the Strausses climbed into the first truck with the yeshiva students.

"Mind your own business," Sigmund shouted back.

Moses pushed Mrs. Lipsky up onto the step of the second truck. Fanny and Aaron pulled her the rest of the way up and set her down next to Ida Bornstein. Lilli found a spot near the truck's opening and sat cross-legged with Shaya in her lap as the two trucks lurched away from the wharf and onto the Bund, the broad sweep of land facing the Whangpoo River.

Corpses, their bodies bloated, floated in the gutters, the mats they had been covered with bobbing along beside them. Some of the corpses had slipped into the center of the road and appeared to be swimming along with the current. Margot Strauss clutched her daughter's hand as a corpse floated by.

"If this is Shanghai, I'd rather be in Germany," Hannah said, her fur muff dangling from her arm like a sopping brown cat.

"They don't bury their dead," Aaron said. "A decent society is one that feeds and houses and buries its people."

"Burial isn't necessary," Moses replied.

"The Talmud says so."

"But you said a decent society demands it, not the Talmud. There's a difference."

The trucks stopped, and Rachel, in a too-large raincoat, rain-soaked hair hardening into a mesh of straggly blonde strings, hustled everyone into a two-story building filled from floor to ceiling with sheetless, pillowless hard bunk beds. The odor of unwashed bodies and dirty clothes, of vomit and feces and urine, ravened the air. Rats skittered across the floor and up the walls. The space was a web of narrow aisles, of clothes and boxes, of people standing, leaning, kneeling, smoking, talking, kissing, arguing. Some were sprawled on the beds making love fully clothed except for unbuttoned trousers and a raised skirt. Some beds were curtained, the limp mesh black-hemmed where it had been dragged through rat droppings and leopard-spotted from the pull of dirty fingers.

"Welcome to the Seward Road *Heim*," Rachel said.

"Is this where we'll live?" Aaron said. "Like animals?"

"Yes, and you're lucky to be here. You'll have a bed and a blanket and a pillow. And there's food. Not much of it. I'm in charge of food procurement and I do my best. This isn't a home, and I won't pretend it is. It's a place for you to be. You'll have to figure out how to live here for yourselves. Don't ask me for any favors. I don't have any to give. I don't have time to baby anyone. We get by on what we beg and steal. My job is to try to keep you all alive."

"I can't stay here," Hannah said.

"Unless you have money to go elsewhere this is where you'll stay. You can do it easily or you can do it with difficulty. I don't give a damn either way. And if you've heard that the other heime are better, that you're getting stuck with a shitty one, believe me when I tell you, they're all shitty."

"Such a mouth," Aaron said when Rachel had gone. "She speaks Yiddish, but she must have learned it in a toilet somewhere. It's obvious she's not Jewish. It's not possible. Jewish girls don't talk like that. *Tznuit* prescribes that a Jewish girl behave and speak with modesty."

Hannah was trembling, her knees bumping the edge of a cot.

"Give her a pill, Sigmund," Heinrich said.

"I can't swallow pills without water."

"Try, darling," Margot murmured.

The yeshiva students were still holding their suitcases, swaying in place, jerking their shoulders and shaking their heads like loose-limbed carnival dolls.

"It's just a place to sleep," Lilli said as she picked out beds for Fanny and Mrs. Lipsky and slid Aaron's suitcase under a bed in the corner. Ida Bornstein was now shouting that she was hungry, she was dying of hunger, she was starving to death. Lilli gave her a piece of bread and sat her down on a bed, then picked a bed out for herself and Shaya. She was careful not to choose one too close to the stairs or against a wall. Stairs were noisy; rats might drop down a wall onto a bed that was too close to a wall. Shaya had taken off her shoes and climbed up onto the top bunk and was jumping up and down on the stained mattress.

"Look how high you can jump," Lilli said.

"What does a child know?" Mrs. Lipsky said with a shrug.

"Well, it isn't the worst thing," Lilli said. "I'm sure there are worse things than this."

"Where?" Aaron asked her. "Where is it worse?"

The yeshiva students still hadn't put their suitcases down. Moses gathered them together near the stairs. "Listen to me. You have to sleep, you have to live, and if you accidentally hear or see things that shock or offend your religious sensibilities, God will forgive you."

"But where do we undress?" Hannah moaned.

"Here," Heinrich replied. "You undress here."

"Where will I put my things?"

"Don't be a baby," Sigmund told her. "Leave them in your suitcase. "When you need something, put your suitcase on the bed and take what you want out of it."

"I can't do this, I can't," Hannah cried.

Margot, who had been standing in shocked silence, one hand clasped to her mouth, finally said, "Heinrich, I don't think I can ever forgive you."

*   *   *

At dawn women lined up at the sinks on the second floor, slivers of carbolic soap in their hands. They squatted over blue enamel buckets in the second-floor washroom; some retched into them. Those with dysentery no sooner got up than they had to squat again. The men used the toilets in the basement. Breakfast was at eight o'clock: two thin slices of bread, a cup of coffee, and a dab of margarine in the dining room, an undecorated hall as blighted as the rest of the building, the signs of Japanese bombs still visible in the shatter of ceiling plaster. The line began on the first floor and snaked up the stairs. Tin plates were washed and kept to be used from meal to meal. Five dollars a month from Jewish relief for toothpaste, notebooks, playing cards, razor blades, and soap for the washhouse on the roof. The soap didn't lather. The water cost money. Nothing got clean. At night coughs and snores and babies' cries tore sleep to pieces.

"I heard that people are dying of typhoid and cholera here," Moses told Lilli. "They take the very sick and the dead away before it alarms the rest. Make sure you eat only cooked food. It's important that you keep well."

Chapter 7

Shanghai
February 1941

Edward Statham was Sir Elias Mansour's secretary. He arrived at the office in the Mansour Bank Building at seven in the morning and left promptly at seven in the evening. Trained in service to a London barrister in the 1920s, he had been Sir Elias's protector for eleven years, managing the daily list of appointments with the eye of a hunter in the veldt, ready to dispatch anyone whose appointment was overlong or in any way disrupted Sir Elias's flow of hours. Although he had no particular likes or dislikes, that Sir Elias Mansour was a Jew had been a shock at first. (His view of Jews was a Lilliputian one compounded of myth and suspicion.) He had managed to put his prejudices aside, which amused Sir Elias, since he knew that if anything out of Edward's range of duties were to occur, his devotion would go no deeper than the skin of an apple.

He now opened the door to Elias's office and crossed to the window, pulling the blinds halfway down to shield the Persian rug from the morning sun.

"How many are waiting?" Elias asked him.

"A representative from the White Russian Committee, Sir Elias. Also the president of the Jewish Community of Central European Jews, a deputy from the Japanese Foreign Ministry, fourteen refugees from the Ward Road Heim, eighteen from the Seward Road Heim. There is also a man and his son. The father claims to be a friend of yours. He wouldn't tell me his name. Shall I give an excuse?"

"No."

Excuses were of no use. Refugees hid in the lobby, slept on the street in front of the doors to the Mansour Bank Building, pounced and shrieked when Elias stepped out of the elevator. They grabbed at him on the street, begged him for help, tried to kiss his shoes. They moved like wraiths, sliding sideways through cracks, emerging unbidden from hiding places, ashen-faced facsimiles of real people, their bodies boneless, unsubstantial, their voices all the same, their stories identical, an endless army of caught-on-the-wind apparitions rising out of the Whangpoo fog to moan, to press photographs into his hands, to tell stories of murder, torture, escape, missing children, dead wives, dead husbands, dead mothers, dead fathers. Yesterday a woman cut her wrists and no one noticed until the blood soaked through the seat cushion of the chair she was sitting in and puddled on the floor beneath her.

Elias had already seen twenty-three refugees and four foreign ministers today and it was only ten-thirty in the morning.

"Who else?"

"Rachel Shapiro."

"Tomorrow. I have no energy or patience for her today."

"She insists on today. She says she won't leave. She says you'll have to step over her body if you try to leave without seeing her."

Elias had seen Rachel the day before his trip to New York. He had returned yesterday and here she was again. She refused to give him a moment between onslaughts. *I want, I want, I want.* Her wants were acid, they ate through the skin to the bone, they sucked out the marrow, deprived cells of oxygen, veins of blood. He had nothing new to tell her, nothing she didn't already know, but she would shrill and carp and harangue over the few things that lay in the gray zone between maybe and never, would pepper him with facts and figures, would name-call and swear and rage until he fell under the weight. Putting her off didn't work. She sometimes followed him home. Three weeks ago she camped overnight in the rose garden on the Mansour estate clutching a list of more refugees for him to consider, to process, to sponsor, to give money to.

"You might as well let her in."

"And the gentleman and his son, Sir Elias?"

"Later."

Rachel came through the door explosively, as though a giant wind were at her back, a bulging, ink-spotted briefcase in one hand, a sheaf of papers in the other, wearing the same dress she was wearing the last time he saw her (he remembered the rip in the sleeve at the elbow, the uneven hem of the skirt), plopped into a corner of the yellow silk sofa, dropped the papers on the floor next to the briefcase, gave Elias a half smile, bent over, opened the briefcase, rummaged through folded, torn, crushed pieces of paper, and quickly read one after another, her fair skin flushing from chin to forehead, her unpinned, honeyed hair tumbling into yet another part of her face with each movement of her head. "This," she said waving a paper at Elias. "Read it. We've had to cut the food allotment again. Did you know about this, Elias?"

"Funds are low. We have too many people to feed."

"Bullshit! If you'd stay around and attend committee meetings instead of farting off to New York to have dinner with rich Jews we'd get something done here."

"I saw your parents in New York. I told them how committed you are to working for the refugees in Shanghai—how intensely you're committed."

"Don't patronize me, Elias."

Elias knew her parents well. He had worked with her father, Martin Shapiro, in the effort to help Jews emigrate to Palestine. Just a few days earlier he sat in the Shapiros' Park Avenue apartment listening to Rachel's Gentile mother describe in her soft American South drawl how disappointed she was that Rachel had become, as she described it, a Jew worker.

"There never were any Jews in her life growing up, except for Martin," she said "She's had every advantage. I really don't understand why she wants to live the way she does. She was our pet, our adored Rachel, Martin's darling girl. I don't know how it happened that she's turned out the way she has. It's truly beyond me. And you know, of course, of her terrible illness last year. I worry constantly about her health in that awful place."

Rachel had now emptied the briefcase out onto the floor and was on her knees on the carpet riffling through reams of paper. The soles of her shoes had holes in them. She never wore stockings, and there were deep scratches on the calf of her left leg, probably from scrabbling through brambles in his rose garden. Mean scratches, scabbing over, the demarcated edges bumped up like cookie crumbs.

Elias didn't tell her parents that he thought she had come back to China too soon after her illness. It would have done no good to tell them. She directed her own course, listened to no one's advice.

She was now reading aloud from a creased piece of paper.

"'Dear Miss Shapiro: The London Council for German Jewry would like to aid further in relief efforts, and we promise a grant of two thousand five hundred American dollars. We must, however, have a firm assurance from your committee that they will exert their influence to prevent other refugees from coming to Shanghai.'"

"I have a copy of the letter, and one just like it from the U.S. Secretary of State," he said.

"Have you answered them?"

"There's no need."

"No need? What the hell are you talking about, 'no need'? You sit here and tell me there's no need? You should be outraged."

In New York the week before Rabbi Lewin had asked Elias how conditions were in Shanghai. "I mean, how are they really? Can the Jews hold out to the end of the war?"

"It depends," Elias had replied.

Elias had *meant* to be vague. The American Jews had their emissaries here in Shanghai. Let *them* tell the rabbi about the appalling conditions in the heime. When asking for money from American Jews, Elias's preference was for more evasiveness and less honesty.

"There are a few less Jews since you left," Rachel said now. "We've had ten suicides, fourteen cholera deaths, and four typhoids, which leaves us with approximately seventeen thousand. And whether your Municipal Council succeeds in limiting emigration or not, I don't think there'll be many more arriving. There've only been a few who've managed to leave Europe since the beginning of the year."

"That will be good news to the Council. The Japanese have been demanding that I find a way to limit emigration. The fewer refugees we have to deal with, the easier it will be."

"Easier how, Elias? To look for reasons to lessen your support?"

"Easier to deal with the Shanghai Jews. The refugees are a burden, Rachel, an embarrassment."

"You know what, Elias? You're a self-hating Jew. You won't admit it, but you are. And I don't care how many times the king taps you on the shoulder, you're still a Jew. Have pity, for chrissakes. And while you're talking to the Japanese about their demands, tell them there's more anti-Semitic propaganda turning up on the streets and more attacks on refugees and you want them to do something about it."

"While I was away I had the strongest desire not to come back," Elias said. "I've been thinking of moving my business interests to Bombay."

"Bombay? What the hell are you talking about? We need you. American Relief can't support the refugees alone. You can't leave. And we need more money in the account for entry permits. Some of the refugees are keeping the deposits instead of turning them back. Some of them only keep a few dollars of it, and others keep the whole four hundred. I can't blame them, but we're short. And the yeshiva students need more books, and a complete Shas—I don't know what that is, but whatever it is they need it."

She stuffed papers back into the briefcase, crawled across the carpet gathering up assorted pieces of paper. Despite himself, Elias admired her persistence and lack of shame. Her methods sometimes burned bridges, but she got what she wanted. He should have said something to her parents about the state of her health. Her arms and legs were too thin. She neglected to eat while worrying about fattening others.

"I'm glad you're not leaving Shanghai," she said.

*   *   *

Sigmund picked a chair near the window, Heinrich settled into the sofa. Elias hadn't seen Heinrich Strauss since 1933 in Munich. It was at the opera. *Tannhäuser*. They spoke at intermission. Heinrich was somewhat stouter then. His wife Margot, slim and glittery in a beaded gown, had mentioned something about inviting Elias to their ski lodge in Bavaria that coming winter. Sigmund was at the university in Berlin, Heinrich had said, and interested in medicine. "A talented boy, quite disciplined, a great joy to his mother and me." Hannah was away at school in Vienna, Margot had added. "It's too soon to discern her talents, but she shows a genuine aptitude for music. If you strike a note on the piano, she can identify it exactly and promptly without any coaching or peeking."

There was no mention now about what had happened in the intervening years, no explanation of why the Strausses were in Shanghai. Hadn't Elias read somewhere that Heinrich had moved his family to New York, that he was negotiating to buy a newspaper chain? Or was it a bank?

"I meant many times to contact you over the years," Heinrich said.

"Of course."

"Hitler was a problem."

"If I remember, you thought he would be good for Germany."

"In 1932. By 1933 I was sure he would be its ruin. I should have left then, but I had hope that things would change. I underestimated his grip on the German psyche." He crossed his legs in the relaxed, knee-grazing manner Elias remembered.

"How is Lady Sybil?" Heinrich said.

"Very well. And Margot?"

"Splendid."

"And Hannah?"

"High strung, but very well."

"I thought I heard that you left Europe in 1940."

"We didn't manage it. We went into hiding in a cottage on Count Logronski's estate. You remember Count Logronski."

"Very well."

"It didn't last. We were found out."

"We arrived in the village in a touring car," Sigmund said. "We weren't potato farmers, we didn't tend sheep or goats. Father looked like a Jewish merchant in his fine clothes, Mother was wearing her best jewelry, Hannah paraded around like a prize chicken with her matched set of luggage."

"We had the protection of Count Logronski."

Sigmund shook his head. "A nonexistent protection. I spent a year in Dachau."

"I got you out. I liquidated everything to accomplish it."

"We should have left in '39."

"You wanted to study in Berlin."

"You knew the political situation better than I did."

"I won't take the blame for your choices in life, Sigmund."

"But you saw what the Jewish situation had become."

"I didn't believe it would affect us. Our Jewishness has always been nothing more than a description. There is no reality behind it other than the name, no blind attachment to tradition or observance, no filial branches to accommodate."

"How could you say that? The Strauss name is as dangerous as a knife to the throat. You could have predicted I would be expelled from the university."

"I thought we would be exempt, that the laws wouldn't apply to us. Besides, Hannah was in the sanatorium for most of the year and too frail emotionally to travel."

"Hannah uses mental aberration as a refuge. You indulge her."

"She wasn't well. She couldn't travel."

"That wasn't why we stayed. Mother wouldn't leave Germany."

"She would have if I had insisted."

"But you didn't."

"No, I didn't."

Heinrich turned toward Elias and smiled. "Sigmund mistakes concern for indulgence. Due to the Jewish laws Hannah was expelled from the music conservatory and her Aryan fiancé broke off their engagement. She had a breakdown. I'm afraid Sigmund makes too much of my ability to alter events. I've tried my best to influence his attitude. His attraction to defeat is foreign to me. I have always risen to the top, my confidence intact. But there it is. You see us as we are, at each other's throats because of what has happened to us, what we did, what we didn't do. The strain threatens to overtake us at times when we think of what we've come to, what we've lost. We are a family without a country, without funds. But, I'm sure, not without friends."

"Of course, not without friends," Elias said. He avoided staring at the oblong oily stain on Heinrich's overcoat, at the soiled collar of Sigmund's shirt. "Have you been in Shanghai long?"

"We arrived yesterday. It was a difficult trip. There were no more ships from Italy. We went overland through Manchuria and then to Japan. I'll be frank, Elias. We have no money, none at all. There, it's said. We need your help. We are living in the Seward Road Heim. Temporarily, of course. I've promised Margot I'll find someplace else for us as soon as possible. I intend to publish a good German-language newspaper here, but I'll need some backing, which, of course, is why I've come to see you. It will be paid back to you with interest. I'll need a place to work from. Someplace small at first will be sufficient, but when circulation improves I might call on you for interim loans, all of which, of course, will be calculated and paid back with interest. To start again in a new place isn't easy, but I've told Sigmund that with determination we can succeed here in Shanghai as easily as anywhere else."

"There are three German-language newspapers in the refugee community already," Elias said. "They're barely surviving. They give away free copies in their reading rooms."

"They don't have my experience. The knowledge and ability to run a newspaper has been hard won by me. If they give away free copies, they're not approaching readers appropriately."

"They're all run by refugees like you. And I must be frank with you, Heinrich, friend or not, your story is no different from a thousand others I've heard. I can give you five dollars a month. It's more than I'm authorized by the Joint to give. It's my personal present to you, not a business arrangement, and there is no need to calculate anything or pay me interest. I make this gift to you as a friend, and will continue to do so for as long as you need it. Five dollars will supplement the diet in the heim and will see you through. My only request of you is that you not mention it to anyone."

"You're telling me you want to give me charity?"

"Thousands of refugees have descended on us, all wanting to work, all needing money."

"'On us'? What does that mean, 'on us'? You're a Jew. You could be sitting here sweating despite the cold instead of me."

"You don't understand the situation I have to deal with. A million starving Chinese have flooded Shanghai trying to escape the Japanese in the north. The Japanese control the Chinese section of the city and blame the Jews for the increase in crime. The White Russians complain they're losing jobs to the refugees, that Jews are working for nothing just to get a toe in the door. There are Nazis in the Shanghai German community undermining everything I'm trying to do for the refugees. I have delegates and representatives and committees and councils on my head day and night. I'm walking a fine line, Heinrich."

"I don't give a damn for your fine lines. What do you think I am, a fool? Why do you think I came to see you? To listen to your excuses? You're my friend."

"Take the money I offer you. It will help. I know what the food is like in the heime. Take the money."

"You take it."

*   *   *

Seven o'clock. Edward gone. Office empty. Quiet. Elias poured himself a tumbler of brandy, downed it, then lay down on the sofa and studied the porcelain chargers lined like full moons across the marble mantle. Elias collected antique Chinese porcelains. He favored dragons and court scenes. He was known in all the auction houses in Shanghai, all the shops. He was tenacious when he wanted something. He once spent a thousand Shanghai dollars on a two-inch inkpot. He owned a tea set that belonged to Empress Tzu Hsi—twenty-four pieces, with matching garniture, that he had seen at the home of one of Sybil's friends about to leave for England and later found in a small antique shop in a building near the race course. The owner of the antique shop, an opium addict, let Elias have the set for five hundred Shanghai.

On the wall to the right of the mantel was a portrait of Elias's ancestor, Mansour ben Abdullah ben Daoud, who fled to Mesopotamia when Jerusalem fell to the Romans in 70 AD. He was standing in a garden, a finely woven cascade of cloth enveloping him. The Caliph of Baghdad told his subjects that ben Daoud was a descendant of King David, a Jewish Prince in Exile, what the Jews called a *Nasi,* and must be paid respect. Mansours lived in Mesopotamia for twenty-four hundred years and were advisers to the great Valis of Baghdad until the anti-Semitic Turks drove them out.

Next to ben Daoud's portrait was a painting of Elias's wife Sybil. She was beautiful then. Narrow-arched nose, rose-petal skin, wide-set blue eyes. She was still beautiful, despite the small lines that had begun to lap at her cheeks.

When they met at the Prince of Wales' country house in 1925, the Prince informed Elias that Sybil's father was an earl without a fortune and that she didn't mind that Elias was a Jew.

They were married in Shanghai in 1926.

"I warn you that although Mansours have lived and prospered in Shanghai since 1843, Gentiles don't seek out my company," Elias told her. "I'm called Sir Elias to my face, but the Jew Mansour behind my back."

Sybil invited two hundred people for a six-course dinner, hired an orchestra, a troupe of flamenco dancers, and a Chinese magician. Each guest had his own "boy" to serve him. After that Sybil's address book was as full as the Shanghai telephone directory.

A self-hating Jew? Rachel was mistaken. Until the refugees began pouring into Shanghai, Elias rarely even thought of himself as a Jew. His grandfather Mansour ben Daoud ben Ezra came to Shanghai when the Bund was still a muddy towpath and rope-tied coolies strained to pull junks upriver to the Yangtze. Opium had brought them their fortune, but cotton had brought them respectability. Elias owned the Mansour Bank of China and the Mansour Shanghai Insurance Company. He was a member of a trading partnership and sat on the boards of five international corporations. He owned silk factories and carpet mills and had been knighted by King George for service to the British Crown. On the wall were framed commendations and medals and royal citations.

Why should he listen to anything Rachel says? She's a beggar, someone who would say anything to get what she wanted. When the refugees started pouring into Shanghai in 1938 and the American Joint Distribution Committee in Shanghai asked Elias to head the Refugee Relief Committee, they said he would be working with an American woman. He hadn't thought they meant anyone as difficult as Rachel Shapiro.

The worry was the Japanese authorities. What they intended to do about the refugees was unclear. The Japanese promulgated new laws, but made no effort to target the Jews. The Joint still did their work without interference. Of course, if the war went on too long and the Germans persisted in pressuring the Japanese to dispose of the refugees in some way, what then?

He stood up and poured himself another brandy.

Heinrich Strauss penniless? The owner of the *Tageblatt Hamburg*, the second-largest newspaper in Germany, reduced to begging for money to publish a refugee newspaper that would, unread, end up as stuffing for worn-out shoes? His flaxen-haired wife Margot, *Die Dame's* 1932 Fashionable Woman of the

Year, living in the Seward Road Heim? And his son. Well, what could be said about a son who spoke to his father with such contempt? Elias was glad he had no children, if children meant the possibility of a son like Sigmund.

He lifted his glass to his ancestor's portrait. Elias's eyes, large black spheres, had the same buttery shine, but he flattened his curly hair with scent-less pomade instead of wrapping it in a coil of cloth. And he wore no flowing robes. Only suits he had tailored for him in England.

"To the Prince in Exile," he said aloud. "To the Jew of Jews."

Chapter 8

For several months no additional refugees had arrived. Letters from Europe stopped. Those refugees who once talked about returning to Poland or Germany when the war was over now spoke despairingly about those they left behind.

The last letter from Mama was in May.

> *Dearest Lilyichka,*
>
> *I bought a map and I press my finger on the dot that says Shanghai, and then I kiss my finger and thank God you're safe. The Germans dropped bombs on Kovno in June, and the Russians stole from the stores and took the peasants' food and then ran like rabbits. They left the prisons open, and the criminals ran, too. We are safe for the moment in Slobodka with the baker and his wife, but it is a stillness such as will be when the Mashiach comes. We sit in the dark, full of fear and sadness. The Germans will come soon, and what will happen then we don't know.*
>
> *The baker and his wife want us to leave Slobodka with them and follow the Russians. I would go, but Papa quotes Talmud: "Should those who live in the valley fear the evil spirits?" And so we stay.*
>
> *The village is beautiful this time of year, and the berries are ripe. Remember the beautiful berries we ate together? I depend on you to remember those things.*
>
> *Take care of Aaron, and remember me to Moses and the yeshiva buchers. Be kind to everyone, and, God willing, we will see each other again.*
>
> *Mama*

* * *

Dear Mama,

   Do what the baker said and follow the Russians. Make Papa go. You can do it. No one but you can do it.
   This is a strange place, but we are well.

Lilli

*   *   *

This was the letter Lilli didn't write:

Dear Mama,

   Aaron goes to the synagogue on the Bund every morning. When the yeshiva students come back to the heim in the evening he isn't with them. At night I hear him pulling his shoes off and getting into bed. When I ask him where he's been he won't tell me. How can I take care of him if I don't know where he goes every day?
   The yeshiva students go to the synagogue every day and Moses goes to work in a bicycle shop in the French concession. Three dollars a week. He gives me half. I love him, Mama, but the world is upside down and what can we do?
   Save yourselves.

Lilli

*   *   *

Farmers came from the countryside. They set up their crates in the fetid lanes of Hongkew and swished heads of lettuce in the foul brown water of the gutter until the leaves were sopping and the curled edges relaxed. Sometimes, like today, there were round, nubby-skinned oranges for sale.

Lilli looked the oranges over and then pointed to one. "I'll give you two coppers for that orange."

The farmer waved a head of lettuce in Lilli's face. "Two coppers."

"I don't want lettuce, I want an orange."

"No can do two coppers. Can do eight coppers."

"Three."

He picked up the orange and rolled it around in his grimy hand. "Five can do."

"Three."

"No can do."

She turned away.

"Four can do," he said.

She hurried through the narrow lanes with the orange, past mangled buildings held together with broken cement, shards of glass, chipped bricks, past a Chinese woman washing her long black hair in a bucket of pale green water, past a Chinese man pouring the contents of a urinal into the brown stream the farmer rinsed the lettuce in, past old men playing mah-jongg in the shade of a bombed-out factory, past a rickshaw tucking its wheels into the cobbled cracks. Laundry flapped from every window and from roof to roof. Coal smoke and walls shaved the sunlight, except for an occasional streak the width of a straw. The lanes thrummed with noise, the fevered air a floating scape of peddlers' barks and bicycle bells, of slamming hammers and squalling animals.

Hongkew, the industrial section of Shanghai, had been bombed by the Japanese during the takeover in 1937 and now rats as big as dogs haunted the ruined buildings. Lilli had seen them in the heim at night when the heat kept her awake. They climbed the rough walls and prowled the floors and beds looking for food, their eyes hard and bright. One crawled into the sleeve of Aaron's coat. In the morning when Aaron went to put it on, Lilli heard the rat's crepitant creep along the jacket's stiff lining. Aaron refused to kill it. He said the rat was God's creature, too, to throw the coat away. Moses took the coat out into the lane and beat it with a rock until it was flat and silent. By then the coat was a bloody mess. Lilli tried to scrub it clean, but the sleeve ripped where the lining was chewed away. Now she not only examined their clothes for lice and bedbugs, but checked for rats.

But now the cold was forgotten; the summer heat was here. Stealthy heat that one day suddenly appeared, as though it had been lying in wait. The refugees lay on their beds in their underwear fanning themselves with sheets of paper while mosquitoes fed on warm skin and welts were scratched to runny sores. The heat clung, rose up, hovered overhead, then laid itself down on sweaty, itchy bodies as neatly as a second skin. Lilli sometimes thought that the heat had a shape, that she could see the outline of its body, a thick cloud clinging to the walls.

The food in the heim had been reduced again. Watery stew at lunch, no dinner at all. Some of the refugees had set up stands in the lanes and were selling their winter clothes and remaining possessions to the Chinese for money to buy food. The elegant shops in the Concessions were filled with German woolens, gold wedding bands, fine Italian leathers, Swiss watches, music boxes that play Brahms's lullabies.

Aaron wouldn't allow Lilli to sell her coat.

"God has not changed the weather. Winter always comes."

"I know that winter always comes, but where do you go every day, Aaron?"

"Where do I go?"

"Yes. Where do you go?"

"And why should you ask me where I go? Is it your business where I go?"

"You never went anywhere in Kovno."

"I'm not in Kovno. I'm in Shanghai."

"Tell me where you go."

"To the Public Gardens. I sit on a bench and look at the Whangpoo and smell the flowers and the good, fresh air."

"You go there at night?"

"Will you tell me I can't? Will you call a policeman? What I do is up to me. So don't ask questions. A girl who asks too many questions is sure to get into trouble."

She had now reached the heim. Children were playing on the steps. Fanny and Shaya had gone inside, one of the children said. Lilli should have taken Shaya with her to buy the orange. Worry brayed her when they were apart. Ida had turned clever, could pretend a cheerful spiritedness, but madness sometimes came limping behind it as slyly as the rat that scurried up the sleeve of Aaron's coat.

Up the steps. The ambulance, or clinic, was on the first floor to the right of the entrance. There was no one in there now but the dentist from Austria who tended it. He had a chair for doing extractions and a dissecting table where corpses were laid out for burial. A watchman kept vigil over the corpses for two days to make sure they didn't wake up. Fanny said she heard that the dentist and the watchman stole gold out of dead mouths.

Up the stairs to the second floor. A string quartet seated on chairs in the hallway, half-dressed in the muzzy light, were practicing for a recital, baroque motifs knitted into rainbow waves of sound.

A right turn past the stairs into the maze of beds.

Relief. All was well. Shaya was playing with the doll Lilli bought from an Austrian woman on Studley Street, its cracked skull and bare head set crookedly on its cloth body. Fanny was applying tincture of iodine to a scratch on Hannah's arm, Hannah fussing, Fanny telling her to hold still, Hannah yanking her arm away, Fanny telling her to go ahead, get infected, the women playing bridge four beds down telling them both to shut up. Ida was asleep, her right cheek bound to the pillow, her hair hanging over the side of the bed in a squashy snarl.

"Look, Shaya, a beautiful orange," Lilli said. She peeled the orange, one piece for Fanny, one piece for Ida when she woke up, two pieces saved for Aaron and Moses, the peel for herself, the rest for Shaya.

A trickle of orange juice ran down Shaya's chin. Lilli leaned forward and licked the drips away with her tongue.

"Do you know how to dance, Lilli?" Hannah said.

"No."

"It's really easy to learn. You just stand on two feet and kind of shake and jiggle. It's fun. You know Esther Burger, the girl from Munich, the one with the long side teeth?

"I don't know her."

"She's on the first floor."

"I don't know her."

"You do. A German girl."

"I don't."

"You must know her. She speaks to Poles. She doesn't mind at all. I've seen her do it. She even has a Polish boyfriend. Her father died of typhoid and her mother has gone to work as a maid in Frenchtown. Can you imagine that, Lilli, a German girl with a mother who works as a maid?"

"I don't know her, Hannah, I really don't."

"I suppose being a maid isn't the worst thing. Mutti spends her days on the roof, sitting next to the dirty laundry and reading the same book over and over, and Vati just stays in bed and studies the cracks in the ceiling, and Sigmund has ruined my life. It's his fault, you know, that there are no photographs of me to put up on the wall of the cabaret. A German camera for a broken-down bicycle? I'm ashamed to say he's my brother. I wonder if what Ida has is catching. It might be. I once read that people can catch all sorts of diseases. I think it's a disease when someone like Sigmund, who was almost a doctor, rides up and down lanes on a bicycle slapping the fenders like he was riding a horse." Hannah lowered her voice. "She took me to this new place, Lilli."

"Who took you to a new place?"

"Esther Burger, the German girl on the first floor. Haven't you been listening to anything I said?"

"I've been wondering whether there will be any dinner. Half an orange isn't enough for Shaya if there isn't going to be any dinner."

"Her name is Esther Burger, and I've been going there every night. You should come. Really you should."

"Is that how you got the scratch on your arm?"

"Don't be silly. No one gets scratches dancing. You talk to people and dance with them. The men pay you. I made eighteen dollars. I bought American cigarettes. If I don't smoke them all, there's a Polish girl who will give me twice what I paid for them. She's a profiteer, Vati says. He says I should stay away from her, that either the Japanese will arrest her for profiteering and send her to Bridge House, or they'll want a share of the profits. It's really wonderful, Lilli, what a person can do with money in Shanghai. Black market, Lilli. Aren't those exciting words? Like a novel. I wouldn't do anything like that, of course, because I don't want to go to Bridge House and be tortured to death or share what I have with the Japanese. The Japanese are strange, don't you think? I rather like them, though. They don't argue with you when you tell them you're a good girl. It makes me laugh the way they don't argue with you about it. Isn't it a wonder what a girl can do for herself just by being pretty? And you *are*, you know, if you'd fix yourself up a little more and not look so sour. Men hate girls who don't smile. Come with me and I'll show you how it goes."

"I can't."

"I don't know why not. You need the money. You're wasting away. All your good looks will be gone before you know it. A person can die just sitting here thinking about all the food they're not eating, all the things they're not doing. It's really not a good thing for you not to eat, Lilli."

"I eat. I eat all the time."

"Crumbs. You spend the money Moses gives you on food for Shaya. You eat orange peels, crusts of bread. You lick out her bowl. It's disgusting."

"I eat as much as I want to eat. I feel myself getting fatter and fatter. Look at all the meat on my arms."

Fanny had finished with Hannah's scratch and was studying her English lesson. She had been attending a class at the Chaufoong Road Heim to learn English so she could read the book one of the refugees who died of typhoid left behind. (When she dipped the book in iodine to disinfect it half the words disappeared.)

"Go dancing, Lilli, I'll take care of Shaya," Fanny said.

"You see," Hannah said. "Fanny knows that what I'm saying is true. She would come dancing with me, too, if she had the figure. Men like girls with good figures. You ought to do it before you lose any more weight, Lilli, and your figure disappears, before no one will want to dance with you no matter what you do. And if you don't care about yourself, think of what you can buy for Shaya with the money."

* * *

The door of the bicycle shop closed behind Moses. He was through for the day, spinning out the door into the crush of people on the street. The noise in Frenchtown at this time of day increased: the drub of rickshaws, the hiss of dry leaves beneath the slap of shoes on the blistering pavement, the competing notes of foreign languages, the plunk of music from the girlie bars.

He was part of the onward rush of whirling bicycles, passing the boulevard shops, heading into the residential section of Frenchtown, past the large chrome-yellow apartment houses, the awninged mansions, then over the Garden Bridge to the heim.

He always felt uneasy until he saw the steps of the heim, concerned that something had happened to Lilli while he was gone.

Lilli and Shaya were sitting on the top step near the door. He handed Lilli the bag of sticky buns he had held in the hot murk of the bicycle shop since noon and pressed his lips against her cheek. She didn't pull away, but showed no flicker of interest.

Lilli broke a bun into pieces and fed it bit by bit to Shaya.

"I want to see you eat one," he said.

She ate half a bun and put the other half back in the bag.

"Do you know where Aaron goes every day?" she said.

"To *shul.*"

"Where does he go after *shul?*"

"After *shul?*"

He didn't care what Aaron did after *shul.* He didn't care about the yeshiva buchers, who now spent their time in a religious trance in the synagogue. He cared about Lilli. He had tramped the streets of the Concessions looking for more remunerative work so that he could supplement her diet in the heim, but there were too many like him, everyone scrambling to find a way to make money. And now Lilli wanted him to worry about Aaron when his concern for her left no room for anything else.

"Where does he go, Moses?"

"Ask him," Moses said.

Chapter 9

Lined up on the wall to the right of the Crystal Cabaret's bandstand were the White Russians, painted dolls in too-short skirts and low-cut blouses, wrinkled skin barely ironed out by the blinking lights.

French girls, bosoms drooping, were in one corner. They flashed their legs, ribbon streamers trailing from bias-cut hems, their eyes muted flames that sparked when they wiggled.

On the wall to the left were the Chinese, Korean, and Japanese in embroidered gowns, jade combs raking twists of charcoal hair, small mouths partially open buds revealing betel-stained teeth.

Refugee women were in a section of their own, shabby dresses hanging lank and formless on their thin bodies. They shifted their weight from right foot to left and cradled their elbows in their hands. Lilli recognized a mother and her thirteen-year-old daughter from Alcock Road Heim. Lilli had traded her a scoop of rice for a faded skirt. The mother was wearing a purple scarf and what looked like a bathrobe. The daughter was in a cotton slip, a frayed shoestring governing her teak-brown hair, her lipsticked mouth a drop of blood in her narrow face.

A rope held the men back. They pressed against it, eyes keen, feet tapping. The Crystal Cabaret's proprietor, a Russian with thick fingers and slicked-down hair the color of wood embers, gave a little speech to the girls while the band warmed up. He switched from Russian to Polish to German in a voice as harsh and metered as a marching song in a key Lilli had never heard before.

"Make sure you take the ticket or I can't pay you afterwards. Any gifts handed to you on the premises belong to me. Don't try to hide them in your skirt or pass them off to accomplices. My men watch the floor all evening. If someone invites you to sit down at a table, say yes. If he asks you to have a drink with him, order champagne, we'll give you cider. If he wants whiskey, we'll give you tea. If someone wants to take you somewhere and you still have tickets, you can cash them in the next day. What you do when you leave here is up to you; you can charge whatever you want and do whatever you want, but in here you act like a lady."

He pulled the rope free and a horde of swift-moving bodies larded the leaden air with pomade and garlic and sweat. In seconds the mob was tamed, frenzy bottled. The men prowled the periphery of the cabaret, dog-like, some marking their route by an ass pinch or a hand swipe between a girl's legs or a quick snatch of breast.

An immense man speaking Russian clutched Lilli around the waist and yanked her out onto the dance floor, her cheek flattened against his belly, his belt buckle digging into her chin. Hannah had showed her how to move her feet, but there was no need, he held her up, her feet above the floor, and carried her around.

He dropped her where he found her, handed her his ticket and another Russian seized her. After the two Russians, a Korean man, mouth reeking of garlic, then a Japanese man, who held her so close she could count the buttons on his shirt. A German man, whose stomach growled and snorted, grabbed her breast. She pulled away. He called her a dirty Jew.

The music stopped. Acrobats were on the stage.

"How many tickets do you have?" Hannah said.

"Six. I'm leaving."

"Oh, look, can you believe what they're doing? Eight men on a bicycle."

"I told Fanny I wouldn't be late. Ida's been acting strangely."

"Ida is always acting strangely. I'm having too good a time. Aren't you thirsty? I'm dying of thirst."

The acrobats were gone, the musicians were playing again. A tango, the thump of drums as rackety as boot kicks against the walls. Men made their pick. A gritty shuffle of shoes across the polished floor. Heat percolating beneath tight clothing erupted in circles of sweat on stinky bodies. The blinking lights were dimmer now, filtered through woven strings of cigarette smoke. Exhausted women laughed but made no sound.

"There's someone coming this way now, Lilli. Maybe he'll buy me a drink. Chinese. Handsome, too, but not to my taste, too polished for a Chinese, they look down on you when they're too polished, although they're not as stingy as the Japanese. He's looking at you, Lilli. Smile at him. Show your teeth, for godsakes."

"Please," he said and pressed a ticket into Lilli's hand.

They moved out past the tables, his hand hot against the small of her back. The Chinese she had seen in the lanes of Hongkew wore cotton trousers and cloth shoes and carried their possessions on their backs. They didn't cut their hair in the European style or wear tailored suits or speak to her in English.

"Jewish?"

"Yes."

"I like Jewish women. They're very congenial. What's your name?"

She didn't answer.

His name was Li T'ien, he said.

The dance was over.

He picked a table and sat opposite her.

"Schnapps?"

"Yes."

The cold tea in her glass was the same rich color as whiskey. There was no nourishment in it, no sensation of filling her empty stomach, merely a cold draft channeling a course past her ribs. She looked across the dance floor. Hannah had been near the door a moment ago. She didn't see her now.

A bare-breasted Negro girl in a feather skirt was up on the bandstand doing an Apache dance. She dropped the feather skirt and danced nude, her long legs the color of cinnamon, her pubic hair shaved into the shape of a star.

Hannah appeared, welts on her neck.

"I looked for you," Lilli said. "Where were you?"

"I was here."

"I think we should go."

"I'm having too much fun. I saw you dancing. You didn't look too unhappy. You could smile more. But you do know how to move. You'll have regulars in no time. Regulars can keep a girl busy the whole evening. You should stay at least for another hour. A magician is coming on at midnight. You'll miss all the fun."

"Are you coming with me?"

"No. I'm having too grand a time."

Lilli cashed in her tickets. The Chinese man followed her.

"How will you get home?"

"Rickshaw."

"I have my car and driver here. Come home with me and I'll give you five dollars."

"I'm not a prostitute."

"Then I'll take you home. Do you live in one of the heime? Ward Road? Seward Road? Chaufoong Road?"

"Seward Road."

An automobile was waiting at the curb.

Li T'ien got in back with Lilli.

The leather seats were cushioned and deep. The driver wore a uniform. Lilli kept her hand on the door handle as they drove away from the cabaret.

"I've seen your friend before," Li T'ien said. "A lot of refugee girls are prostitutes. Prostitutes have to register. It's a criminal offense not to register. If your friend is a prostitute, you should warn her. Shanghai is a dangerous city. Jewish girls can lose themselves here."

"You shouldn't make up your mind what people are just because they're in a place they shouldn't be. I came to dance to make money to feed my little girl. Not everyone is a prostitute who's starving to death."

She let her hand drop, sat back, looked out the car window, counted windows lit by candles. She had never said that before out loud, *my little girl*. It shamed her that she had said it, taking possession of a child who wasn't hers, pretending, if only for a moment, that she was Shaya's mother.

The lanes looked different at night, quaint houses, buildings, shacks, all in a row, silvery roofs overlapping, garbage and dead bodies swept away from the curbs, tucked into corners, ugliness blunted, sharp edges smoothed out, the quarter moon a lustrous spot in the dark sky. She had sixty cents in her purse. Money she didn't have that morning. She thought about what she could buy with it. A banana for Shaya, two oranges, maybe even a tomato.

When they reached the heim, Fanny was outside standing in the middle of the lane, ghost-faced and trembling.

"Ida jumped into Soochow Creek. Sigmund was passing on his bicycle and jumped in and pulled her out. Sigmund is in the hospital. Ida, too. She won't talk to anyone, won't tell anyone what she did with Shaya. Moses is out looking for her now. Sigmund didn't see Shaya in the water. He said he would have seen her. He was right there when Ida jumped. I thought Ida was asleep. You know how she sleeps, like a dead one, but she was awake, and she took Shaya."

Li T'ien had gotten out of the car.

"Chinese children play in Soochow Creek. They're used to it. But the water's bad. Foreigners who fall in are dead in two days." He handed Lilli a small white card.

"For the man who jumped into the water. If he lives."

* * *

Beds in the hospital ward were jammed together, every bed occupied. Patients lay with wet towels spread over their naked bodies, the heat so intense it was almost visible.

The Strausses were at Sigmund's bedside, Heinrich at the head, Margot at the foot, Hannah at one side, the three of them pinned in the narrow aisles as snugly as clothes in a closet.

At the other end of the room near the bank of smeary windows Lilli found a few inches of space beside Ida's bed. She bent forward, her knees pressed against the mattress.

"Ida, can you hear me? It's me. Lilli." She took Ida's hands in hers, felt the fever heat in the fingers, the slow crawl of blood in the wrists. "Where is Shaya, Ida?"

Ida's mouth opened, a cavernous dark in lips frothed with spittle.

"Sold."

"You sold her? You sold Shaya?" Lilli felt the beginning of a toppling fall, an upright faint.

"Sold, sold, sold," Ida said. Her eyes opened wider. "You won't let them take me there, will you, Lilli? It's a strange country. Don't let them. No one will be able to find me if you let them take me there. I was supposed to leave today on the train. Mandel said to watch out, the boat leaks, it might sink. You won't let them take me there, will you?"

"I won't let them take you there," Lilli said.

*   *   *

Moses and Aaron stood in the hospital corridor, out of the way, looking in. Too many people, the nurse said, as if two more made a difference

"Who would have thought he would jump in after her?" Aaron said. "A selfish man like him. Why did he do it?"

Moses shrugged. "It was a reaction. People react in all sorts of ways when there's a threat."

"A reaction? That's what you call it?"

"What do you call it? Fated? *Beshert?* Do you think it's written somewhere that Sigmund Strauss was destined to come to Soochow Creek at the exact moment that Ida Bornstein jumped and that he was to jump in after her—like in a play, like in a drama?"

"No. What he did was stupid, it went against what God wants. God would not have written in Sigmund's book of fate that he should risk his own life for Ida's. Saving one's own life takes precedence over saving someone else's, especially a crazy woman who did God knows what with her own child. And look how he ends up for his troubles. In a bed in a stinking refugee hospital for no reason, no purpose."

"Are you saying he would have been right in the eyes of God if he had let her drown?"

"Absolutely. It's God's law, not mine."

"Even though Maimonides demands that you stop a murder?"

"It wasn't a murder, it was suicide, and the Midrash says it is not for courts to decide, that Heaven will deal with the one who kills himself."

"Maimonides says do not stand by the blood of your neighbor."

"To apply that to what Sigmund did is a misinterpretation. And I'm not going to argue Maimonides with you. When you come back to the synagogue and become a good Jew again, a pious man, we'll discuss Maimonides."

"Where do you go every afternoon?"

"My business. No one else's."

"Lilli worries about you."

"Lilli worries about everybody."

Lilli had turned away from the bed and was walking toward them.

"What's the matter?" Aaron said. "Your face is white. She didn't make you sick, did she? Did you let her breathe on you? You didn't stand too close to her, did you?"

"She sold her."

"What?"

"She sold Shaya."

"You see, Moses? That is the woman he gave his life for. I ask you, where in the Talmud does it say a man should do such a thing?"

Chapter 10

Rachel Shapiro's office was in a cubbyhole off the kitchen in the Ward Road Heim. No matter how many times she told the cooks to quit banging the pots and pans and not to slam the screen door, they didn't listen. And the cooking, my God, all that cooking and steaming in the August heat, as if two ex-jewelers knew how to cook and were really producing something tasty for the pittance the Joint Distribution Committee gave them, instead of just making her miserable.

She pushed her chair away from her desk, got up, and yelled across the courtyard.

"Don't you ever stop boiling things? Do you know how steamy it is in here? Do you know what misery you're putting me through in this god-damned box?"

She sat down at her desk again and lit a cigarette. She smoked too much. She promised herself she would quit soon. She woke up in the morning with green slime coating her throat. But she had to do it gradually; it couldn't be done all at once. She could probably do it overnight if she were in New York, but not here, not in China with the whole refugee situation so big she didn't know which part of it to grab first.

Maybe she had come back to work too soon. "Typhoid was a snap," she now tells anyone who asks her how she is. It hadn't been a snap. It had been a full stop, ragged, clutching fall. It had been six months of hell lying in bed in her parents' New York apartment, an alternate universe of flowers in crystal vases, of measured footsteps on parquet floors, of slipstreams of cooled air, of the plangent tones of the doctor's voice ringing as flat as a wooden rattle.

"Tell her she can't go back to China," her mother told the doctor.

"I can't do that. But I will say she ought to live a more conventional life. She'll have a weakened constitution at best."

"She'll do what she wants to do," her Jewish father, the rough-hewn law-yer and doer of good works, said.

Her father had always stood behind her, from capricious child, dirt eater, explorer of subterranean worlds, to the erratic student who read books on mysticism and economic theory and went to the Yucatan to analyze the distribution of food between indigenous and European populations for the Mexican government and came back from the jungle with her fair skin ruddied by tropic sun, rid herself of material possessions, became a fundraiser for crippled children charities, and in 1936 was named Director of the Jewish Orphans Guild of New York.

"Rachel Shapiro has spent her life dedicated to the solid burn of cosmic compassion" the Guild wrote in their promotional brochure.

But China? She had never thought of China as having anything to do with Jews until the rep from the Joint Distribution Committee visited Rachel in her office in New York in 1938. "We've seen what you've done with American-Jewish orphans. We could use your organizational skills with the European-Jewish refugees in Shanghai."

"What do you really do for the Jews in Shanghai?" her mother asked in her last letter.

"I do everything but kiss donkeys' asses to raise money. I'm a professional beggar, Mother, a *schnorrer*. You know, like the ones you see kneeling on the street with their hands out."

Did the Joint even know what was going on here? The appalling conditions? The food shortage? She told them and told them, but did they read the reports she wrote?

Well, the day was young, anyhow, good health or not, heat or no heat, food or no food. This afternoon she had three committee meetings to attend, one for Central European Jews, one for German Jews, one for Eastern European Jews. Every day it seemed there was another committee she had to deal with. The committee chairs had all at one time or another accused her of taking over, of pushing everyone else around, as though that weren't what they wanted from her. Their criticisms made her screamingly, violently nasty. What did they expect? She was a professional bully. That's what they wanted, that's what they got.

She was way behind on her ledger books. This morning she was determined to catch up. It was so hot in the room that the glue she used for sealing envelopes had dried in its pot, and the rag she kept beneath her hand to keep perspiration from smearing the ledger pages was nearly soaked through. The entries, a scrawly script only she could decipher, were a record of how many begging letters she sent to organizations in the States each month and what money, if any, she received. If she didn't receive any money within two weeks of receipt of a begging letter, she sent another letter, and another one after that and another one after that. There were envelopes now on her desk postmarked

New York, Chicago, St. Louis, Detroit, San Francisco, Tampa, even one from an orthodox synagogue in Phoenix. All with donations in them. Not enough. Not nearly enough.

"This Jew work is ruining your chance of ever finding a husband, sweetheart," her mother said.

"I don't want a husband."

Husbands seemed to Rachel to be a waste of resources. All that slavish devotion her mother spent on her father could have been used for something worthwhile.

Enough with the ledger entries. She picked up the meat bills. She was behind on payments. Lots of dunning notices. There wasn't enough meat for all the heime. How long could they live on rice and wormy bread?

A note from Rabbi Gurvitz at the Seymour Road Heim. "Send meat back to purveyor. Not kosher."

Not kosher? Oh, God, not kosher? Good meat? She tossed the note into a pile of similar notes. She wasn't throwing any meat away.

A note from Elias. "Talmud and Mishnah on way from England. I put a rush order on it. Hope our conversation wasn't too antagonistic. I never mean them to be. Circumstances dictate. Elias."

Poor Elias. She wished he'd say what he really thought.

"We'll feed every Jew who comes to Shanghai," he said in 1938, when there were still only a couple thousand refugees, mostly prosperous Germans who just needed a hand settling in. "And then we'll send them to the United States."

He was a generous man, she had to admit that. And he had kept his word. He and his Refugee Relief fed a few hundred refugees and then sent them off to the United States and Canada. But when the Americans started restricting emigration and refugees began arriving at the rate of two thousand a month, and they were poorer and needier and no one knew what to do with them, he began distancing himself from the effort.

God, the heat was awful. It made her fingers swell.

"Come home," Rachel's mother wrote in February.

"I will," Rachel wrote back.

She didn't say what month or year. She didn't like to be pinned down. In her own mind she actually thought she'd be home before the summer, but summer was here and so was she.

A young girl was in the doorway, a slender refugee in a faded blue skirt, asking if she could come in.

"No, you can't. This isn't the office you want; you want the Joint Distribution Committee office upstairs. Whatever it is you need, they'll help you."

"I was up there. They sent me to talk to you."

"This is unbelievable."

"What is?"

"That they sent you down here. You don't belong down here. This is my office and I don't do individual cases. Go back upstairs and tell—who'd you speak to?"

"Mrs. Friedman."

"Right. Sandra. Tell her to take care of it, that I said so."

The girl sat down. They usually left when you told them to leave. They didn't sit down.

"I won't take too much time."

"That isn't the point—what's your name?"

"Lilli Chernofsky."

"That isn't the point, Miss Chernofsky."

"Lilli."

"Lilli."

"I just want five minutes."

"Shit. Where are my cigarettes?"

"Next to the ashtray."

"Right. Smoke?"

"No."

Rachel took a Chesterfield out of its crumpled pack and lit it. "Five minutes. I'm timing you."

"There was a woman in the heim . . ."

"Which one?"

"The woman?"

"No. The heim."

"Seward Road."

"Go on."

"Aaron didn't want me to have anything to do with her. Aaron's my brother, very smart, a yeshiva student. But I didn't listen to him. He's very smart about books, but very dumb about people."

"Time's running," Rachel said impatiently.

"Her name was Ida Bornstein. She jumped into Soochow Creek and died of cholera this morning. Sigmund Strauss also lives in Seward Road Heim.

He saw Ida jump and he jumped in after her and pulled her out. He has cholera too and probably won't live either."

"You need the burial society. Talk to the director of your heim. Was she orthodox?"

"I don't know. I don't think so. I never saw any sign that she was orthodox."

"Then it doesn't matter."

"Ida had a daughter, two years old, named Shaya. Before Ida jumped into Soochow Creek she sold Shaya to someone."

Rachel stubbed out the cigarette. "No one told me anything about selling babies."

"I told the Refugee Affairs department upstairs about it, and they said it happens all the time, that some of the Russian women don't want to spoil their figures, so they come to the heime and buy children from the refugees. They said that sometimes a refugee will get pregnant just so she can sell the child. Ida didn't do that. She came to Shanghai with Shaya."

"Look, I'm sympathetic, don't think I'm not, but I . . ."

"Before she died I asked her who she sold her to, and she said she couldn't remember. Mrs. Friedman said to talk to you, that you knew everyone in Shanghai and could help me. Ida's husband is still in Russia. He doesn't even know his wife is dead."

"Give me an address. I'll write him a letter."

"He's with Intourist. He works for the Soviet government."

"Fine. I'll take care of it."

"No, you won't. I can tell you have no interest in it. You want to be polite. Everyone wants to be polite, but I can't be polite now. But I understand. You didn't know Ida and you don't know Shaya and you don't know me, so why should you care? You have all these people in Hongkew to take care of. Shaya isn't that important to you."

"I'm not a detective."

"And children can't be sold. Civilized people don't do things like that. Ida was insane. She didn't know what she was doing. She wouldn't have done it if she knew what she was doing. Shaya has a father. She has me. I take care of her. She shouldn't be with strangers. She should be with me."

"I'll ask around. I promise."

"Did you write down my name?"

Rachel sighs. "No."

"Write it down. Lilli Chernofsky, Seward Road Heim."

Chapter 11

No one saw Lilli leave. It was easy to come and go in the heim. No one noticed. The day began with the first quivering rays of the sun and ended in the creep of dark, but real time in the heim meant nothing. It was yanked in all directions, turned inside out, laid sideways, bounced on its head. There were always people sleeping or playing cards or arguing. The sick retched into tin pails at all hours. Babies shrieked at midnight and purred at noon. Everything that could be done in private was done out in the open. No one noticed.

She was out on the street now, being shoved along, jostled on all sides, nearly tripping as she rushed to keep from being caught in the fleeting spaces between the scurrying feet where the beggars and lame hovered.

The heat was beginning to bloom, converting the stew of sewage and decaying corpses into breath-sucking rot. The Garden Bridge, a graceful suspension of metal arches spanning Soochow Creek, was ahead, aswarm with people and automobiles and rickshaws heading for the Bund. There was a rhythm to the traffic on the bridge, a loping loose-hinged dance, quixotic and mercurial, no one leading, no one following, everyone on their own, cranked forward, as though gravity were vacuuming up the morning traffic and getting ready to disgorge it on the Bund.

She turned onto Nanking Road. The noise and congestion lessened. Lilli had been in this part of the city before, had pushed open the polished brass doors of foreign-owned shops and asked well-dressed sales people guarding cases of silver and leather goods and jewelry if they had any jobs available.

Not today, they said. Not tomorrow. Not next week.

The Race Course was ahead, an oasis of green in a forest of tall, sun-scorched buildings. Chinese faces. Chinese music. Lottery tickets. Money lenders. Jumbles of merchandise in shop windows. Carved jades and ivories, shriveled roots in satin boxes, dried frogs by the bundle, herbs and fish bladders and snakes in jars, preserved animal parts tied with string. The aroma of sesame noodles clamping onto flights of super-heated air.

Lilli was offered a job in an underwear factory on this street. Four cents for nine hours' work.

The street narrowed. No automobiles, just pedicabs and rickshaws hurrying past workshops fabricating umbrellas, filing brassware, hammering silver into miniature pagodas. Women sat at benches in open doorways stitching bright thread onto sheer fabric by hand, their eyes straining for light, a silvery shadow of sun on their bent heads, the fabric held close and pulsing with each exhalation of breath.

A sign on the side of a small concrete building, *Hong Shin Kee Tailoring*. A sallow-skinned old man hunched over a sewing machine next to a clouded window, a mound of silk pajamas on the floor at his feet, the workers behind him snipping and sewing, machines whirring, scissors slashing through fabric with metal-gnashing clanks.

He looked up at Lilli. His right hand rested on the wheel of the machine, the other held a tail of red thread to his lips.

"Is Mrs. Danoff here?"

He licked the red thread to a point, threaded the machine, gave the wheel a spin, touched his foot to the treadle and the needle darted invisibly across the silk.

"I want to speak to Mrs. Danoff about a little girl."

He pulled the fabric from beneath the needle guard, examined it a moment, then threw it onto the pile.

"Who told you to come here?" he said in Yiddish.

"Rachel Shapiro from Jewish Relief. She said she had heard Mrs. Danoff was someone to see if I wanted to buy or sell a child."

"Through the curtain in back. She's in there."

A dark hallway. Lustrous bolts of silk stood as straight as cigarettes against the walls. Fabric dust hung thick in the air, clung to the bolts of cloth, flew up with every step like startled formations of tiny white gnats.

She opened the curtain at the end of the hallway. A small room with no windows. A cot against a wall. Baby clothes atop a wooden box. The floor a spill of fabric scraps and trodden slips of paper. The air soggily humid and smelling of baby feces and old vomit.

A middle-aged woman, her huge bulk overflowing an upholstered chair, cradled a baby on her lap.

"Are you Mrs. Danoff?"

"Keep your voice down. This one hardly sleeps at all. Now look what you did, you woke him up. Did you have to come in right then? Now he'll be screaming when the woman comes to look at him."

"You bought a little girl two weeks ago. The mother's name was Ida Bornstein from the Seward Road Heim."

"The crazy woman. I remember her. She wouldn't take the money."

"She's dead. I want the child back."

"You're too late. You should have come sooner. A beautiful child. Sweet. They're not always so sweet. Sometimes they cry so much their faces swell and then it's hard to sell them. But she was very easy, very quiet. I had several women who wanted her. If I had waited there would probably have been more women who wanted to buy her, and then I could have gotten more money, but I have no help, and this one was due."

"Who bought her?"

"Don't worry, she's in a good place."

"You had no right to sell her."

"Don't be so rough. A pretty young girl like you talking like that to someone who could be your mother. I have children. My children don't talk to me that way."

"Where is she?"

"Would you want me to tell someone if you bought a child? My business could be ruined. I have a reputation. Leave her be. Her mother wanted to sell her. She didn't want her any more. I didn't force her. I didn't make her do it. I tried to give her money and she said she didn't need money, so I kept it. Is that why you're here, to get the money she wouldn't take?"

"I don't want your money. I want the child."

"She's gone. You can't get her back. You'll just make trouble. I knew that woman would bring me *tsoris*. And here you are, breaking my back, wanting something that isn't even here. I talked to her one minute and I knew I would be sorry, but I took the child anyway. I knew if I didn't, she would put her in the street. A Jewish child in the street is a dead child in no time. So I sold her. Jews in Shanghai have to make a living the best way we can. I don't apologize. I do what I have to do. So leave me alone. You're unhappy? I didn't do anything to you. I don't even know you. The mother sold her. That's it. *Fartik.* Finished."

"If a mother in her right mind gives away a child, that's one thing. If a mother who has no mind gives away her child, God notices. Would you take a chance that the child the crazy woman sold you will be the one to bring God's wrath?"

"There is no God in Shanghai. Everything is for sale. Why should a child be any different?"

Lilli sat down on the dirty floor at the woman's feet, put her arms around the fleshy legs, laid her head against the fat-cushioned knees. The baby was whimpering, one leg fallen out of its blanket and resting on Lilli's head. Was this what Mama felt when Masha died, this mournful emptiness, this enveloping horror, this icy barrow of despair?

"I'm begging you."

"Get up."

"No."

"You can't stay here. The woman will be coming. You'll ruin the sale."

"Where is Shaya Bornstein?"

"Is that her name?"

"Yes."

"A pretty name."

"I want her back."

"Oh, my God, you make me sick."

"Tell me where she is and I'll buy her back."

"Six hundred Chinese dollars the woman paid me. Who says she'll sell her to you, and where would you get that much money?"

The baby was crying. The woman rocked it back and forth in her jelly arms.

"Such fools come here," she said.

*   *   *

It had been raining all day. Not hard enough, Elias knew, for Sybil to cancel the party, although she had prepared for the possibility by having the oriental rugs in the entry rolled up and put away.

The automobiles were coming up the drive now, servants running out with umbrellas, car doors opening, guests dashing inside, now shaking hands with Elias, then kissing Sybil, then handing their wraps to a servant and remarking how hot it's been, how welcome the rain, then proceeding into the flower-filled ballroom.

Informal dress, the invitation said. A small celebration in honor of our new daughter, the invitation said. Elias had to smile. Everyone knew that Sybil never did small celebrations. The women were in long spangly gowns, the men in evening dress, stiff collars cutting like dull razor blades into their necks.

Sybil had bought an electric train at the Peking Treasure Shop on Nanking Road and the servants set it up last night in the middle of the ballroom floor. This morning the amah brought the child downstairs and at the train's first coruscating flash of lights and whistles she screeched as loudly as she might have if the amah were about to feed her to lions at the Shanghai Zoo.

Mr. Northbrock and Mr. Pernod, members of the Shanghai Municipal Council, were down on their hands and knees now watching the string of cars and locomotives bowl along the silvery track while the amah, Elizabeth in her arms, followed Sybil around the ballroom, past the buffet tables to the adjoining lounge where the guests were gathered at the mahogany bar. Elias wouldn't have done it this way, inviting guests to a party to show off a child that Sybil insisted Elias would learn to love, but whose presence he found eerily, remarkably alien.

But he couldn't complain. Sybil was radiant, her normal pale a fervid pink. And the child *was* pretty. More like a doll than a child in her white lace dress, the blue ribbon in her burnished hair a match to her eyes. Elias hadn't realized the depth of Sybil's disappointment at not having children. She never spoke of it. He had thought her content with the way things were and was bewildered at her almost magical attachment to the child (a child whose existence she had only discovered a few short weeks before) and perplexed by the tears and stammerings and evasions that met his every question about the child's origins.

"Are you suggesting I stole her?"

"I'm not suggesting anything. I'm not trying to find fault with you or the child. I merely am asking where you got her."

"Does it matter?"

"Of course it matters."

"A woman gave her to me."

"What woman?"

"I don't know who she is. I can't remember every little detail. The amah went and got the child and brought her home. I've longed for a child, Elias. I hope you'll love her."

The upstairs suite had been Sybil's mother's, intact since her death eight months before, now turned into a nursery. Staffordshire figurines, Battersea boxes, china tea cups, closets full of fur-trimmed suits and long capes and feathered hats, all of it gone, replaced by hobby horse and doll house and picture books, closets flush with dainty dresses, embroidered blouses, hand-sewn shoes, silver spoons, lace-edged sweaters, stuffed animals.

It was apparent that the child's name was not Elizabeth (she seemed puzzled when called that). She didn't respond to French, and although she seemed to understand some English (a startled move at certain words, a quiver of lips at a particular phrase), she was, by the look of her pinched cheeks, most probably a refugee child.

"How does it feel being a father, Sir Elias?" Mrs. Northbrock asked.

"It feels fine."

It felt nothing of the sort. It felt as if Elias had wandered into the wrong house.

In the evenings after dinner the amah would bring the child into the dining room and place her on Sybil's lap. The child would stare at Elias, as if waiting for him to say something. He could think of nothing to say. Of one thing he was certain: there was something suspicious about the way Sybil had acquired her. He should have made inquiries of the heime, should have checked with the foundling society, should have asked Rachel Shapiro if a refugee child was missing. He did none of those things, for he was reasonably certain that this was just another one of Sybil's passing passions, the amusement of the moment, and one morning he would come down to breakfast and the child would be gone.

At any rate, he would have sent out a simple announcement and left it at that.

*   *   *

English hedgerows and leafy laurel trees soldiered the drive so that the gabled house was only partly visible from where Lilli stood at the gate. There was a party inside, cars in the drive, silhouettes in the windows slipping in and out of the dancy light.

She moved back. Another car. People stepped out and up the stairs. A man, as dark-skinned as an Arab prince, stood in the doorway of the house, a fair-haired woman at his side.

"Don't offer her money right away," Mrs. Danoff had said. "Too soon and you will make her angry, and the anger will make her stubborn, and no matter how you plead, no matter what story you tell her, she won't let her go. A month or two, even three, and she'll be tired of her, and then she'll be willing and you can offer to buy her back. She'll sell her. Don't worry. I have had dealings like this before."

Chapter 12

A sunlit reception area on the twentieth floor of the hotel, men in business suits playing mah-jongg, ivory tiles clattering as they tumbled across baize cloths, the fumy smoke of cigarettes painting white shadows on the oak walls. A Chinese woman in an embroidered cheongsam and cloth shoes, silvery hair a soft confection of gathered braids, glanced at Lilli, then led her down a long corridor past rooms with closed doors.

The last room was an office, tall windows facing the Bund. Walls, leather couch, desk, chairs, wooden bar, all the same shade of brown, as though the room had been buried for a time and then dug up.

Li T'ien was at the desk, his beige suit a dull glow against the dark wall, his hair as slick and shiny as rain-washed tin.

He didn't remember her.

"A woman jumped into Soochow Creek," she said.

"Ah. Of course. A man jumped in to save her."

"Yes."

"Did he live?"

"Yes."

"You gave him the card?"

"Yes."

"And the woman?"

"She died. Ida Bornstein. Her daughter's name is Shaya. Ida sold her. I want to buy her back."

"And you've come here for money?"

"Yes. I remembered what you said."

"Why do you want her? She isn't yours."

"She *is* mine. I made her mine."

"What is she worth?"

"I don't know."

"But you had a figure in mind?"

"The child was sold for six hundred Shanghai. I don't know if the woman who bought her will sell her to me for that or want more. I'm not even sure she'll sell her. People sometimes hold onto what they don't want when some-one else wants it."

"I can spend a week in a brothel with fatter girls than you for two hundred Shanghai. I'll give you twenty."

"I've never been with a man before. I'm more valuable than a prostitute. If you give me fifty today, I'll do it for twenty next time."

"I may not want you again."

"You will. I learn very quickly."

"You would do this for someone else's child?"

"Yes."

"Fifty Shanghai is a lot of money for someone as skinny as you are."

"Fifty Shanghai is not too much for a virgin. I won't do it for less."

"You're a businesswoman."

"My price is fifty Shanghai."

He looked at her the way she used to look at the chickens in the crates in the marketplace in Kovno, wondering if they knew that when the *katsev* picked them out of the crate they were going to die.

The money was in a desk drawer. He fanned the bills out on the desk like a deck of cards. "Fifty Shanghai. And I'll give you a carton of American cigarettes. Hold on to them, they'll be worth four times as much next week. Maybe next time I'll have sugar from Free China for you."

He ignored her now, concentrated on his zipper, then sat down on the couch, zipper open, flesh exposed, feet angled straight out in front of him and motioned for her to undress. She looked out the window while she pulled the loose skirt from around her waist, stepped out of it, slipped her arms out of her blouse, let the gray underwear drop to the floor. She touched the window glass, felt its heat. Can anyone see her up here, someone walking on the Bund? Her whole body was in the glass, the liquid image of a girl she didn't know, a twisted image, cruel and imprecise, of an underfed stranger that darkened as she gazed at it. It was a poisonous idea, coming here. Repugnant, grotesque, a sort of madness.

He called to her.

He wanted her mouth on him first.

She had seen this done before, women kneeling in the aisles of the heim, their backs as bent as footstools, garlands of hair cloaking their heads.

She did what he said, choked once, stopped, he touched her head, she continued.

The men in the heim hid their pleasure, made no noise. He moaned.

When he was finished he gave her a handkerchief and told her to wait.

She sat in a chair, her skirt a cape around her shoulders while he talked on the telephone and wrote Chinese characters on a long sheet of paper. He pinched the pen close to the nib, his knuckles sinking inward as though compressed by the weight of his fingers. He didn't show his teeth when he talked, the contour of his face never changed, no smiles, no scowls, no worried brow. His suit jacket was on the floor, his trousers wet at the crotch, and his hair, shaken loose from its pomade set, jutted up like a flag at the back of his skull. His fearful presence was altered. She had altered it. He was now as ordinary as any beggar in the street.

The Chinese woman came into the room with a tray of sweets.

"Too skinny," she said and put a sugary bun on Lilli's bare leg.

Lilli nibbled at the edges of the bun until the taste of him was gone.

He was off the phone, standing over her. He wanted her to lie down on the floor.

The carpet, thick and spongy, gave with the pressure of his body on hers. The sun was moving more rapidly in the sky now. It came into the room at a slant, rested softly on her bare skin, laid a hazy red coat across the windows. She was being crushed, pummeled, bitten in some places, licked in others. This is not what she had seen in the heim; those shadowy couplings, quick and furtive.

"Bend your knee," he said.

Someone had come into the room and was watching, but it didn't matter. A spidery jolt of pain and she felt herself disappearing, sliding into that thin space between wakefulness and sleep, moving across an airless plane. She knew she was here because she had brought herself here. A circle of sun darted across the bole-colored ceiling. A reeky cloud roiled up out of the carpet beneath her head. No one she cared about was here to see her shame. If she kept her eyes closed she could imagine herself lying on a carpet of dry leaves in a forest in Kovno when the blackberries were ripe and the first frost was a long way off.

*   *   *

The building was behind her now, the window where she stood a short while ago looking down at the street lost in a yellow fog of dust and charcoal smoke. The Chinese woman in Li T'ien's office had given Lilli a rag to put between her legs. She could feel the ooze of blackening blood staining the rough rag, its nubbed pile chafing tender flesh. Way inside her in some hidden cavern something had cracked. She walked awkwardly, thighs tight against the rambling pain. She had seen thievish couplings in the heim, heard the riffles of barely stifled moans, the yelps at hymenal rips. Blood and pain were small matters, unimportant. She had fifty Shanghai in her pocket and a carton of Lucky Strikes wrapped in brown paper safe in her arms.

She passed the cigarette store. There was a queue out onto the sidewalk. American cigarettes. "Hold onto the cigarettes," Li T'ien had said. "In a week they'll be worth four times as much."

She glanced around her at the press of people on the street, everyone intent on going somewhere, the well-dressed and the beggars tilting for space, insensible to the grime and pluming smoke. It was a marvel that a person could do what she has done and walk out onto a fog-raddled street and there would be no outward sign, no visible blot. A yeshiva bucher rushed by her on the way to the synagogue, *tzitzis* whipping like wet noodles against his trouser legs. He had once slept on the floor in her father's house. He didn't look at her now lest God glue his feet to the pavement.

The pain was smoothing out, receding. A bit of sun dazzled through the murk. There was no one to tell her what to do now. She had severed forever the chain from Papa to Aaron to her. The echo of their imprecations were for some other Lilli, a girl without mastery of herself, a girl without daring. This Lilli was cunning enough to find water in the desert.

* * *

The first time Rachel came to the hospital to see Sigmund Strauss it was out of curiosity, a desire to see the person who had risked his life for someone who didn't want hers. But Rachel was captivated by his disinterest in everything around him and by his stark seething anger. It repelled Rachel to be like other women, spiders at their webs catching whatever ventured in. She had always chosen her prey, which in the past had produced a chain of unsuitable men. But Sigmund stirred her heart. She wasn't a fool about who he was, this German Jew, this spoiled hero sunk in misery and holding onto life with both hands, who looked at her with befuddlement, who sometimes forgot her name, who called her "Ramona," or "you." Mostly "you."

"Sigmund."

He opened his eyes.

"You."

"Yes. Me. I brought you some rice cakes. I ate a few. I was hungry."

"I don't want any." He had kicked the sheet away and was lying on the bare mattress in urine-stained undershorts, a spray veil of perspiration on his bare chest. None of the unsuitable men had been as beautiful as he was. The long torso, the slim hips, the arrogant brow above steel-blue eyes.

"You want to be able to get out of this damn place, don't you? You won't if you don't eat."

The nurses didn't like her visits. She yelled at them about the stench of the place, made a scene when his sheets weren't changed or the bed pan wasn't emptied.

"I left in the middle of a committee meeting, just got up and said fuck it, I've gotta go see Sigmund Strauss. Maybe today he'll know my name."

"Was my father here?"

"I haven't seen him."

She knew his father, had seen him in her office, not to talk about Sigmund and what was to be done with him when he left the hospital, but to listen to his complaints about the food in the Seward Road Heim, to hear him tell her again about his important past, his estate in Hamburg. She didn't know whether he had visited Sigmund in the hospital or not. She had seen the mother here once with her daughter. The mother, refined and emotionless, stood, an impassive onlooker, at a distance from the bed. The daughter began to weep as she came through the door, then threw herself across Sigmund's body, lay there clutching him, straightened up, shut the tears, wiped her nose, looked at herself in her hand mirror, asked Rachel who she was, didn't listen to the answer, asked Rachel for a cigarette, then sat at the foot of the bed and smoked it.

"You're certainly not Siggie's type," the sister had said. "Siggie likes pretty, petite girls who dress well."

"Little Siggie doesn't get his choice in Shanghai, honey," Rachel had replied. "He gets me, because I'm here and I'm all he's got."

"He'll drop you when he's well. He always does that, even with the pretty ones. He's very fickle."

More beds had been brought in since yesterday. Patients were housed like table legs in rows of beds that ended in snarls of wheelchairs and X-ray machinery and slop buckets. Newly sick patients crowded out the freshly dead who languished unclaimed behind hanging sheets, their bodies ripening in the heat, the odor joining the smell of pus-filled bandages and sweat-stained bedding. Patients called out, their voices as muzzy as the vibrations of distant motors. It maddened Rachel that she couldn't bulldoze the building and build a better one, couldn't turn on a spigot and make money flow.

She eased him into the crook of her left arm and fed him bits of cake. People died of typhoid. He had had typhoid and cholera and was still alive.

"Did you get up today at all?"

"No."

"You're getting up now."

"Oh, God."

She lifted him up and half-held, half-dragged him along the side of the bed. He felt weightless, body parts loosely packed and useless.

"No more," he said.

"Everyone knows about you," she said as she eased him back onto the bed. "I think the Central European Committee is going to give you a medal. I said, 'He's such a snob, he won't take it unless it's from the Council on German Jewry.' Of course the woman you fished out of Soochow Creek was Russian, so maybe I'll tell the Committee on Russian Jewry to give you the medal. You did fish her out, didn't you? You didn't just trip and fall in, did you, Sigmund? Your name is in the ghetto papers. No medals. Lots of free papers, though. I'm saving them for you. You can read about how brave you were when you're out of here. Shit, Sigmund, you should have thought about what was going to happen before you jumped in. If I had been there I'd have stopped you. I'd have told you the water'd kill you. I'd have told you heroism doesn't pay."

Chapter 13

Hannah sat up in bed. "I hear something." She walked barefoot to the lattice screen and looked out into the yard. It was mid-afternoon and Madame Cheng, the Chinese woman who owned the house, was squatting beside a bucket of used water, dipping dirty dishes in and out, a cloud of flies buzzing in the heated air.

"Come back to bed, Hannahla, and let me hold you a while longer."

"I heard a man's voice, Aaron."

"There are men in the rooms, so you'll hear their voices. We still have half an hour's worth of time. Come back here. I don't want to waste a minute. I still have more in me to give you."

"I'm sure I heard something."

"You heard the *kurvas* with their men upstairs. Come. I'm lonely."

There was nothing in the room but an iron bed, a sliver of mirror hanging on a string from the bamboo ceiling, and a bucket with the same toxic slime in it that Madame Cheng was using on the dishes. Aaron didn't care where they were. If he were asked, he wouldn't have been able to describe anything about the room except the way the lantern light outside the door grazed Hannah's breasts when she turned and walked back toward the bed. She had never been here with anyone else, she told him. He believed her. So what if she was lying? Was there anything in the Mishnah that could turn him deaf and blind the way she did?

She lay down on the damp sheets beside him.

"I saw Marlene Dietrich yesterday in a movie at the Odeon. I met her once at a party. She told me I had beautiful hair."

"You do have beautiful hair, the most beautiful hair in the world. I dream of your hair. Then I wake up and I'm alone on a stinking cot in the heim, a dead man, a corpse, because you're not there next to me. I can do without food and water, but without you . . . here, touch me here."

"Like that?"

"Yes, *mein tayer* Hannah, like that. Now turn on your side. I want to try something."

A few fierce shakes and the thin mattress slid halfway to the floor.

"Did that feel good?"

"You finished too soon. I felt nothing."

"I have to rest. Give me some time, we'll go again."

"You spill onto the bed and make it smell."

"Where should I spill if not on the bed? Did you know that the Torah says to spill one's seed is a sin? Do you know that you have ruined me as a Jew?"

"I don't need a baby, Aaron, so don't even think about anything like that."

"I'm just explaining."

"Don't explain so much. Let me sit on you and we'll do it that way."

"All right, *mein tayer*, all right, we'll do it any way you want."

Their efforts in the heated room heaved sprinkles of wet breath against the papered walls.

"Oh, oh, oh."

Aaron rolled away, exhausted.

"You make too much noise," she said.

"I make noise because I'm happy. Are you happy?"

"I'd be happier with more to eat."

"I look for work every day."

"You stand in front of the synagogue every day."

"And one day someone will come and offer me work. I'm sure of that. Everything is possible." He placed her hand on his chest. "Feel how fast my heart beats. I'm emptied out. Finished. Nothing left of me. How did I not know of such pleasures before?

"Because you didn't have your Hannah, that's why."

"Why do you love me?"

"I'll make a list."

"I'm serious."

"I love you because you're not like my father and not like my brother, because I'm the first woman you've ever had, because I love your red hair and I like the way your beard tickles my nose. And you're kind to me. Men aren't always kind, Aaron. They've said and done things that have hurt me and made me sad. I was sad in Germany for a long time. I don't want to be sad anymore." She raised her head. "Did you hear something?"

"Just my heart. I wonder how many times a minute it beats when I'm with you."

"We can time it."

"I sold my watch."

"I'll buy you a new one."

"With what? How do you always have money? Where do you get it?"

"I told you. Men give me gifts when I dance with them. They like the way I dance. There, it's a man's voice."

"I hear it now."

Aaron pulled on his trousers while Hannah peered out at the jungly garden. Two Japanese policemen were crossing the soggy ground, shouting. Their voices were small explosions, whip cracks, meteors punching a hole through a turgid sky.

* * *

Hannah and Aaron stood where other people had stood before, where other feet had gouged the floor to splinters. Behind them a queue of prostitutes reached almost to the outer door. There were no windows and half of the blades of the ceiling fan were broken, the whole ones barely churning the air.

The Japanese police captain looked appraisingly at Hannah, his broad brow hidden by a billed cap.

"Name?"

"Hannah Strauss."

And to Aaron, "Name?"

"Aaron Chernofsky. Talmudic scholar, skilled practitioner of *halakhic* discourse, fierce defender of *yidishkeit*." The policeman's eyes, two fig-shaped cocoa-brown globes behind wire-rimmed glasses, bore right into Aaron's heart. He couldn't breathe. His beard was so heavy on his neck it nearly closed his throat. "Have pity on me. I've spent my life in the synagogue. I'm a stranger to the world. Half the time I don't know what I'm doing or where I'm going. My head is always on other things. My torture at being here is extreme, my mortification complete."

"It's all right, darling," Hannah whispered. "You can wait outside, if you want. This won't take long."

"You've been here before?"

"Not exactly here."

"Exactly where?"

"In the Chinese sector and a few times in the British sector, but they were all mistakes. The Chinese always let me go and the English didn't even care. They served me tea."

Now his head hurt, the pain as sharp as knife points.

The policeman was talking to Hannah again. "You are a prostitute?"

"No, no, no. I dance for a living. In the International Settlement. The Chinese sector."

"But you are a prostitute?"

"You have no authority over what I do in the Chinese sector."

"The house is in Hongkew. Japanese sector."

"I can't be bothered about geography."

Aaron's hands had begun to shake, his right thumb drilling into the palm of his hand, his left thumb jerking as spasmodically as a defective engine.

The police captain handed Hannah a printed form.

"Sign."

"I won't sign that. I'm not a prostitute."

"You were with him in the room."

"We're getting married. We were making love because we're getting married soon and there was no other place for us to go."

"Sign."

It was dark when they left the station, stars streaking the sky like showers of broken glass.

"You should have defended me," she said as they picked their way along the rutted lane. "You didn't even say that you love me, that I'm not like the other girls. I can't believe you just stood there and didn't say anything."

"What could I say?"

"That it was a mistake."

"Was it?"

"Of course it was.

"I don't think so."

"How can you say that to me, your Hannah, the one you fondle and kiss and touch all over? How can you?"

"How can I? It's easy. I just open my mouth and say it. My God, what will Moses say when he finds out what I've been doing? I've fallen so low I don't recognize myself. I was a *frumer yid*. I lived a life of Torah. Do you know how embarrassed I was in there? It was like I wasn't even a person. And now when I think about what we did just a few hours ago I fight the urge to pull you into one of these dark corners and touch you and do what I want to you. I'm lost. I'll never be the person I was. I disgust myself."

"Moses probably does the same thing with Lilli."

"Watch your mouth, Hannah."

"I don't know what all the fuss is about, anyway. You make such a big thing out of it, like no one does it, like we're the only ones. Well, Aaron Chernofsky, I'm here to tell you that everyone does it. Everyone does it all the time."

"Who else do you do it with?"

"No one. A little cuddle in a pedicab is all I will allow."

"Are you a prostitute?"

"Of course not."

"I don't believe you."

"Then don't."

"I want to believe you."

"Then believe me. Who's forcing you either way? I'm the same person I was yesterday as I am today. We were caught. So what? Do you want me to tell you I'm a prostitute? I won't. I'm Heinrich Strauss's daughter. Do you think a daughter of his could be a prostitute?"

"Then where did you learn everything about—you know—about how . . ."

"In books. I've read a million books. You're not the only one who reads, you know. I'm just not interested in all that Jewish stuff. My interests are different than yours. Did you know that a person can learn anything from books? You can learn a language, you can build an automobile, you can even take someone's appendix out. You don't have to go to school anymore. It's really amazing what people write about."

"You told him we were getting married."

"I told him that so he'd leave us alone. You don't marry someone just because you do it with them. Why, people would have to get married a thousand times a day. And you haven't got any money, and we have no place to live, and Mutti and Vati don't like you."

"What do I care what atheist Jews like or don't like?"

"Then I won't marry you."

"I didn't ask you."

"And I can't sleep with you anymore."

"Oh, God, you drive me crazy."

* * *

Moses had him cornered in the smelly washroom of the heim, wouldn't let him go, wanted to know where he had been, why he looked so terrible, what he's been hiding.

"Nothing. I'm not hiding anything."

"I hear you don't go to synagogue anymore."

"Neither do you."

"I'm different. I don't believe. You're a believer, Aaron. What's going on with you? What's happening?"

"It's not what it looks like."

"What does it look like?"

"Terrible, that's what it looks like. Does Lilli know I don't go to *shul*?"

"Yes."

"What did she say?"

"Nothing. Lilli has her own problems."

"What problems does Lilli have? Lilli has no problems. Don't tell me about Lilli and problems, because she doesn't have any. There are no problems but mine, they're the worst, the most terrible. What problems does she have?"

"I don't know. She won't talk about it."

Aaron put his head in his hands. "Shanghai is a ruinous place, Moses."

"Where were you?"

"If I tell you, you won't believe it."

"I'll believe it, Aaron. There's nothing you can tell me that I won't believe. You're an honest man. I think you want to tell me what's going on. Where were you?"

"At the police station."

"Every day?"

"No. Just today. It was horrible. They made Hannah register as a prostitute. If God's watching me these days, even if I stay away from her for the rest of my life and do nothing but pray, I'm still a doomed man. I'll rot in hell."

"Hannah Strauss?"

"Hannah Strauss."

"You're crazy."

"I am. I'm crazy."

"She hates Jews."

"She makes an exception for me."

"All this time you've been with Hannah?"

"All this time."

"And she's a prostitute? Is that what you're saying?"

"Yes. No. She's not a prostitute. It was a mistake. Usually I'm only there a little while. She rents the room for an hour, two hours, then she goes back to the cabaret. Sometimes I fall asleep, and if there are empty rooms, Madame Cheng leaves me alone, lets me sleep. Today we stayed too long, and the police came."

"If she's not a prostitute, why was she arrested?"

"There are prostitutes in the house. I heard there were policemen around the neighborhood, but I didn't pay attention. All I could pay attention to was Hannah. You don't understand. She's poison to me, Moses, sweet poison. And it started so innocently. We met in the Public Gardens. The Shulchan Aruch states that to even sit on a bench next to a woman is forbidden. Did I obey? No. I sat on the bench next to her and we looked at the flowers and I told her about the Megillah and the Mishnah. I told her about what she could do to become a good Jewish woman. And all the time she was bewitching me." He brought his lips close to Moses' ear. "She's a *dybbuk*, Moses. She comes inside your body and takes over and makes you do what she wants you to do. She's like the blood in my veins, like my own bones, like the spit in my mouth. She's inside me. My soul will rot. It's unholy. It's ungodly. She's not a Jewish woman at all."

Moses' laugh rang through the bathroom. "You, the Talmudic scholar, the innocent who examines every aspect of life for possible damnation. You squeeze the life out of Lilli for every word she says and you lie down with Hannah. You have wasted all these years interpreting God's role in your life, and in one moment it's all over. How do you explain that, Aaron? How do you see yourself now as a Jew? Are you still good? Are you still worthy? Has the world stopped because you've thrown the rules away? Or are they just thrown away for you?"

"What do you know about it? I've struggled. I didn't just give in to lust. I was bewitched. If you had ever known a woman in the biblical sense, you would understand what I've just told you."

"In the biblical sense?" Moses said and laughed again.

"Fornication. Do you know what I mean by fornication?"

"I know what you mean."

"You've done it?"

"I've done it."

"You didn't do it with Lilli, did you?"

"And if I did?"

"Then I'll kill you."

"You'll kill me? Do you even know what you're saying? Have you ever killed anyone before?"

"God forbid."

"You wouldn't want to do it, Aaron. When you kill someone, you kill a part of yourself. You never forget it. It stays with you. You dream about it. You look at a stranger and say to yourself, does he know I've killed a person? Can he smell it on me?"

Aaron's eyes fluttered, his lashes as red as bloodstained moths' wings.

"Ah, I see the joke now. I've told you how far I've fallen, and you try to make me feel better by a recitation of imagined misdeeds of your own. I thank you, Moses, but it doesn't relieve my suffering, my humiliation, my embarrassment."

"Then I withdraw it all," Moses said.

Chapter 14

Elias toyed with the blancmange in front of him. He didn't put the spoon to his mouth. This was the best dining room in the best club in the French concession, but it was cholera season and in the sweltering heat not even the best dining room was exempt. He imagined fleets of cholera germs wiggling off the cook's fingers and diving into the milky mix before it was baked.

"I have no quarrel with the Jewish people," Colonel Yazuka said. He had already drunk a half bottle of wine and devoured a sauced veal cutlet and was starting in on the suspicious blancmange. "It's a historic fact that there are two nations within every Western country, the native one and the alien Jewish one, with its own loyalties and own interests. It's commendable, Sir Elias. Don't misunderstand me. Jewish bankers financed our war with Russia. We have gratitude and will express it in any way we can, but you must realize that we face great opposition from the Germans for our lenient attitude toward the refugees. Even your own British turn the Jews away from Palestine, while I have personally signed entry permits into Shanghai. I intend to save lives, Sir Elias. The destruction of such a wise, ancient people is abhorrent to me. We merely want the Jews of the world to be aware of Japan's position in Asia. It would be foolish of Jewish leaders to question Japan's determination to prevail in China."

There had been no discussion about "the Jewish people" up to that sentence. They had been talking about refugees. Generic. A discussion of humanitarian exigencies. Wasn't that what they agreed the discussion would be about when Elias consented to meet with him? And now these stealthy remarks.

"As a British subject I support Chinese sovereignty," Elias said.

"But you are also a Jew, and you care about what happens to your fellow Jews. What do you care about what happens to the Chinese? Don't be foolish about where you place your allegiance. Your leaders are in a position to endorse Japan's presence in China. Jews listen to other Jews. They're very clannish. Like the Japanese." Yazuka's usual expression was a sullied smile, but he laughed now, great salvos of laughter, holding his hand to his clicking front teeth, fingers spread like a child's in a game of hide and seek.

"Jewish leaders are not likely to endorse Japan's adventure in China," Elias said.

"You must not characterize it as an adventure, Sir Elias. We are brothers to the Chinese, here to help them exploit natural resources. I merely ask you to understand that the Japanese want the goodwill of the Jewish people. They have great influence with President Roosevelt and can convince him that we have no quarrel with the Americans."

"The Jews of the world are not of one mind. They're not easily led. They have a tradition of examination and analysis. Some may support you and some may not."

"You have influence in your community. If you help, I'm sure you'll receive the Order of the Rising Sun from the Emperor himself."

"You overestimate my influence."

The billiard room next to the long bar was full, in the adjacent women's parlor afternoon tea was being served, and here in the flower-filled dining room the sun's rays pierced the crystal dome and pasted flamy spots on the walls. Business was being conducted at every table, expansive conversations going on where Elias was sure that nothing said was the truth, where there was the smell of deceit on the papers being inked, where handshakes were no more than perfidious graspings. Yazuka's upper body was reflected in the restaurant mirrors, shoulders and back composed of angles and planes, his face an amalgam of friendliness and unalloyed conceit.

Elias longed to be away from here. Jonathan, Elias's new chauffeur, a Scot who was stranded in Shanghai in 1932 when his merchant ship left without him, was waiting at the rear of the club where the lawns wound down to the tennis courts and swimming pool.

"I beg your indulgence a while longer, Colonel. Your position is very clear, but my response will require more thought."

*   *   *

Rachel was sitting in the grass next to the car.
"I was accosted three times by guards wanting to know what I was doing here. I could have told them it wasn't any of their damned business, but then I decided they'd probably arrest me, so I used your name."

"Do you want a lift?"

"If you're going to Hongkew."

"I'm not. I can drop you off at the bridge."

Elias held out his hand to help her up. She pushed it away and struggled to her feet, her skirt flaring up to show the frayed stitching of her under slip. As they got into the car, Elias felt a momentary annoyance at her rough-hewn behavior and vulgar language. There was no way he could rid himself of her.

Jonathan maneuvered the car into traffic.

"Very nice car," Rachel said.

"You followed me, and then lay in wait."

"I did. That's what I do. That's what I am. Well, what did he say? I waited an hour in the broiling sun for you to finish your damn meeting. What did he say?"

"His position is the same as the last time I spoke to him."

"I don't believe it. He's lying. The Japanese want to control all of Shanghai and don't know how to do it. He didn't want to talk to you about what you already know, and I can see it in your face. He said something entirely different, didn't he?"

"He wants me to get the Jews on his side against China."

"Christ, no one has that much influence."

"The Japanese are worried about war with the United States. I could feel the pressure that's been put on him from higher up. They'd like to continue nibbling away at China without American interference. He promised me a medal from the Emperor."

"I hope you bowed and scraped over that one."

"He put forth the proposition that if I told American Jews how innocent Japanese expansionism in Asia really is he would continue to see to the safety of the refugees."

"He said that to you?"

"It was more subtle than that."

"Did you ask him about The Protocols of Zion? He's been spreading copies of that anti-Semitic shit all through the Japanese officer corps. It has his fingerprints all over it. And he wrote an article for *Shanghai Today* claiming the Jews are behind a Bolshevik conspiracy to rule the world. I nearly pissed I was so raving mad when I read it."

"Must you talk like a dockyard foreman?"

"Yes, I must. Well, did you talk to him about it? We're working here and he's undermining everything we're trying to do."

"We didn't get to it. It was too delicate a subject. I didn't think it was the time."

"Why the hell did you agree to meet with him if you weren't going to tell him anything?"

"I wait to hear what he has to say, Rachel. I'm not in charge. I have to keep his goodwill. There is no official change in the Japanese position and that's what counts. If I confront him, no telling what they'll do. The Japanese control the Council, we could see restrictive laws, *J*s on passports—God knows what they could think of to do."

"I give up, Elias. You are too much for me. All these months I thought I knew you, I thought you had a backbone."

They had almost reached the bridge. Traffic was stalled, two overturned rickshaws up ahead, their passengers spilled like grains of rice across the road.

"Thanks for the ride," Rachel said. She hopped out of the car and was gone.

* * *

Colonel Yazuka at noon, then Rachel, and now Heinrich Strauss standing on the sidewalk as Jonathan let Elias off in front of the Mansour Building. He was thinner, his clothes dirtier. The sleeves of his jacket, as though grown longer since Elias saw him last, covered his hands to the fingertips. And the change in his demeanor was evident. Elias had seen it all before in refugees who at first clung to their former status: the blustering pronouncements, then the lowered expectations in the face of reality, and finally the loss of dignity. He had thought it would take Strauss longer than most to lose the last of his swagger. It embarrassed Elias to see that it hadn't. He wished they hadn't known each other in that other life; it would have been easier to deal with him.

"I need to talk to you, Elias."

"Not here on the sidewalk. Come up to the office tomorrow."

"I don't want to bother you."

"It's no bother, Heinrich. We're old friends."

"I can talk to you here just as easily."

"In the morning. I'll be happy to see you tomorrow morning."

"I'm only here to tell you I'm sorry our last conversation ended so badly. I was wrong to say what I did. I took advantage of our friendship. I didn't understand your position. I understand it now. Everything has become clear. My position. Yours. There is no room in Shanghai for human feelings. It's a place of pain and disappointment. You were right to treat me the way you did. There is only so much one man can do."

"Before ten. It's always quieter before ten."

"No. I won't be back to bother you. You can rest easy on that account. Our friendship doesn't entitle me to impose on your good nature."

"Is Sigmund improving?"

"So I'm told."

"And Hannah?"

"I don't know. Her life is hidden from me."

"And Margot, is she well?"

"She's very thin. Dysentery runs through the heim like a fire. I have no doubt as to your disgust at the sight of me. I won't bother you again."

"I feel no disgust at all. It's only that I hear your story a hundred times a day."

"But from your friends, Elias? Do you hear it from your friends?"

"I offered you a monthly stipend. You refused it."

"It's not enough. Nothing you can give me will be enough. I want what you have. I want your life. When I leave this piece of sidewalk, this street of fine buildings, the garden on the corner that someone luckier than I am tends to, I will walk back to the filthy streets of the heim, and Margot will ask me if I have found work, and I will tell her no, and she will cry and turn away from me. But you—you will go up to your clean office, and later your chauffeur will bring the car and carry you home to some palatial estate, and you will sleep in a fine bed with soft sheets, and there will be bountiful food and fresh fruit. You don't know what a humiliation it is to stand in line with a tin plate to receive a bit of inedible stew. We bathe out of a sink because we don't have the thirty cents Shanghai for a proper bath. I thought I understood the world. I thought I controlled events, but now I see that they control me. You sit up there in your beautiful building high above the street, safe and secure, and you control me. You steal my pride, you leave me with raging anger at your good fortune."

Elias was exhausted. By Heinrich, by everyone and everything. There were no alleyways to escape into. He was caught wherever he went, followed, hounded.

Elias reached into his pocket and handed him five Shanghai dollars.

Heinrich put the money in his pocket. "I always told Margot that Elias Mansour was a man of noble intentions, someone to emulate. Give me your hand, Elias. There, like old times. We are still friends, aren't we?"

"We are still friends, Heinrich."

"I sometimes think of that autumn day in Upper Silesia on Count Logronski's estate when you and I stood side by side shooting grouse out of the sky. Grouse neither you nor I would even eat. My soul for one of those dead grouse. You can't imagine what it feels like to say that to you. You can't know what it is to see your family being destroyed before your eyes. You have no idea what's become of us."

*   *   *

Moses waited until he heard the faint click of the heim's front door before he stepped out of the shadows and headed down the steps. Lilli was already melting into the morning crush. He waited until the distance was right and the babble and clack of the streets was sufficient before he started after her.

She was crossing the Garden Bridge. There was meaning in her bold stride, in the charged angle of her shoulders. He wasn't surprised that she traveled alone. In that way she was like him, isolated in the task she had set for herself, thinking that there were no witnesses, that what she did had no ripple effect, made no difference to the equilibrium of the planet.

He had watched her make this trip twice weekly through the fervent heat of summer and now into the cooling weeks of September. He knew her now in a way he hadn't known her before. He felt as though he could reach out and tell her that. "I have ways of knowing where you go and what you do," he would say. "You have no secrets."

They walked in tandem, she ahead, he behind, both moving headlong through the maddened downtown streets, the wind off the sea salting the rancid air, the raucous sound of beggars and peddlers and trackers and horns and bells as discordant as the shriek of wild birds. His expert dodgery was the result of long, hard, mean training. He had ways of insinuating himself into strange places, of collapsing his body into nothingness, of observing from hidden recesses, of finding out things that no one wanted him to know. The assassin's trade, the burglar's arsenal of tricks, he owned them all. She would run from him if she knew what he was capable of, would condemn him if she understood the extent of his hatreds, would shrink at his touch if she knew the ferocity of his feelings.

The building was ahead, the sun striking the grid of windows and the bronze lions beside the main door.

From the shelter of the plane trees on the Bund's promenade he watched her enter the building. He envisioned her in the lift, the motor whirring, then the stop at the Chinaman's floor, her undressing near the window, her nude body sun-spangled and obedient.

While he waited for her to leave the building, he imagined the clock on the Custom House tower didn't move, that he controlled time, that he managed the living and the dead. While he waited, his eyes never strayed from the building's entry. He had seen her enter, he would see her leave.

The steel-plated door finally swung open and she stepped out onto the Bund, the string bag that had been empty when she entered the building now heavy on her arm. How long had it taken for her to debase herself in exchange for a full bag of goods? A half hour? An hour?

He headed down the towpath toward the heim, keeping her in sight as he walked. It didn't matter how long it had taken. He breathed more freely now, relieved that whatever degradation she had endured in that windowed office was over.

*   *   *

It was milky dark, almost light. The heat rose before the sun, blanketing Hongkew with a sulfurous layer of coal smoke, an acrid smell that cat-crept through open windows to choke and stupefy. There were stirrings in the beds, random coughs, groans, peevish voices. Lilli stood in the narrow aisle in a square of space between slop basins and shoes and overhanging bare toes and watched Moses sleep. He slept prettily, one hand cradling his cheek, oblivious to sound and smell. He lay in undershirt and trousers, arms and back sweat-glistened, thin-veined eyelids sketching some secret dream. He was here and yet not here, a mysterious man who rooted easily in shallow soil, a brooding man who livened when he looked at her. If he would stay asleep she would kiss him and whisper in his ear that today the schedule was changed, no peregrine streets to follow her through, no plane trees to stand sentry beneath, no sun-beaten windows to study. Today she would leave him behind, no spying on where she went, no chance that he would see the person she was meeting and frighten her off.

*   *   *

"I've arranged for you to meet Malka," Hannah told Lilli. "She's smart and, like you, she understands money. She wants me to be her girlfriend. She has given me a few presents, but she has no delicacy, no refinement. Besides, reputations are important, don't you think? And if I'm going to do something like that I'll want to get enough money for it to live in a big house in Frenchtown with servants. She lives in a lane apartment in Hongkew, with no hot water, and a toilet on the roof. What would I gain? I mean, men are one thing, but women can ruin you and then where are you?"

Lilli hurried through the slowly waking lanes to where Malka was waiting at the Ward Road Heim. There was no greeting, merely a sudden stop in the middle of the lane and a stealthy exchange of names. She was just as Hannah described her: a short-haired girl with a flat nose, her graceless body wrapped in men's clothes.

Malka's manner was abrupt, her Polish clipped and shorn of formalities. "Hannah says you have a friend who supplies you with goods from Free China," she said.

"That's right."

"But are you willing to do things?"

"What kind of things?"

"Things that will weigh on your conscience."

"My conscience is numb. The last few slivers of it are flickering and close to death. I need money and will do what I have to do."

"Everyone says that at first, but most drop away. Robbers are on every corner and the Japanese will bayonet you for a sack of sugar."

"I won't drop away."

"You do seem more eager than some I've seen. Did Hannah tell you that I want a share of whatever you sell?"

"No, but I figured you would want something."

"I want more than something. I want half of what you earn for a year. It's only fair if I'm to show you what to do."

"Six months. No longer. And half is too much. I'll give you twenty percent."

"Twenty-five."

"For twenty-five I'll teach myself."

"You have to know where to get the goods, and there are some stores that would kick you out onto the street. It will take you a long time to get customers on your own, not everyone will want to buy from you without my guarantee."

"I don't want you to complain that I cheated you later so we have to agree now. Twenty percent for six months, and you'll keep no secrets."

Malka grimaced. "Hannah didn't tell me that you would squeeze so hard."

"I will go on my own if you don't agree. You seem a reasonable girl, someone I could be friends with. We could talk about things. I could tell you about Kovno. Where are you from?"

"Warsaw."

"You see, already we have something in common. My family came to Lithuania from Poland. There is no difference between us that can't be bridged. So do you agree?

"Your talk has mixed me up. I don't remember what you offered."

"Twenty percent for six months."

"All right, all right, I agree."

They started down the narrow lane. The beggars were rising out of their night's sleep, misshapen accretions of bodies and rags, an army of ghostly garbage shuffling along in the heat.

"You look weak," Malka said when they reached the Garden Bridge. "A short walk and your cheeks are red."

"I'm very strong. I can carry a sack of rice with no effort at all. It's not possible to tell what a person can do by looking at them."

They continued on across the bridge, past trucks carrying squally geese, past dunnage-laden cars and rickshaws threading like wooden spiders through the crush. Below, through a dulcet haze, sampans lay as neatly as lily pads on thin sheets of water.

The bridge was behind them now and they were on a broad street margined by plane trees, green-leafed branches umbrous and papery in the fitful breeze. Apartment buildings with stone facades and iron balconies speared up into the poisonous sky, the passages between as dark and silent as notches in a mountain range. Malka stopped at a building where several young children were at play in a gated interior garden.

"This is where the smuggler lives. Last month I bought sewing needles from him. Very strong needles. I made forty dollars and now I have enough to buy condensed milk and writing paper. When I'm through here we'll stop at some stores, I'll show you how to sell. I'm known in all the shops. Robbin's Kiddie Store, Bendel's Pharmacy. Everyone buys from me. Russians, Germans, Dutch. Even the Chinese. Some in the black market cheat their customers, sell broken goods and medicines that are nothing more than talc, but I have a reputation for fair dealing. You say you have a carton of American cigarettes?"

"Lucky Strikes. Also two boxes of flints."

"Good. When we meet tomorrow, bring them. Now I'm going inside and you're going to wait here. If you see anything unusual, come in and tell me. Apartment 12, first floor.

Lilli wasn't sure what constituted anything unusual. Was it the young couple standing at the garden gate peering in at the children, or the rickshaw that had just disgorged an elderly man in front of the building's main door, or the Chinese delivery boy who had propped his bicycle up against the building wall and was padding after Malka through the door?

Nothing ugly could happen in the quiet of morning on a clean street in Frenchtown in a building with limpet balconies clinging to stone walls. Wasn't disaster the sum of noisily cascading events? Wasn't catastrophe always situated in other regions?

In minutes the door opened again and the delivery boy, a large red smear on the right leg of his trousers, ran out, jumped on his bicycle, headed for an opening in the enfilade of buildings and disappeared as quickly as a lump of meat down a dog's throat.

A few steps and Lilli was in the building, orienting herself to the heated gloom. There was a weariness in the fallow light, a sense of momentum stalled, of caution bedeviled. Past the entry and into a long hall, the shadowy glare of dimly lit sconces, fretted screens painting patterns on the walls. There were no halls like this in the heim, no unoccupied space frozen in silence. A foggy brume of steamy air swam in waves across the carpeted floor and cut visibility. Lilli felt the soft punch of tangled clothes against her legs and stopped at the sight of Malka's blood-drenched body stiffening in a ray of dim light.

The door to Apartment 12 opened and a man stepped out.

"Help me take her inside."

Malka seemed lighter in death, as though the knife had carried away more than her life.

"On the couch."

There had been other people laid out on the couch, the stains of other bleeds, the scraps of package wrappings and scribbled notes tucked into the cushions from other frantic times.

"Did you come with her?"

"Yes."

The light was brighter here than in the hall. A disheveled room, a desk, oddments of fabrics, rolled rugs, closed boxes, open bins, and standing over Malka, wild hair as stick-stiff as goose quills framing his large face, the gruff Russian Jew Lilli had seen in the heim bringing bags of sweets to the children.

"That's Jacob Rossitsky." Aaron said when Lilli asked who he was. "Like a bird he flies into the heim, drops a little money, some candy and flies away again. A Russian. He's not stateless like us. He lives in Frenchtown. Not a real Jew, I'm sure. What real Jew never goes to the synagogue? I'll tell you who. A brutish lout who isn't interested in *yiddishkeit*. I have no use for a man like that. He's probably a *goniff*, a thief. Who knows how he makes his money? A smuggler, I've heard. What do I care about such a lump of a man? Stay away from him, Lilli. I'm telling you, he's a *shande* to decent Jews, a disgrace."

The apartment was cooler than the hall, the clack of an electric fan stirring the air. Jacob was now talking to someone on the telephone.

"Come through the back."

Lilli laid her hand on Malka's arm, smelled the salt sweat and crusting blood. Malka's face was changing, her cheeks scalloped with spots and blotches. She was Lilli's age, like her a Jewish girl bent on survival. It was a certainty in Lilli's mind that they would have become friends, both of them grasping at life, but now there was nothing left, merely a remnant of the live Malka spiraling up out of some common root and twining itself around Lilli's heart.

Jacob was through with the telephone.

"You live in one of the heime?" he said to Lilli.

"Seward Road."

"Better go. There's nothing here to see. The burial detail will come and take her. *Fertig*. Finished."

"I have a carton of cigarettes."

"So what? Smoke them. You want to be a profiteer? Look at Malka. It's not such a picnic. A man is better able to take care of himself than a girl, no matter how smart she thinks she is. I told her 'be careful, you talk too much, you let people know you carry money. A *gonif* finds out you have a dollar in your pocket, he knifes you in a building.'"

"Cigarettes will bring a good price," Lilli said. "I have flints, too. The price is going up. When it's high enough I'll buy rice with it, but rice is twenty dollars Shanghai and going up, so I have to wait longer. I won't make enough money anyway with the goods I receive from my friend, and Malka was going to . . ."

"American cigarettes?"

"Lucky Strike."

"Bring me a pack of cigarettes, I'll give you some tinned milk and sardines, maybe some sugar. Now go. Get out. This whole thing is making me sick."

Chapter 15

October 1941

The coolie padded along behind Lilli, his intermittent whistle of breath scraping through the Whangpoo's seeping yellow mist, the day's trades suspended from a bamboo pole whisking against his thin back. The last stop of the day: the Luxury Goods Store, beggars curled onto mats on the stoop, an old Chinese woman crawling between people's feet, scooping up spilled rice and dropping it grain by grain into a bucket. The old woman moved away to let Lilli enter, then swatted at the coolie's heels with the bucket as he followed Lilli into the store.

The store was once owned by a Chinese man who sold dried herbs and Chinese newspapers. A German refugee bought it from him in 1938. He stocked the store with what he could buy legitimately. He also bartered goods and sold stolen merchandise on the black market.

English teas and American tinned goods and French cigarettes were displayed like rare gems on glass counters. Shelved books were arranged by language (English, French, German, Dutch). A large table in the middle of the store held Belgian lace tablecloths and silk sheets. In a special section in the back of the store (far away from the door where the beggars squat) were the scented soaps and perfumes and bath salts, the shampoos and combs and toothbrushes. And behind a partition were the pawned goods: used shoes, old clothes, broken toys, tattered magazines, German-language physics texts, dinged and dented baby carriages, hand-carved canes, briar pipes, ratty fur boas, precariously tilting stacks of dust-covered cracked crystal, dented silver, broken musical instruments.

The owner came out from behind the counter, a large white apron wrapped high up around his fatted waist almost to his ribs, felt house slippers on his feet.

"What do you have for me today?" he said.

"Two packages of American razor blades, Gillette. A sack of sugar, refined. Two jars of apricot preserves. Thirty-six hard candies, English, all flavors. A few other things, too. It depends on what you have that I want."

"I can give you some tinned milk. Carnation. Just delivered on the docks. An Italian shipment. I can only spare four."

"Do you have any shoe polish? I have a customer who wants shoe polish, with real wax in it. Brown."

"If I had it, I'd only have it in black. But I don't have it."

"You should really think about shoe polish in colors. Shoes aren't always black. Women wear all colors. And fancy shoe buckles. Rhinestone ones. You can make money on rhinestone shoe buckles. Silver ones, too. I'd trade you two cartons of Chesterfields for one silver shoe buckle, one carton for rhinestone."

"No shoe polish, no shoe buckles. I'll give you the milk and a hundred thousand Shanghai."

"Not enough. What else have you got?"

"Soap. Lux soap. Two bars."

"Five bars or no deal."

"I only have three."

"Not enough."

She looked around the store. Checked the linens and fountain pens. Stopped at the bookshelves.

"Three bars of soap, four tins of milk, three English-language Bibles, and five thousand Shanghai," she said.

"You want too much."

"I'll be bringing you a gold cross next week, Italian, very fine. Be flexible today and I'll give you a discount next week."

"You make me dizzy."

She smiled at him.

"Who can resist?" he said.

She gave him the razor blades, the sugar, the apricot preserves, and the hard candies, put the Shanghai dollars in her string bag, packed the milk and soap into the basket with the goods she hadn't offered him and stepped out into the now darkening mist of late afternoon.

Another productive day. She had already sold a square of Flemish lace to a tailor in Frenchtown who designed gowns for the wives of British diplomats. Next time she would persuade him to buy chocolate creams to serve his clients when they come for fittings. From there she had walked to Robbin's Kiddie

Store in the Russian sector, then to a paper factory in a godown on the Bund, and finally to the Luxury Goods Store in Chinatown.

The feathery mist was rapidly turning to fog, muffling the sounds of cars and rickshaws, layering shop windows with a chalky dew. The Chinese lived in huts on these streets, whole families with scarcely an inch apiece of living space, holding their babies out over the gutter to defecate, cooking over open fires. She walked quickly. Roving thieves ran slip-fingered through these streets.

This morning when she was checking Jacob's new merchandise, he had lectured her about safety.

"Nothing bad has happened to you so far, so you think you're a *knaker*, that you're made of iron, that no one and nothing can touch you. You think a few words from you, a little smile, and no one will do you harm."

"I'm careful."

"And I'm telling you to watch out for traps. You go from one place to another every day and you think no one notices. Have you forgotten what happened to Malka? Malka was careful. And even Malka didn't walk where you walk, take the chances you take. You won't know who it is or where it comes from. Just watch out. I don't want to call the burial detail to pick up what's left."

Papa's and Aaron's Talmudic scoldings had once railed her in, but Papa was in Kovno and Aaron no longer paid any attention to what she did. Now it was left to Jacob to lecture her and Moses to bloodhound her through the Shanghai streets.

Two weeks ago Moses had confronted her in front of Jacob's apartment.

"You risk too much. You aren't safe."

"Go away. Leave me alone."

She had spoken to him roughly, but she had to admit that she liked that he followed her. She liked to turn around in a crowded street and see his head floating dark and stern above all the other heads.

"It's obvious he's drowning in love," Hannah said.

"Love is for another time, another place," Lilli replied.

Besides, she didn't need anyone to tell her what she was doing was dangerous. Yesterday she was stopped by two Japanese soldiers in the Russian sector who accused her of terrorism. They could have shot her right then, right there, but she gave them each a small pack of cigarettes and they let her go. Malka was murdered for the six thousand Shanghai—three hundred American—in her pocket. Lilli carried as much in her string bag. If what Papa said was true, that all happenings in life were *bershert,* fated, then there was no reason to worry, whatever would happen would happen. Besides, she had no time to contemplate disaster when she was occupied by how much could be gleaned from a piece of lace or a half dozen eggs, what profit could be made from a dozen fountain pens, eight buckets of coal briquettes, what customer wanted writing paper or flints or ten spools of silk thread.

The coolie had fallen behind. She couldn't see him through the fog. She called out, "Chop, chop," her voice spiraling through runnels of water-laden air. Then a bruising blow to the side of her head. Not a blow. A hard slap. She felt no pain, merely a dull headache. She stood upright for a few moments, sure she must have bumped her head on the iron pole in front of the Luxury Goods Store, and while she was contemplating how she could have done that when she knew exactly how far above her head the Luxury Goods Store pole was and had never bumped into it before, she realized that she was now being dragged along the street, her cloth shoes etching wavy lines in the pavement. Oil lamps flickered in open doorways as she passed, then the sharp squeal of a rusted door hinge, a shove in the small of her back, and she was sitting on a cold floor in a dully lit room, brick walls sweating in the airless space.

"You give me ninety percent of what you make, you pay it once a week, you pay it here in this place."

She had seen him before. A fugitive soldier she had given cigarettes to. He was the danger Jacob had warned her about. Not a starving refugee from the heim or a gangster who rose up out of the streets when the fog was at its thickest, but a Japanese thief not much older than she was, with hairless skin and eyes the color of coal bits, his half-moon mouth filled with teeth as beamy as polished bone.

"I make very little. Not enough to bother about. I'll give you what I can today, and that will be all you get."

He didn't reply.

He obviously had no experience at thieving. He had seen her on the street and thought she would be a simple target. What he didn't know was that she was expert at persuading people. She had made a business of persuasion. A no from someone always encouraged her to press harder. She waited now. It was always a good thing to let a proposition settle in. Some people took more time in answering than others did. She wouldn't rush him. There was no advantage in rushing. To rush suggested a weak position. He had even begun to smile at her. Despite her headache, she was already reorganizing her thoughts. This wasn't as bad as it could have been. She would make him understand that she couldn't be told what to do. She would make him understand that this was the only time he would get something from her and that he would have to be satisfied with the amount.

"Look," he said and pointed toward a shadowy corner.

Her eyes weren't clear. Small gray blotches obscured her vision. She walked unsteadily toward where he had pointed. The body of a man lay crumpled against the wall. It was the shopkeeper in Frenchtown who specialized in Victorian jewelry. She had sold him a set of silver shoe buckles.

"He didn't pay," the soldier said. "He was a profiteer like you and he didn't pay."

Chapter 16

This was Li T'ien's gambling enterprise, a metal cage in an abandoned underwear factory. White Russians guarded the doors, but no guard was as expert as Li T'ien at identifying spies, at spotting Japanese agents or rivals who would ask for a percentage. One nod of his head and the unwanted were gone.

Two fighters were in the cage, one crouching, thick-necked, knees spread, the other one tall and fat, his thighs as large around as truck tires, both men in white cotton trousers, feet bare, a strip of red cloth tying their straight black hair to their foreheads. The signal hadn't been given to begin yet; they pranced and posed while they waited.

Ten rows of seats circled the cage, a spider web of woven metal illuminated by a bank of lights overhead. Every seat was taken. Li T'ien, his two bodyguards, and Heinrich were in the front row.

It had been raining for two weeks, soaking fields, turning streets to rivers, and fouling the mud walls, but still the autumn heat had not broken; it festered in the windowless noxious space, gauzy growths as brown and furry as caterpillars oozing out of sodden walls and leftover bales of cotton cloth.

"Record the bets, memorize the faces," Li T'ien said to Heinrich. "Watch carefully. Each finger is a thousand they're betting against me. Remember where they're sitting. Remember the number of fingers. My fighter is from Hunan, the other one from Szechuan."

The job had been meant for Sigmund, for the man who jumped into Soochow Creek to save Ida Bornstein.

"Sigmund is still sick," Heinrich had told Li T'ien, "and even well would never do for money what I will do. I will do anything. I have no boundaries, no requirements, no shame. I was successful in Germany. I know about money. I understand politics. I see patterns in the way events unfold. I speak German, French, and English. I will do anything you ask me to do."

The betting began, fingers flashing. Heinrich's head swiveled. He stood up to see better, wrote numbers on a piece of paper, this face two fingers, that face three, one in the back ten. He attached faces to numbers, was sure his heart was running loose in his chest.

Hands were up now in all the rows. Three fingers. Five fingers. In the rear someone flashed both hands twice.

"Four to one," Li T'ien yelled.

A man in the first row, corner seat, turned and raised three fingers. Someone behind him held up five fingers. The betting was still going on when the fight began.

Hunan kicked first, a smash to the head, a slashing blow with a foot to the chest.

Szechuan stumbled, caught himself, slammed a fist into Hunan's nose.

"Fifteen to one," Li T'ien cried as Hunan jabbed two stiff fingers into Szechuan's eyes.

The fighters flailed at each other, geysers of blood and mucus sliming the wooden floor of the cage.

Hands were up, an excited roar, a waving of fingers and fists. Heinrich was breathless. There was no air. A crabbed scribble on the paper replaced a number, faces blurred into each other, were in danger of disappearing.

The fighters beat at each other. Bones breaking resembled fracturing glass. Betting escalated. Gamblers pushed their elbows into each other's faces. Small brawls broke out.

Szechuan fell to the mat. He tried to get up, but his left leg flopped. Hunan shot-kicked Szechuan's bobbing head, then jumped, body straight, hands reaching up to the top of the cage, and flattened Szechuan's head beneath his feet. Blood nozzled up and a spray as fine as pencil points found the front of Heinrich's shirt.

Heinrich handed the scribbly paper to Li T'ien, bets were settled, the body taken away, the cage washed clean.

"You did well, Heinrich," Li T'ien said as gamblers vanished into the humid night. "Perhaps I can find more work for you. Fifteen American dollars a month. Three for tonight."

Heinrich walked back to the heim exulting in his newfound fortune. Fifteen American dollars a month. Every day black-market rates changed. Today an American dollar was worth ten Shanghai, tomorrow it might be worth five hundred. Sigmund was young and would find another job, and Heinrich would be able to buy Margot whatever she wanted to eat. She would be the way she was before. She'd let him touch her. He would rent a room in a lane house. He would be a new man. He had lived out of the empty suitcase of memory for too long. Homeland, culture, status were gone. What he was or did in the past had no value here. A man had to change if he wanted to succeed.

*   *   *

Heinrich searched through the cinder-gray smoke of the café for a glimpse of Margot's blonde head. He had never been inside the café before. Only someone with fifty cents for a meal could come in, sit down at a table and listen to the musicians. He had imagined it to be a grander place. It was hardly better than the heim, tables jammed together so tightly there was no more than a foot of space per person. There were laughs and sudden shouts, conversations as brittle as whip cracks, chairs scraping across the cement floors, waiters shouting orders across the room to the kitchen, echoes crushing the room, closing it in.

He saw her. She was in a blue dress, sitting at a table with a long-necked, soft-faced man in a fairly clean suit. Heinrich made his way toward them.

Margot stared at the blood spotting the front of his shirt.

"My new job," he said.

"A butcher?"

"No, not a butcher."

"My husband Heinrich," she said to the man beside her. And to Heinrich, "You remember Gerd Franck, Heinrich. We heard him play in Berlin in 1932."

"A Brahms recital," Gerd said.

Someone had stepped up onto the small stage and was thundering through a Chopin Étude. The crowd grew quiet.

"I haven't seen you in the Seward Road Heim," Heinrich said to Gerd.

"I have a room in Chapei, not too far from here."

"I didn't know they paid refugees to play the piano in Shanghai. May I sit?"

"Sit and shut up," someone shouted.

"Listen to the music, Heinrich," Margot said. "You can talk later."

Heinrich sat staring at the back of his wife's head, at the familiar brown mole on her neck.

"He's very good," Gerd whispered to him.

The piece was over. Applause rippled, rose, then gave way as the noise of the place sneaked back in.

"If you had come earlier," Margot said, "you would have heard Gerd play Scarlatti. It was lovely."

"I have never been able to decide whether my heart belongs to Scarlatti or Brahms," Gerd remarked. "Scarlatti is so contained, Brahms so unashamedly romantic."

"Do you live in Chapei with your wife?" Heinrich asked him.

"With my daughter and her husband and their two children. My wife died in Italy while we were waiting for the ship."

A waiter asked Heinrich for his order.

"I'll have a slice of rare beef and braised potatoes."

"We only serve Russian food."

"Then why did you ask me? Serve me whatever you want."

Heinrich turned sideways in his chair, his arm resting on Margot's shoulder.

"How did you find me?" she said.

"Hannah told me you come here often."

Gerd lit a cigarette. "Your wife is a fan of mine."

"I have no money to pay for your meal, Heinrich," Margot said. "You should call the waiter back."

"I have money."

The waiter returned with a bowl of borscht and a small dish of sour cream. The sight startled Heinrich. He had not tasted cream or milk for seven months.

"You must have some first," he said to Margot.

"I've eaten. Gerd bought my dinner. Is it blood on your shirt?"

"What difference does it make? I've found work with a Chinese gambler. We can afford a room, have some privacy."

"Be careful who you work for," Gerd said and flicked cigarette ash into his empty coffee cup.

"Is it your business?"

"Heinrich, please," Margot said.

"The job is a start, Margot. If I prove myself, he'll keep me on. Bitterness spreads, Margot. We can make the best of our situation or we can claw at each other."

She reached one hand up to neaten stray strands of hair fallen out of its bun. He took her hand, but she shook it loose. She once loved him. Sweet pet had been her name for him. How different the world was now, so distant from the world of tennis tournaments in Bremen and golfing in Scotland, of pet names and picnics and *gemutlichkeit*. When he met her he had nothing but a Mercedes sports car and a lust for Jewish women who resembled Swedish princesses. She thought him clever, her father thought him worthy of investment.

"Watch yourself," Gerd said. "Some of those Chinese gamblers are in the Green Gang. You don't want to involve yourself with gangsters."

"Gerd works for the Joint unloading provisions at the wharf at Pootung," Margot said.

"I'm in charge of distribution to the heime. I have first choice of everything that comes off the ship."

"You take food from other refugees' mouths," Heinrich said. "You should be pleased. Keep lifting boxes with those delicate fingers, you won't play the piano for long."

Gerd pushed his chair back and stood up. "I'll speak to you tomorrow, Margot."

Margot watched him leave, her lips white.

It had pleased Heinrich to insult him. He would have liked to have stomped on his head and cracked it open like the Szechuan's.

"You should have warned me you were seeing another man."

"We enjoy each other's company."

"I have a job now. You can enjoy my company."

"He treats me well. Think of me for once, Heinrich."

"I think of you every minute of the day. It's for you I've tramped the streets all these months. I now have a way to make money. It isn't what I've done in the past, but none of us can do what we did in the past. I've learned humility here, Margot. I'm not the man I was. I no longer take anything for granted. I'm grateful for every advantage. I want us to be together, to have a life."

"I want a divorce."

"Here? In Shanghai, you want a divorce?"

"You can't be surprised, Heinrich. Even in Germany you and I were no longer good together. I was unhappy. I told you that, but you didn't listen. You've never listened to me. The great Heinrich Strauss listened only to himself. It was like I spoke to the air. And when we had a chance in 1933 to go to England, you made excuses. Your business, your money, the time wasn't right, Hitler would soon be gone, everything would be the same as it was before."

"Sigmund was in Dachau. I couldn't leave him."

"We could have left before that."

"You wouldn't leave before that, and I couldn't force you. You fought with me about it. You don't remember that, but I do. There is nothing I wouldn't have done for you. If you had said you were willing to go to England in 1933,

I would have sold the newspaper and the house and the lodge. I would have salvaged some of our real estate holdings. I would have had a better plan than what you left me with. Don't tell me what we should have done. And don't argue with me over what's lost. There's nothing I wouldn't have done for you if you had but asked me."

"You're a liar, Heinrich. You've always been a liar."

"I would snap your neck if I could."

"No, you would have it done. You've always kept yourself clean in that way. Anything dirty was done by someone else."

"Do you love him?"

"He treats me well."

"So that's the measure of your love, that he treats you well. I gave you everything and you look at me with disgust. I'm happy to know how cheaply you can be bought."

The waiter brought *shashlik* and a cup of strong tea and set it down in front of Heinrich. The aroma of the skewered beef overwhelmed him. He saw the edge of her blue dress move away from the table, but didn't look up. He picked up the knife and fork. The meat's juices filled the plate. He took a bite. The taste made him lightheaded. He chewed carefully, slowly, savoring the flavor.

Chapter 17

Chinese fleeing the marauding Japanese poured into Shanghai. Their waste floated in the swollen gutters. Their starving children begged in the streets. In the past eight months a hundred thousand Chinese corpses had been collected from the city's sidewalks. In the refugee community, people died of hunger and disease. Those who sold their winter clothes in the summer now walked the streets wrapped in blankets. Most of the refugees found the strength to persist. The truly despairing found a beam and hanged themselves.

*   *   *

There wasn't enough room at the table in Rabbi Salkowitz's study for all the men who had been invited to the pre-wedding *tisch*. The yeshiva students stood in a group behind Aaron's chair, mufflers and prayer shawls swaddling their necks, earmuffs buried under their hats. Heinrich and Sigmund were on one side of the table, both in new suits, Heinrich bullishly jovial, Sigmund as pallid as bleached muslin. Aaron and Moses were on the other side, Aaron's white shirt a frame for his red beard, and Moses' shabby suit grown shabbier. Rabbi Salkowitz was at one end of the table, a mummified figure in embroidered *tallith*. The seat nearest the door was occupied by Elias.

Rabbi Salkowitz was standing now, *tallith* swagged around his shoulders. "Rabbi Hanilai has said that a man who has no wife lives without joy, without blessing, without good. Rabbi Eleazar has said that a man who has no wife is not even a man. And Genesis chapter two, verse eighteen says 'I will make man a helper to set over against him.'" He raised his glass. "A long wedded life to Hannah and Aaron. *L'Chaim.*"

The men blew on their raw fingers before they lifted glasses of schnapps to their lips.

"What kind of rabbi is he?" Aaron murmured to Moses. "Certainly not orthodox. I don't care what he says, he isn't orthodox. His beard is trimmed and his *payes* cover his ears too neatly. Head of a yeshiva in Poland? What proof? Who vouches for him?"

"No one. The yeshiva was destroyed."

"Would a *roshei* yeshiva save only himself? I don't know, Moses, I have my doubts. And would he marry me to Hannah if he were truly a *roshei* yeshiva? No. He would ask questions first. He would want to know about her, about me. He wouldn't marry us without asking questions. How can he be orthodox? It's not possible. He doesn't separate the men from the women. Everyone will sit in the sanctuary together."

"Do you want them separated?"

"I don't care. But to say you're orthodox when you . . ."

"The man says he headed a yeshiva. Maybe he did and maybe he didn't. Maybe he's orthodox and maybe he isn't. Maybe he isn't even a rabbi. We're not living in HaShem's Torah now. You're not in your father's house. Everything has changed."

"The yeshiva students are the same. Still hungry for Torah, still with their eyes on heaven. They could be on the moon for all the difference the world makes, yet they still rely on the word of God as it's written, and as it's interpreted and as . . ."

"Such a whispered conversation going on over there," Rabbi Salkowitz said. "Let us partake. Perhaps we can learn. The Torah says to listen is to learn."

"The Torah says to listen to God, not to Aaron Chernofsky," Aaron replied.

"Aaron is overjoyed, Rabbi," Moses said. "He questions his good fortune."

"Ah. Very good. And can we hear from the father of the *kalleh*?"

"Look how her father hesitates, Moses," Aaron said. "It pains him to be here. The German part of him has come out already. He told me in so many words just a few minutes ago that I wasn't his first choice. His first choice. Can you imagine? In Shanghai he could have a choice? Even with a fine suit and money in his pocket, what choice is there?"

"He'll soon be your father-in-law. Then you can ignore him."

"Maybe Hannah and I will just do what we've been doing without marriage. Is it so terrible?"

"I have no opinion. I've told you already that if you don't want to marry her, don't."

"She'll be unhappy."

"Then marry her."

Heinrich is on his feet now, legs planked against the rounded edge of the table.

"Look, he's going to open his mouth," Aaron said to Moses. "Watch what he says. You'll see, it won't be good. I can guarantee you he won't even say my name."

"Thank you, Rabbi, and welcome to all my guests. My daughter Hannah has made up her mind to marry. I have no control over it, but I give her my blessing. And my son Sigmund is a hero. He didn't have to do what he did. He suffered for it. But he did it. Perhaps you would like to say something, Sigmund?"

"No."

"Did I tell you?" Aaron said. "The father disposes of me with two words, and the brother insults me with a measly 'no.'"

Heinrich swayed in place, looked around the room, planed his hair with fanned fingers.

"I'm glad Sir Elias is here. Forget I ever asked you for anything, Elias. It was only a moment of weakness on my part. I lost confidence in myself, but I'm recovered. Keep your charity for someone else."

"You see the arrogance of the man, Moses?" Aaron said. "He chooses this day to relieve himself of some festering hatred. On my wedding day, with Hannah in the sanctuary waiting for me. To him I'm barely alive. He looks at the clock, he looks at the ceiling as if somewhere between the hour and the roof he'll find some decent words to say. Everything about him offends me. And that bold gleam in his eye, is it possible that I will be related to him?"

"This temple was built for the Jews of the Far East by David Mansour, Sir Elias's father of blessed memory," the rabbi said, lips pursed, tiny hairs quivering beneath his nose. "It was empty for many years and now it lives again to comfort the Jewish exiles. Sir Elias is our honored guest and will honor us with a few words."

The rabbi placed a coaxing hand on Elias's shoulder.

It was an accident that Elias was even here today. The meeting in the synagogue of the Committee for Central European Jewry had been set for the following day, but Rachel had changed it at the last minute. Yet another opportunity for her to badger Elias about the food shortage, that it was his fault they had been caught short, that it was his job to shake money from the coffers of the rich Shanghai Jews, that he shouldn't have taken the job if he hadn't intended to devote himself to it, and on and on. And now this, the rabbi asking Elias to speak, as though he would have been here as a guest if it hadn't been for the meeting, as though this were a proper wedding when Hannah Strauss's name was on a weekly list of registered Jewish prostitutes.

My golden child, Heinrich once said of her. Elias had seen her and her mother on the steps of the temple before the *tisch* began, Hannah too thin, but still pretty, although, from what Elias knew of her, hardly golden, and Margot Strauss, once the beauty of Hamburg, sag-skinned, temples blue-veined, cheeks basined and lined, her hand in Gerd Franck's. Margot Strauss holding Gerd Franck's hand? Sybil had once invited the pianist to dinner. A dry, literal-minded man with an opinion on every subject. Heinrich Strauss had bounded up the steps ahead of them while Sigmund, who had been a gifted athlete, needed Aaron's help to climb the steps.

"Thank you, Rabbi," Elias said and stood up. "It's an honor to be here. I'm sorry Lady Sybil isn't present, but I'm sure she would join with me in wishing the bride and groom much happiness."

There was more lifting of glasses, more *L'Chaim*s.

"What is he, a duke or an earl?" Aaron said to Moses. "Can a Jew be called Sir? It's not in the Torah, that much I know. He's very polite, but he didn't mean a word of what he just said. Can you see the way his eyebrows lifted when he said the word 'happiness'? I've heard that about him. He tells people what they want to hear. He's a businessman and a politician, nothing more. If he helps Jews, it's because somehow or other it will be good for him."

"Who told you that?"

"What? You think he's sincere?"

"I don't know if he's sincere or not. What difference does it make? He wished you well."

"Then I won't believe anything you say either."

"Who says I'll say something nice?"

"Then don't."

When Moses stood up his head with its massive clump of hair reached nearly to the ledge of the tall windows.

Everyone was waiting for him to say something. If not profound, then at least comforting. What could he say to them? That they were fools? That Aaron's marriage was unimportant, a ritual designed to distract them from the ugliness on the other side of the synagogue doors?

He pitied the yeshiva students, shivery in their threadbare suits, smiling as though they were children snug at home in Vilna or Warsaw on a *freilich* Hanukkah, handkerchief-wrapped *gelt* in their pockets, a plate of sweets waiting for them on the dining room table. Only Heinrich was cold-eyed. Moses hadn't yet determined what had brought back his old swagger. It certainly wasn't faith. It must be money.

He cleared his throat. "Aaron is a good man. He has read the Torah and believes in God. Now he has found a wife. Proverbs chapter eighteen, verse twenty-two says he who finds a wife finds something good. I wish you happiness and *mazel*, Aaron, in equal measure."

"Did you have to say I read the Torah, in the past tense?" Aaron said when Moses was seated again. "You could have said I read the Torah, in the present tense."

"If you want me to lie, I'll get up and make it present tense."

"The rabbi is looking at me."

"It's your turn."

"What should I say?"

"Whatever you want."

"I'll be seen through. Anyone listening to me will know that I'm an apostate, that I've lost my way, that I shouldn't be married in a synagogue, that I'm a fraud."

"You're no more a fraud than anyone in this room."

"I'm not *frum* anymore."

"It doesn't matter. Just stand up and say something."

Aaron swiped his hand over the top of the table a few times—deep, concentrated swipes, as though the ground-in stains were his fault—and stood up.

"My marriage day. I never dreamed of it. I didn't dream at all. I had my nose glued to the holy books. I ate them for breakfast, lunch, and supper. Sometimes I swallowed them whole. Where did it get me? I can quote Midrash, Mishnah, Maimonides, the Pentateuch, and Prophets, but the real world eluded me until I met my Hannah. She is my world now. I need no other." He paused and rubbed his beard. "It's difficult," he said and sat down.

"I made a fool of myself," he said to Moses.

*   *   *

Rabbi Salkowitz took his place under the *chuppah*. He had exchanged his tall black hat for a fur one that sat on his head like a reclining beaver.

"We could have frozen to death waiting, Aaron," Hannah said from beneath the drooping laurel boughs of the *chuppah*. A man's overcoat covered her short yellow dress, a yellow chrysanthemum pinned a sheer veil to her hair.

"Everyone had something to say," Aaron said.

"Mutti. Where's Mutti?"

Margot came out of a shadowed spot near the door. "Here I am, darling."

"Lilli, take my coat," Hannah said. "You'd better put it on, you're shivering. Why are you so pale? Are you sick?"

"I'm all right. I'm just very cold."

Elias felt as though he had seen the bridegroom's sister before, the blaze of hair, the blue eyes, the blushy tinge to her skin. Possibly a committee meeting. Rachel sometimes brought people to help carry files.

"Are we ready?"

"I am," Hannah said.

"Yes, ready," Aaron said.

"You ought to be up there next to your wife, Mr. Strauss," Fanny said. She was wearing two sweaters like a winding cloth around her plucked body.

"I'm fine where I am."

The rabbi had begun. "May He who is supreme in might, blessing, and glory bless this *kalleh* and *chosen.*" He looked around. "Where's the wine?"

Rachel handed the rabbi the Kiddush cup. "Don't let them drink it all, Rabbi. I'll pour what's left back in the bottle and you can use it for Sabbath *kiddush.*"

"Praised are You, O Lord our God, King of the universe, who sanctified us with Your commandments. The veil, please."

Lilli held Hannah's veil up.

"Kiss me, Aaron," Hannah said.

"Now?"

"Of course now."

The rabbi tapped his foot impatiently. "I haven't finished."

"I just want a kiss. It will only take a second."

When the kiss was over, the rabbi continued.

"Praised are You, O Lord our God, King of the universe, who created man and woman in Your image, fashioning woman in the likeness of man, preparing for a man a mate, that together they might perpetuate life."

The rabbi paused.

"Is that it, Rabbi?" Aaron said. "The whole thing? What about the seven blessings?"

"Be patient. I'm taking a moment to reflect on the meaning of marriage. You should reflect also. It's good for the soul of a man about to become a husband to reflect."

The rabbi then recited the seven blessings and pronounced Hannah and Aaron man and wife. Moses laid the cloth-wrapped glass on the floor at Aaron's feet. Aaron stomped on it and it crinkled anemically. Everyone hollered *mazel tov*, then followed the smell of roast chicken into the sanctuary kitchen.

Moses stayed behind with Lilli, who was still standing under the *chuppah* holding Hannah's coat, the sleeves bunched and crimped, snaggy loops of hem unstitched and hanging.

"You followed me for months. I've missed seeing you in the street behind me."

"I have no words for what you're doing."

"I do what I have to do."

"What you're doing is dangerous, Lilli. If you die, whatever you think you are accomplishing will be forgotten."

"I didn't ask for war, Moses, I didn't ask for Hitler. I do the best I can with what little means I have. This is me. This is who I am now. Too thin, too hungry, sometimes too angry. You should have taken me on the train. I wouldn't have been as accomplished a lover as I am now, but I didn't have an instructor then. There is roast chicken in the kitchen. You should go now and eat some before the yeshiva buchers swallow everything."

The yeshiva students had linked arms and were dancing, a line of black-coated young men joined together as tightly as a knotted string, leaping ecstatically through doorways, tall hats bouncing as the line snaked from the sanctuary to the rabbi's study, to the kitchen and back again.

*　*　*

Everyone crowded into the synagogue kitchen, the crush of bodies in the small space warming the air. Fanny Lipsky was slicing a braided loaf of bread, slipping every fourth piece into the pocket of one of her sweaters. The yeshiva students, out of breath and flushed, surrounded the table, some of them leaning in so close to the pans of roast chicken their beards floated in the gravy. Elias noted the way Rachel tended to Sigmund, bringing him food, fussing over him, whispering. Rachel and Sigmund Strauss. She was full of unexpectedness.

"Have something to eat, Elias," Heinrich said. "This is not as elegant as some of the parties you attended at my home in Germany. You'll have to settle for bread and chicken."

"There are too few such good times as this, Sir Elias," Gerd Franck said. "Too few indeed."

Margot was now at Gerd Franck's side.

"It's so good to see you again, Elias," she said.

"It's always a pleasure to see old friends."

"I'm afraid Shanghai has taken its toll on me. You see me at my worst."

"I see you persevering."

Gerd said, "With inflation as it is, one wonders how a refugee could afford such a lavish wedding. Of course, Heinrich is no ordinary refugee now. He's speculating in currency, I hear."

Elias couldn't be sure, but was the bridegroom's sister the girl who stood at the end of the drive every morning and stared at the house?

"Cigarettes were to arrive today," Gerd said. "They were stolen before the ship could dock, and now they're five dollars a pack. Can you imagine the money that's being made on stolen goods?"

Sybil sent one of the servants out on Wednesday to ask the girl what she wanted. *Nothing,* she said.

"Then again, if the Americans come into the war, goods will stop coming in altogether," Gerd said. "I pray they let the Japanese carve up China in peace, or we'll all suffer."

"The Americans are very lucky," Margot said. "No one there uproots you from your home."

It wasn't possible it was the same girl. It was someone else.

"I don't think the Americans will be foolish enough to fight the Japanese over China," Gerd said.

"What?"

"The Americans. I don't believe the Americans will get into the fight. They send dollars to Chiang Kaishek to fight the Communists and pilots to man his Air Force. That's all they're going to do. They'll never go to war with Japan."

Maybe she was someone he met in New York. Or at a Joint meeting in Shanghai. Or in a shop in Frenchtown. She couldn't be the same girl who watched the Mansour house every morning as though something inside belonged to her.

Chapter 18

At midnight an open boat left the dock at Pootung Point, a bombed-out village of flattened houses and abandoned godowns across the Whangpoo River from the Bund, and headed toward the mouth of the Yangtze. Li T'ien was seated in the prow between his two Russian bodyguards, Heinrich behind them. Zhong Tu was at the wheel, piloting the boat the way he drove a car, erratically, and smoking a cigarette that fumed and fizzed in the enveloping wet.

A flotilla of sampans, firefly lanterns blinking, verged toward them out of the frigid vapors of the river, snugged the boat, wooden timbers nearly touching the hull, and the reformed flotilla, now as wide as a floating island, made its way upstream past Japanese cargo ships and dark godowns. Heinrich watched the lights of the Bund dim behind them, buildings now chess pieces on an inky board. He had forgotten his hat in the car. He should have worn a sweater under his overcoat. The iced spray gathered around him like a tent, a cloistered coldness, wind-driven and biting.

There was no cage fight tonight. A business deal instead. *Your special services are required*, Li T'ien said. But there was no explanation of where they were going, what special services.

A steamer was at anchor ahead, searchlight sweeping its molten beam across the chop of the river. Heinrich felt the boat slow, then heard the gentling of the wave slap. Sampans broke away and Zhong Tu zipped through the scant passage and pulled alongside the steamer. In a few minutes a man in a Japanese Army uniform dropped down onto the deck of the boat.

"Colonel Yazuka, it's a cold night for business," Li T'ien said.

"With a good coat, a man can be comfortable," Yazuka replied.

"What do you have?"

"Manchurian opium. Best quality. Guaranteed."

"Two million Shanghai for the shipload."

"We want American dollars."

"One hundred fifty thousand American dollars, then."

"You're a thief."

"Rifles and ammunition included."

"I can't do that."

"One hundred fifty-five thousand American dollars. My final price."

"I can't take less than one hundred seventy thousand."

"Ten thousand for you and one hundred fifty thousand for your superiors. That's my offer."

"I accept."

Oilskin sacks were tossed into the water, grappled with bamboo poles and pulled onto the sampans. A crane lowered crates of guns and ammunition from the steamer onto the boat. Dollar bills, sodden with salt spray, were passed from Li T'ien to Yazuka and the floating island, now heavy in the water, headed back to Pootung Point.

By dawn the flotilla was docked at the Point and sacks and crates were being unloaded by coolies into an abandoned factory. Zhong Tu and the Russians stationed themselves on the roof, occasionally popping up from behind the wooden parapets like birds in a nest.

When the unloading was finished Li T'ien stood at the open door with Heinrich.

The sun wasn't full up yet, the remains of the moon suspended from golden wisps of cloud. In a few moments a car pulled up in the alley and parked. A tall man stepped out of the car, a red muffler around the collar of his well-cut topcoat, his forehead in the dawning light as broad and shiny as a swath of parchment.

"This is Herr Webber," Li T'ien said to Heinrich. "He speaks only German. You will translate. Tell him I want two hundred fifty thousand American dollars for the opium. No bargaining. That's my price. And he must remove the bales by tomorrow night."

"Two hundred fifty thousand American for the opium, and he wants no bargaining," Heinrich said to Herr Weber.

"Your accent, northern Germany," Herr Weber said. "Hamburg perhaps."

"Exactly."

"Although on second thought there might be something else, a hint of something Slavic."

"German is my mother tongue."

"I meant no disrespect. Some that Li T'ien have found speak a poor German that hurts my ears. Yours is the German of a cultured man."

"Perhaps you've heard of me. Heinrich Strauss."

"Ah, the newspaper magnate. Of course. Who in Germany hasn't heard of Heinrich Strauss?"

"And you?"

"An industrial chemist." He laughs. "And a victim of wanderlust. We must have a meal together sometime. Two hundred fifty thousand dollars, then. The money is in the car."

"He wants the bales removed by tomorrow night."

"I can accomplish that easily."

Heinrich watched Herr Webber walk back across the alley to his car. The Slavic remark was meaningless. If he was aware of Heinrich's Jewishness, he gave no sign of it. He hadn't spoken to Heinrich in the filthy, low German that the Gestapo officer spat at him in Berlin when he pleaded for Sigmund's release from Dachau. He hadn't called Heinrich a *Saujud*, Jew pig, or a *Verfluchte Juden*, a damn Jew. He talked to Heinrich as an equal, recognized Heinrich's good breeding, acknowledged that such things matter.

Herr Webber had reached the car and started back carrying a bundle as large as a bed pillow in his arms. The firecracker snap of bullets split the quiet sky. Men ran toward the factory, their figures a blur of padded blue trousers. Flurries of bullets rained down from the broken windows of an adjacent factory, from the men in the alley, from Zhong Tu and the Russians on the roof of the godown, a rising squeal and screech of metal skittering along the alley stones, the noise mimicking the pained barks of fighting dogs. When it stopped, Herr Webber and five blue-trousered bodies lay like knots of old clothes on the wet stones.

Li T'ien kicked at the blood-soaked package. "Empty. He brought the Red Gang here to steal from me, as if I had not prepared for this, as if I didn't know that he had stolen from others and would one day turn his eyes on me."

Heinrich stared at Herr Webber's corpse. The gore surprised him, the number of bullet holes, the amount of blood. The blood didn't fountain, it slid, flowing out of the shadows, a thick red stream seeking the sun. He had seen the corpses of beggars on the Shanghai streets and the bodies of fighters beaten to death, but this was a man he had a conversation with in German, who told him that he was cultured, who appreciated him, a man who wanted to have a meal with him.

He vomited into the gutter, then leaned against the wall of the factory, chest burning, and watched as Zhong Tu hopped down from the roof, and as expertly as a seamstress cutting a new hem, sliced off the heads of the corpses. He hung the Chinese dead by their hair to a lamppost. Herr Webber's close-shorn head was flung like a ball toward the wharf. It bounced and jumped as if there were a will involved, as if there were still life in it.

*   *   *

Chungking, China

The boat moved up the Yangtze, leaving Shanghai nine hundred miles behind. Heinrich hadn't eaten the rice balls Zhong Tu offered him, or stood in the prow of the boat with Li T'ien, but sat cold and miserable in the ice-prick air, sleeping on and off, but mostly sitting dumb silent and wishing himself somewhere else. He once would have enjoyed the journey, would have relished the sensation of float, the smooth slip of the boat's wake, the parade of flickering towns and green-rowed paddies, the yoked water buffaloes grinding through alluvial plains, Chinese peasants loping up and down the sides of sloped cliffs. He once would have stored up every image. He had no appetite for any of it now. He had made a mistake. He could see that now. He of all people had always understood that there was always and finally some form of payment to be made for unearned wealth, that position was no guarantee of safety, that the easy ascent could end in a trap, but he had forced himself to ignorance, shut warnings away, told himself that glimpses of violence were something less than sinister, possibly warranted, most probably accidental. He had folded doubt as neatly as a pocket knife and stowed it away, convinced himself he couldn't have succeeded on his own, that speculating in currency was risky, that without Li T'ien's backing he might fall and be as wretched as he was before. He had told himself that events had to be placed in context, that this was China and these were difficult times. All of this he had told himself. And then Herr Webber's brains slid out of his severed head onto a filthy street and for the first time since Heinrich left Germany he felt truly lost, his carefully calibrated control wiped away.

They landed at Wang Lung Men in Chungking on the third day. A Chinese Army officer met the boat, and Li T'ien and Heinrich and Zhong Tu climbed the pyramid of steps up through the fog to a waiting limousine. The crates of guns and ammunition were brought up behind them and loaded onto a truck.

The main road was bomb-rutted and layered with mud, people wandering through the muck on foot while fleets of official cars honked and splattered their way through the maze of bamboo lean-tos and patched tents. Steep steps and narrow lanes radiated from the road down the hillsides. Most buildings were piles of rock. Bamboo poles propped up still-standing walls and bare electric wires ran up the sides of windowless structures before they abruptly ended, dangling free, electrifying nothing. Everything was gray. Gray buildings, gray fog, gray people. Japanese bombs had scorched the banyan trees so that even the leaves of the trees were gray.

They headed up a mountain road, the city dropping away behind them, the fog breaking up into pearly bits that spun aimlessly in the sudden sunshine. At a guard house a gate opened and the car drove through into a bamboo forest. Armed soldiers lined the road. Another turn and they were on a walled drive, private and cool. A scarf cloud drifted over a moon gate leading to a tiled roof house.

Servants greeted them at the red door.

It was not a Chinese house. It was an English house. Its chintz sofas and dog paintings might just as well have been in Surrey. There wasn't even a whiff of China here, not a hint of the dried fern smell that in a Chinese house hugged the embroideries and drifted from freshly opened ginger jars.

Generalissimo Chiang Kaishek, a small, thin man, sat in an armchair in the large living room, his pointy-jawed face stern above the high collar of his military uniform. His head sloped, hair bristling up as short and stiff as chicken quills out of the grooves in his neck. Madame Chiang, a pretty woman with a moon-round face and cheerless mouth, her black hair slicked into a chignon, her slim body jointless in its tight satin gown, sat in a straight chair at his side. Aides and bodyguards were stationed around the room, two at the door, one behind the Generalissimo's chair, three more at the windows.

The Generalissimo, his gaze clouded by suspicion, pretended not to remember meeting Heinrich in Paris in 1923. In 1923 the Generalissimo was a Communist, one of Sun Yat-sen's aides, and had a homely Russian wife who bobbed her hair and wore trousers. He had wanted Heinrich's newspaper to treat his cause favorably and was plaintive in his need and want. Now stolid and graceless, he glanced at Heinrich as through a smudged pane of glass, waved whip-thin fingers in the air as though dismissing his presence, as though forgetful of a time when he faced Heinrich dipped in humility.

"You are one of our few visitors," Madame Chiang said and invited Heinrich to sit down on the couch. "As you saw, the Japanese have caused great devastation to China. Hospitality is difficult. Are you an American?"

"German. A refugee."

"You are Jewish?"

"Yes, but not religious. Not at all. I never have been."

"Jews are very intelligent. Very Chinese."

Madame Chiang paid no attention to Li T'ien, who hovered over Chiang's shoulder, Li T'ien probably telling Chiang what had happened at the Point, the aborted sale of opium, the loss of money for Chiang's coffers. Heinrich couldn't tell; Li T'ien's words were cropped, Chiang's face a dogged mask, his hawk-like shadow a glossy blot on the white walls.

Li T'ien turned toward Heinrich. There was a request. The Generalissimo had a new plan to fight the Japanese and wanted Heinrich's help. Heinrich was not ignorant of the stories about Chiang and Li T'ien—the secret society, the murders—or the self-indulgence of Madame Chiang, the luxury and corruption surrounding her, her pleas for money from the United States.

Heinrich was caught, held suspended in Chiang's limpid stare. He wanted to lie down. Or walk away. Just amble through gardens, past walls and down the pyramidal steps. His mind scanned for ways to extricate himself. *I'm a Jewish man, a publisher, a person of importance. I sat at the King of England's table. I don't belong here with criminals,* he longed to say.

"I would be happy to be of service in any way I can," he replied.

Chapter 19

All Aaron would say was that he and Hannah had rented a room in house number 14 on Alcock Road.

"Just a room," he said, "a nice little room. Nothing fancy. A Jewish woman, Mrs. Blitzstein, owns the house. She has other renters, too, some Russians, not all Jews. White Russians can be as poor as Jews these days."

Aaron hadn't described the slubby yard, the fifteen little mud-brick houses flung as haphazardly as clods of dirt against the bamboo fence, the reeking trash barrels beside a stagnant pond, the lean-to with a single tub for bathing, door missing, sides falling in, remnants of thatched roof open to the sky.

A Chinese woman, long black gown cleft at the ankle, was on her knees beside the pond, washing clothes in the mossy water. Lilli rattled the gate latch and the woman toddled toward her on bound feet, let Lilli in, then ambled back to her washing.

House number 14 was a timbered ruin, ravaged by weather and age, a portion of the roof scorched, peeled back, sheets of tar paper clouting the ashy shingles. A piece of paper nailed to the door listed the occupants. *Chernofsky, 12* was penciled in second from the bottom.

The door felt spongy to the knock, soaked and resoaked by troughed water falling from the eaves. A pinch-faced woman wrapped in what looked like a fringed table cloth, her light-blonde hair pin-curled to her head in rows that showed her pink scalp, opened the door.

"Hannah Chernofsky?"

"Follow me."

Lilli followed the woman into the dark entry. A toilet was to the right of the door, women standing at the row of sinks arranging their hair, spitting into mascara boxes then brushing black goo onto their eyelashes, powdering their faces, grimacing at the mirror as they tugged and yanked at too-tight skirts. Some of the women were young, faces plump and smooth, their viridity as yet unblemished; others were older with witchy looks partially masked by heavy makeup that had sunk into their wrinkles like finely sifted flour. Lilli followed the woman past a small parlor where the odor of cooked cabbage drifting from baffled transoms had cleaved thick as cheese to old sofas and damp wallpaper. Beyond the parlor a long dreary hallway wove past doors with chiseled-out numbers, some of the numbers colored in with red nail polish. Mumbly sounds oozed through loose-fitting door frames. Objects resembling sacred offerings lay in front of some of the doors. A dead plant. A violin with a fractured neck. A single slipper with a note peeking out of the toe. A small pile of dirty dishes. Pages of a handwritten letter. Somewhere in the house a woman was singing in a sweetly husky voice, the words squeezed and shredded by the noise of a radio at high pitch. A man in a checked suit, jacket buttoned wrong, face pocked and gouged, coarse gray hair a springy mess, came out of an open door. He brushed past Lilli, the odor of stale cigar smoke trailing.

"That's their room," the woman said.

Chernofsky, written on a Chinese postcard, was tacked to the carved lintel of the room. The whole poor scheme and scope of the room was visible from the hallway. Iron bed, wooden chair with rush seat, chamber pot, boxes of clothes lined up against the mildewed wall, Aaron's books stacked on the floor.

Hannah was smoothing the rumpled red coverlet of the bed, her breasts swaying like Chinese lanterns beneath her silk kimono.

"How long have you been standing there?"

"I just came."

"Mrs. Blitzstein usually warns me when someone comes. I'll have to tell her about that. She knows I don't like it when people just come anytime they want. And look at this place. If I had known I would have swept the floor."

There were sheets of paper on the floor covered with Aaron's familiar handwriting, a piece of bread covered with ants, a pair of high-heeled shoes (one buckle missing), a pile of dirty clothes that had been rolled into a ball and shoved in a corner.

"Well, you're here, so sit down. Take off your coat. Make yourself comfortable."

"I'll keep my coat on. It's colder inside than it is outside."

"The heater is broken. It's been broken since we moved in. Mrs. Blitzstein says wait for summer, it won't matter."

Hannah's right eye was swollen, a clump of mascara hanging as limply as a blackened sow bug from one eyelash. There were small welts on her wrists, an orangey bruise above her lip, and her rouge had smeared from the center of her cheeks all the way up to the sides of her forehead so that she looked as if she had a fever.

Lilli sat down on the chair.

"I would offer you something to eat, but this morning Aaron ate the last of the crackers." Hannah picked a sheet of paper up off the floor and fanned her face with it. "You're cold and I'm warm. I'm never cold. Aaron goes to bed with two pairs of socks on his feet, a coat, and a scarf. 'Warm my feet, Hannah. Give me a little of your heat, Hannah.'"

There were loose dollar bills on the bed. Hannah scooped them up, shoved them into the pocket of a coat in the pile of clothes, then sat down on the bed, a hand tucked beneath each thigh, and swung her bare legs back and forth.

"I meant to invite you over. I was going to. I even told Aaron that it was time we brought Lilli to see our little home. I said, 'Won't she be happy to see our little love nest?' He's too busy to do anything, he says. He stands in front of the synagogue waiting for someone to hire him to do electricity. I don't think he knows anything about electricity. He says he does, that he read about it in a book. I think he just likes to be close to the synagogue but not in it. He says he doesn't go inside, but I think he does. That Jewish stuff is hard to get rid of. I hear him dreaming in Hebrew sometimes. At least I think it's Hebrew. It certainly isn't German or English."

"Aaron said you were still dancing in the cabaret."

"He visits you in the heim? What a good brother. Not like mine. I haven't seen Sigmund since the wedding. But that's the way the world is. All changed." She stood up and placed her hands on her hips. "Look at my figure, Lilli. Not eating much makes my waist small and my hips like a young girl's. Juicy. That's what everyone says about my hips, that they're juicy." She sat down on the bed again. "I can tell you don't like our little place. You don't have to say it. I know how terrible it is. I can touch three walls from the bed. My bathroom in Hamburg was three times the size. I don't care. I won't be here long."

"What do you mean? Where are you going?"

"Don't be silly, I'm not going anywhere *now*. After the war, Lilli, that's what I'm talking about. After the war I'll go back to Germany and everything will be the way it was before. Vati will run his newspaper again, and Sigmund will get his medical degree and cure nervous German women, and Mutti will glide elegantly through all the rooms of our big house, smiling at the servants and checking the tables for dust. All my old boyfriends will come calling, and they'll say, 'Oh, my, Hannah, what juicy hips you have.' And the sun will come in through the windows, a blazing sun with bits of gold in it, and if there are any Nazis left they will grovel at Vati's feet and apologize to him for all the meanness and inconvenience they've caused."

"But we're here now, Hannah. You have to think about how you can do the best you can right here."

Hannah shrugged. "Yes, this is where we are. Mutti with her German pianist, Vati with his Chinese gangster, and me with Aaron. Aaron says wherever I am it's paradise. If you want to know the truth about your brother, Lilli, I think he's lost his mind. Everything to him is perfect. I'm perfect, the room is perfect, every morsel he puts in his mouth is perfect. I feed him pork and tell him it's baby lamb, and he doesn't ask where in the world I would get baby lamb, he just eats it and licks his fingers and tells me what a perfect wife I am."

"Fanny's going to Mozambique."

"Oh? Where is that?"

"Africa."

"Africa? Why would she do a thing like that?"

"She has Polish papers. With Polish papers she can go to Africa. Thirty-six people in the heim are going. She'll be better off there."

"I'd never go to Africa. I don't know anyone there. Anyway, I know how things run here." She lit a cigarette, took a few puffs, then pinched the end of the cigarette with her fingers and slipped it back in its pack.

"There was a man in the hallway," Lilli said.

"There are always men in the hallway."

"Your door was open."

"So there was a man leaving the room. So what? It's a little thing I do to keep us alive. No one would rent a room to me without a husband. Now I tell the men in the cabaret to come and see me here, that my husband is away all day, that we'll have comfort and privacy. If it weren't for Aaron, I would still be standing up against a wall for a few dollars in all kinds of weather. Or on the ground under the bushes near the park, watching out for policemen. A married woman has privileges, Lilli. At least I don't starve and Aaron doesn't have to pick worms out of bread before he eats it."

"You'll break his heart."

"And what of my heart? Who cares about me? And you have no right to lecture me. I know what you do. Vati saw you. You're the same as I am. Why are you here, anyway? What do you want? You look sick. You *are* sick, aren't you?"

"I'm pregnant."

"Oh, Lilli, are you sure?"

"I vomit every morning. But I'm not sick all the time."

"It could be something else. When was your last monthly?"

"Three months. There's no doubt. It's a fact. I'm sure of it."

"If you had come to me, I would have told you how things go, what you should do, and how you should do it. Tell Li T'ien. Maybe he'll set you up in a house. He's very rich. Vati lives in one of his apartments in the Crown Hotel. It has a tile bath and hand-woven rugs, and he doesn't even pay him any rent."

"I'm rid of him. I make more money on the black market. I'll soon have enough to buy Shaya back."

"Shaya is probably not even in Shanghai anymore. She's probably with some rich family in England right this minute, being pushed around Hyde Park in a pram."

"She's in Shanghai with Sir Elias Mansour and his wife. I see her in the car with them. His wife wanted a child, so she bought one, but she doesn't like children. She doesn't look at Shaya, she doesn't touch her."

"The Mansours? Do you know how rich they are, how important? Leave her alone, Lilli. She'll have a good life."

"A child shouldn't be given away even once, and she's been given away twice. And now to people who don't love her. Who goes to her when she cries at night? Who comes when she calls out?"

"Why would you even want her, someone else to worry about, to watch starve?"

"She needs me."

"I don't understand you at all, Lilli."

"I don't want you to understand me."

"What *do* you want?"

"Medicine."

"Medicine is dangerous, and it doesn't always work. Maybe it gets rid of the baby, but it can get rid of the mother, too. Aaron will kill me if something happens to you."

"Who will tell him? You lie to him about everything else, you can lie to him about this, too."

There were no windows in the room, no air. Lilli leaned her head onto her knees, felt Hannah's hand kneading the back of her neck. Then the sound of a purse clasp snapping, of something liquid being poured into a glass.

"Drink this. I got it from a Chinaman in a shop on Bubbling Well Road. You'll feel a little sick, and your stomach will ache like you've had too much to eat, and then something will come out and you'll be like you were before. I've been caught a few times myself."

The liquid tasted like very sweet tea and had a yeasty smell, as though something had been growing inside the bottle.

Lilli lay down on the bed and Hannah sat in the chair.

"I feel dizzy. It wants to come up."

"Don't let it, Lilli. Hold it in."

Lilli leaned over the bed and a long blue liquid stream jetted onto the floor.

"You should have held it in," Hannah said. "I don't have any more."

*　　*　　*

The rickshaw stopped in front of the synagogue, the swaying motion stilled, prickly cold rain washing Lilli's face and puddling around her feet. Aaron leaned over her, his beard as soft as a clutch of fine feathers brushing her cheek.

"What happened? What's going on?"

"She's sick," Hannah said.

"Sick? What do you mean sick?"

"She drank something."

"Something? Did you give her something?"

"She asked me to. And then she vomited it back up and fainted, and I didn't know what to do with her."

Aaron was lifting Lilli up, carrying her.

"Be careful, don't drop her."

"Why would I drop her? She doesn't weigh a pound, how can I drop her? What did you do to her, Hannah? If she dies, it will be on your head."

"Yell at her. Don't yell at me. She came to me because she's pregnant. What was I to do? And what do you know about Lilli? Nothing. Do you know that she sleeps with a Chinese gangster for money? Do you know she sells things on the black market, that she could be killed at any minute? You don't live in the real world, Aaron, you don't listen, you don't see."

Up the steps of the synagogue. The rabbi talking to Aaron now, *Come this way, follow me, take her into the study,* Hannah calling Aaron blind, Aaron calling Hannah brainless, the yeshiva students crowding around, damp wool socks pulled up around skinny legs, their breath like potatoes in oil, like onions they couldn't digest.

She was in the rabbi's study now, sitting in a hard chair, long rivulets of rainwater sliding down her legs and disappearing into cracks in the floor.

"Look what's happened to you," Aaron said. "Aren't you ashamed? What's going to become of you? You've ruined your life. It's finished. Over. Do you hear me? What's going to happen to you now?"

"Don't yell at her," the rabbi said.

"I'll yell if I want to yell. Who are you to tell me what to do, when to yell, when not to yell? She's my sister. Mine. I'll yell if I want to yell."

"Yelling won't cure it," Hannah said.

"You keep out of it. You've done enough damage today."

"This has nothing to do with Hannah," Lilli said.

"And you have to be another worry for me to handle? I don't worry enough as it is?"

"You don't have to worry about me."

"And who will, if I don't? Tell me that. What's wrong with you that you should even think of doing such things? What is going to happen to you? I have nothing to give you. I'm a broker, a worthless broker. I've fallen into a hole so big I'll never be able to climb out. How can I save you when I can't even do anything to save myself? *Oy, gotenyu.* How could I know it would be like this when we left Kovno? I didn't think about anything. Just go, that's all I thought about. I didn't know about ugliness until I came to Shanghai. I didn't know what could happen to people here. I was supposed to take care of you, and look what happened, the two of us lost, the two of us ruined."

He started to cry, tears worming their way into the channel beneath his eyes, vanishing into the red beard. Lilli regarded them with horror. In her cunningness and daring she had tossed a stone onto a lake and thought that nobody would notice, that its dead weight would take it straight to the bottom, but it had skipped along the surface, riffles fanning out, unintended, unguided, unwanted, as steady as the arc of the moon, as visible as the sun.

"It's not the end of the world to have a baby," she said. "Even here in Shanghai. Even now when everything is so terrible. Babies come when they want to. We're not ruined, Aaron. We changed a little, but how else would we have been able to live?"

She put her arms around him, felt his shoulder blades as sharp as broken chicken bones poking up out of skin and gristle.

"He's a bigger baby than you'll ever have," Hannah said.

Chapter 20

Rachel was thinner than when Elias saw her last, the curve of her cheek deepened, the shank of her neck a veined rod in its bony cape. She was taking her coat off now, tossing it onto the couch next to her purse and briefcase, settling into the chair on the other side of the desk, pointing to papers he had to sign, bills he had to okay. She stood up again, took a cigarette out of her purse, lit it, exhaled a smoky sigh. He remembered the dress. A polka-dot affair. It was loose on her, needed to be taken in at the shoulders and waist, floated around her knees, an unfurled flag that whipped between her legs when she walked. And her hair had a peculiar shape. Uneven. As if she had taken a scissors and snipped a nuisance lock too close to her scalp, then cut away some more to make it symmetrical and ended up with something resembling a patchy lawn.

The dress caught in the heel of her shoe as she sat down again. She disentangled her foot and the hem ripped, a zippering sound that stalled at a knot of thread, then ripped some more, until the hem was attached by one fierce scrap of cloth. She didn't look down, didn't check the extent of the damage, smoked her cigarette, nicotine fingers flagging certain pages, sometimes one turned-down corner, sometimes two for emphasis. She smoked negligently, had a brash of burn holes all up and down her sleeves, some no larger than a dust mote, others as big as a fingernail.

Elias watched her as she read. Her eyes were feverishly bright.

"You're not eating well," he said.

"I have no time."

"You won't spend the money."

"Well, so."

"I insist that you eat better."

"Insist away."

"I'll send food over to your apartment."

"I'll take it to the heime and distribute it."

"I'll write your mother and tell her."

"My mother likes me thin and she doesn't like you at all. She thinks you're an Arab. She doesn't like Arabs. They irritate her. Italians irritate her, too. All that pasta."

"I'm serious."

"Do you know that Heinrich Strauss is in the waiting room?"

"Yes. He comes here every day."

"You see him every day?"

"I don't see him at all."

"For chrissakes, why not?"

"I don't deal with gangsters if I can help it."

"If you can help it? What does that mean?"

"It means if I have a choice in the matter, I don't deal with gangsters."

"Not clear, Elias. You either do or don't deal with gangsters."

"I'm not going to argue with you, Rachel."

"Well, anyway, I can't afford to call him names. He brokered five hundred cases of powdered milk for the heime at a bargain-basement price."

"You would have gotten the milk free if the Green Gang hadn't stolen it off the docks."

"I don't give a shit who stole what, as long as we got the milk. Jesus, Elias, don't be so stubborn. The man can be useful."

"He's gained a footing in the Green Gang. He works for thugs, Rachel. He's dangerous."

"He's only being himself. Heinrich Strauss at work. Making his way. Promoting himself in any fashion he can. Isn't he your old friend Heinrich? Didn't you shoot pigeons or something with him in Germany?"

"Grouse."

"They're not pigeons?"

"They're grouse, Rachel. Just grouse."

"Are they tasty?"

"We never ate them."

"You shot them and didn't eat them? My God, what a waste."

"Are these all the bills?"

"Do you want more?"

"They seem incomplete."

"We got an infusion of money from Chiang Kaishek, of all people. A friend of Heinrich Strauss, the note with it said. How about that for your old friend, Elias? Not someone to be thrown overboard so easily."

"Heinrich Strauss is the worm in the apple."

"For chrissakes, Elias, we have no time for that shit. He gets things done. Will I see you at the meeting of the Joint tonight?"

"Yes. Should I pick you up?"

"No. I can manage."

Elias didn't see anyone for a while after she left. Why did their encounters always end so badly? He expressed concern about her not eating enough. In return she was contrary and irritating. The remark about Elias and Heinrich Strauss being friends. They weren't. They never had been. They had been parallel acquaintances, moving in similar circles, knowing the same people, at times being in the same country at the same time at the same earl or duke's castle. And so what if Chiang Kaishek sent money for Jewish refugees with Heinrich Strauss's name attached? Was that a reason for Elias to jettison all his scruples?

Elias saw eight more people, answered ten telephone calls, dictated three letters. At four o'clock Edward brought the afternoon telegrams into the office.

"Is Strauss still here?"

"He is."

"Send him in."

It was distasteful to see him looking so well. The well-tailored suit and topcoat, the neatly trimmed gray hair.

"You're a new man, I see," Elias said.

"You might say I've been raised from the dead."

"Sit wherever you like. The couch, a chair, it doesn't matter."

"Ah, I see you're still angry at me," Heinrich said and picked the couch. "And fully justified. My lack of propriety in our recent dealings was deplorable. I was at a low point and I couldn't resist the urge to retaliate at anyone who was available, but I assure you that I'm fully recovered and now realize that none of my bad fortune was in any way connected to you. I hope you receive my apology, Elias."

"What is it you want?"

"To present a business proposition."

"On whose behalf?"

"Li T'ien. I understand that you have had dealings with him."

"I pay him not to burn down my warehouses."

"And he is satisfied with the arrangement. He holds you in the highest regard. He thought that since you and I are old friends, that if I explained his proposal to you . . ."

"I'll leave China and abandon my interests here before I'll become involved in his activities."

"It is to your mutual benefit."

"There can be no such mutuality between us."

"You want the Japanese to leave the refugees alone?"

"Yes. And so far they do."

"Not for long. If the Japanese go to war with Britain and the United States, there'll be no more International Settlement. You will be the same as I am. A refugee, Elias. The Japanese will pour out of Hongkew and swallow all of Shanghai. Do you think they'll leave you and your Jewish businesses alone? They might even put Jews in concentration camps. I've seen their anti-Semitic posters. I saw posters just like them in Germany. Li T'ien wants you to help him form an underground to fight them here in Shanghai. The Generalissimo will provide some of the funds and armaments. Opium will supply the rest."

Elias stood up. "I think that's enough."

"You deny that your family's money derives from opium?"

"I think you should leave now."

Heinrich remained seated, crossed his legs.

"Please sit down, Elias. I've waited a long time to see you. Have the courtesy to hear me out."

Elias walked to the window. He couldn't stand to look at the man. It galled him that he was here, that he brought up the past, that he stepped uninvited into Elias's life. Even the smell of him, slinking its way up through layers of wool to join the scent of barber's lotion, nauseated him.

"I make no judgment on you or your family, Elias. They did what they had to do to survive. A natural circumstance, one that someone like me can readily appreciate. I myself have had to come to an accommodation with my natural bent for scrupulous business dealings. Out of necessity. Just as your family once did. Not that I compare myself in the least to the importance of your family, but I do have some standing now and understand all too well how necessity can bring about startling revelations as to man's true nature. None of us is a saint. We figure and refigure what we have to do to get on in the world. I am now of the opinion that there are no rules that can't in the name of survival be broken. The sale of opium in Shanghai to those who care to use it is a case in point. We need make no moral judgments on its addictive properties or the harm it might do to society. That is for others to determine. But I'm sure you can see the benefit to the refugees if opium is once again moving freely through the Settlement to its distribution points. There will be more money for food and medicine for the heime. I know that the fate of the Jewish community rests on your shoulders, Elias, and that you would do whatever you could to see to its survival. I need not tell you that greater aims must always be kept in mind when contemplating difficult, if not illegal, adventures. Opium is but a small pest in this nasty war. Bullets and starvation are deadlier."

Elias sat down at his desk. He was exhausted. Could it be that he was getting ill?

"You suppose I have more power than I do. I know nothing about opium or distribution of it. That is all in the past. I had nothing to do with it."

"As president of the Municipal Council you can find a way to exempt Li T'ien's trucks."

"I can't do that. If it's known to the Japanese that the Jews are engaged in underground work against them, that I'm involved in opium smuggling, the whole community could be destroyed. The fate of all the Jews of Shanghai hangs on what a few of us do. Tell Li T'ien that my answer is no."

"Come now, Elias. You know that's not a good answer. Look at me. I was a pitiable beggar a few months ago. I understand the nature of status and dignity as only one who has lost both can understand them. I also understand imperiousness. I was a master of it, someone who thought himself well protected from the afflictions of the common man. I see the way the world works now as I never did before. Exceptions must be made. Detours must be taken. Subterfuge must be encouraged. You weren't in Europe. I couldn't believe what was happening even while it was happening, and I'm an intelligent man, as intelligent as you are. This is a dangerous world, and unless we act with fearless resolve, we are no safer than a butterfly in a windstorm. Take heed Elias. Plan what you do carefully and keep in mind what I was a few short months ago."

When he was gone, Elias lay down on the couch and closed his eyes. He *was* feeling ill. He ran his fingers across his stomach. Right there in the center, near the navel, pain flicked, raw and mean. An old ulcer trodding along a well-marked path, shifting shape now beneath his fingers, the exact location clouded by a contrecoup of scar tissue, the whole stomach a symphony of pinches and tweaks.

Rachel said the important thing was to get what we could for the refugees and ignore everything else. Take Chiang Kaishek's money, join forces with gangsters, and save the Jews of Shanghai. He wished she weren't always so right.

Chapter 21

*O*ne-thirty, **Heinrich had told Aaron.** *In front of the Royal Café in the French Concession. And bring Moses with you.*

They had been waiting an hour now in their light jackets. It was almost one-thirty, a fleeting sun pocking the streets, a single cloud hovering like a puckered balloon overhead. The past few weeks, along with rain and sleet, dank winds had begun to howl into Shanghai from the Himalayas, searing through layers of clothing, flash-freezing tender skin.

The street was crowded, women in smartly layered clothes and scarves, hats, and gloves, stopping to gaze into gleamy shop windows, then hurrying on, stepping over the beggars squatting on the sidewalk, placing the toe of a shoe here, a slim heel there, backing up, going forward, then sideways, stepping on as few fingers as possible as they marked a path. Men rushed along the street without care, preoccupied, not looking down, not noticing the smite of shoes on arms and legs.

"If he ever shows up, there's no way I'll eat anything he pays for," Aaron said to Moses. "His money comes straight from the Green Gang and that criminal Chiang Kaishek. Can you imagine, Hannah's father, the good German, consorting with gangsters? I'm not eating, but you can hold your nose and eat his lunch if you want to."

Moses had no qualms about being here or eating lunch paid for by Heinrich Strauss. He didn't scruple in his dealings with criminals. Even the fact that Li T'ien was probably the steersman of whatever proposition Heinrich would set out today was of no importance. Moses, cold almost to the personal, had discharged any connection Li T'ien had to Lilli. He was intent only on discovering the tentacle reach of Li T'ien and the Green Gang before he declared them an enemy.

A Bentley pulled up to the curb and Heinrich got out.

"A cold day," he said and rubbed his gloved hands together as though swilling them of something greasy.

"We're not eating," Aaron said. "You can tell us right here on the sidewalk what's so important."

"Of course you'll eat. And you shouldn't be so disdainful, Aaron. When have you had fifty cents to eat in a restaurant? You're a poor Jew. A poor Jew can't afford to turn down a meal."

"A poor Jew doesn't have to eat with gangsters."

"You should watch your mouth. I'm still your father-in-law. Don't be stubborn. The food is kosher. Just the way you like it. Jew food, isn't that what they call it? For myself, I like a little atmosphere, a potted plant or two, a linen napkin."

"I knew we shouldn't have come. I said to myself, put a few dollars in Heinrich Strauss's pocket and you'll see that he's still the same big shot he was before, stepping on everyone's head. What do you have to say that's so important?"

"Let's just go inside and you can order some food or not, as you like, and we can talk." He nodded to Moses. "You have no such objections to my money, do you, Moses?"

"I have no objection to anyone's money."

A bakery was on the ground floor of the building, then a flight of stairs that curled around itself and ended up on the roof. The wind was unobstructed here, lappets of tattered tarpaulin flapping and buckling overhead with each cold blast, puddly spots of rainwater on the tar paper floor where the tarpaulin gapped, bits of newspaper floating in the puddles, a few draggled refugees sitting at round metal tables sopping gravy up with thick slabs of bread.

"Maybe I will eat a little something," Aaron said.

"Have the veal plate," Heinrich said. "And dessert. Their apple strudel is very good. Don't worry about the money. Just enjoy yourselves. And how is my daughter?"

"Beautiful. A perfect wife."

Moses watched the waiter bringing food to the other tables. He was hungry. He went to bed hungry, woke up hungry. It was a chronic disease.

"This is no place to be for a hungry person," Aaron said. "A person like that should stay away from places like this, should be in a room by himself where it's easy to put hunger away in a drawer, in a corner, on a shelf. Are you going to eat, Moses?"

"Of course. I never said I wouldn't."

"My father-in-law is generous. He says to have the veal plate when it's twenty-five cents more than the chicken."

"Bring everything on the menu," Heinrich told the waiter.

The waiter brought so many plates of food they shingled the table like a nest of roof tiles.

Moses didn't know what to eat first, the veal or the potatoes or the chicken or the blintzes or the pancakes, whether to eat politely or to pick up one of the plates and let everything on it slip into his mouth, whether to cut squarely with a knife and fork or rip at the food with his teeth. It was a sight, all that food in one place. He started cutting and chewing and swallowing, stabbing at whatever was closest to the fork, nearest to the spoon, easiest to get at. He jabbed at a chicken leg, held it on the end of his fork. The skin was a glossy brown. Fat ran down the tines of the fork onto the plate.

Aaron ate in intervals, stuffing his mouth, then breathing hard, as if he had been running for miles, but always keeping his plate close to his beard, letting the gravy slop over onto his lap.

Heinrich didn't eat anything, but sat at a corner of the table watching them.

"It takes a while to fill up an empty stomach," he said. "The first money I made I sat right where you're sitting and ate like a lion."

One plate after another was emptied. The table became a graveyard of chicken bones and veal chop gristle, smouched with congealing fat and dribs of potato. The other diners had gone except for an elderly couple at a table beneath a swinging strip of tarpaulin, the husband reading a Jewish newspaper to his wife while she sipped tea and took little bites out of a piece of bread she retrieved from her purse.

The waiter cleared away the dirty dishes. Wrens had come out of the linden trees along the street to scavenge, and their oily feathers were mirrors in the moisture-laden air. Moses held a handful of crumbs out, and one of the birds, its piked beak as curved as a baby's lip, pecked at Moses' palm, scrabbling it clean.

"So now we'll talk," Heinrich said. "I have a proposition from Chiang Kaishek. He's forming an underground to fight the Japanese. You know about electricity, Aaron. You can figure out how to blow up buildings and bridges. Moses, you're strong, you can carry things. No one will suspect orthodox Jews of sabotage. There'll be extra food for you, money in your pockets."

"Who says we're still orthodox?" Aaron said.

"It doesn't matter. Just don't shave your beards."

"The lunch was good, but not that good. Did you ask Sigmund to blow up buildings?"

"I'm asking you."

"Ask Sigmund first, then we'll talk."

"I hear the Japanese have plans for the Jews," Moses said.

"It's possible. For now they tolerate them."

"And the Jewish underground, will they have a part?"

"This is about explosives, not Jews."

"Everything to me is about Jews. What I want to know, is blowing up buildings good for the Jews, or will they be blamed? There has to be a reward for sabotage, an improvement in conditions, more food, less harassment, not a wanted sign hung around a Jewish neck."

"Do you have something better to do? Look at me, how I've risen, and you, still a nobody. You put chains on bicycles and don't earn enough to buy a decent meal. That I have even had to approach you with this makes me angry. I knew in advance what Aaron's answer would be, because I know the crookedness of his thinking, that for him words take the place of deeds, but you…"

"Who profits on the sale of opium?"

"Such questions."

"There are Jews involved in sabotage already. Why would I join Chiang Kaishek?"

"Because there is money."

"Does some of it go to Jewish coffers?"

"It goes to the coffers of those involved."

"A slip can mean death. Loyalty is important. Without loyalty there is no security."

"You're playing a game now. I thought you would see the merit of what I propose and would understand."

"I know of no alliance between Chiang Kaishek and the Jewish underground."

"I told you, there is no Jewish underground." Heinrich shoved some folded bills toward Aaron. "For Hannah. Take it."

"We don't need it. We do just fine. God provides."

Heinrich put the money back in his wallet.

"I hope you enjoyed the lunch," he said and headed back down the stairs.

Aaron wrapped the rest of the bread in his handkerchief, put it in his pocket and drank the last of the tea.

"I shouldn't have eaten. I'm sorry now. Already my stomach is rebelling. Are you thinking?"

"I am."

"And?"

"If blowing up bridges and buildings will put a hoodlum like Chiang in control of China, then I say it's a bad idea."

"Still, when all is said and done, a person could find a little sense in what he says, Moses. Don't you think he made some sense? The Japanese might turn on us at any time. What guarantee is there that they'll let us live any longer than Hitler would? The Japanese let us live this long, but who knows for how much longer? It could possibly be a good thing. Even fools and gangsters sometimes have good ideas. Should we just sit here like poor *nebechels* and wait for the flood to come and drown us?

"You have trouble lighting a match, how will you blow up buildings?"

"How hard can it be?"

"You'll get caught."

"I won't. I'm very swift on my feet. Have you ever seen me run? I can run as fast as a gazelle. So are we going to blow up buildings or not?"

"He didn't answer my questions."

"He doesn't know the answers. He pretends to be a *macher*, but he's a *pisher*, a nothing."

Moses understood the value of acting alone; he had learned the art of covertness in the bitter way a wounded hare in a coppice learns it. He carried the unbundled, raw images of the past with him. Sounds paced his days: the cry of a child, the baying of dogs, the creaky shift of loaded trucks on uneven ground. His nights were sundered by nightmare dreams of endless chases and broken bodies.

The birds, finally free to roam the tables at will, perched now on the backs of chairs and padded boldly beneath table legs.

"I don't want to be responsible for your death," Moses said.

"What kind of answer is that?"

"It's my answer."

Chapter 22

Heinrich stood at the edge of the parade ground and watched the Jewish Brigade march up and down the muddy field, Mogen David emblems on their sleeves and hats, arms swinging in rhythm to the captain's shouted commands. Sigmund was third from the right, his back as straight as a sheet of cogged steel, face sun-blushed, hat tipped toward the nape of his blond head. Heinrich's eyes misted at the sight of his son in a uniform, the same age as Heinrich had been when he enlisted in the Kaiser's army during World War I.

The exercise ended, soldiers scattered.

Sigmund walked toward him.

"You used to let out a wild whoop when you saw me," Heinrich said. "You would run across the play yard toward me, eyes dancing."

"How did you find me?"

"Major-General Chester. A new friend of mine. I told him about your heroism and he was quite impressed. I heard that you had approached the British Volunteers and I wanted to help, to make sure you were accepted. Major-General Chester said they wouldn't take a German, so I had to settle for the Jewish Brigade."

"You talked to the colonel on my behalf?"

"Of course. Military experience will benefit you in many ways. The discipline, the comradeship, all of it very important to a man's development. A British or German brigade would have been better. But one can't have everything. At least there are no yeshiva buchers like your brother-in-law, with beards and side locks, long black coats dragging in the dirt, arguing about whether to drill on the Sabbath. These boys could pass for Gentiles."

"We're not boys."

"Come, don't be petty. I'll buy you a meal. It's been a long time since I've seen you."

Sigmund looked back at the boot-tramped field. Rain had begun to fall, a sudden rain that glistered the weeds at the edge of the field, a hard rain that in minutes could turn a dent in the ground into a mud-chucked ditch.

"Spare me an hour of your company," Heinrich said. "I've missed you."

The Bentley was waiting at the edge of the parade field. Zhong Tu opened the passenger door and Heinrich got in. Sigmund hesitated.

"Come. One hour for your father."

Sigmund stepped in beside his father, the engine started, the banyan trees slipped swiftly by.

"You live like a king," Sigmund said.

"That's the way life is. One minute up, the next minute down. The important thing is to keep moving."

"Is what I heard about you true?"

"What? That I'm eating? That I don't have to grovel for crumbs in the heim? We are in no position to make moral choices, Sigmund. When and if life resumes some day and this is all behind us, then we can be moral and put ideals above necessity."

"Then it *is* true."

"Exaggerated. But you haven't done too badly yourself. I've heard that you've found a woman. Good for you. Have you seen your mother? Does she ask about me?"

"I've seen her. She doesn't ask about you."

"You mustn't blame her."

"I don't."

"Good. So who is in command of your brigade?"

"Colonel Weiss."

"I'll talk to him, tell him you're my son, and that I was in the Kaiser's Army and won a few medals myself. It could be just the thing you need to make yourself stand out, make them pay attention. I'm not completely useless to you, Sigmund, although you might think so. I want to help you. I have a certain standing now. I have privileges. People defer to me, move aside when I ask them to." He rested his hand on Sigmund's shoulder. "It's not exactly the way it was in Europe, but sometimes I think it's better. Here I'm a new man, not tied to any one path, free to explore many possibilities. What I've learned is that there are always ways to improve one's lot."

Sigmund shrugged Heinrich's hand away. "I once admired you. I tried to emulate the way you spoke, the way you thought. I wanted to be just like you. There is no excuse for what you really are."

"No excuse for trying to stay alive? Is that how you think?"

"I hardly think at all. I float. I have no emotion. I once had heat in me. Now I'm just hollow."

"You're a hero and I'm proud of you."

"You're proud of your son. Your son could be anyone. You don't think of me at all."

"That's a lie."

"It's the truth. You deal in possessions, not people."

"I will forgive that because I know that it comes from the misery of your experience in Dachau, and that you don't mean it, that you wouldn't say that to your Vati if you meant it. What you need is what I needed, to make yourself useful. Look at me. Your mother left me and I'm still alive. There's much to savor in life, Sigmund. Merely to breathe air is a marvelous thing. But first I had to stop judging the morality of opportunities before I examined their practical value. If you were kinder to me, if you treated me with respect, I could get a position for you with Li T'ien. He has a reverence for heroes."

Sigmund leaned forward. "I'd like to get out."

"What are you talking about? We're going to have a meal. Can't you have a meal with your father? Is that so terrible? I won't talk about Li T'ien. We'll talk about the Army. We'll talk about anything you want to talk about."

"Tell him to stop the car."

The car stopped and Sigmund got out.

"You're not a man, Sigmund, you're a boy," Heinrich hollered after him. "You can fuck a woman and march like a soldier, but you're still a boy."

*　*　*

Sigmund couldn't sleep. Rachel was snoring, her arm across his chest. He touched her arm and she turned onto her side. He wished he slept as easily as she did. *My sleep is like death,* she told him. *I don't dream. I don't worry. When I'm awake I do the best I can and fuck the rest.*

He sat on the edge of the bed, head in his hands. She wasn't what he would have chosen. He liked soft, compliant women. She was hard and unyielding. He couldn't fool her and that made him anxious, nervous, touchy.

You can't go back to the heim, she said when he got out of the hospital. *Come live with me. I won't interfere with you at all. You may come and go as you please. So we're not in love, so what? I've slept with men I didn't love before.*

She didn't have to be in Shanghai. She could be in New York. She could be anywhere she wanted to be. He resented that he was here with her, that he took everything she gave him and waited for more. He forced himself to be nice to her, not to snap at her for her vulgarities or carp at her for her messiness. The apartment had been a rubbish heap before he arrived, her clothes tossed on the floor if they were dirty, thrown across a sofa if they were clean. He had brought order, hung her clean clothes in the closet, put the dirty ones in the basket for the boy to take to the laundry, arranged her classical records alphabetically, lined her books up neatly behind the glass doors in the French bookcase. He made himself useful, tried to earn his keep.

He went into the bathroom and leafed through one of her sociology books while he sat on the toilet. She had no decent books. *Man in Developing Societies.* He sat on the toilet until his legs went numb. He washed his hands and face, peered at himself in the mirror, noted the hairless space at the sides of his forehead. A receding hairline. Was it possible he would end up resembling his father?

He went into the living room and looked at the lantern-lit junks on the river through the window. The apartment was on the eighth floor of the Blackpool Hotel, high above the noise of the city.

"Sigmund?" She was in the doorway, yawning.

"I can't sleep."

She stood at the window with him.

"They look like fireflies."

"I saw my father today."

"Oh."

"I don't ever want to see him again."

"Don't be stupid. He's your father. Do you want something to eat?"

"No."

"Then I'm going back to bed."

He heard the toilet flush and then she was back, sitting on the couch, her legs under her.

"He wanted to spend money on me, buy me a meal. I couldn't stand to look at him. I once thought he was God. Literally God. He got me out of Dachau. Nothing stopped him. No one. He was ferocious. I never saw him once show any sign of discouragement, any flagging of optimism, not even when the Jewish Committee told him he had paid three hundred English pounds for worthless visas, not even when we were all declared stateless and I had to report every day to Gestapo headquarters so we all wouldn't be deported. 'I'll take care of it, Sigmund,' he said. The Gestapo wanted copies of this and copies of that. I didn't know what they wanted. My father said, 'Here, these are the ones they want, today they'll let us leave.' But they were always the wrong ones. And every day he sent me to the Gestapo with the wrong papers, and every day I was beaten, and every day my father told me the next day would be better, he would get the right papers, and so every day I went, because I believed in him. He was the one who soothed me when I was hurt, who encouraged me to succeed, told me to be proud I was a Jew, that we were special Jews, not like the rest, that I could do anything, be anything. I thought he knew everything, that the world was wrong and he was right. But he's a fake, a liar, a fraud. Nothing is what he says it is. Nothing."

"What the hell do you want from him, Sigmund?"

"I don't know."

Chapter 23

December 8, 1941

The telephone call came before dawn, Edward's voice on the other end. "The Japanese have bombed Pearl Harbor, Sir Elias, and are making a move into the city."

"Has the *Petrel* left Shanghai yet?"

"Not yet."

"Have Jonathan bring the car."

Elias dressed quickly. The Americans, the great monolith of dogmatism and domination, battered by the wily Japanese. A quirk of coincidence, Elias planning Sybil's departure just as the Americans were about to join the fray. He thought fleetingly of the dead Americans (sad for them, but probably all to the good in the long run), then of Rachel. No time to call her. She probably already knew.

He awakened Sybil.

"I'll be back as soon as I can. Have Elizabeth dressed."

"It's so early, Elias. You said noon."

"The Japanese have bombed the Americans and are moving into the Settlements. Take the photo albums and my mother's letters. Leave everything else."

"I still don't understand why I have to leave. I don't want to, Elias. I don't know why anything has to change for us just because of the Japanese. You've been talking for months about the Japanese taking over, and it didn't happen, and you frightened me for nothing. Even if they have taken over, why would they care whether I stay or go? It's not fair to rush me like this. I promise, I'll leave next month. Elizabeth has a slight cold. It isn't wise for her to travel when she's ill."

"No argument, Sybil."

The car was parked in the drive, Jonathan, in his British Brigade uniform, in the driver's seat. He had been mobilized, he said as he started the car and wheeled down to the gate. "Spent thirteen days in a rain-soaked tent at the race course in the last mobilization waiting to fight Communists, and no one to fight. Went home without firing a shot. Probably be the same with the Japanese."

The streets were quiet, blanketed by a frosty mist, debris and papers kicked up from the sidewalks, swirled across tram tracks and sleeping beggars, plastered against the windows of the stores along Nanking Road. On the Bund there were thin lines of lime powder drawn across intersecting roads into the International Settlement. Some of the streets were barricaded. The Japanese cruiser *Idzuma* was anchored offshore. Except for the USS *Wake*, the American Navy boats were gone from the harbor. The only thing left to protect British interests was the gunboat HMS *Petrel* steaming up and down the Whangpoo. Across Soochow Creek, north of the Garden Bridge, helmeted Japanese soldiers waited in their fenced garrison. The signs, unmistakable for weeks, that the Japanese were about to make a move into the Settlements were now drawn on the morning streets and in the muddy waters of the harbor.

He should have made Sybil leave months ago. He shouldn't have listened to her pleading. All the indications were there. Signs on the American-owned businesses gone, employees and equipment moved to Manila or Hong Kong. The British Embassy advising its nationals to leave. At the end of October, he had for a few days convinced her of the coming danger and booked passage on the *Anhui* for her and the child, but at the last minute she refused to go. The *Anhui* left for England at the end of November, the last passenger ship out of Shanghai.

He had no illusions that Sybil had stayed for his sake. She liked Shanghai. Her life here was successful in ways that, as the wife of a Jew, it never could have been in England. She ignored her servants' thievery, the chaos of the city, the increasing belligerence of the Japanese. And even now when the warnings had been made concrete, she begged and cajoled, talked about Elias's lack of fairness, his false-alarming.

There was no longer any question about whether she should leave. The line between possible danger and outright catastrophe had been removed yesterday when Colonel Yazuka made a surprise visit to Elias's office. It was a short visit. He didn't suggest that he and Elias have a drink at the Shanghai Club or that Elias intercede with Jewish leaders in the United States on Japan's behalf. He merely bowed stiffly to Elias, and said, "I think your family should leave Shanghai at once."

They had now reached the Mansour Bank Building. Everything was the same. The large lobby, the marble walls. The lift gliding smoothly upward.

Edward was already in the office going through the files, a bonfire of paper and folders and envelopes blazing in the fireplace, the Kerman carpet spark-hit and smoldering, the smell of burnt ink and seared glue choking the air.

Elias threw off his coat and scarf. "Have you gotten rid of all references to American Jews?"

"Yes, sir."

"And correspondence with Chinese officials?"

"Yes, sir."

Elias opened the safe behind the mirrored door and began tossing fistfuls of documents into the fire. Bank statements, corporate ledgers, shareholders meetings, trade reports. Ash hung in the air, landed on Elias's hair, tasted bitter on his lips. Twisting curlicues of ash bronzed the wood walls and coated the windows. The room was a coffin, closed tight, the life squeezed out of it, every scrap of history that could prove its existence being cremated.

"I certainly hope this is necessary, Sir Elias. I would hate to think we were destroying everything to no purpose."

"I should have done it before."

By eight o'clock there was nothing left but debris. Edward was gone. Elias didn't wait for the lift, but sprinted down the stairs and into the street.

The car wasn't at the curb. There was no sign of Jonathan, and there were more barricades on the Bund. Elias started to run. He hadn't run since he was at Cambridge, wasn't wearing proper shoes. The soles of his feet were soft, no callus, the pavement not for running, no give, no elasticity, each step striking his back, shocking his shins, the world running alongside him, dead-ending and turning around, heading in directions they didn't want, rickshaws and automobiles a giant clot across the city, traffic and people congealing into one, being carried along, finding openings where they could, slipping through.

*   *   *

Sybil wasn't ready. She hadn't done what Elias told her to do. She was in her sitting room lying down.

"I have a headache."

"Where's Elizabeth?"

"With the amah. All the servants have gone, Elias. Just walked out the door."

"Is Elizabeth dressed?"

"I don't know. I'm not leaving."

"You are. Get up."

The child was in the kitchen, the amah washing jam off her face.

"Get her dressed," he said. "Pack something to eat, crackers, some fruit. Call a taxi for us and then you can go. Hurry."

Up the stairs again. Sybil was standing at the closet looking at her clothes. Elias pulled out a dress, a fur coat, a pair of shoes.

"Put these on."

"Oh, Elias."

She began to dress.

A few toiletries in an overnight bag, the packet of food, Elizabeth in Elias's arms, and they were soon in the taxicab, driving through the iron gate. An old taxi, the roof liner sloughy, a straggle of rust-stained strings cobwebbed from front windshield to back, the Chinese driver reeking of garlic. The engine sounded distressed, pinging, exhaust reeling from engine and undercarriage and smoked rubber into the open windows. The driver knew the streets, skirted the traffic on the Bund, drove through and around barricades, onto sidewalks, slipping into rat spaces, oblivious to the honking horns, his head and shoulders bouncing as if to some spherical music, the taxi a small planet spinning through a meteor-strewn sky.

Elizabeth was crying. Elias tried to soothe her. He didn't know how to soothe a child. The city had fallen. It was only nine-thirty. It surprised Elias how little time it had taken to undo their lives.

Captain Polkinhorn was waiting on the jetty. The wind was more frenzied now, whitecaps in the water like dropped handkerchiefs, the gunboat's hull grinding against the wharf as though trying to climb up out of the water.

"It's very good of you on such short notice to take my wife and child aboard."

"We have room for you, Sir Elias, if you change your mind."

"Please come with us, Elias. I don't want to go alone."

"I'll be with you by April, I promise."

He kissed her cheek and reached for Elizabeth, tried to take her in his arms one last time, but she had turned away from him, was looking past the seawall to a young woman getting out of a rickshaw at the foot of the quay.

"Someone else to come aboard?" Captain Polkinhorn said.

"No, no one else," Elias said, watching.

"Who is it, Elias?" Sybil said.

"I'm not sure."

"She's saying something. What is she saying?"

"'She's mine.'"

"Who is?"

"Elizabeth."

"Ridiculous. Don't let her near us, Elias. Keep her away."

"I'm doing you a favor, Sir Elias," the captain said. "I'm not interested in smuggling children out of Shanghai."

She had reached them now. It was Lilli, the bridegroom's sister. The one who had appeared at the end of the drive to mourn something precious she had lost. She was wearing a yeshiva student's black coat. It drooped off her shoulders, the sleeves covered her fingers, but the buttons strained across the front, the cloth molded around a bulging fullness.

Lilli had hold of the child now. They were whispering to each other in Yiddish. The child was laughing, an unrestrained full-bodied laugh that raised her up so that she was almost standing on Lilli's arms, so that the two of them seemed to be floating above the wharf, about to dance away over the river.

"She's mine," Lilli said. "You can't take her away. Everything can be explained."

"It doesn't matter."

"How can you say it doesn't matter? You should care that I'm taking her away from you. You should want to know the reason why."

There was nothing he wanted to say to her. The child was hers. There was no argument to be made, no bartering or negotiating, no contractual revisions. Hers. It didn't matter how Sybil found the child, how Lilli lost her. It happened. That was enough. He didn't want to look at her. He was pained by his part in it, the unwilling abettor, the one who held the ladder while the thief climbed into the house.

"The child stays," the captain said.

Sybil was weeping.

"You'll have to decide now if you're coming aboard, Lady Sybil," the captain said.

"She is," Elias answered.

"No, Elias. Please."

One of the seamen took Sybil's overnight case, and there were no words after that. A quick kiss from Elias, a tearful wave to the child, and Sybil was on the gangplank, stepping carefully along the jaggy wood, rising higher and higher until she was on the deck, leaning over the rail and waving.

There was a wanton, untamed quality to the scene. As if this were the night before the end of creation. A purple sky and the end of the world. A scurrying city, the Japanese in their garrisons, the beggars in their holes, the wealthy taipans like himself waiting to see what happens next.

The ship moved away from the wharf, a single gliding motion, as though a hand were beneath its flat bottom smoothing it along, making way, grunts of steam spiraling from the single stack, the masts tremulous sticks in the wind.

Lilli was still there, still holding the child, as if there were more to say, more explanations, excuses, reasons. And he didn't care, didn't want to know, because everything was moving, the gunboat, the river chop, the wind like escaping steam in a kettle cascading in linear bursts from the east, and what could be so important about whether a child was hers or not, or whether Sybil stole the child or bought her or found her? Everything in Shanghai would change now. Even the shape of the land would be different.

A bright blaze and stark rumbling from the shore. Rattles of light crossed over the water toward the gunboat. The masts fell first, a fragile falling, dainty and polite, and lay crosswise across the upper deck. The ship's silhouette flattened. It was all very slow, a resignation, a bending at the water line, huge gaps, and then the explosion. Whump, whump, whump. Fiery splinters skated along the water, and the gunboat shuddered, as though reluctant to die, then floated free of itself. Flaming pieces, a starburst on the surface of the river, torched the sky.

Elias dove into the water, felt the icy lick under his jacket, and began to swim.

*　　*　　*

"Twenty-three units in the Volunteer Corps," Commander Weiss said, "and no sign that any of them have been called out. There's no use in fifty Jewish boys dying for nothing. Get rid of your rifles and ammunition and run."

Sigmund headed north through the cat's cradle of blockaded streets. Patterning smoke and scudding clouds of throat-choking ash painted a slaty blanket over the solid mass of cars and trucks and people heading away from the river, going somewhere else, pushing, shoving, trampling. A stage set lit by burning ships. A mountain, everyone aslant, losing balance, being sucked backward for every forward foot. Sigmund could see the roof of the Blackpool Hotel above the crazed streets, but couldn't reach it.

A rifle was aimed at his chest, a Japanese officer gazing intently at the Star of David on the jacket of his uniform.

"Shanghai Volunteer Corps," Sigmund said.

"Spy," the officer replied.

* * *

Heinrich awoke to the boom of cannons. The Chinese girl who had been in the bed when he fell asleep was gone, and the windows were alight, rays of starry orange and glazed purple shooting into the room. Wakefulness was slow. Awareness pricked his consciousness limpingly, unwillingly. Phantasmagorical shapes, as from a fevered dream, floated across his vision.

He sat up. Knowledge poured in.

The Japanese were on the move. Like bees, they had come out of their hives and were swarming. He would go home to his apartment, wait it out, see which direction was best, analyze the circumstances. He was very good at analyzing circumstances, at maneuvering, at finding the correct answer to any question. That was his usefulness. He had always thought his success lay in his intellect, but it was his wily suborning, his coldness in adversity, his analysis and deductions that distinguished him, set him apart.

He had had too much to drink. He was heavy in his movements, plodding, the dullness still there in his head. Shoes and socks were under the bed. Trousers, shirt, tie, vest, jacket draped over a chair. His hat. He had lost his hat.

He stepped out into the hall. All the doors were open, the men patrons gone, the Russian and Chinese girls running half-dressed down the stairs.

Out on the street it was pandemonium. He buttoned his coat and began walking quickly toward the north, away from the Bund. On Avenue Roi Albert, Japanese troops suddenly appeared. An officer pulled a man out of the crowd, examined his identification papers. Heinrich wasn't worried. He had nothing to be worried about. The man was obviously a refugee. The beaten look. The downward gaze. Heinrich was not that man. He could look anyone in the face, match wits with anyone, talk his way out of anything. He patted his tie and kept his gaze steady and his back straight. He had always reminded Sigmund to keep his posture erect, that a man who yielded to a bent spine was a man who would lose.

He remembered where his hat was. In the brothel's living room, that grand space fitted out like a cheap Russian drawing room, noxious clouds of perfume caught in the silk lampshades and velvet drapes, trapped in the shadowy swags above the windows. His hat would be ruined. A fine felt, hand stitched.

Soldiers encircled him. He was startled. Had he been dreaming? About what? His hat?

He held out his wallet. "I have no papers. No need to bother with me at all."

The liquor had worn off, his mind was clear. He instructed himself. Precise thoughts. Casual conversation.

"I'm Heinrich Strauss. German. An ally of the Japanese. I have no papers, but it's easily explained. To be stateless is no mark of inferiority. It's a political moment in history. I'm not a refugee either. Refugees are what's left when the corpses are carried away. I have good connections in Shanghai—friends, all of them conciliatory and willing to work with the Japanese in any way they can."

He was put in an open truck, dumped into it like an old rug, thrown against those who had no friendly connections or precise thoughts or casual conversation.

* * *

Moses was out of breath when he reached the synagogue. Aaron was already there, waiting in the street.

"Did you get it?" Moses said.

"No. There are soldiers in the sanctuary. What if they find it?"

"Where did you put it?"

"On a *shtender*, under *Maimonides.*"

"I'll get it."

"Leave it. It's just a book. Anyone can have a book."

"Not a book like that. What row?"

"Thirty-three, in the middle. The *shtender* sags to the right."

Moses walked into the cold room. A Japanese officer was trying to organize a line. The older worshipers were silent, but the Mir Yeshiva was here in force, the last yeshiva out of Poland, a small army, eighty at least, eighty-five counting the rabbis, the students talking and gesturing and asking questions. A line? What kind of line? Where do you want the line? At the door? Near the *bimah*? Is it a line with two people across or three? A line with only one across will snake into the street. Two people across will bump into the desks. Should the line go closer to the *bimah* or toward the rabbi's study? The *bimah* will fall over with the pressure. The study door is locked. Should we open it? An open door creates a draft, people are sick with colds, the sick will grow sicker. Neat lines? A neat line can mean many things. Is it a neatness like the pages of a book? How can a book be neat? Pages shift, you turn them over, they face another direction. The officer was torn apart with questions, fragments coming from everywhere, answers before questions, comments and commentary, logic and reasoning. He tried to gather everyone up, to herd them like sheep, but they wouldn't be herded, slipped out of his grasp, he couldn't find the center. It was like a drop of oil, push it this way, and it bleeds out somewhere else.

Moses found row thirty-three. *Maimonides. The Guide for the Perplexed.* Beneath it was the stiff blue binder. *Detonators and Explosive Devices.* He slipped the binder beneath his coat and, with the walls echoing with the cunning sound of obfuscation and the noisome lilt of Talmudic debate ringing from rafter to rafter, walked out the door.

*   *   *

Rachel didn't know where Sigmund was. No one answered at the Volunteer Corps offices. And when she tried to get through to Elias at the Mansour Bank, no one answered there either. She heard one short radio transmission about the Japanese bombing Pearl Harbor, and then the radio went dead.

She left her apartment and stepped into the maelstrom of the streets. The press of people was like a blanket thrown over her head. She stood on tiptoes and looked for landmarks, navigated by buildings, that spire to that cupola, then to the right, then to the left, a glimpse of wharf, then to the right again.

The Cathay Hotel. The door was barred. No cablegrams to New York. The Japanese had taken over all the cable and telegraph lines. From the Cathay she made it over to the offices of the Chinese Government Radio Administration. The door was blocked there, too, a sign on the building proclaiming it the property of the Japanese Empire. *Do not remove furniture. Do not remove vehicles.*

She couldn't feel her feet any longer, but her legs still moved and the streets were beginning to clear. Everyone had given up, gone back to where they started from, or been arrested. Elias was probably at home. Why would he be anywhere else? He was too smart to have ventured out into the streets.

*   *   *

The gate was open, no automobiles in the drive. Rachel rang the bell, heard chimes inside but no swish of cloth shoes coming to answer. She pushed the door open. She had never been in Elias's house before. A silent entry. Marble floors. Chinese screens.

"Elias?"

Two steps down into a reception area. A round table with a vase of wilted flowers, a wall of long, narrow windows, family photographs on the grand piano.

There were always at least seven servants in every British house in Shanghai. In a mansion such as this there should be twelve, maybe even fifteen. No sign of even one.

The library door was open. A wall of books, a claw-footed desk, a leather couch. French doors to a back rose garden. To the right of the stairs the garden room. To the right of that a ballroom, straight chairs arranged like fence posts against the walls.

"Is anyone home?"

Someone at the top of the stairs. A window at the figure's back, the shimmery radiance of a fire-licked sky turning face and features into a mosaic of beaded light. Rachel moved out of the glare. It was Lilli, hair like molten copper, a small, giggly child in her arms.

Chapter 24

Afternoon, December 8, 1941

The trucks kept coming, spilling their captured prey onto the sidewalk where they were prodded by Japanese soldiers up a flight of stairs to a room in the Municipal Council building. When Heinrich arrived there had been room to move around and chairs to sit in. People were polite. *Excuse me. Pardon me. Do you by chance have the time?* It was now an hour later, and there were so many people the walls vibrated and the too-high windows were clouded with exhaled breath. Heinrich gave his chair to an elderly Chinese woman. The low-lying stink of putrid air was somewhat lessened standing up.

Sigmund was sitting on the floor, head down, legs drawn up to his chin.

Elias was here. Someone had found a chair for him and he sat hunched over, shoes gone, the sleeves of his suit stained with oil. His wife was dead. Drowned, someone said, when the *Petrel* was sunk. Elias had jumped into the water to try to save her. Elias, the aristocrat, leaping into the flaming waters of the Whangpoo. It mystified Heinrich. What was the impulse that made a man turn his own life into a commodity to be spent for someone else's benefit when this was the only life there was, there was no other and no hope of another beyond this? Heroes were universally admired, but they secretly infuriated Heinrich. Heinrich wouldn't have thought of Elias as one, but Sigmund had always shown signs of it. He always reacted without thought, didn't treasure his own life. He gloried in despair, searched for meaning in selfless action. He would have been a doctor (saved only by Hitler's malign intervention), handling diseased flesh, touching it, examining it, dipping his fingers into its rot, when it was clear he wasn't up to its rigors, had no objectivity, saw no difference between the burden of his own body and that of others.

"If you had asked me, I would have told you that wearing a Jewish uniform is dangerous," Heinrich said to him now. "If it had been a British brigade they would never have arrested you. Believe me when I tell you they won't keep you here. They're looking for spies. Anyone with half an eye can see you're innocent of any wrongdoing. What have you done but march around in a uniform? I guarantee we'll be released before supper. One must look at the psychology of a conqueror's mind, Sigmund. A city like Shanghai is hard to govern. A little terror, a few arrests, is good for instilling respect and enforcing discipline. The Japanese are merely demonstrating their newfound power. Look around you. There's no pattern. It's not like Germany. If they wanted to harm us, there would be a pattern. This is only a temporary situation."

"Can't you for once admit that what's happening is beyond your control?"

"Beyond my control? What do you know about it? Do you know what you're talking about? I have more influence at my fingertips than you will ever dream of. I know people who with one word can set armies on the march. You don't know half the things I am capable of. You are a spoiled child, Sigmund. I spoiled you by shielding you. I'm convinced of my guilt in that regard."

"You shielded me from nothing. I went to Dachau without your help."

"You would have died there if not for me."

"I wouldn't have been there in the first place if you had exerted your authority with Mutti and made her leave Germany when there was still time. You didn't stand up to her."

"Your mother is delicate. I deferred to that delicacy. And it was her pampering that kept you an infant, prevented you from developing properly. You were her beautiful boy, the anointed one. But I invested everything in you, gave you the best I had, hoped to mold you into something worthwhile. I see now that you are an impossible subject for molding. Stubborn. Stubbornness is a form of defeatism. No one is anointed, Sigmund. No one. A person makes his way by his wits."

Another truck arrived. Refugees in mildewed coats, British sailors in brine-soaked uniforms, Chinese women with slicked hair and ankle-straddling gowns, Chinese men with chin hairs and notched teeth, gray-suited diplomats holding tight to leather valises. There was no room for another body, but somehow they squeezed in, flattening themselves into a jigsaw puzzle of legs and arms and heads, the whole mass like a wheat field rippling in the breeze.

The Japanese Embassy was in an adjoining room, the silhouettes of desks and filing cabinets canted shadows on the frosted glass. Heinrich pushed his way through the crowd, let himself be carried from one faintly yielding spot to another until he reached the embassy door. He would put an end to it now. What purpose was there in being held here? He would speak to someone in charge, make them aware of who he was. He would tell them about Sigmund's fragile psyche, advise them that the boy's state of mind was perilously close to disintegration.

"I'd like to speak to the officer in charge," he said to the soldier guarding the door.

The soldier put one hand out and gave Heinrich a shove. It was a surprise, the slam of the man's flat palm against his chest, then the sensation of falling backwards, of wanting to hold onto something, of waiting for the crack of his head against a hard floor. But there was no room to fall. He was caught by a cushion of soft bellies, felt the poke of hard-boned limbs, swayed back and forth a few times, and, like a self-righting punching bag, bounced up as straight as a picture frame.

In late afternoon a Japanese official made an announcement:

"All civilians will receive a slip of paper and may go home. You will be notified later where to register as enemy aliens."

The solid squirming mass of people now gradually broke apart. Those qualifying for the slip of paper formed a line separate from the rest. The line stretched around the room four times, a loose-limbed shuffling line that jerked and stopped an inch at a time. Heinrich looked around for Sigmund, but couldn't remember where he had last seen him and couldn't move from his place in line to look for him. The official said the slips of paper were for civilians. He didn't say what someone in the uniform of the Jewish brigade would get. If Heinrich had known there was to be a distinction made between civilians and others, he would have given Sigmund his suit jacket to cover his uniform, he would have pulled him into line with him, he would have done something.

It was dark by the time Heinrich received his slip of paper.

He teetered on one of the now-empty chairs to see if he could spot Sigmund's blond hair, but was knocked to the floor by the crush of people trying to get to the door and onto the stairs and out of the building. He scrambled to his feet, but was then caught in another onslaught, this one more desperate, as if some rumor of impending disaster had run through the room. He felt himself moving toward the stairs, propelled by some unseen engine, his legs useless, his feet akin to a tap dancer's, shooting out from beneath his knees as though there were a rhythm to the random foot stamp, as though he had mastery over where he went and how he got there.

He was on the stairs now, his feet sliding from step edge to step edge, his arms pinned. Two Chinese women fainted. An old man collapsed. There was no stopping, not to breathe, not to holler, not even to die. It was a river heading downstream, people caught in it, being carried along like flotsam. A corpse could have been swept down the stairs and no one would have noticed. Heinrich tried to climb out, but the tide was too strong. All he could do was hold on and let himself be flung like a broken chair down the stairs and into the street.

Chapter 25

Sigmund and forty-five British sailors, five Americans, and a balding White Russian furrier from Minsk were taken by truck to Kiangwan Prison, a gray stone building a few miles north of Hongkew, near the railroad station. There were no accusations, no charges, no reasons given. They were brought through the gate, marched across a muddy field to an office and told to hand over their valuables (Sigmund's last valuable, the gold watch Heinrich gave him for his twenty-first birthday, had been confiscated at Dachau), after which they were each handed a metal cup, a rice bowl, and chopsticks, and led back across the field to a barracks building and locked in.

* * *

In Dachau Sigmund had been starved and beaten, but the barracks had been clean, cots neatly made, white-tiled shower room scrubbed every day, the whole a testament to the Germanic ideal of *gesunde Wohn*—healthy living. By contrast, the barracks in Kiangwan were mud-floored, the beds lumpy damp sacks of straw, the corrugated tin roof seamed and sieved, so that cold wind barged in at will. Lice knit themselves into the threads of the rag blankets. Rats shambled across the roof at night, the drum of their feet on the tin like the wild tapping of a thousand sticks.

The British sailors wrote letters and griped among themselves about having to march to meals (three scoops of rice a day with a few morsels of fish thrown in), about eating standing up, about wet that seeped into shoes and turned to ice.

The Americans played cards and told each other jokes. Sometimes they sang songs that made their eyes glisten. The leader of the Americans, a redhead named George (he was covered with freckles, and his teeth were as long and white as piano keys) spoke English with a soft, slanty accent. Sigmund heard him tell Vasily, the furrier, that he was from Atlanta, Georgia, and had a dog and a girlfriend and was going to buy a boat when he got home.

Sigmund kept to himself. What was the point of joking and laughing and singing when he knew they were all going to die, when the knowledge was in the air, as strong and true as if it were written on the Japanese flag at the entrance to the prison?

*   *   *

On an icy morning at the end of December, Sigmund and Vasily and the five Americans were taken out of the barracks, given shovels, and told to dig a trench on a frozen piece of dirt not too far from the barracks. The spot might once have been a vegetable garden. Shriveled plants still clung to the earth by brown, twisted roots.

Three Japanese soldiers armed with bayonets and rifles watched as the men dug. The Americans weren't singing now or telling jokes. They didn't look at each other as they dug. Vasily dug as though he were being paid. Sigmund dug methodically, painfully, each thrust of the shovel accompanied by a gasp. The trench grew slowly, but by midmorning it was deep and wide.

The guards brought hot tea. Vasily was the only one who took a cup. Sigmund and the Americans stood staring into the pit as though they had dropped something valuable into it in the digging.

Sigmund had gone slightly mad in Dachau dreaming of death, but it never came. Here is where it will be, he told himself. He now waited for the shot, the bayonet thrust, but the soldiers stepped past him, tied the five Americans into neat bundles and shoved them into the pit.

Screams curled upward. Sigmund was sure he had been here before, had stood over a pit like this one, had heard the same screams. What should he do? Jump into the pit? Cover the Americans with his own body?

Vasily put a shovel in Sigmund's hand.

"We have to put the dirt back," Vasily said.

"They'll die."

"Of course."

The Americans' bodies had changed the volume of the pit. It took less work to fill the space. Each shovelful slid easily from one place to another. When all the dirt had been replaced, Sigmund got on his knees and began to smooth the surface the way a farmer might after planting radishes.

"Enough, Sigmund," Vasily said.

Had George been in that spot over there where a wet cold floated upward? Was that George's voice worming its way up through clods and stones and bits of ice, his face beneath that last shivery layer of dirt, his breath causing the gentle rising that was as tentative as the flutter of a bird's wing nearest the edge of the pit?

"Get up, Sigmund," Vasily said. "It's finished."

The Japanese soldiers laughed, but Sigmund kept smoothing, rushing to keep ahead of the grave's little cave-ins, hurrying to quiet its convulsions, not content until there was nothing more than a bumpy rash on the dirt's surface.

* * *

On a blustery evening in March of 1942, as they waited in line to receive their bowl of rice, Vasily said, "My friends have come, Sigmund. It's time to go."

As the searchlight swept across the lunar scape of rocks and ice, they ran toward the fence on the western boundary where two dark figures on the other side were working at the ice-clad mesh with wire cutters. A section fell away in a cascade of broken metal. Sigmund looked back once at the place where the Americans were buried, then stepped through the breach to the other side.

Chapter 26

March 18, 1942

Dear Dad,

I don't know if you'll ever get this letter. I'm here, still alive, money nearly gone. The Japs are now controlling everything—every day a new edict, a new restriction. We're up to our asses in restrictions, and I can't get my damn money out of my own account, except for five hundred Shanghai a week, which is twelve dollars fifty cents, for which they line us up in the cold outside the banks so that we're half frozen by the time our turn comes. Twelve fifty a week and the little I had in cash will keep me in my apartment a while longer. For how much longer, I don't know.

Only the damn French, with their Vichy protection, go on unmolested. And, of course, although to a lesser extent, the White Russians and the Germans and the Chinese. The rest of us are turning into something subhuman, scrambling and scraping to keep ourselves alive.

Pedicab and rickshaw rates go up hourly, so except for the tram when I have to go to the office or the heime, I depend on foot power. The French have been able to keep their automobiles, but have had to resort to charcoal gas instead of gasoline, since that's being hoarded by the Chinese and resold on the black market for American dollars. So now, besides the corpses and garbage, which the Japanese don't seem to care about picking up off the streets, the sky is full of black fumes that suck the oxygen out of the air and turn everything and everybody a dirty, gritty gray.

There's an American and British Relief here to help foreign nationals, but with funds from overseas cut off they're as bad off as the people they're trying to help. All they can do is hand out sacks of wormy rice and heads of wilted lettuce.

I now have to have a pass to go to the heime in Hongkew, which the Japs have turned into a military preserve by dumping radio transmitters and arms caches there, and my poor Jews, down to one meal a day and starving, are even more isolated than before. The staff at the heime are now working without pay, and the refugees are selling their last few belongings to buy food. Our tailoring shop turns Red Cross grain sacks into shirts and dresses. You can tell whether someone is a refugee when you see the faint imprint of the Red Cross on their clothes.

Since the Japanese takeover there have been notices in the newspapers, "Enemy Aliens Must Register." The idea of being categorized galled me. I decided not to register. Then last week a Japanese official showed up at my office. He didn't take off his hat or overcoat, didn't accept my offer of a cup of tea, merely said, "Register." I told him I didn't think I would. He said he thought I'd better. I asked what would happen if I didn't. "Bad," he said. "Very bad. Spies go to jail." Very comical. But also menacing. In a cryptic sort of way. So I went to the Municipal Council and registered. It was ridiculous. They asked me if I had guns, if I knew any spies. They took my shortwave radio and told me not to change my address.

We've been able to get some funds from the New York Joint through the Red Cross, which is helping keep us afloat. But month to month we're not sure what funds we'll have, so we're cutting services and food to the barest. Could you check and see whether Adler got my letter? He's to try to shake my donors up for more money. I don't have money to buy postage, and wouldn't want to put the names down on paper even if I did, in case the Japs are opening my letters. We can now send cables through the Red Cross, but limited to twenty-five words. What could I ever possibly say in twenty-five words?

Despite all, I'm still trying to do what I can here. I hope money arrives soon. Same address.

Love, kisses, and hugs,

Rachel

P.S. Tell Mother the usual and give her my love,

R.

Chapter 27

Rachel kept to the open doorway of the tram. The tram jerked and shuddered. Blasty winds and skirls of rain pelted her bare legs. There were empty seats, but she didn't sit down. In January she had sat down next to a Russian woman wearing a fur coat and didn't notice the lice scuttling along the silken shreds until too late.

She got off the tram at Seward Road and crossed the trash-littered street to the gray building on the corner, its rickety balcony draped with laps of sodden paper banners from the Chinese herb store next-door. It was raining harder now, beggars and refugees and pedicabs and bicycles slopping through brackish gutters the size of small lakes. Refugees walked with newspapers draped over their heads, soggy sheaves of melting newsprint trailing behind them.

The relief committee meeting was in Dr. Blau's dental office on the first floor. Four walls, a cement floor, and a window looking out onto the street. A 1925 extraction chair (large, bloated pads of leather covering seat and back, the tilting mechanism broken, the stamped-metal footrest dragging on the floor, the sliding side tray for instruments missing, the velvet headrest merely a few plush strings on hard metal), and a dental engine (its treadle like the treadle on a sewing machine), both the gift of a retired missionary dentist from Xian, occupied the center of the room. On a chipped enamel workbench against the wall was the set of dental tools Dr. Blau had carried in his suitcase when he fled Munich in 1940. The vulcanizer, sterilizer, and X-ray machine donated by the Joint were on the floor. A few hard chairs were scattered around the room.

Rachel had a note somewhere in her file. *Blau. No anesthesia since last December. Get him some whiskey.* She hadn't yet. Whiskey was in as short supply and as expensive as nitrous oxide.

Dr. Blau, a slight man, meek, undemanding, easily outshouted, was at the sink washing his hands with lye soap, his fingers red and chapped, the skin peeling away from the nails, the nails themselves ridged and soft.

There was a rougy stain on the wall behind the sink (blood splashes from jaw dissections), slivers of jawbone in a limpid solution on a tray table, stacks of dentures taken from corpses heaped in a bucket on the floor. Everything was in disarray. Spotted, finger-stained, phlegm-clotted towels had been flung around the room, debris from muddy shoes had left tracks on the cement floor.

Rachel wrote in her notepad, *Get help for Dr. Blau.*

"Jesus, it's cold." She poured herself a cup of tea from the tin pot on the stove next to the sink, then sat down in the extraction chair.

Abe Milstein, the representative from Ward Road Heim, thin and gray, his bulgy, goiterous eyes the size of pigeon eggs, was sitting in one of the hard chairs next to Elias Mansour. (She hadn't seen Elias since the memorial service for Sybil four months ago; his gauntness now shocked her.) Moses Zuckerman, who had taken Sid Brownstein's place from the Seward Heim (Brownstein died last month of typhoid) was standing near the sink. A hard-eyed man with a perpetually graveled expression, as though he would be elsewhere, as though the company in which he found himself didn't suit him. And what did she hear about him from Dr. Lewin in the Alcock Heim? That he was in the resistance in Poland? *Be careful,* Dr. Lewin said. *He's done things. What kind of things?* Rachel asked him. *Just be careful,* Dr. Lewin replied.

Fuck that. She couldn't throw out healthy men who were willing to help relief efforts any more than she could throw out meat that wasn't kosher.

"First order of business: we need money," Rachel said.

"Where's the money we were supposed to get from the Joint?" Milstein said.

"We have enough for another month, but that's it. The U.S. has a new law, something to do with trading with the enemy."

"Who's the enemy here?"

"You asked me about money, I'm answering you. I don't make the rules. I'm just reporting. What about you, Elias?"

"The Japanese locked my accounts. I had some gold bars in a strongbox at my office, but they've locked me out of there, too. They took my automobile."

"How about the Russian Jews?" Milstein said. "There are some very rich Russians. Let them give."

"I asked Jacob Rossitsky if he'd speak to his people about it," Dr. Blau said.

"What about the cracked wheat?" Rachel said. "The Red Cross ship arrived and the wheat was on it and now it's rotting in a warehouse on the Bund. The Japanese won't release it. I tried every damn thing I know to convince them they should, but they won't. We need that wheat." She tapped her foot for emphasis. "Well? No one has any ideas? So what was the purpose of this meeting?

"I can make inquiries," Milstein said.

"Inquiries? What about? I've already made inquiries. We need money. We need that wheat. It's very simple. How many ways do I have to explain it?

"Rossitsky says he can get things done," Dr. Blau said.

"He likes to hear himself talk," Milstein said.

"I have some dollars," Elias offered.

"How many?" Rachel asked him.

"Five hundred."

"Not enough. Keep it for yourself."

Rachel put the empty cup on the arm of the extraction chair and stood up.

"Look, if anyone knows how we can get the wheat, then we'll have a meeting. Right now I'm cold and wet and tired and hungry and my time may not be worth anything, but I'd rather sit in a chair in my apartment and stare at the walls than listen to this shit."

*   *   *

Four months without a word from Sigmund, and when Rachel got back to her apartment there he was, on her bed, sleeping.

She shook him and he rolled toward her.

"The door was unlocked."

"Well, you can't stay here. You'll have to find another place to live. I can't feed you. I don't have enough money. I looked for you. No one in the heime had seen you or knew what happened to you. You could have let me know where you were."

"I was in Kiangwan."

"Well, I'm really sorry about that, Sigmund, and I wouldn't kick you out if I could afford you, and I know terrible things must have happened to you there, but terrible things are happening to everyone in Shanghai. Did they hurt you?"

"No."

"Look, I don't want to be mean, but I can't take on another burden right now. It's different than it was before."

She sat down on the edge of the bed. The muscle in his calf jumped at her touch and the brightness was gone from his eyes, the color mulled to a watery gray. Other than that, there were no signs of mistreatment, no healing wounds or scars. He was probably better off in Kiangwan than he would have been in the heim with food rations reduced and disease rates soaring.

"You know I like you, Sigmund. It isn't love, I won't pretend to that, but I like you. I was irritated when you disappeared, but I got over it. Now I'm irritated by other things. I'm fighting bureaucracies day and night. There's no milk. There's no flour. I haven't seen butter in a month. The Japanese squeeze me a little bit more every day. They want me to slink away, to forget about the Jews. Everyone argues with everyone else about who did what, who said what. I send begging letters to every agency I can think of and get no replies. The money's dried up or caught somewhere or no one cares about the Shanghai Jews anymore. And I'm infuriated by everything. Big things and little things. I hate everyone, Sigmund. I can't stand people. I'm completely helpless and enraged. You've come back at the wrong time. I'll fix you something to eat, but you've got to leave in the morning."

He rolled back onto his side, his face now in profile.

"Let me stay," he murmured.

Chapter 28

Heinrich tried to prevent the meeting. **"Moses is hard and unyielding,"** he told Li T'ien. "Unpredictable. A dangerous intermediary."

"If he has a proposal, I want to hear it. Are you afraid of him?"

"Afraid? How can I be afraid of such a man? He has no power, no position . . ."

"Then what?"

"There are rumors about his past. He's not an eccentric, not a religious zealot, but he has doubtful allegiances. I don't trust him."

"Trust has no meaning to me. Business has meaning."

"He doesn't think of business in the same way you do. He would be an unsuitable partner."

"Invite him."

*　*　*

Heinrich stood at the door out of the way, Moses was seated on the earth-hued leather couch, Li T'ien at his desk. There had been no conversation when Moses arrived. He strode into the room, as though he had been there before, and now, without letting Li T'ien speak first, began.

"There is wheat in a godown on a quay near the Bund. It belongs to the American Joint Distribution Committee. The Japanese won't release it. There is also rice in the godown. If you provide the Jewish underground with a truck to load the wheat, you can take the rice."

"We don't need your permission to take the rice," Li T'ien said.

"Then we'll steal a truck and take the rice as well as the wheat and give you nothing."

"If you do that, there will be no chance of cooperation between us in the future."

"You asked for my help before and I refused it. You can have it now. We can help each other."

"In what way?"

"Aaron Chernofsky is expert in explosives. He memorized the book. He went into the fields and practiced detonations the way a pianist practices scales. Many things can be accomplished with explosives—diversion, shock, destruction."

Heinrich moved closer to Li T'ien's side. "Aaron can't be controlled."

"I can control him," Moses said.

"You permit his eccentricities," Heinrich said.

"He looks to me for direction."

"After the fact. His impulses are reactionary. His Talmudic training has rendered him useless."

"He can be shaped. I know how to do it. I know his mind. He's like an idiot who has suddenly discovered the world and is intent on itemizing and categorizing and arranging it."

"And I say he's useless."

"He's only useless in the way a diamond is useless; it has no value except for what it can be sold or bartered for."

"You describe his abilities well," Li T'ien said.

"I *know* him well."

"We should wait," Heinrich said.

"We will do it now or the wheat will rot," Moses said.

"Heinrich doesn't trust you," Li T'ien said.

"And I don't trust him."

"How much rice is there?"

"An estimate . . . half a ton."

Li T'ien nodded.

"This is a mistake," Heinrich said.

*   *   *

The rice was piled along the far wall of the godown. The wheat, in burlap sacks, lay in a slattery heap beneath a tarpaulin, skid marks and footprints in the spilled wheat like the scat of wild animals.

Zhong Tu pulled one of the trucks close to the warehouse wall. The other truck was parked close behind, Li T'ien's body guard driving, six coolies standing in the truck's bed. Aaron and Moses and Sigmund had arrived early, Vasily a half hour later with five others, all young refugees.

Li T'ien and Heinrich got out of the truck.

"How much time do we have?" Moses asked Li T'ien.

"An hour."

The men started to work, carrying the sacks through the godown door, then heaving them up into the bed of the truck while Li T'ien gave instructions to the coolies. Heinrich stood silently beside him and listened. His Chinese was improving. He had been an excellent student at university, had mastered any subject presented and was sure he would be fluent in time. University classes. What did they teach him that was of any importance? That Hegel was a rational man? That Goethe said the personality is everything? No. Rationality and personality were nothing. It was the will that was important. Without an indestructible will, a man was an empty shell.

He watched now the way Sigmund was struggling to carry a bag, wheat dust powdering his padded jacket and thickening the runnels of sweat on his cheeks. He carried the bag a few wavery steps, dropped it, stopped to rest, then dragged it along the cement floor to the opening of the godown where one of the coolies took it from him and pitched it into the bed of the truck.

Hannah should have been the son and Sigmund the daughter. She wasn't worn down by every challenge. Her frailty in Hamburg had been merely a part of adolescence. She had Heinrich's spark. She wasn't afraid to do what needed to be done to survive.

"Remember, you take only the wheat," Li T'ien said.

"We're not here to take anything but what belongs to us," Moses replied.

Aaron said. "The Talmud says that once you commit one crime, the second one is easier, and the third one takes no thought at all."

Chapter 29

March 1942

Mitzui was waiting for Lilli in the street. He was not in his uniform today. Today he wore a western suit. From a distance he had a pleasant face, his nose foreshortened but not flat, a creased upper lip, a narrow chin. He held out his hand for the week's money. His fingers, delicate as a woman's, flicked the bills as he put them in his wallet. His share ravaged what Lilli earned, leaving barely enough for milk and rice.

"The baby will be here soon," she said. "My legs can't carry me miles through the city and Shaya has grown too big for the basket. There will be no more money for you, no more squeeze."

"When you have the baby, you will be back," he said.

*   *   *

Through the French doors Lilli could see Shaya on her rocking horse beneath the shade of the plane trees. The sun was a butterfly flame, flitting in and out of the dried plants. Tall grasses, feather stalks topped with cottony boles as delicate as spider webs, flared like small torches. The trees struggled on, conserving water by dropping leaves, but didn't rot or fall. They braided their branches and hovered protectively over the roof of the house and out into the grove that stretched past the gardener's shed to the gabled roof of the neighboring mansion.

Elias sold the kitchen stove two weeks ago. The place where it stood against the wall was as greasy as an oiled pan. (Lilli now cooked their meals in the ruined rose garden, lighting a handful of coals beneath a clay pot, then fanning the embers with a straw whisk until they glowed.) He sold the piano for twenty-five American dollars. Sofas went for fifteen, artwork and porcelains for bags of rice and tins of milk. In Shaya's bedroom only the large walnut bed with its flower-carved headboard remained. The French bureau was gone, as well as the bird's-eye maple wardrobe and the brass hangers and satin quilts and percale sheets. Sounds were magnified now that the dampening furniture and heavy rugs were gone. Whispers were as shrill as shouts, the slide of Lilli's slippered feet on the bare floors as loud as the rustling of trees in a brisk wind. The house was a skeleton, the timbery frame, bereft of flesh and skin, moaning and creaking.

Elias couldn't afford to pay for the water in the flush toilets in the bathrooms. Lilli had watched him dig a privy where the roses once bloomed. He used the shovel awkwardly at first, but then got the rhythm of it and soon was measuring and nailing boards as if he had been constructing privies all his life. He could have left Shanghai when the Swiss were still able to exchange American and British diplomats for Japanese. He wouldn't go and his last chance to escape had vanished along with the furniture. He behaved as if nothing had changed. He dressed in the morning as if he were going to his office in the Mansour building, drank a cup of tea, ate a small portion of rice, then opened the front door to the line of people waiting to ask his advice, beg for food, or merely weep. In the afternoons he was in his study writing articles for the underground newsletter (distributed hand to hand at night and tacked to the walls of buildings in the morning).

She didn't know how it happened that she was here. She didn't remember the first day. Had she planned it? She didn't know. But she had found herself in the house, wandering through the rooms. And then Lady Sybil died in the explosion of the Petrel and Elias, sunk in misery, was hardly aware of Lilli's presence. By the time he had recovered there was no question of her leaving.

She prepared the meals (Elias forgot to eat if she didn't remind him), made sure he got enough rest (she limited the number of people he saw each day), rationed the amount of rice he could give away to half a cup per person.

"We have barely enough food left for ourselves," she told him. "You won't be able to help anyone if you starve to death."

Shaya's shiny laugh rang across the yard. What would Mama say about Shaya, this child that Lilli loved so much, or about Elias, as dear to her as a brother, who sold the furniture in his house a stick at a time so they could all eat? What would she say about the child yet to be born?

Mama's letters had stopped, but Lilli's to her continued, thrown like confetti into the whirlwind.

Chapter 30

April 1942

Moses had just left the bicycle shop when he spotted Lilli coming out of a grocer's on East Nanjing Road, holding Shaya by the hand and carrying a small tin of milk.

"Moses, don't you know me?"

"Of course."

"You pretended not to see me just now, would have turned away without speaking. When I ask Aaron about you, he says you won't even mention my name. This is no time for friends to turn away from each other."

"I haven't turned away. I think of you all the time. If you want to live with Mansour, then live with Mansour, and I hope everything is better for you there than it was in the heim."

"Why are you so angry?"

"I'm not angry."

"You make it sound like Elias and I are . . ."

"It's not my business."

"You used to follow me everywhere. I would see you darting in and out of the shadows of buildings. I sometimes couldn't see you, but I heard your footsteps. I even knew the sound of your shoes on the pavement. I felt safe knowing you were there. And then you stopped. Of course what I do is your business."

He looked away. The street had become thick with people coming out of their houses for morning rituals, a young girl combing her wet hair, an old woman washing her feet in the gutter water, women waiting in line at an awninged kiosk to buy fried dough sticks. A sidewalk doctor had set up office on the curb and was spitting snake water onto the chest of a sick patient.

"Aaron worries about you," he finally said.

"Aaron exhausts me with his worrying. If he doesn't hear from me for two days, he thinks I've died. And if I'm not dead, he's sure I will be, that I'm starving to death, that I should be with him in the heim. He doesn't trust Elias, can't understand why he would let me stay in his house, that it's a *shanda* to live with a man who no longer has a wife, that I'm lost to everything decent and good. I don't even listen. When you get back to the heim you can tell him you saw me, that I'm fine, I haven't fallen into the life of a *kurveh*, that there's no sign of damage at all."

It was a cold morning, the wind blowing ramparts of leaves across the sidewalk and swirling them into the air. Lilli knelt down and tucked Shaya's wool scarf more snugly inside her coat. When she straightened up, Moses saw the swell of her stomach beneath her jacket.

"Are you still angry?" Lilli said.

He shook his head.

"Then you have to walk me home. Elias has gone to look for fuel for the clay stove, but he'll be happy to see you when he gets back."

Shaya tugged at the hem of Lilli's jacket.

"Shaya wants to kiss you, Moses."

He leaned down, waited, and then felt the moist imprint of the child's lips on his cheek.

*   *   *

The interior of the Mansour house appeared to have been looted of anything of value. A large bare entry, then a sweep of hollowed-out rooms that echoed each footfall. A few forlorn chairs in each room, walls gouged where paintings had been removed, bookshelves emptied of books.

"So this is where the famous Sir Elias Mansour lives," Moses said. "In an empty palace that is colder inside than it is outside. A person can get lost in such a palace. A person can forget where the door to the outside world is because he's so busy deciding what part of the palace he should sit in. Is he still a lord now that he has no money?"

"He's kind to me, Moses."

"And Li T'ien, is he kind to you?"

"He doesn't want me now."

She unwound Shaya's scarf but left the little girl's coat on.

"Your cheeks are so cold, *bubala*," she said. "Are you hungry?"

"*Ya, mameh.*"

In the kitchen, cabinets had been torn out of the wall, pamphlets and maps and Japanese proclamations tacked in their place. Shaya's eyes followed every move Lilli made as she poured milk from the tin into a glass and tore a piece of bread from a loaf in the cupboard.

"I would offer you something to eat, Moses, but . . ."

"No, no."

While Shaya ate, Lilli licked her own lips as if she could taste every morsel.

"Look how sleepy my little girl is," she said. "She chews and sleeps at the same time."

She wiped Shaya's mouth, then held her in her arms for a few moments, swaying in place.

"Do you want to take a nap, *bubala*?"

"*Ya, mameh.*"

*   *   *

Shaya was asleep in her room across the hall. This was Lilli's room. Note paper, pen, photographs, nubby pencils, and a bottle of ink in a box on the floor beside the bed. The door to the closet was open: two blouses, one skirt, a heavy coat with patched sleeves, a pair of Chinese cloth shoes. Dents in the floor of the room marked the places where bureaus and armoires and credenzas had been. There was no sign that anyone lived in the room with Lilli. Aaron was wrong when he said that Lilli and Mansour were lovers.

He sat down on the bed.

Lilli stood quietly facing him.

"I once lived in a house no larger than this room," he said. "A house with lights that flicked on with a finger touch and sisters who called out in the morning that I would be late for *cheder*."

"Sisters?"

"Three. Eliana, Bluma, and Faigel, and a brother Avrum. Bluma was the youngest, the baby. She was born with a twisted foot and was never able to walk without pain. I used to carry her from place to place on my shoulders. She was a beautiful child, never complained about what she couldn't do. Sometimes I think I hear her voice in the morning when I'm not yet awake, but it's not possible. She's gone. Mother, father, sisters, brother, they're all gone. I couldn't save them."

He felt the press of her fingers on his arm.

"I joined the partisans and killed Germans with the same ease I once killed chickens," he said.

She didn't take her hand away.

"You don't care?" he said, looking up.

"No."

She began to undress. "That you killed Nazis to stop the slaughter of innocents was righteous. You fought evil the only way you could."

The clothes she had taken off were now in the closet and she stood naked, back arched as though the weight of the smooth swell of belly were too heavy for her slight body. He remembered her bud-tipped breasts from an accidental moment in her parents' house in Kovno. She had stared at him with such boldness then, as if to say *take me if you dare,* but he had stopped himself. She was a rabbi's daughter, said her prayers morning, noon, and night, covered her hair with a scarf and began every sentence with a bright-eyed, innocent smile. Now her breasts and stomach were small pillows on a fragile scaffold, and there was a weariness in her eyes that he had seen in the eyes of girls who fought beside him in the Polish forest. In time they became *vilde chayas,* wild women. No, Lilli wasn't like them. She was hard, yet loving; a stranger's child called her *mameh.*

The room air was a stagnant cold, undisturbed by their bodies' warmth, only their breath alive in the moisture streaking the windows. The house was far enough away from the city streets that Moses could hear birdsong and the crisp rustle of tree branches. If he lived in this house with Lilli, he would keep the world outside the walls and greet each day with joy.

"Since there's no one left of my family, I want you to make sure when I die that I'm buried in a Jewish cemetery," he said.

"I might die before you."

"Then it won't matter."

Her shadow fell in a slender crescent across the bare wall, wavered there, then sank as she got into bed beside him. She smelled of fragrant herbs and spiced ginger, and in the gloomy light it seemed to him no time had passed between the time on the train and now, that he could honestly tell Aaron that he had seen her and she wasn't damaged, she was the same as she had always been, that they were all the same as they had always been, that at least in moments like this there was no war, no death, no sorrow.

She pulled the covers over them and tucked her body so close against his he felt as though his skin covered them both.

"Have you always loved me, Moses?"

"Always."

Chapter 31

July 1942

There was nothing in the high-ceilinged dining room but the mahogany table. Moses had brought a chair in from the kitchen for Lilli to sit on, but everyone else had to stand. They had been standing for two hours now, studying the map spread out in the middle of the table, going over and over the plan.

"The map isn't current," Aaron said. "The distances aren't to scale."

"What are you talking about?" Vasily said.

"I'm talking about the map."

"It's a good map."

"I'm telling you it's no good."

"It's the same map we've been using," Elias said.

"I thought we were only here to go over last-minute details," Sigmund said.

"We are."

Lilli hadn't liked the plan from the beginning. Elias's contacts in the American OSS had told Elias that Japanese oil tankers were carrying synthetic fuel that could harm the Americans, and this was Elias's solution: blow up the tankers. He had even been the one to decide who would take part.

It's too sketchy, too undefined, Lilli had told Elias. *There are too many ways for your plan to go wrong. And where did Vasily come from that he's included in this, when there are so many things he doesn't tell you about where he's been, what he's done that made the Japanese angry enough to put him in prison? He's a Russian. He's protected. He doesn't need to do this.*

He's also a Jew.

"I need some water," Lilli said now.

Moses followed her into the kitchen.

"Are you all right?"

"I'm all right. I just couldn't sit there any longer and listen to the bickering. And Vasily doesn't know how to talk to Aaron, he makes Aaron nervous;

when Aaron is nervous he tries to overdo, overthink, overprepare. What will happen if he falls apart? Elias won't be there to pick him up. Anything can happen. It's a crazy scheme. I don't like it."

"I'll be there. He'll calm down once we start."

Elias looked up when Moses came back into the dining room.

"Is she all right?"

"Just thirsty."

Sigmund said, "If we're only here to go over details, why are we going over the whole thing?"

"To make sure everyone understands," Elias replied.

"Aaron thinks he's King David," Vasily said and lit another cigarette. Carelessly discarded lit cigarettes had embroidered lacy black grooves in the table's glassy finish.

"If I'm King David, I'll smite Goliath," Aaron said, "but only lightly enough to injure him. I won't kill him. If it will help Americans end the war, if it will destroy Hirohito and Hitler, I'll blow up whatever I'm supposed to blow up, but killing I won't do."

"*Now* you think about that?" Vasily said.

"I'm just making it clear. I won't kill anyone. I won't be an assassin."

"We're not asking you to assassinate anyone," Elias said.

"I don't want any misunderstandings."

"You want a guarantee?" Sigmund said.

"I'm making a statement."

"To what purpose?"

"For clarification."

"It's possible that something might happen and someone might get killed," Moses said.

"That's my point."

"People die, Aaron. If you bump into a man on the street and he falls into the path of an automobile and is killed, are you then an assassin?"

"That depends on my intentions. If I accidentally push a man into the path of an automobile and he dies, then I am merely an instrument of God's design. God allows for accidents. But if I rig dynamite and electrical charges . . ."

"The wharf is patrolled by guards," Elias said. "To get close enough to the tankers to blow them up won't be easy."

"I'll take care of the guards," Vasily said.

"How will you do that?" Aaron said.

"I will do it."

"Kill them?"

"It's possible."

"Either you will or you won't. Which is it?"

"Then I won't."

"I don't believe you."

"Calm down, Aaron," Moses said.

"I'm calm. I'm very calm."

"Then is it all settled?" Elias said. "Are we agreed as to what you're going to do? Aaron?"

Aaron didn't answer.

"Moses?"

"Agreed."

"Sigmund?"

"Agreed."

"Vasily?"

"Agreed, if Aaron promises not to remain behind to admire his handiwork."

"If you insult me again . . ."

"Are you agreed, Aaron?" Elias said.

Aaron nodded.

"You have to say it, Aaron. Are you agreed?"

"Agreed. I'm agreed. I'm agreed. *Gottenyu*, let us all live and be well."

* * *

Aaron had been quiet since they got off the tram, no dissection of the difference between murder and accidental death, merely an occasional stertorous breath as they made their way through the hutongs to the jetty.

There were no lights, not even the blink of an oil lamp through an open doorway. The docks were up ahead and the sharp outlines of the two Japanese tankers, giant metal bodies floating like steel cerements at the confluence of Soochow Creek and the Whangpoo River, silky beams of light flowing from rusted portholes.

A wooden bridge curved to the right, straightened out, bent back into an arc and ended at the water line. No sign of sentries. Slack water, no breeze, a raft of pearlescent stars overhead.

"I could have blown up ten tankers in the time it took you to get here," Vasily whispered.

"Should I give you a medal?" Aaron said.

"Is everything here?" Moses said.

"Everything."

"Where is Sigmund?"

"At the south end of the pier. How much time will we have?"

"Enough," Aaron said.

"Set your charges close to the hull," Vasily said.

"Are you an expert? I'll pick the spot."

"Do what you want, but give us at least three minutes after the flares go off to get away."

He sprinted across the wharf and was gone.

Moses had nothing to do with picking the proper spot or setting the charges. He left that to Aaron. Aaron was the one who had studied the explosives book, who could quote from it, page and line, who now knew the chemistry and physics of detonation as well as he knew the Torah.

"Have you picked a spot yet?" Moses asked him.

"Give me time, give me time. I'm still thinking." He took a pad of paper out of his pocket and began writing equations. "Wind direction is very important. I want to make sure the initial explosive force doesn't stall in its trajectory."

He took a tape measure out of another pocket to measure distances and made more calculations.

A truck rumbled by on an access road, soldiers with rifles standing in its bed. The truck didn't stop.

"I can feel you rushing me," Aaron said.

"I'm not. Take your time."

"Two charges. Close to the hulls. That's where the force will be the greatest. And I still say that to speak of murder is to avoid the real question, which is can men be of the world and still keep their souls?"

"You're not doing murder, Aaron."

"It's possible."

"It's not. Place the charges."

Aaron placed the charges. Moses laid the cable.

"The fittings are loose," Aaron said.

"They're not loose."

"They are." He spun the fittings, ran his finger around the machined edges, then reconnected them.

"It's enough, Aaron."

"It has to be right."

"It's right. Believe me, it's right."

"Then let's go."

They started to run, Aaron carrying the detonator, Moses reeling electrical cable out behind them. At a hill to the west of the docks Aaron set the detonator on the ground.

"Is the cable still connected?"

"It's still connected."

"Are you sure?"

"I'm sure."

"How can you tell? It's too dark to see."

"It's connected, Aaron."

"Maybe God will punish us."

"He won't. He doesn't even see us."

"He sees everything."

"Not when it's dark."

"You shouldn't make jokes like that."

"You don't even pray anymore, Aaron."

"I still believe the *meshiach* will come and good will triumph."

Sigmund's flare shot up first, a dying comet snaking across the sky. Vasily's followed close behind.

Aaron pulled the detonator handle, then rammed it flush to the black box.

"You should have waited," Moses said. "They needed time to get away."

"They had time. They had enough time. There was plenty of time."

A delicate band of crimson spread out over the docks, then a roar as loud as a million hammers filled their ears.

"You did it," Moses said.

"I didn't."

"The dock is on fire."

"What do I care about whether the dock is on fire? It's the tankers I want. They're not burning."

"They'll burn."

"They won't. Someone moved the charges."

"No one moved anything, Aaron. You set the charges close to the hulls, just the way you said you wanted. There was no mistake and no one moved anything."

"They did. You don't think I know how to do this? I could do this unconscious. I could do this asleep."

He started running back to the jetty. He was a madman, jacket flapping, showers of multicolored cinders falling around him, his red beard glowing orange as a fireball in the bright sky.

Chapter 32

August 1942

A warm wet pool spread out beneath her. She sat up. Was it a pain she felt? She had felt small contractions before, mild ones that grabbed and released, as though they were daring to be caught. This was different.

She lit a candle (to save money, lights were turned off at nine) and went into the small adjoining bathroom.

There's typhus and diphtheria at Ward Road Hospital, Rachel said. *Stay away from the hospital.*

Another pain. Below her navel now. She leaned against the sink, took quick sips of air. It was deeper this time, lasted longer.

Chinese peasant women give birth to their babies in the fields where they're working, she read in a book when she was twelve. *African women give birth leaning against a tree.*

She stood still a moment, resting. Her body was cumbrous, unstable, her stomach foreign to her, a pendulous attachment chained to her midriff.

How long had it been? It felt as though hours had passed, but there were no signs of dawn. The shadows hadn't shifted; there were no rays of light against the tiled walls.

The full heat of summer had come. It stuck like wool cladding to her skin. She had cut her hair short, the remaining curls clung damp and springy to her forehead.

She pulled the nightgown off, twisted it the way she would if she were wringing out a cloth, tied it to the chrome pipe beneath the sink and lay down on the floor.

Another pain. She pulled at the tail of the gown, arms stretched, body sliding backward along the floor.

Then rest. Dream. Doze.

The canny light of dawn hatched the walls and single spasms joined into a stiffening ball of pain. She had chewed the gown until it was ripped along the seams and was as thin as a skein of yarn, as supple as taffy.

She dropped the ropy gown and sat doubled over, knees to her chin. She was as dizzy as if she were lying inside a glass bowl that someone had set to spinning. She imagined she smelled *challah* baking and heard Mama telling her it will be done when the crust is brown and shiny.

Everything takes time, Mama said. *You have to be patient.*

She gasped, pushed, felt a mountain moving inside her, and in one eager burst, a girl, eyes shut, lids half moons, gave a delicate cry.

Chapter 33

September 1942

Hannah looked around at what was once the garden room and was now a damp bricky shell, empty except for the small settee she and Lilli sat on. Outside the wind gusted in harmonic bursts, tree branches cudgeling the windows to be let in.

"This place is awful. You'll all get pneumonia here. It's colder than a mausoleum."

"I can get you a sweater," Lilli said, baby Anzia asleep on her lap.

"I don't need a sweater."

Shaya, sprawled on the floor at Lilli's feet, was drawing on one of Elias's notepads with colored chalk.

"Oh, how sweet, is that a drawing of me?"

"It's a bird," Shaya said.

"Well, isn't it pretty. And so are you. I wish I had eyes that color. You'll be a dazzler when you grow up." She turned to Lilli. "She *is* right in the head, isn't she? I mean, there's no sign of her, you know, what her mother, you know . . ."

"She likes to draw. I think she'll be an artist."

"I don't know how you do it, Lilli. She isn't even yours. What a sacrifice. And now you have another one. The whole idea is depressing. You have to do everything for them, and they can't tell you what they want or who they are, and it all just seems such a waste of time when they're only going to grow up and forget all about you."

She pulled the blanket away from Anzia's face, studied the tilt of the eyes, not quite Asian, not quite round, and the black hair, cleaved with red, that cambered and dipped the way Lilli's did.

"Blends are very much in demand these days," Hannah said. "Men like the idea of cross-breeding. It's exotic to them." She touched her fingers to her forehead. "Did you notice my brows? I've plucked everything away and drawn an arch. Penciled brows with high arches are all the rage."

She tilted her head so Lilli could see the reconfigured eyebrows, two thread-thin lines angling up toward her temples, the dewy eyes beneath embedded in kohl-rimmed sockets. Her once translucent skin had darkened. Musky splotches as coarse as sand peeked through the heavy powder.

"The pencil doesn't come off. It's a special kind made for eyebrows. The trick is to get them both looking the same."

"They're very nice."

"You may think it strange, but Jewish women are in demand. The more Semitic my face looks, the better business is. You should think about doing something to yourself, Lilli. A little rouge and lipstick wouldn't hurt. And you don't eat enough." She stood up, straightened the seams of her silk stockings, and sat down again.

"I haven't seen Elias in the longest time. He always manages to be out when I'm here. I think he avoids me."

"That isn't true."

"It certainly seems that way."

"He hardly knows you. He's out every day making inquiries about Aaron and Moses."

"I can't imagine why he bothers. It's obvious they're dead."

"Don't say that, Hannah."

"It's true. Sigmund, too. It's been months. He's never been gone this long before. I never thought I'd miss him, but I do. He's the only one who lets me be myself. Besides you, of course."

"Guessing at the bad is as foolish as guessing at the good. We don't have any news, we don't know what happened, and it's stupid and a waste of time to mourn or celebrate before we find out. I think Moses and Aaron are both alive, and if you want to think they're dead, then that's your choice."

"You don't have to snap my head off. Men don't like women with sour personalities. And I know what I'm talking about. I used to have one and I didn't have half the business I do now. I'm just like a little baby now, sweet as can be to everyone. Being anything else just doesn't pay."

She angled one shoulder toward Lilli. "I hope you're sweeter to Elias than you were to me just now. Now that Moses is gone, you have to look to the future."

"Elias isn't like that."

"My God, Lilli, all men are like that. Elias is no different. I have clients like him, most of their money gone, the Japanese swarming all over them. They're particular about the women they speak to on the street, but they're not ashamed to come and see me and tell me all their dirty secrets and cry over what they've lost. I pretend to care when I really want to laugh. It's just a matter of time before Elias shows you who he really is. Mutti knows all about him. She says he only married Lady Sybil because she was titled and he wasn't. His own title came later, of course, and Vati told me it was probably paid for with the millions of pounds sterling that he made in the opium trade. And all that underground business, it's a wonder the Japanese haven't arrested him by now. I've heard that they've already interned some British men."

She smiled, slippy red lipstick parting to show nicotine-stained teeth.

"I told Madame Liskaya about you. She said anytime you want a job I can bring you into the house with me. I have a good following and anyone I recommend will be brought in and welcomed. The girls will share with you until you get established. You can even bring Shaya and Anzia. We have amahs to take care of the children. It's really quite homelike, not like you would imagine at all. Prostitution is in vogue now. You should come and visit me, Lilli. It's not a place where men fondle you through your underpants behind a gauze curtain. It's very stylish, very discreet. The men are investigated and credit is established. They pay by the month. They're very respectable and have to be recommended. We're really like sweethearts. I've been to the jai-alai on Avenue du Roi Albert and bet on the games, and I've seen the greyhounds race at the Canidrome. I've even been to the dinner dances at the Cathay Hotel. Li T'ien is always there with different girls. I think you're foolish not to ask him to help you. After all, Anzia is his daughter. If you're nice to him, he might set you up in a house with servants and fancy clothes. Chinese gangsters own Shanghai now. The Japanese may think they do, but they don't. And Li T'ien is the biggest gangster of them all. Ask anyone. I don't know what your arrangement is with Elias, except that it seems peculiar to me. If it's just a place to live you want, why, there are a million places, and you won't have to worry that Elias will throw you out or die or get arrested. You really have to think about your future, Lilli."

She hiccupped, stared at the rhinestone bows on her shoes, and blinked her eyes. A tiny tear driveled out of the inside corner of her left eye.

"My father saw me at Madame Liskaya's. He has a Chinese mistress there. I didn't even know it until the night he came into my room by mistake. There was a Russian girl and a Frenchman in bed with me. I thought I would die right then and there."

She folded a corner of Anzia's blanket between two fingers and held it to the tear for a moment.

"Are you sure he knew it was you?"

"He said my name, then called me a whore."

"He just had a reaction, Hannah, that's all. People get shocked and surprised and they say things they don't mean. He loves you. Nothing changes that."

"Here you are, two children, living in a bare house with a man who's lost everything, and your sweetheart has disappeared and you talk about love. There is no love in Shanghai, Lilli, none at all. It's so depressing." Tears, free as river water, flashed across her powdered cheeks. "Mutti hates me. And now Vati . . ."

"No one hates you, Hannah."

"I've ruined my makeup." Ant trails of mascara blotted her cheeks. She took her compact out of her purse and powdered over them, a thick layer that turned her skin as crackly as an old vase.

"It's so strange. When I used to stroll down Peking Road looking for customers, I was happy. Now that I'm in a house with regular working hours I feel sad. I suppose I could open a bakery or a beauty parlor with the money I've made, but I have no talent for business."

She probed her purse for a handkerchief.

"I married Aaron and made him miserable and now he's gone. You never told him about me, did you?"

"Never."

"I think I wiped away my eyebrow. Is there anything left of it?"

"Most of it's still there. Wipe a bit off the other one and it'll be fine."

The compact was out again. A swipe of one eyebrow, then the other, then an evening up.

"It's so strange, Lilli, the way life is. I wish I could be as perfect as Mutti. Even living with another man, she's still perfect. Some women are like that. Nothing they do can stain them. Like you. You're as bad as I am, but people don't talk about you the way they do me. You live with Elias and so that makes everything you do all right. Poor Aaron with a wife like me. And I suppose he loves me, but he thinks I'm someone else, someone pure, who only fools around a little bit. Siggie always said I couldn't control my impulses. I just get an idea and I do it. A man says something to me and I go with him. And I think about Aaron, I really do. Sometimes I imagine that he will come home, but I don't know what he'll come home to. Someone else lives in our little room. He won't even find me there. I wonder if the Japanese have him in one of their terrible prisons or . . ."

"Just think of the best, Hannah. If something had happened to Aaron and Moses, I would feel it. And I don't. One day when we're not expecting it, they'll come in the door as if they've never been gone. Aaron will tell me that Anzia isn't a Jewish name, and Moses will argue with him about what a Jewish name is, and everything will be like it was before. I see it all in my mind. I hear their voices. It has to happen."

Hannah's eyes were dry now, the remains of her penciled eyebrows short and uneven.

"You're so smart, Lilli. You always know just the right thing to say to comfort me."

Chapter 34

October 1942

It was raining. An anonymous rain, indiscriminate, anointing every-thing—pavement, beggars, bicycles, corpses—with the same oily wash. Elias's shoes were wet (stuffed with paper to cover the holes in the soles), the bicycle wobbled and clacked, the wool jacket, rain-shrunk by half, rode up his back and left his wrists bare. (Lilli had traded Elias's tailored suits for the bicycle and the jacket, a sack of sugar, and four chocolate bars.) He had been to the Japanese Consulate, the police station on Yates Road, the Red Cross office in Frenchtown. The Japanese official at the Consulate didn't look at him while he was speaking. The officer at the police station said Elias was becom-ing a nuisance. The official at the Red Cross office made him wait an hour and then had an assistant come out and tell him there was no news. He was no longer Sir Elias Mansour. He was merely a fifty-year-old man on a bicycle with an armband on someone else's coat sleeve and a cap pulled low on his forehead against the rain asking anyone he could think of what had happened to two particular Jews out of thirty thousand.

Elias blamed himself. What did he know about espionage? What did he know about Vasily? A Russian furrier from Minsk was all he knew, with a sis-ter in Russian Town who said she thought her brother went north. North. As if north were an address. And Rachel still hadn't heard from Sigmund.

Elias used to ride in an automobile along this street, seeing only what was to the side and front, never noticing the shape of the sky above the buildings, or the buildings themselves or the way the trees looked from season to season. He saw everything now. Pendulous gray clouds teasing the spires and domes along the Bund, shifting and swinging in the saturate wind; the slow trawl across his vision of liquidambar trees flanking the street, camphor-scented, their apple-green leaves jade ornaments a few months ago and now the color of melting rust; the glaciate gleam of shop windows in the rain, lights inside burning outward like welcoming torches.

The bicycle was running well today. Moses had promised to find him another one, a better one, but Moses was gone and Elias liked this one, anyway, liked the rip of its dangling fender on the scabrous sidewalk, the erratic harmonies of its squealing brake. He bicycled everywhere, his leg muscles now smartened and blood-fed and as strong as when he sprinted across schoolyards as a boy.

Sybil wouldn't have been easy in this Shanghai, her possessions gone, friends sorted and culled, some to be interned, some left alone to starve, Elias living in his decaying house with a stranger and her two children.

At odd moments he imagined Sybil coming down the stairs to greet their guests, candles flitting in her gown's brisk wake, her cheeks fired with excitement. Or sitting in the car next to him, a cashmere throw over her legs, her back and neck all angles and shadows. But memories of that other life lay fallow in the thickening past; they stuttered and stalled; their brilliance faded.

He glanced at the people on the street, watched for a glimpse of beard or a long black coat, as though Aaron and Moses would be strolling along Nanking Road looking in shop windows. No sign of them today. Only Chinese faces. Here and there a European with a sleeve branded B for British or A for American or H for Dutch. A line of red armbands waited in front of a bakery on Avenue Joffre to buy their day's ration of bread. Europeans, identity sewn to their arms, waited in line for everything, even for cigarettes filled with lotus leaves and dirt.

Up ahead a small sign at the entrance to the bar: Enemy Aliens Not Allowed. Elias pulled his bicycle through the door past the cases of Chinese rice wine, leaned it against the cloakroom wall and stood in the smoky archway looking in. Snatches of German and French conversation melded to the rhythms of ragtime being played by a Chinese man on a scarred grand piano.

Colonel Yazuka was waiting for him in a wood-paneled booth, a bottle of brandy and a half-full glass on the table in front of him.

Yazuka greeted Elias by his first name. He didn't call him Sir Elias. He didn't tell the waiter to bring another glass.

"I risk arrest by being here when the sign tells me to stay out," Elias said.

"You risk arrest by being in Shanghai when most of your countrymen have been interned. I have never been able to understand why you didn't leave. Men like you who have everything and here you stay, on the edge of disaster."

"Maybe it's because I couldn't make up my mind what to take with me. Or it might have been that I was enjoying myself too much. In any event, you see me now without my armor. It should please you."

"It doesn't. I liked you better the other way. You were someone to admire. Now you're ordinary. I'm holding your internment off as long as I can, but there is only so much I can do. Sooner or later you will have to leave your grand house, and then it will be taken over. The young girl who lives there with you. A relative?"

"No. A Lithuanian refugee."

"There will be an edict in February. She'll have to move with the rest of the refugees into Hongkew."

"No exceptions?"

"None. You also have a friend, an American woman."

"She's an American with a passport."

"An enemy alien like you."

"She has a relief-worker exemption. She's vital to the refugees."

"She's breaking the law."

"What law? She's here helping people when she could be safe in New York. She gets nothing for being here, no money. She's suffering like all the rest."

"She solicits funds from the enemy. A capital offense."

"There are no funds. Everything has dried up."

"She persists."

"She does not persist."

"She writes letters."

"They're intercepted. They don't reach their destination."

"A technicality. When we find her she'll be sent to Bridge House and executed. I can't do anything to prevent it. She's too visible."

Yazuka flicked cigarette ash from the lapel of his uniform and gazed around the room. He had no profile. His cheek eclipsed his nose. Only his eyebrows jutted out, a spatial collection of single hairs ringing a slight brow. The pianist was playing the Horst Wessel song, a drunken chorus of German voices riding tunelessly from table to table, the bar girls dancing, two by two, on a speck of floor. Yazuka leaned heavily against the back of the booth and it creaked like an old bed.

"Four men blew up the wharves in Yangtsepoo," Yazuka said. "Two were religious Jews with long beards and black coats. You've been asking about the two Jews. I would advise you to stop."

*   *   *

The elevator wasn't working. Elias dragged the bicycle up the eight flights to Rachel's apartment. She was in pajamas, her hair snarled, a pillow crease on her right cheek.

"What time is it?"

"Eleven-thirty."

"And I was having such a good dream. Since you woke me up, you might as well come in."

Her apartment was a hodgepodge of account books and cardboard boxes and piles of dirty laundry in the small entry; file cabinets, a three-legged couch, an overflowing garbage pail, an ebony upright piano piled with books in the living room.

He wedged the bicycle in between a cardboard box and the garbage pail.

"If I can find my way to the kitchen, I'll fix you something to eat."

The kitchen was in an alcove off the dining room. A small sink, a hot plate. Over the bare window a braided red rope was strung with fraying Chinese baskets.

Sections of the floor stuck to his shoes. A single overhead light striped the walls. It was obvious she had no interest in her surroundings. The apartment was tornado-struck, the remains scattered.

She mixed cold rice with a curdled looking brown sauce and spooned it into a small bowl.

"I can't afford to turn on more than one light at a time. I make some strange concoctions as a result."

She handed him the bowl and a spoon and he followed her into the dining room.

An orange cat padded over the cluttered table, testing its footing on ledger books and typewriter and stacks of correspondence. An electric iron, cold face planted on the sleeve of a wrinkled blouse, had photographs propped against its side.

She sat across from him.

"There are problems," he said.

"The understatement of the world, Elias."

"New problems."

"If it's about Sigmund, I haven't seen him. I don't know where he is. He came and he went. I'm glad he's gone. He requires too much attention."

"I think you should give up the apartment."

"And go where?"

"With me and Lilli."

"What's going on?"

"You're on a list."

"For what? What the hell did I do? What are the charges?"

"Soliciting funds."

"Soliciting funds? What does that mean? That's why I'm here, that's why I've stayed."

"You've been writing letters, contacting Americans. The Japanese aren't in a mood to parse the difference between that and your relief activities. If you stay here, they'll arrest you. They can execute you, Rachel."

She folded her arms on the table and laid her head on them.

"Everything is compromised now," he said. "The walls I thought were keeping out the barbarians have been breached."

She murmured into the bend of her arm. "Shit, Elias, I should have gone home when I had the chance."

Chapter 35

November 1942

The apartment building seemed to have aged since Lilli was last here in August: interior garden overgrown, the iron grillwork balconies rusted, bronze streaks meandering over the cracks and crevices of the stone facade. Inside, in the long hall, people with British, Dutch, and American armbands were spread like laundry over the tiled floor, everyone costive in the cold, their exhaled breath wisping the frigid air. Lilli knocked on the apartment door and Jacob Rossitsky opened the door.

"Come quick before they follow you in." He ushered her into a living room that had disappeared beneath an avalanche of boxes and bins, toppling sacks of sugar and rice, sets of crutches, wheelchairs, and bedding. He cleared a space for her on the spotted couch, and he perched on a tall crate of tinned biscuits.

"Is it my fault they didn't leave Shanghai when they had the chance? Before they became enemy aliens I was that Russian Jew, now I'm the messiah. They think I can get them Soviet papers. I give them some rice and tell them not to send their friends, but every day they come and sit and wait. For what? What do they think, that I have no problems, no difficulties? You're thin. You don't eat."

"Money for food is scarce." She began probing boxes and cartons. "What have you got that's interesting?"

"The black market again? You're lucky Matsui let you walk away, he could have killed you. Times are worse now, everyone out for themselves. Look out in the hall. Who could have seen it coming? Who would have predicted? You're lucky. He could have cut you in half. I'll give you sugar and rice, take it home, and *zei gezunt*."

"I'll take the sugar and rice. And insulin and digitalis. Also beans and peanut oil and tinned fish. If you'll please give me money for the rickshaw I'll repay you."

"Will you take two children with you now, walking the streets with a baby and a little one hanging onto your leg? It's craziness."

"I already have people who come to the house and ask me if I sell this or that, and with a few stops in the shops I can feed us and maybe more. And what I do with my children is my business. Don't be stubborn, Jacob. I've planned out what I'm going to do and how I'm going to do it. Everyone in the house is hungry all the time. Elias tortures himself because he can't help. Rachel writes begging letters to the U.S. and gets no answer. Also boxes of matches, people need matches, I hear that over and over, *do you have matches?* And chocolate, dark if you have it. And spices, especially salt and pepper. Also vanilla bean."

She straightened up.

"You are a wonderful friend, Jacob. I depend on your friendship. I could use silk cloth, any color or pattern, it doesn't matter. I think that's all I can think of right now. If I need something else, I'll be back."

"Matsui didn't hurt you enough? You didn't see enough of what he could do? Two bodies in the Whangpoo just this month. Both of them had been paying him squeeze, both of them not making enough, and so, *pfft*, he kills them."

"He won't kill me."

"What makes you so sure?"

"He just won't, that's all."

*   *   *

December 1942

Since the internment law went into effect, the Mansour house had become a small island on a vacant sea, the last of its neighbors having been arrested and interned by the Japanese. Military trucks scouted for enemy aliens on arrest lists, mopping them up as tidily as a housewife on cleaning day.

Although meetings were now punished by imprisonment, they continued in the Mansour house. Today the only ones besides Rachel and Elias at the dining room table were Abe Milstein from Ward Road and Jacob Rossitsky, head of the Russian Jewish Welfare Society. Lilli no longer attended meetings. Son Li, the new amah, took care of Anzia and Shaya, and Lilli was free to come and go as she pleased, sometimes leaving the house early in the morning and returning late at night. Not only did Rachel now worry about Elias, who was new to risk-taking, but she worried abut Lilli, who seemed oblivious to the perils of the black market.

This afternoon the meeting was about crematoria in Pootung. Fritz Flechtman, the German Embassy attaché, had provided Elias with a copy of the plans.

"Maybe the ovens are for baking bread," Milstein said.

"A bakery in Pootung, far away from the city, in a place you can only get to by boat?" Elias said.

"Burning Jews in ovens, no one would do such a thing," Rossitsky said. "We're willing to help Jewish refugees all we can. We can give them meals at low prices and bury the dead, but about ovens and burning I have nothing to say."

"You talk about Jews as if you weren't one," Rachel said. "Do you think your Soviet passport will protect you forever?"

"A Jew is a Jew," Milstein said. "If the Japanese want to, they'll kill us without ovens. Who needs ovens? They just want to frighten us, keep us in line. Last week they were going to put all the Jews on ships, take them out to sea and push them overboard. Now this. It's nothing but propaganda."

The door opened, then the sudden rush of Lilli's sandals on the bare floors. "Japanese soldiers in a truck."

Elias and the two men raced down the front drive. Rachel grabbed Shaya, Son Li carried baby Anzia, and they followed Lilli out the French doors and down the steps into the garden. They waited in the cold, damp garden through the afternoon. At the last skim of sun overhead they went back into the house.

"They didn't come inside," Lilli said. "Nothing was touched."

"Are you sure you saw soldiers?"

"They were in a truck. I saw them."

Hours went by. Rachel sat on the front steps and waited for some sign that Elias had eluded the Japanese. Behind her through the open front door she could see Lilli at the dining room table working on invoices. Aaron and Moses had disappeared and Lilli no longer mentioned them. Now Elias was gone, and her emotions appeared to be as folded as a fan. Her eyes were often red-rimmed, but that could have been from lack of sleep.

Rachel wrapped her coat more tightly around her and stared through the iced trees and dying privets along the drive for any sign of Elias. She had never thought of herself as the anxious sort; news was either good, which was a relief, or bad, and she dealt with it—at times rudely, impulsively, and fool-hardily, but dealt with it. Now she was helpless.

"You should come in, Rachel. There's hot tea."
"No, I'm fine. I'm fine."

*   *   *

Elias was back before morning, loping up the drive with the ease of someone who had just been out for a walk.

Chapter 36

January 1943

It was too much to believe that Matsui would forget Lilli, that he wouldn't see her in the shops when he did his rounds, that he had grown so generous he no longer required squeeze, no longer bartered lives for money. She knew he was somewhere around, watching her from a distance, counting the number of stops she made, approximating the amount of time at each place, estimating from the merchandise he knew she now dealt in what amount of money she was making, then calculating how much she owed him. He knew her business was growing, that her inventory had grown so large it had escaped the small box in the kitchen of the Mansour house, had snaked into the pantry and from there spread out like a terminal disease, and that in the past few weeks enemy nationals and refugees had been tromping through the weedy yard to trade with her. She sensed his presence somewhere in the neighborhood, was sure that he peered into the French windows from the sun-striped yard. His circuitous behaviors were no mystery to her. It would be what he would do, follow her home and watch from a distance, waiting for the right moment before confronting her. He hadn't shown himself because he knew she expected him to. In response she became bolder in her transactions, selling goods to customers right out on the street, open to view, inviting customers into the house so that, if he were watching, he could witness the extent of her business, could more accurately estimate its value.

On a brisk, sunshiny day at the end of November, he appeared at the front door of the Mansour house. He had come on a good day, a fortunate day. Elias and Rachel were at a meeting of the Joint. Son Li had put the two children in the pram and taken them for a walk.

He swept past her, letting his arched neck lead him forward. He already knew the inside of the house by the shape of its outside walls, by his peerings through the windows. He wasted no time in rooms of no importance, but headed to the kitchen pantry where the goods were stored. Lilli followed a short distance behind him, assessing his mood, although it didn't really matter

what his mood was. The level of threat was always the same, a seething vol-
cano calibrated by some primitive rationing of fury. There was no fury like his,
the silently pleasant expression suddenly erupting in violence. She held her
left wrist crookedly because of him. Her ribs ached because of him.

He had found the money, was counting it out, beads of perspiration on
his sun-lit forehead. He was engrossed in his counting, holding the bills in
his left hand and slicking them with his right. He wore his uniform today,
smart-looking in its olive finish, a red sash around his waist. The uniform gave
him the imprimatur of officialdom, gave him the right to rummage unde-
terred through a stateless refugee's cupboard. He was engrossed, forgetting she
was there, unmindful of the sun glare or that the curve of his back was to her.

She had no feeling for him as an enemy. An enemy was a concept, a set of
ideas. He was a thing, a hindrance, an impediment to be stamped on, crushed,
destroyed. As he counted out her money, she felt time telescoping, seconds
turning in on themselves. If she waited, he could turn toward her, and the
moment would be gone. The kitchen was the hub of the house, the warm center. There were onion peelings in the sink and bits of cheese on a plate. Rachel
had left a pack of cigarettes on the table next to a bowl of oranges that had
cost a sack of sugar and a box of matches. Could she do it here in this familiar
place where they ate their meals? Would there be a spectral tinge to the air
afterwards, an oppressive shadow on the walls?

"You've done well," he said, and dug further into the pantry, began pulling
out tins of sardines and sacks of sugar and packages of cigarettes, absorbed
in each fresh object. The pantry door hung loosely on its hinges and made a
noise with each bump of Matsui's shoulder against it. He didn't hear the long
drawer slide open.

"I have children to feed," she said.

Matsui took a step backward and tins of sardines tumbled to the floor.

It's always best to shoot more than once, Jacob said when he sold her the gun.
What's one more bullet when you're not sure the first one did the job?

He lay on his back, blood budding on his chest, the fabric of his jacket
drinking it in in a ragged circle, then spreading out like the unfolding of an
exotic flower. She fired once more, put the gun down, removed the sword
from his belt, washed the blood off at the sink, put the gun and sword in the
pantry, then went into the study, sat down at the desk, and waited for Elias
and Rachel to return.

*   *   *

They dug a hole for Matsui's body near the privy and covered it with dirt and dried leaves.

"Are you sure no one saw him come into the house?" Elias said. He had erased the shock from his face, but his voice was hoarse.

"I'm sure. And I would have done it some other way if I could have."

"Well, I don't want to know a goddamn thing about it," Rachel said, her face flushed.

Lilli felt a pang of sorrow that there had been no way she could have kept this from them. Especially Elias. He was much more tender than Rachel, who in the future would probably think of what had happened in some clouded way, details blurred, the totality of it irrelevant to her affection for Lilli. But it would lie between Lilli and Elias forever. When he looked at her, he would see Matsui's body. He might say to himself that she must have had a good reason to do what she did. He might blame it on the war, say that she had been worn down by adversity, had been bludgeoned by hardship. He might decide she had been defending herself, that she could not have killed coldly, intentionally. *The sword, wasn't that proof of his own murderous intentions?* he might retort if challenged. Or *She did it for us*, he might say. *It was an act of courage*, he might even add. He would ponder and guess and mine for explanations. He would try to purge the memory, but it would resist. And although Elias and Rachel would each approach an explanation from different avenues, approach it they would, and although Lilli had no regret for what she had done, it saddened her to know that by her actions she had done them both some indefinable harm.

A bright breeze stirred the garden weeds, and the sky seemed to Lilli to be the bluest she had ever seen.

Does the Torah ever permit murder? Lilli asked Papa.

To preserve life, Papa replied.

Chapter 37

July 1943

The truck stopped close to the steps of the house. An old truck, stake-body, crammed with those British, American, Belgian, and Dutch citizens who had been exempt from internment until now because of age or illness or special privilege, or for one reason or another had been overlooked in all the assemblies that had come before. Elias with his British passport and Rachel with her American one, were two of the last to be picked up.

Elias handed up the two valises, the iron bed frame (*No double beds permitted; no jewelry, antiques, or electric appliances*, the instruction sheet said), the large twine-wrapped package of food.

An Englishman with a Japanese armband was in charge of stuffing people and bed frames and valises and pots and pans into the truck.

"Move over, make room, that's it, that's it."

Lilli and Rachel stood at the foot of the steps, their arms forming a tent, Shaya in its ambit, the baby's blue blanket trailing across Lilli's arm onto the morning-damp stones, which would be sun-shot by noon. Since there were no summer clothes of Sybil's left, all of it turned to Lilli's inventory and sold, Rachel was wearing the last of Sybil's winter suits, a beige cashmere, its fur collar lying like a long-haired cat across her shoulders. Her hair was buried as tight as pillow wadding under Sybil's yellow cloche hat and she carried Sybil's purse, a square leather envelope with a gold-lipped clasp that closed with a satisfying little smack, now empty of Sybil's perfumed handkerchiefs and filled with bandages and iodine and cough syrup and aspirin. Despite the borrowed clothes, Rachel still didn't resemble Sybil. She had none of Sybil's grace. She walked with bruising force. She clutched Sybil's purse in her fist, carried it as though it were a sack.

The Englishman barked, and Rachel pulled away from Lilli, the move like stitches ripping along a seam.

"I sewed twenty American dollars into the lining of your suit," Lilli said to Elias.

"You'll need all your money."

"I have enough."

"They'll be taking the house when you move into Hongkew."

"I'm not moving into Hongkew."

"For God's sake, Lilli, they'll make you go."

"Don't worry about me. I've made other plans. You just take care of yourself and Rachel."

"You'll be careful?"

"I'll be careful."

Elias climbed into the truck and held out his hand for Rachel. She hitched her skirt and sprinted up into the truck as easily as a boy.

The men were sullenly stoic, the women draggy and silent, but slowly, reluctantly, moves were made, and as though the truck bed were a chess board, positions rearranged. Those on the truck first took up the most space. There was no more room to sit on valises. Elias and Rachel joined those standing. Everyone finally settled into the new configuration and tuned their body to the lurch of the truck as it headed to the Bund.

Elias looked back. Lilli was still standing there. All stateless Jews in greater Shanghai had already been forced to move into Hongkew, one square squalid mile now designated the Shanghai Ghetto. *I've made other plans*, she said.

He had forgotten his wallet. Everything was out of order this morning. The sudden rush to get ready, Rachel blithely continuing the letter to her father, Lilli wrapping rice balls in one packet, salt duck and noodles in another, oranges in a cloth bag, then hunting the pantry over until she found the dried peaches, Elias meeting for one last time with Jacob Rossitsky, handing him his will, giving him the names of people in London to contact in the event of his death.

There was nothing of value in the wallet. A small telephone book with numbers for people who no longer had telephones, a piece of paper listing closed bank accounts, a small snapshot of Sybil standing on the Great Wall looking cold and preoccupied.

The wallet was on his desk. He had been about to pick it up, had his hand out. What happened? It was so strange how insignificant missteps can torture you, how just the act of mulling and retracing could both calm and bedevil.

Rachel was very quiet, looking out the truck's wake at the coolies and beggars spitting and jeering as the truck passed.

"So how old are you?" he said.

She turned toward him. "What?"

"How old are you?"

"They're not going to ask me that."

"They will."

"Forty-three in January."

"Where were you born?"

"London."

"Mother and father?"

"Shit, Elias, no one cares how old Sybil was or who her parents were. I'm wearing her coat, for chrissakes, and carrying her goddamn purse."

From the Bund they turned west onto Bubbling Well Road. There had been nothing in the notice about where they were to be taken first. Most of the information gleaned was by inference, words parceled out as charily as gold bars.

The boulevard widened to meet Western Road and sturdy Victorian mansions rose up as suddenly as clouds in a thunderstorm. The dome of a church was ahead. Elias and Sybil had attended a performance of Handel's Oratorio there three Christmases ago. It had been snowing. Pilgrim snow, in exile from Manchuria.

The truck stopped without slowing, the occupants caught in the sudden deceleration whipped back and forth, the sound of crockery breaking, the snap of the tailgate latch, people, packages, valises, bed frames, pots and pans dumped out onto the sidewalk, the sharp commands of soldiers, the way blocked by the fallen-down elderly, the stubborn children, the spilled lotions brought in contravention of orders.

Elias had lost hold of Rachel's hand, couldn't see her. Other trucks had now pulled up, were disgorging, the mix on the sidewalk mob-like, loose, a rout as fierce and driving as a wimpling wind gone wild.

"Elias!"

"Over here."

They were shoved through the church doors. The semblance of a line, explosive, ragged-edged. Hands out for printed forms, pencils.

"Write neatly," a Japanese officer standing in the pulpit said sermon-like, the pen in his hand a baton.

Everyone rushed for a seat. There were murmurs and scribbling sounds of the tracks of dull pencils on cheap paper, every cough a shot in a tunnel.

The interviewing began. A large-faced Japanese Naval officer at a desk, aides on either side of him, questions as teasing as a board game, memory-ridden, inconsequential, revealing, every answer as burdened as though it led to the guillotine.

Their turn. They were on their feet, Rachel clutching the purse. Elias suddenly hated the purse, hated the idea that she had to do this. She wasn't Sybil, couldn't pretend to be, and might say something flippant, might turn obstinate, might even swear at the examiner if he pressed too hard.

"Name?"

"Sir Elias and Lady Sybil Mansour," Elias said.

"And this is your wife?"

"This is my wife."

"Your parents' names?" he asked Rachel.

"My father was David, Earl of Southwold. He was an international banker with business interests in New York. My mother's name was Edith. She was Winston Churchill's American cousin." She smiled. "On his mother's side, of course."

*   *   *

Ash Camp, a cluster of tin-roofed wooden barracks buildings surrounded by barbed wire, was once used by the British as a parade ground and military base, the swampy ground stabilized by the application of tons of ashes. The blanket of ash held firm for a while, but then ash and water turned to mud, buildings creaked and tilted, mosquitoes flew up out of the gelled ground to torture the soldiers, and they were forced to abandon the place.

*   *   *

The air was sepia, everyone sluggish and slow in the heat. Captain Masako, the bristle-haired commander of the camp, ordered the new prisoners to stand at attention in the yard while possessions were sorted and identification papers collected.

"We will be fine friends if you obey rules, but remember that the velvet glove can hold an iron hand. Some of you will be housed in the barracks, some in the huts, but when you walk on the campgrounds you must remain ten feet away from the fence or you will be shot. My office is in the main building near the gate. Do not come there to ask for anything. We supply no equipment. We will give you six ounces of bread daily and two ounces of meat. There will be roll call twice a day. You can cook what we give you or eat it raw. The well water is bad. You may wash clothes in it, but if you drink it you will get sick.

The water cart will bring water once a day for boiling. We have no tea. We have no sugar. We have no medicines. We have no hospital."

At dark they were allowed into the buildings, scrambling to take possession of the allotted fifty square feet of living space per family.

Elias set the iron bed up near the window, then lay down on it, his hand over his eyes. Rachel untied the parcel of food. She had no appetite. She tied the parcel up again, wrapped it in Sybil's hat, then stretched out beside Elias.

The moon was bright, snatches of clouds, as full as ships' sails, visible through the glassless window.

She could have been in Free China by now. Lilli had arranged it with a Polish rug dealer in January.

He has connections with Chinese smugglers, Lilli said.

Elias said, *Smugglers will turn you over to the Japanese before you reach the crossing at Wuhu.*

Rachel had wanted to prove him wrong. She packed a suitcase and went to the rug dealer's shop, then stood outside and stared at the silky carpets that lay like sculptured fields of flowers across the gray windows and didn't go in.

And now she was here, Lady Sybil Mansour's impostor, lying next to Lady Mansour's widower on the web of an iron bed, no room to move, the sound of crying all around them, ravenous mosquitoes in a frenzy of feeding on virgin flesh, the brittle slaps at blooded, itching skin, the shouts and shushings, the soft suck of nursing babies, the slow float of repressed terror. A continent of woe sinking into the ashy mud.

Elias didn't stir. He slept without movement or noise. Sybil would be forty-three. How old was he? Not old. He had no temperament. She didn't have to fight him.

She closed her eyes. She was too exhausted to sleep. She could hear her heart. It ticked in her ears, each beat the click of a latch. She counted the beats.

Elias hadn't kept her from leaving. She just didn't go. Sometimes she thought it was because he said, *Stay with me.* She might have dreamed he said it, a pellucid dream that wrapped the world in light, that married desire to illusion and produced memory. Or he might not have said anything more than that it was too dangerous, which made it so inexplicable why she didn't go.

In the morning the camp was chaos. There was no one to regulate anything, to ensure that food was distributed fairly, that the sick were taken care of, that fuel was conserved and boiled water kept free from contamination.

A contingent of American merchant seamen transferred from the all-male camp at Pootung in March had staked out a portion of the camp for themselves, cooking their own food on a chatti made of a punched-hole, wire-grated, mud-lined five-gallon gas can, scavenging for coal dust that they mixed with dirt and rolled into balls. They looked weak, their energy cropped close. They were no help at all to the newcomers. They regarded them as competitors for the dwindling stores.

"We need to organize," Elias said.

He suggested a secret ballot, names written on scraps of paper and dropped into a barrel in the middle of the yard. A Scottish doctor, Roger McGregor, who had already taken one of the storage sheds as an infirmary, was elected camp representative. Rachel became inspector of provisions, Elias arbitrator of camp disputes. The rest arranged themselves into camp squads. The kitchen squad to see to the communal kitchen, cooking food, stoking fires, and guarding the fuel the Japanese provided (a mix of coal, sand, and pebbles that when burned produced noxious clouds of black smoke), the labor squad to clean the camp grounds, the nursing squad to help Dr. McGregor in the infirmary and bring food to the elderly and sick who couldn't stand in line for meals. Prisoners too old, sick, or weak to take a turn at squad duty were assigned to pick rat droppings out of the rice.

Meanwhile the Japanese were in the gun towers and guarding the fence, Masako was in his office at the gate, and the prisoners were on their own.

Chapter 38

August 1943

The rickshaw slued back and forth across the road, then stopped in the treeless, sun-seared forecourt of the Japanese administration building. Lilli owned a car, an old, coal-swilling car she got in exchange for a load of powdered milk, but she hoarded its use since an Italian customer made a remark about how rich she must be.

There was a long line of Jewish refugees in front of the ghetto administration building waiting to see Officer Ghoya about day passes out of Hongkew. Since May, when stateless Jews were ordered penned in this forty-block section of Hongkew, affidavits proving employment outside the ghetto had been required. Lilli was exempt.

I'll give you money to buy the Mansour house from the Japanese for me and get me Soviet papers, Lilli told Jacob in April.

For you, anything, he said, *but be careful. The Japanese think every Russian in Shanghai is a spy for Stalin and every Russian Jew is a saboteur.*

Lilli showed her Soviet identification to the guard now and walked through the double doors.

One-thirty. Lilli liked to get here no later than one o'clock. Officer Ghoya took lunch at two and his mood turned mean when he was hungry. But she had had other business to attend to this morning. A stop at a shop on Avenue Foch to sell a case of American peanut butter, then to the German wholesaler on Avenue Joffre to arrange delivery of a thousand yards of smuggled silk, then to the Swiss Embassy to buy a Georgian tea set from their envoy. All the pieces of the morning's business assembled as precisely as a Chinese box. But appointments had exceeded time allotted, spilled over, slopped and bled into one another, and now she was late.

It was almost as hot inside as out, ceiling fans stirring the choked air. Ghoya was waiting for her in his office on the second floor, a short man, small-eyed and stocky, who stood with legs spread as though he were on a horse.

She put four packs of American cigarettes and a porcelain jar filled with paper-wrapped candies on his desk.

"You were here twice this week."

Did he make a written record of her visits? *Tuesday, Lilli Chernofsky, a group pass for children to attend Kadoorie school. Thursday, Lilli Chernofsky, eight passes for soccer players at Chaoufoong Heim to attend championship game.*

"The violin teacher you got me is no good."

"I'll find you another one. Have you heard of Walter Kreitzler?"

"Who is he?"

"He was concertmaster with the Berlin Symphony. He's at Chaoufoong Road Heim. If he doesn't suit you, I'll find someone else."

"There was a band at the Libra Café."

"A band? When? There's no band there now."

"Before the ghetto. Before. Not now. I'm not talking about now. A Jew led it, a violinist who played Gershwin. He's the one I want."

"If he's alive, I'll find him."

"The music stand you sold me has a crooked leg."

"It's an antique. Antiques are sometimes not perfect."

"Take it back."

He pulled at his lips with his fingers, shined the toe of his boot on his trouser leg.

"I wanted to talk to you about the Amati," he said.

"I haven't set a price yet."

"It's probably a fake."

"It's genuine. Sixteenth-century. The owner was a violinist. He died in Germany. His wife brought the violin to Shanghai in 1940 wrapped in sweaters."

"People put labels in new violins and call them sixteenth-century."

"In a shop you would pay ten thousand American for it."

"You would guarantee it?"

"I guarantee everything I sell. If you don't like something, I take it back, just like I'll take back the music stand. But not today. I don't have room in the rickshaw today. I'll send the car for it."

He opened his desk drawer. "How many?"

"Two."

He stamped two passes and handed them to her.

"Amati?"

"Genuine sixteenth-century."

"Ten thousand dollars?"

"In Frenchtown I saw one two months ago sold for ten thousand, but I haven't decided what I'll ask for it. Of course, you would be the first one I'd offer it to, and you would get my best price."

Next stop the annex to Ward Road Heim. It had once been a Chinese school. The windows were broken out and the walls had gaping holes stuffed with paper and rags. Bernard Zitlovsky, the administrator (a non-paying position since Jewish Relief had been cut off), was sitting on the steps in his undershirt, the small handkerchief on his bald head sweated hem to hem. Before the Nazis invaded Poland, Bernard taught ballroom dancing in Cracow. Now he lived in one cramped room in the annex with his wife, his wife's widowed sister, his teenage son, his daughter, her husband, and their twin boys.

"I brought you something." Lilli pulled a short-sleeved white shirt out of her string bag. "Cotton. Hand stitched."

He held the shirt up, checked the stitching, tugged at the seams. "How much should I ask?"

"Twenty thousand Shanghai. You might get more if you keep it folded. Shirts look better folded. Are the children ready?"

"They're being cleaned up a little. Margot Strauss, the woman you asked me about last week, is here. The Jewish Committee found her wandering the streets. Are you sure you want her?"

"Of course."

Margot's bed was by the stairwell. There was no spice or seasoning or perfume that could cover the fetor of unwashed bedding and soiled underwear. Her eyes were closed. She was so thin Lilli could see the whiteness of the bones in her cheeks, and her hand twitched on the filthy blanket, a scrawny blue-veined hand with jagged fingernails.

Lilli touched her arm and she opened her eyes.

"Who is it?"

"Lilli Chernofsky."

"Oh." She picked at the lint on the dirty blanket.

"Let me help you sit up, Mrs. Strauss."

Margot was wearing a cotton bathrobe, the front of it unbuttoned, her shriveled breasts bared.

"Gerd died," Margot said as Lilli fastened the front of the robe. "Tuberculosis. I'm all alone now and as poor as the poorest Pole. Well, what's the use? Life changes. Gerd was very talented. Did you ever hear him play?"

"Once. Have you eaten today?"

"We talked about returning to Berlin after the war. He spoke of resuming his concert career. Then the American ships stopped coming. There was nothing to unload, nothing to sell."

"Have you eaten today, Mrs. Strauss? Are you hungry?"

"Hungry?"

"Did you eat today?"

"I don't remember."

Lilli took an orange out of her bag, peeled it, and put it in Margot's hand. "Eat it slowly."

"I don't need instruction on how to eat."

"If you eat too fast you'll vomit."

Margot sucked on the orange, her lips white and withered.

"Have you seen Hannah?" she said.

"Not for a while."

"All a dream. We once had everything. You can't imagine the way we once lived. You shouldn't be here. Lice." She shrugged. "Well, I never would have expected that you would be the one to bring me an orange. I never thought much of you. I remember telling Heinrich that I thought there might be something wrong with you. A typical Polish Jew, I told him, not educated enough to even have an opinion about anything. I don't remember when I last had an orange. I don't begrudge whatever you've managed to have for yourself. I wouldn't ask anyone to live in a place like this. A slice of bread in the morning. Soup with worms in it at noon. They tell me I should eat the worms, that protein will keep me from dying. I don't care if I die or not. I have no one. Hannah is a whore and I don't know what's become of Sigmund. Heinrich I hear has become rich selling goods to the Japanese, then stealing them back."

Orange juice streamed down Margot's arms. Lilli handed her a handkerchief.

"I've been looking for you for weeks. I left word at all the heime. No one knew where you were. Then someone said you had moved into an apartment in the ghetto. I went there, but you were gone."

"Gerd's daughter Sonia and her husband paid key money to the Chinese who had the apartment. Eight thousand yuan. Gerd had no money to give them, and Sonia cursed him. She has no delicacy, no feelings. I made aprons and Gerd tried to sell them on the street. He didn't sell one apron. No one buys aprons in the ghetto. People with not enough to eat don't buy aprons."

"I would have bought your aprons. Eat another piece of orange, Mrs. Strauss."

"His daughter had no pity. She saw how difficult it was for him and she had no pity at all. A friend from the Berlin Philharmonic got him a job making coffins. Thirty coffins a day and he didn't earn enough to buy food. We still had to go to the communal kitchen. Sometimes he would buy a half ounce of margarine, but by the time he brought it home it had melted into the paper and there was nothing left. He was standing and making coffins in one-hundred-thirty-degree heat the day he died. He had a hemorrhage."

"I'm so sorry I didn't find you before now."

"What could you have done? He would have died just the same."

"There are always things that can be done, Mrs. Strauss."

"Don't be foolish. We couldn't pay for a doctor."

"You wouldn't have had to pay."

"And who would have paid?"

"I would."

"With what? Anyway, he died. Sonia had him buried in the orthodox cemetery. He wasn't even religious. I wouldn't go, and she told me she didn't want me there, anyway, that I wasn't his wife. I never saw him put into the ground. I'm glad I didn't go. She threw me out of the apartment. It was a disgusting apartment. I couldn't stand to live in it. Four adults and three children in one room. There was no toilet, just buckets lined up on the roof, one per family. And Chinese thieves all around us. They stole our clothes when we washed them and hung them out to dry. They came in when we were asleep and took our money out of our pockets. And when we walked in the street they dipped their fingers into our purses as smoothly as if they had no hands at all." She stared at Lilli. "What would you have done with the aprons?"

"I know people who like good needlework."

"Well, now you've found me, but you're too late. I have no aprons. I have nothing. I should have stayed with Heinrich. I made the wrong choice. But how was I to know what would happen?"

Lilli found Margot's shoes beneath the bed, the backs broken down, rat droppings on the toes. On a hook behind the bed a dress large enough for two Margots.

"I don't know why you were looking for me. What do you want?"

"To take you home with me."

"I can't pay. I told you, I have no money."

"I don't want any money from you and I still have errands to do, so don't waste time questioning and arguing. Put your dress and shoes on while I go talk to Bernard."

Bernard and the two children were waiting in the annex office, a cubicle with cracked walls and corroded pipes.

"The boy is Austrian, about four years," he said. "His father was a Gentile. He divorced the mother when the ghetto decree was announced, and then she died of scarlet fever. The girl is maybe three. The mother's a prostitute. The father's a gambler." He tapped his bald head with two fingers. "No brains. He gambles away what his wife makes on the street. The child was dropped here without clothes. They even sold her coat. And look here." He lifted the girl's shirt to show Lilli a puckered scar running across the thin chest. "One of the mother's men. An accident, he said. He was bringing a kettle of hot water to the mother as a gift and didn't want it to cool off. God knows if she'll ever have breasts now."

"How much?"

"For the boy, nothing. Fifty thousand Shanghai for the girl. The mother might have given her to you for nothing, but the father interfered. He heard about you. He knows you'll pay it."

"Write down their full names and anything else you know about them and I'll pick her up tomorrow. I don't have the money with me today."

"You can still take her. You'll owe them the money."

Lilli knelt down so her eyes were level with the little boy's head. An army of lice marched through his hair. She asked his name. Kurt, he said. Then the little girl. She was barefoot, her toes as black as stubbed-out cigarettes. Her name was Hilda. Two passes today. Bernard said she didn't have to have the money for her today, so which one should she take and which one leave for later? The boy winced when Lilli touched his arm; he hadn't eaten any of the raisins she gave him; his eyes brimmed with sadness; hopelessness flared with each rise and fall of his chest. The girl leaned her stomach against Lilli's knee and smiled. She was eating the raisins, picking them daintily out of her hand with thumb and finger.

"I'll take the boy and Mrs. Strauss today. I'm out of cigarettes. I'll bring you some tomorrow when I come to pick up the girl. Try not to tell people about me. It makes everything harder than it has to be. Is there anything else besides cigarettes that you want?"

"And sugar. I'm dying for the taste of sugar."

Bernard half-carried Margot out of the building and into the rickshaw. Lilli placed the little boy on Margot's lap and got in beside them.

The rickshaw rolled forward.

The ghetto was vivid in its ugliness, streets crowded with vendors selling the last of their possessions, the blunt roughness of despair in every face, the rubbing desperation of the quest for advantage, any advantage—a better price, more food, a slim strip of sidewalk that no one else had claimed yet, a narrow mantle of shade.

Stateless Refugees Prohibited to Pass Here Without Permission was posted at the ghetto gate. Lilli showed her identification papers, handed the Jewish policeman the two passes, and he waved the rickshaw through.

They were stopped once more at the Garden Bridge guardhouse. The Japanese sentry looked at the passes, at Margot, at the little boy.

Lilli bowed. She had become expert at bowing, at showing respect, at bending her waist as though it were hinged, then letting her torso drop parallel to her legs and staying that way, forehead skimming the ground. At times when she had felt that a bow from the waist, even one as luxurious as hers, wasn't respectful enough, she had lain down on the dirt on her stomach, breathing in road dust, arms outstretched as though she were trying to gather the street up into her arms. She once stayed in that position for ten minutes while the sentry weighed whether the pass she was carrying was for the child in the rickshaw or had been issued to someone else. It meant everything to the Japanese to see her degraded; it meant nothing to her if it got her across the bridge.

She stayed bent over now, studying the pores in the bridge floor, listening to the traffic going through on the other side of the guard house, the squawk of chickens in a truck, the honking horns, while the bridge heat burned into the soles of her shoes.

A tap on her shoulder. Back in the rickshaw and over the bridge.

* * *

It was the first blush of sunset, the doors of the house open to catch the breeze, the sound of children like the glide of bird flocks overhead. The children were fit tight and glowing in this clarion space: Anzia walking on baby-canted legs; Shaya, Emma, Freda, Nathan encircling Lilli, exploring her pockets; amahs soothing crying infants, Son Li, slot-toothed and twig-haired, holding Kurt despite the animals in his hair; Son Li's daughter Mei-Bo, her neck as graceful as a flower stem, jade combs in her lacquered hair, calling orders to the cooks in the kitchen.

"This is Mrs. Strauss," Lilli told Mei-Bo. "The boy's name is Kurt. They'll both need delousing. Burn their clothes. Mrs. Strauss will take my room. I'll sleep downstairs. Did the doctor come for the new baby?"

"This morning. The rash is from the heat. It isn't typhus."

"Good."

Margot, hard-jawed bewilderment in her face, hadn't moved away from the entry door.

"You'll have a nice bed and clean linens," Lilli said. "The adjoining bathroom has hot water and the toilet flushes. You may use all the soap and water you want, and if there is anything you need, tell Mei-Bo. She runs the house. If Mei-Bo isn't here, Son-Li can help you."

"But why me?"

"You're part of my family. Maybe someone somewhere is taking care of my parents. You can make yourself useful or not, it doesn't matter, although when you're feeling better, you can help in the kitchen, if you want to. There are no rules, but if you would talk less about your disgust with Polish Jews, you will fit into the house better. Most of the children here are Polish Jews."

Margot took Lilli's hands in hers and kissed the tips of her fingers. "No one has been kind to me since Gerd died."

"Kindness has nothing to do with it. I left kindness behind in Kovno. Just be glad you're here."

Lilli walked through the house, Mei-Bo and children following, a jabber of languages, toys spatting like raindrops, through the dining room, mahogany table stacked high with diapers, talcum powder, vitamins, soaps, lotions, to the ballroom, the rows of baby beds as staggered as stepping stones on a snowy field.

"The boy from Bubbling Well Road brought orders for canned peaches, shaving cream, and French perfume," Mei-Bo said.

Lilli picked up one of the babies and patted its back. Baby bodies were so supple, they yielded as though they had no bones in them. Their heads, merely wobbly knobs on shortened sticks, nodded and dipped.

"You said you would bring two children," Mei-Bo said.

"I left the girl behind and brought Mrs. Strauss instead. I'll get the girl tomorrow. Did the Belgian chocolates arrive?"

"Yes. And fifty bottles of Scotch whisky."

"Did you check the cartons?"

"Yes. None of them had been opened."

By nine o'clock the house was quiet and Lilli was at her desk in the study (Elias's desk, Elias's study) going over her accounts. Jacob Rossitsky would be here soon with work passes for five men in the Ward Road Heim. He always came late in the evening when the children were asleep.

It was this time of day when forward momentum faded and it took all her will to battle her mind's strangling chatter and solve what could be solved. Like who owed her money or goods, who had made her promises in exchange for favors she had done, who preferred one type of cigarette to another, who needed insulin, morphine. She kept records on the children: where found or from whom bought, approximate age, parents' names (if known), language (if any). Records had to be updated daily. She counted the names. Besides Shaya and Anzia, there were now eighteen children. Tomorrow the little girl would make nineteen.

Jacob brought the first one. *She has a tubercular mother*, he said, *a Russian Jew with no family.*

The others came as barter for goods, left like starvelings in lumpen rags for Lilli to resuscitate. Still others she bought. Like a piece of fish. Quitclaim. Hers. A few were on loan, temporary, to be redeemed.

Children made belief in God a possibility. *Tikkun olam*, the Jewish prayer said. *Go out and repair the world.* Children gave Lilli a reason for repairing the world. Mrs. Strauss didn't fit that reason. There were worthier people to help, gentler people, people who were of value to others. *Why me?* she said. There was no why. Lilli had heard that she was on the street, battered and despairing. Their lives were intertwined. For saving this one unworthy refugee, she now promised herself to save four.

Her head ached. She hadn't been sleeping well lately. She dreamed too much and would awake in the mornings exhausted. The dreams were always the same. Mama waiting at the window of the house in Kovno for Papa to get back from synagogue, Moses and Aaron in the dining room arguing about Talmudic interpretations. Her dreams were visits from the ether, more real than waking time, every little dish and doily, Papa's hat resting on a chair, a pot of *knaidlach* boiling on the stove, Mama's wig on the nightstand, all of it small pictures of the past reeling out across sleep's realm.

At ten-thirty, Jacob arrived. He was a rough man, and usually as quiet as a brick through the window, but he sat silent in the darkened study. He said yesterday that he might have a buyer for the two tons of printing stock Lilli found in an abandoned godown on the Bund. But he hadn't mentioned it. He was uncomfortable, and Jacob was never uncomfortable. He was always nerveless and brazen. Business deals gone sour meant nothing to him. He wouldn't have hesitated to tell her if the buyer had changed his mind or wanted to pay in dollars instead of gold bars. But he didn't bring it up. His silence was understated, ripe, his body alarmed, head sloping so far forward it was as though dread and gravity were one.

A sheer slip of cool air peeked through the open door as he took Lilli's hand in his and told her that the Japanese had Aaron.

Chapter 39

August 1943

The American bombers were flying off, the mewl of their engines spinning away over the water. They had hit the city dead center tonight, rupturing buildings, blasting streets into a fiery pattern of incendiary gorges. The Americans up to tonight only bombed the wharves. Bombs that fell anywhere but the wharves fell only by accident. Bombs that fell on innocent people were only a terrible error, a miscalculation of instruments, a confusion of geography, a tragic misreading of maps.

When the first bomb hit, Mei-Bo braked suddenly and in the blindness that followed, Lilli had the disorienting sense that the car had been struck. Mei-Bo sat still as a painting, rue-faced and shaky. In a few moments she was easing the car forward again through the upside-down streets and wailing sirens, past a skeletal catacomb of piked timbers and scorched walls, past the cork-hued glow of a burning automobile, the grotesque blur of melting figures inside, the scene as flat as a slide show, all movement done, finished, the remains left to the lazy flicker of flames.

People on the streets, buckets of water passing hand to hand. There was no stopping for the mobbing of the car, the frantic knocking at the windows, the dart of faces in the windshield's spark of wrinkled light, the dead and wounded buried beneath crackling debris, draped over bicycles, sitting sightless and mute on shards of metal and chunks of concrete.

A few more turns and Bridge House was ahead of them, an undamaged stark-white mausoleum on a street of smoking buildings two blocks from Soochow Creek, nothing to distinguish it from the eight-story apartment building it once was except for bars like shark's teeth on the windows.

Mei-Bo stopped the car.

Lilli hadn't expected to die tonight, but it was possible, and so she had spent the afternoon at her desk writing out her possessions, her children, her love, in letters and putting them in envelopes.

Mei-bo, a prostitute until Lilli bought her contract from the brothel owner, had five hundred dollars in her envelope, to be shared with her mother, Son-Li. She was also to receive all of Lilli's remaining inventory.

A letter to Jacob. He was to have custody of the children and use the money hidden in the bottom of the onion crate for their care.

A letter to Shaya's father care of Intourist in Moscow, giving him Jacob's address, although the letter she wrote in December came back with "No Identity" stamped on it in red ink.

A letter to Mama. Lilli had written letters to Mama for three years and gotten no reply, but this letter was different; for the first time she told her about the children, recited their names, their ages, where she found them, and how, despite everything, they could still laugh and play.

A letter to Moses. *I love you.*

"There are letters on my desk," she said to Mei-Bo and stepped out of the car.

No one entered Bridge House willingly. It was a hole into which enemies of the Japanese were thrown. Lilli had been here before to pick up a body, a Dutch Jew named Linveldt. She had bought sugar from him in April; in May he was arrested; in June he was executed. Not for black marketeering, but because he had forged Portuguese papers. Jacob worried that Lilli would be arrested by coming here, that she was as vulnerable as Linveldt had been.

"I have an appointment with Officer Tanaka," she told the guard at the door.

He disappeared into the dark interior.

A faded poster was tacked to the wall. *A Warning to All Chinese, Japanese, and Gentiles Alike: The "Chosen People" Have Invaded Shanghai. Be Prepared to Resist an Economic Invasion and Be Prepared for an Era of Crime, Sin, and Intrigue.*

Officer Tanaka appeared. He bowed to Lilli, she bowed to him. He had spoken to Officer Ghoya, he said, everything was arranged, but this was a special case, unusual, not to be repeated, they were both in danger, but he was willing to do it because he was a man of honor, did what he promised to do.

She followed him through a set of locked gates into a main corridor. A maze of offices reeled out from the core of the building, walls and floors smelling as if they had been liquored with antiseptic. Another locked gate led to offices, sleeping quarters, communal hall. American music on a radio somewhere, a loud pulsing hiss trammeling all other sound.

Down a flight of stone steps, odors rolling up, muffled coughs, the rankness of damp, the gagging smell of excrement, rot that climbed the stairwell and clung like ivy to the walls.

A basement corridor, cells on both sides. Chinese and foreigners, men and women, squatted on their haunches or were curled into fetal positions, body to body. Light was discomposed, raying randomly from slitted grates and first-floor openings, over all a hazy pall as though dirt were slowly seeping in to gray the air. So this was where Linveldt was kept before he was beheaded and delivered to Lilli in two pieces.

She was alert now, felt sharply the vulnerability Jacob worried about, the foolhardiness of letting herself be known by face, by name. The keen edge of danger flashed silvery and bright in the fetid air.

The last cell, a key in the iron door, and Lilli was inside. An overflowing commode had fouled the stone floor; the slime ebbed and flowed like the tide. Clambering hands grabbed at her ankles.

Aaron was sitting at the rear of the cell, bent over, arms on his knees, as though resting. Was it Aaron? Officer Tanaka was waiting outside the cell telling Lilli to hurry. She couldn't hurry. She had to think. She had risked her life to stand here without knowing for certain. She had thought of this moment as accomplished without having really examined the geometry of it, the discrete arrangement of its parts. A special case, unusual, not to be repeated. An Amati violin to Officer Ghoya for Aaron's life. She would have given ten Amati violins for one true Aaron, for her beloved brother, for Mama and Papa's treasured son. But was this Aaron? Even at his leanest she was certain she would recognize the outline of Aaron's body, the way it occupied its own intimate space. But would she know him by the simple tracings of a shadow on the limed-brick wall? Aaron's back was straight; he didn't have this man's warped crescent. And his shoulders didn't slack beneath the weight of his head. It had to be Aaron. Wasn't that Aaron's hair and beard, still as full as a scarf around his head and still the color of carrots? And when she leaned over to touch him, wasn't that her name on his lips?

She nodded to Tanaka and he stepped into the cell. He picked Aaron up gingerly—worried, no doubt, about Aaron's stink blighting his uniform—and carried him up the stairs and down the radiating hall to a rear entrance, then around the building to the car, folding him into the back seat as gingerly as a pile of stenchy laundry.

Lilli handed him a hundred thousand Shanghai.

"Spend it today. Tomorrow it will be worth half."

Chapter 40

September 1943

Aaron's waking periods had grown shorter the past few days. He burrowed deeper and deeper into sleep. He was a grainy photograph, the image fading.

He was breathing evenly now, his fingers clutching the hem of the sheet. He shifted uneasily in the bed and she could see the deep hollow of his cheek against the pillow, the skin taut above the skein of beard.

He was awake.

"Is Hannah here?"

"No."

"When is she coming?"

"Soon."

His muscles were scourged, arms and legs too wasted to raise himself up. Lilli sat on the bed, her back against the wooden rail, and held him in her arms.

"Yesterday a Russian girl, no older than you are, held me on the pot because I was so weak. I had no embarrassment, Lilli, no shame. You see her there, the girl in the corner?"

"It's a shadow, Aaron."

"She hasn't moved all day. There, you think that man over there is sleeping, but he's dead. And there, over there is another one. The dead are collected every day. When is Hannah coming?"

"Soon."

"Well, what does it matter? I'm through with everything. Hannah. Bombs. Talmud. Everything. Finished. *Fartik.*"

He was feverish and confused at night. He didn't remember in the morning that the night before Lilli had sponged his body with cool cloths and sat in a chair beside his bed until he was asleep. In the mornings he pushed the rice porridge away and told her to leave him alone. In the mornings he said the only time he was rid of her was when he was asleep.

"Tell me about Kovno, Lilli, about when we were children."

His eyes were lambent, the life in them wavering. There was a gluey texture to his skin, as though the juice in him were running out.

"You brought me pastries when you went to *cheder*," she said. "And you let me use your skates in the wintertime when the pond froze. You were a very good skater and you taught me how to twirl. Papa took us to Vilna once, and we came back through the forest on a sled, all bundled in blankets. Everything was white. The trees, the sky, everything."

"Oh God, Lilli."

"I'm here with you, Aaron. Don't be afraid."

* * *

Rabbi Salkowitz's suit was threadbare, and he spoke in nervous spurts, hands trembling as he held his beard to one side and shoveled rafts of chicken and noodles into his mouth.

"I walked all the way from Hongkew. A special pass for the dead. Was the chicken kosher-killed?"

"Cook amah doesn't know anything about kosher chickens," Lilli replied.

He smiled at the two amahs spoon-feeding congee to six babies at the other end of the kitchen table.

"So many children," he said, and wiped his mouth with his handkerchief. "Where is the body?"

"Upstairs."

It surprised Lilli to walk into the room and see Aaron lying there, as though he were sleeping, as though she could say something to him and he would answer.

But there was a smell in the room that wasn't there the day before, and his skin, smooth in death's stiffness, enveloped him like a pale blue gown. When she was twelve she had notepaper in a flowered box the color of Aaron's skin.

"Where is his wife? I always consult with the wife."

"The wife isn't here. I don't know where she is."

"So who'll bathe him?"

"I will."

"It's unusual, but I remember once that a son washed his mother's corpse. She was a fat woman with deformed feet and hair that had never been cut. The son removed her wig and the hair fell down onto the floor like a young girl's. An old woman with the hair the color of honey. He washed her hair and her deformed feet and everything in between. There was no one else to do it. I suppose you can wash your brother's body."

Lilli stared at Aaron's shrinking body. There were so many things she wished she had told him. She wished she had told him about how she envied him sitting with Papa in the downstairs sanctuary of the synagogue while she and Mama were banished up a long flight of stairs to the women's section where they sat on wooden chairs on a shallow balcony a foot away from the enclosing filigree screen so there would be no chance that a male praying below might look up and catch a glimpse of patterned shawl or a bit of pinked cheek. She wished she had told him she no longer envied him. She wished she had told him how dear to her he was.

She filled a basin with water and sponged his beard and hair and face and hands. She removed his pajamas and his body lay exposed, the bones aglow beneath the smoothened blue skin, the penis a shriveled purse in its bed of red hair.

The rabbi, who had been reading the prayer for the dead aloud, stopped and looked over at her.

"Finish quick. Don't be too particular. To be too particular isn't necessary. This is symbolic, after all. Do you have a shroud? The women of the burial society always sew the shroud."

"I have the sheet from the bed."

"That'll do. That's enough washing."

The rabbi raised Aaron's stiff body while Lilli wrapped the sheet around him.

"Leave his face open."

She tucked the sheet beneath Aaron's chin so that his beard hung down, red against the white, a flame atop a twisted candle. His face was the blue of an old man's veins now with pale green splotches the size of baby cabbages.

"Put the yarmulke on his head and wrap him in the prayer shawl. Like so. Look at him. Already I see a difference in his face, contentment that things are being handled in the correct way. A Jew deserves a Jewish burial. It's his right."

"His eyes moved beneath their lids."

The rabbi breathed into Aaron's nose, then shook his head.

"You wanted his eyes to move, so you saw them move. This is a corpse. There is no life left in it." He lifted a corner of the prayer shawl and ripped the silk fringe off, kissed it, then slipped it into his pocket. "A religious man should be buried in his prayer shawl, because when he ascends into Heaven God will want to see it. It's proof that he prayed. Of course, this isn't your brother's shawl, what can we do about that, but it was a good Jew's shawl, donated for this purpose. Some dead Jews wrapped in their own shawls weren't good Jews, they faked their prayers, but God can see through fakery, no one can fool him. But a shawl is important if you want to show God that the man was religious. Then God can make up his mind on his own. But the shawl shouldn't be perfect. A person living and breathing can use a perfect shawl to pray to God. But when he dies, part of the shawl dies with him. A living man needs four fringes. A corpse can do with three and still get into heaven."

*   *   *

There was barely a strip of ground that didn't hold a grave. Wood and stone marked each space.

"God full of mercy, who dwelleth on high, cause the soul of Aaron Chernofsky, which hath gone to its rest, to find repose in the wings of the *Shechinah*, among the souls of the holy, pure as the firmament of the skies, for they have offered charity for the memory of his soul."

Jacob Rossitsky and Margot Strauss were standing together, Jacob with a prayer shawl hanging from his shoulders, Margot steadying herself against him. Jacob had found something in her to treasure, the two of them an odd-matched pair, he unfailingly brusque in his consideration of her, she painfully self-possessed in her slow recovery.

Mei-Bo had gone looking for Hannah. If she was in a brothel, Mei-Bo would find her. But the coffin was already in the grave, the prayers said, and Rabbi Salkowitz was closing his prayer book.

"Rip your dress to show your grief for the deceased," he said to Lilli, "but don't grieve excessively. Whoever grieves excessively is really grieving for someone else."

She inserted one finger into the collar of her dress and yanked. The material ripped with a weak mew from shoulder to breastbone. A four-inch tail dragged limply in the breeze, leaving a bloodless gash behind. She knelt down and small avalanches of stones kicked the sides of the coffin, a simple oblong box with rope handles on the sides and holes in the bottom to invite the earth in for one final embrace. She ran her hand across the coffin lid's splintery top. The sun had warmed it so that it felt like freshly toasted bread.

As a child she had worried about death until worry took on the shape of a dream, compressing day into night. *You starve your days of joy,* Papa told her. *When the time comes, death is a friend, not an enemy.*

In Shanghai death was everywhere. In the corpse-covered streets, in the cut-short lives of innocents. She had fought its dominion, had done her best, but it wasn't enough, not nearly enough. This death, this cruel, closed-door, extinguished-light death quaked her soul. This death, Aaron's death, her brother's death, unearned and mean, growled and snorted its anger.

She reached into the fractured loam at the edge of the grave, filled her palm with dirt, and a silvery brown spray landed with a rainy grace on the lid of the coffin.

"I'm so happy Mama and Papa aren't here to see this, Aaron," she said aloud and let the tears fall.

"May he rest in peace," the rabbi said.

ENDINGS

Ash Camp
August 1945

Squadrons of American B-29 bombers blotted the sun over the camp all year, but now there were carrier-based Hellcat fighter planes keening the clouds, and reconnaissance planes so high up only a blur of vapor was visible.

Rumors ran through the camp like omens and charms, part fantasy, part hope, everyone adding another bit of information to the mosaic of gleanings and speculation, and finally the news, as unmistakably true as the sky, that bombs were falling in Japan. Big bombs.

But rations had been cut to one meal a day. The bread was alive with weevils. The water, muddy Whangpoo River water purified with alum, was doled out one tin mug a day per person. The internees were now eating boiled chrysanthemum leaves to stave off hunger.

Rachel had been sick for two months. She lay in the iron bed in the barracks, dreaming of apples, watching herself shrink, feeling as though her bones were rattling inside her skin. Elias urged her to hold on, the war was ending, he was certain of it, all the signs were there, she mustn't go, she had to stay, don't leave me, his words like a chant, so sweetly droning, making her smile, making her want to get up and dance.

*   *   *

Kunming, China
November 1945

Moses had three sticks left for the brazier. Bishop Manning rationed fuel. No more than seven sticks per classroom per day, even on days like this when cold fog ramped over the Kunming hills and sheaves of ice bore through the wood planks of the schoolroom walls.

When Moses arrived, smuggled in on a truck loaded with provisions from American Catholic Charities, he thought he would only be at the orphanage a few weeks—that had been the pattern in Shanghai, Jesuits moving Moses and Sigmund and Vasily from place to place, then finally splitting them up, Vasily to Chungking, Sigmund to Hangchow, Moses to Kunming—but he had been here three years, teaching arithmetic to Chinese orphans, not looking backward or forward, not examining the virtues of forbearance, as he once might have done, but shaving his face, donning padded trousers and shirt, and letting life reel out as solemnly as the Jesuits did, defiance tamped, will motionless while the blackening plague of war howled around them.

And now it was over.

There had been a letter from Vasily. What they had suspected was true: Li T'ien and Heinrich Strauss betrayed them. Aaron's life was sold away for money, the explosive charges were moved, the tankers remained intact. Moses had mulled the letter over and over, studying it for explanation, but there was no explanation for betrayal. Betrayal sacked the soul, plundered what little was left of civilization's true mind. Betrayal sewed holocaust in the seams of faithfulness; rapine rose from its ruins.

He looked at the rows of benches where the boys sat reading their last lesson, their bare feet stained the color of tree bark, faces nipped raw by the cold. He would soon be gone, but he was glad for what he had been able to do while he was here. It had redeemed him in a way that he had yet to measure.

He threw two more sticks in the brazier.

"I'll miss you all," he said.

By mid-afternoon he was on an American C-47 heading for Shanghai.

* * *

Heinrich looked out the taxi window. The driver had stopped to let a convoy of trucks teetering with furniture and food and Japanese soldiers pass. Ownership of the city was still uncertain, a question of whether Chiang Kaishek would arrive first and take possession or the Chinese Communists would sneak in before anyone else. The streets were a twisty knot of bicycles and taxis and people and there was a wakeful shrill in the air, a melee of whoops and shrieks and manic behavior, a sense that the dead had risen up to join the crazed joy of the living. American sailors were on the streets, Japanese soldiers directing traffic. An American Marine pulled a rickshaw while its coolie owner sat grinning inside. Someone had rigged a Union Jack atop the tramways building on Soochow Road. From the flagpole atop Shanghai General Hospital a small American flag limped in the patchy air.

Heinrich had been listening to the news all morning in his apartment while he was packing to leave. A division of American Marines had arrived and the U.S. Fleet was sweeping mines from the Yangtze waterways. Money was flying out of the city, Chinese running away from the communists with fortunes in gold, billions and billions of Shanghai dollars in wheelbarrows and wagons and suitcases buying less and less with every minute that passed. Heinrich had anticipated the fall of Shanghai dollars; a suitcase filled with gold bars, a harvest as golden as the gleanings from a ripened field, rested on the seat beside him.

He was leaving before he had planned. He had thought there would be time to sell his jade carvings and ivories, but then he heard that Li T'ien had been knifed on the street, and there was no time left.

By the time the taxi reached the dock the wind was up. The junk, sails cast loose, was at anchor near the Garden Bridge. He could see it through the fine mist, the roll of the river gently rocking it, the wind kneading its sails. He needed no special identification, no authorizations, no passport to board. He had arranged his connections with money and would slip out of the city unrecognized, the sag of his life already beginning to rise. When the junk arrived in Woosung, he would board the ship to Australia and in a short while turn back the clock, be what he was before: a man of means, a German newspaper publisher, someone to be listened to and respected, the years in Shanghai as gone as if they had never been.

He did feel a slight restlessness, as though he had forgotten something in the rush. He had gone through the apartment several times, opening drawers and closets. He was certain he had left nothing of great value behind.

He dreamed of Margot last night, not as he last saw her, but on their wedding day, her hair sparkling beneath its pearled netting, Hannah and Sigmund as infants, each holding a corner of the floor-sweeping train of her satin gown. He awoke to a pillow wet with tears. He might not remain in Australia. An arid country. A country of ex-convicts. A brutish society. He would have preferred America, would have crossed it to the Pacific, would have planted his back to the ocean for safety, but there were too many forms to fill out, too many opportunities for mistake.

Crewmen were doing something to the rigging on the junk's deck. He studied the way the sails had been stitched. The seams didn't look strong enough to hold.

He should have eaten. His stomach was gnawing at him.

He headed toward the pastry cart near the foot of the jetty.

The pastries looked stale. The pastry vendor had dirt under his fingernails and flies had settled on the trays, thready legs sinking into soft custards. Further down vendors were selling dumplings and rice balls and lichi nuts. Lichi nuts would be nice. A bag full to munch on should satisfy his hunger.

He walked further down the jetty. A woman was cleaning fish, scales heaped like rainbowed pearls around her bare feet. He stopped next to her and put the suitcase down. He was slightly out of breath. The suitcase felt weightier than it had when he left the apartment. There was a sore spot in the palm of his hand and his thumb was chafed and numb.

A crowd of people were waiting to board the junk, satchels in their hands, everyone shabbily dressed, faces lined and corroded by privation, bodies defeated. The children scuffled underfoot, reserved and spindly-legged. There was someone familiar standing at the very edge of the jetty, a tall man, smooth-shaven, wearing the padded shirt and trousers of the countryside.

Heinrich pulled his hat lower over his forehead, grasped the handle of the suitcase with both hands and hurried to catch up to the others. Someone jostled him. He sensed it as a soft nudge against his neck. He began to turn, but heard a rip, as though the handle of the suitcase had been torn off. He looked down at it. It was intact. He stared at it for a few seconds, mystified, then heard someone scream. The noise was a vibratory tremolo as eerily cold as a distant quarrel. His legs folded beneath him. There was a glut of something in his throat, a gorging sensation, and blood as glossy as spilled wine poured onto the suitcase and seeped through its fine stitching. He touched his neck, felt the sliced separation and trembly artery. He was on his knees now, wondering at the brilliance of the day.

BEGINNINGS

December 3, 1945

Dear Dad,

   Don't come to Shanghai. Everyone is trying to get out, so don't come here or you'll get caught in the middle of a civil war. I'll be in the hospital at least another month, and there's nothing you can do here, anyway. Shanghai is falling apart. And I don't care what the newspapers in the States say, Chiang is not winning the war against communism. The U.S. Navy brings in food and medicine and Chiang Kaishek steals it right off the docks, sells it on the black market, then declares that all black marketeers will be shot. And I don't understand why you can't get affidavits. Where are all your contacts? Now is the time, Dad. Lilli and Moses need affidavits. They need to be moved up on the quota list. Two of the children are sick and have to get out of here. Elias and I are planning to take three ourselves—two boys and a girl. The boys are three and four. The girl is two. I know your concerns about parents who having misplaced their children will now want them back. Lilli has contacts with all the agencies that look for missing children. My three are orphans. There are no impediments to their adoption. And don't try and argue me out of it, because Elias and I want them and we need them and they need us, and I don't want to hear anything from you about I'm too sick to take care of children. Lilli brings them to the hospital every day and they're already calling Elias Papa and me Mama.
   It's impossible here. Do what you can and don't worry Mother.

Love,

Rachel

*   *   *

January 28, 1948

Mr. and Mrs. M. Zuckerman
453 Bluebird Way
Topanga, California

Dear Lilli and Moses,

    Everything going well on this end. Freezing through a lousy New York winter. Various doctors seem to think I'm getting better, but I don't suppose I'll ever be entirely well. The kids cheer me up. Sarah is taking piano lessons and Nathan wants to be an ornithologist. He brings home all the injured birds he can find. Moishe and I, the sick ones, comfort each other. None of the children talk about Shanghai. It's as if it never happened. Elias is still working for Jewish Relief, worrying about the world in general and me in particular. We'll see you in the spring, God willing, as they say.

Love,

Rachel

* * *

Hatzerim Kibbutz—Palestine

December 10, 1947

Frau Margot Rossitsky
Victoria 16500
Melbourne, Australia

My Dear Mutti:

I realized as I began to write this letter that two years have passed since I said good-bye to you in Shanghai. I hope the two years have brought good things to you and Jacob, and that your health and Hannah's continue to improve. Here meanwhile a lot has changed. I left Hatzerim Kibbutz in May of this year. The time there was spent drilling for water and waiting for the miracle of statehood. It seemed that nothing would happen, that statehood would never come and the desert would never bloom, and so I took a job in a brick factory near Jerusalem. It was a strange decision, and even at the time I thought to myself that it was yet another attempt to prove my independence. Since Palestine is short of flats, and those that exist are very expensive, I had lodgings in the factory yard, which cost me no money, and I took my meals in a neighboring kibbutz at a cheap price, so that I could save most of my wages. I was happy in my work at the factory. Although the brick oven was hot and the hours long, I stayed there and worked like someone was whipping me to do it. But after several months I found myself longing to go back to the desert, and so I returned to Kibbutz Hatzerim. I live in a small house with six other men. My meals and laundry are free, and I receive a small salary. I enlisted in the Jewish Settlement Police and am on duty every other month. On my rest days I read and hike and think about the past and about the things I now know I had no power to change.

Vati is often in my thoughts. I smile to think of what he would think of how my life is now. Perhaps he would be happy to see that I can live on my own and take care of myself and make my own decisions. Or perhaps he *would just laugh to see that my main concerns in life now are the problems of soil salinity and how to best irrigate date palms.*

I have an interesting story to relate to you. I had taken a weekend holiday in Jerusalem and was having lunch in a café when a man came up to me and asked if I remembered him from Shanghai. It took a few moments, but I finally did. His name is Benjamin Stutzman. He was one of the four yeshiva students that Moses brought to Shanghai with him from Poland. I asked about the others and he told me that they are spread around the world: one in Canada, one in New Zealand, and one in America. I don't think when we were in Shanghai that I ever had a conversation with him, but I was happy to see him and somehow it warmed me to know that he was doing so well. He told me he was married and his father-in-law was teaching him the diamond trade. I don't know what possessed me to ask about Moses, but it always seemed to me very odd that the four yeshiva students stuck so closely to him. He told me that Moses had been a teacher in the yeshiva, that when the Nazis came, he joined the resistance. Guns and ammunition were scarce, so he learned to use a knife, that he preferred it because it was silent. He was the scourge of the Nazis in his village, reaching right into the Gestapo office of the Nazi functionary, slitting his throat and getting away before anyone saw him. And here is the part of the story that horrifies. Because the Nazis couldn't catch Moses, in retribution they locked everyone in the village in the synagogue and set it afire. His three sisters and brother were inside, along with his mother and father. The four yeshiva students were the only ones who escaped. I won't say that Moses murdered Vati, but it's possible.

Please send me detailed letters of what you are doing and how the new doctor is helping Hannah. I traded English lessons for a camera and in my next letter I'll send you some snaps of the Kibbutz and of the friends I've made here. I would be pleased if you would send me a photograph of you all together. It would make me very happy.

Well, the letter has come to an end and there is no more to report. I will close with my best greetings and wishes to you. Remember me to Jacob. And to Hannah, a big kiss.

Your devoted son,

Sigmund

* * *

April 1948
California

The Zuckerman house was on a wooded hill, narrow lanes running down to a brindle-colored beach, the ocean at its feet a blue spark in a white sky. Old women sat on park benches at the edge of the sea watching children play. Anzia was six, bold and mischievous, her eyes the color of chestnuts. Long-legged Shaya was ten, a barely opened blossom. They were two of fourteen remaining—the rest claimed by parents or relatives.

Lilli and Moses, bound in ineffable ways, drifted together. Nights were for love-making, for letting passion obliterate memory and stall suffering. Days were for remembering, for gathering up and storing what could be stored and discarding the rest, for looking at the future and imagining its possibilities.

Doors opened and closed. Mei-Bo drove the older children to school. Son-Li tended the younger ones. Children ran in and out. Moses worked on his book about the Shanghai years. Lilli wrote letters. She had traced Mama and Papa to the gates of Auschwitz and was waiting for the final document, the one with their numbers on it.

The days flattened and swelled as rhythmically as the tide.

About the Author

Nina Vida's writing career began when her children went off to college and she enrolled in the University Without Walls program at California State University Dominguez Hills to pursue a long-deferred degree in English. One of the requirements of the degree was a semester of creative writing. Nina, who had never written fiction before, decided to write a story about her thirty-eight-year-old sister's open-heart surgery. The professor said it brought her to tears. Nina's husband had been a Navy journalist in the Korean War, and when he read the story he said he thought Nina had the makings of a writer and should try her hand at a novel. That was in 1980. *Lilli Chernofsky* is her ninth published novel.

She is a native-born Californian, and lives with her husband in Huntington Beach, California.

Other books by Nina Vida

Scam (Macmillan)

Return from Darkness (Warner Books)

Maximilian's Garden (Bantam Books)

Children of Guerrero (revision of *Maximilian's Garden* for Kindle)

Goodbye, Saigon (Crown Publishers)

Between Sisters (Crown Publishers)

The End of Marriage (Simon & Schuster)

The Texicans (Soho Press)

The Queen of Annam's Daughter (sequel to *Goodbye, Saigon*)